Praise for Denzil Meyrick's Kinloch Tales

'Brimming with bonhomie, bristling with banter and
laced with a healthy dose of fantasy'
Sunday Post

'Meyrick has a delightfully light touch. He delights in his
characters and the places he puts them in'
Allan Massie

'Delves into a bygone era of superstitions and whisky
smuggling. A superb page-turner packed with humour'
The Herald

'The poetic dialogue is brilliantly rendered and
the characters are reminiscent of those of Compton
Mackenzie or Neil Munro . . . sings with the evocation of
time, place and people, and the humour and truth
behind fishermen's tall tales'
The Scotsman

'An open fire, a deep armchair and a peaty dram are
all that is required for the perfect afternoon to overcome
a dreich day'
Journal of the Law Society of Edinburgh

'It's atmospheric, witty, and has a
touch of *Whisky Galore* about it'
Scottish Field

Also by Denzil Meyrick

Terms of Restitution

D.C.I. Daley thriller series

Whisky from Small Glasses
The Last Witness
Dark Suits and Sad Songs
The Rat Stone Serenade
Well of the Winds
The Relentless Tide
A Breath on Dying Embers
Jeremiah's Bell
For Any Other Truth
The Death of Remembrance
No Sweet Sorrow

The Kinloch Tales

The Collected Stories

Denzil Meyrick

First published in Great Britain in 2023 by Polygon, an imprint of Birlinn Ltd.

Birlinn Ltd
West Newington House
10 Newington Road
Edinburgh
EH9 1QS

www.polygonbooks.co.uk

1

ISBN 978 1 84697 639 1
eBook ISBN 978 1 78885 595 2

British Library Cataloguing-in-Publication Data
A catalogue record for this book is available on request from the British Library.

Typeset by 3btype.com

Contents

A Large Measure *of* Snow

To the memory of Robert Black

Was he an animal, that music could move him so?
– Metamorphosis, Franz Kafka

Prologue

The gull was making for home through thick flurries of snow. It battled across the wind-tossed sound, before soaring high above the island at the head of the loch and out over the broad expanse of water that stretched before the small town.

Anyone staring up from the car on the east road to Firdale would have seen it. So would those cold, weary mariners on the ship battling through the grey waves seeking the safety of port, or the hill walker making her faltering way down the slippery slopes of Ben Saarnie. Even the curious seal, who popped her head out of the water just as it flew overhead, might have spied the creature and longed to take to the skies. To them and all who came before, there seemed nothing unusual about the bird, nothing unusual at all.

But this bird was the soul of the place.

Long it had watched over those who huddled around the shore of the sheltering loch. It had seen the first folk arrive, clad in skins and carrying spears. Then the ships with horsehead prows came. At first the people were scared of these strangers with tanned faces. But soon they marvelled at their possessions and the things they could do. Before long the wooden head of the horse became their totem.

It watched over them as they hunted and fished, and made

their first attempts to tame the land. It looked on in the time called the Bronze Age, as these busy folk laboured to erect their concentric rings and dig their ditches, fortified by shaven-spiked tree trunks at their hilltop strongholds. This was their defence against the others who lived beyond the gull's care. Some came from the sea, others the land. This was where his people climbed, seeking refuge from those who would do them harm.

The gull had seen the man in his fine shimmering breastplate and crimson plumed helmet as he gazed out across the short sea and dreamed of Hibernia. It watched as the men with the red hair arrived with their axes and swords. It flew over the dragon ships, their crews laying waste to all before them. Eventually, all of them settled, mixed and wed, melting away and becoming part of the community.

Over the years, it heard the tongue of its charges change. They gathered around blazing fires set to banish darkness and cold, their sweet songs of longing lilting on the night air. They sang first to the accompaniment of the shrill notes of reed whistles and then to the skirl of their pipes. It heard their words and stories, their poems of love, war and deep, desolate longing.

The gull had watched as small boats hollowed from logs and pitch became great ships of billowing sales, as hurdles became wheels on carriages drawn by shaggy ponies. These carriages soon propelled themselves, and before long the people could soar higher than the gull itself, horses almost forgotten.

It eyed the men in the dead of night, as they pushed casks with hoops, silenced by whispering wool, to boats on the shadowed quayside. It saw them slink back to their homes under the dull light of a waning moon, or the shaded flame of lamplight, only to emerge bold and tall under the sparkling sun of the new day.

The gull saw men go to war – many times they went to war. At first they donned the plaid woven in rough cloth, as had their ancestors. They battled men clad in steel; they battled men clad only in the paint that covered their bodies. But still they survived through the ages.

Then men in crimson coats with their sticks of fire and flashing swords came. The bird lowered its head as souls marched off in the dun suits of destruction, heading for battlefields far, far away, of which it knew nothing. It wondered why they fought as, in time, it had to turn its head away, too sad to see the women and children weep their tears of desperation for lost loves and dead fathers. It, too, mourned those destined never to return to the loch that was their home, or back into its care.

When the iron bird flew over the town and brought death and terror, the gull watched as the people huddled in the hills that had always been their strength. It looked down as great grey warships, the descendants of the dragon boats of long ago, filled the loch.

It swooped over the ring-net fishing fleet as they took on the great waves, in tiny boats of ancient line. There were the women on the pier packing salted silver herrings into wooden barrels. It caught the scent of peat, malt and burning coal before the sweet tang of raw spirit flowed like clear, clear water from keen copper stills.

When men came to the hill where once had stood the fort of rings and sharpened logs, to remove the black jet necklace from the ground and encase it in a glass box, out of time and place, the gull could remember the day the king who had worn it so proudly was put to rest in the dark earth, and how the folk had wept. But those tears, like many before and those yet to come, had been and would be forgotten.

And now, from his vantage point high on the hill, the seagull watched over a busy little place of homes, streets, shops and chimneys. Boats still set off to sea, men mined for coal, whisky still flowed, farmers tilled the soil as the seasons turned, and the horseless cars meandered like tireless ants. Women still wept for lost loves and ruined lives, and children still cried, bewildered by absences they could not yet fathom.

The bird tucked his head under one wing against the snow. Perched on one yellow leg, he wondered what would come next for the people he had watched over, seen but unseen, for so long.

1

Kinloch, December 1967

The group of old men huddled in the shelter of the Mission to Seamen that stood sentinel before the harbour at Kinloch. For most of them, having plied their trade at the fishing for a lifetime, inclement weather was no obstacle to standing in the elements having a yarn. But today was different.

As they looked on from under screwed-down bunnets, Breton caps or the odd sou'wester, the scene before them could best be described as being *unusual*, in terms of the prevailing weather of the south Kintyre peninsula. Snow was falling, and it was falling hard. Not only that, it had the impertinence to have already coated just about everything in sight with a white blanket. The palm trees that sprouted along the pier road, testaments to the mighty Atlantic Drift that normally cosseted the inhabitants of Kinloch in an unnaturally benign climate, had been defiled. Now they stood like exotic Christmas trees, frosted by the adorning flakes.

Along the esplanade, all but one bollard wore a white peak like a witch's hat, the only exception being the one near the roundabout, where Isa McKechnie had taken a tumble and landed on it only a few minutes before, flattening the snow like a pan scone. She had been helped to her feet by the passing Reverend McNee, who declared that he had prayed the snow would stop before he took the long and winding road to Glasgow later that day.

At the head of the quay, a light blue Hillman Minx now wore a white roof. Beside it, Michael Kerr the Baker's van bore the legend 'YOUR CAKES ARE SHITE' in the accumulated snow on its windscreen. The culprit, young Derek Paterson, sacked as a Saturday boy at the bakery for clandestinely eating four Danish pastries and some meringues, had been unable to resist the temptation as he passed by on the way to school.

The snowflakes were even fatter and more numerous now than they had been in the previous hour, and the rigging of boats hung heavy white, as did the roof of the harbour master's office, the weigh house, fuel tanks and the fish buyer's new Rover 2000. The latter had been denounced as flash by the maritime fraternity and, in any case, would soon be tainted by that particular scent peculiar to the fruits of the sea.

Being a practical man, Sandy Hoynes had squeezed his bulky frame into oilskins that would have been a perfect fit a decade ago. Now, he looked like a purposeful lemon as he trod gingerly from the *Girl Maggie* moored at the pier and headed towards the gathering by the Mission. However, their collective attention was not fixed on his progress, but on a seagull that was leaving marks with its webbed feet in the snow on the pavement before them. Donald McKirdy swore blind they were spelling out 'The end is nigh', though none of his companions could discern this. The gull eyed them all with disdain before taking off into the pearlescent sky with a loud squawk of derision, ejecting a watery deposit that landed on Hoynes' left wellington boot. Fortunately, the silencing quality of snow disguised the profanity that issued from Hoynes' mouth as he took to the road.

'Aye, I'm sure yous have only one date in mind,' he said, as he approached the group of men he knew so well.

'Nineteen forty-seven,' came back in ragged unison. For that year had seen the worst snow in living memory, sending the town into isolation and its citizens into a flurry of activity. The west road had been blocked at Muirloan for three whole weeks, and it was even longer before the bus could make its way back to Firdale up the twists and turns of the treacherous eastern way.

But the good folk of Kinloch and the villages thereabouts knew that they could weather any storm that blocked roads, because they had an ancient highway on their doorstep: the sea. Boats of all descriptions were despatched hither and thon to collect the necessities of life. They had plenty coal from the mine at Machrie to keep them warm and an elegant sufficiency of food to fill their bellies. So life continued much as normal. This general contentment prevailed despite the inevitable loss of electricity that rendered modern contraptions like electric light useless. It also caused a rush on Rory McQuinn's store in Main Street as those in search of the replenishment of accumulators harried the shopkeeper. And even now, all these years later, the same shop was doing a rare trade in batteries. For the people of Kinloch loved the wireless, and some could barely imagine how life had been without it. Television – well, that was something else altogether – and despite missing *The Andy Stewart Show*, in their opinion, there was little else to bother about.

Peeny, for that was his nickname, scratched the end of his sharp nose. 'Aye, it's the same all over again. Man, I'm fair glad

I've no' to make sail for the Ayrshire coast in this. It's a blessing that my days in the wheelhouse are done.' Then, in a more reflective tone: 'But mind you, I've tae listen to my dear Elspeth all day now, and that's a task any decent man would find daunting.'

His companions nodded in silent agreement, for most of them had been at the wrong end of the said Elspeth's tongue at one time or another. But, on a positive note, she was well known for her skills as a cook. They'd all sampled her mince and tatties, undoubtedly the best around. Though none would dare admit it to their own wives lest they be accused of something much more damning than marital infidelity.

'It's set for the day, and no mistake,' said Hoynes. 'You wait, the cry will be out for those of us that are left to take to the sea and feed the toon.' He stared mournfully at the loch before him. He'd not long been skipper of the *Girl Maggie* the last time such a calamity had hit. In those days fishing boats sat in rows, filling in the gap between the twin piers with no room to spare. Now, these vessels populated only half of the harbour. A sad reflection on the times, he thought.

As though picking up on these thoughts, Malcolm Connelly sighed. 'Aye, you youngsters will be fair inundated by errands of mercy if this is as bad as it was back then. And precious little thanks you'll get for your endeavours, neither.'

Sandy Hoynes liked to be called a youngster, even though, now in his early sixties, he was the second oldest skipper in the fleet. 'Och, we'll just have to manage. But it will need to be better arranged this time round, that's for sure. Though here's hoping this is just a wee minding. Hamish says it will be fair melted away by the afternoon. And as yous all know, he has the sight.'

8

This statement was greeted by a general murmur of what could best be described as scepticism, as white clouds of breath billowed out from the little crowd only to be punctured numerously by flurries of snow.

'Come on, Sandy,' said McKirdy. 'Does it look to you as though this will stop any time soon? Take a gander at the sky, man. It's fair heavy – fit to burst, no less. By this afternoon, it's mair likely to be a blizzard.'

This suggestion seemed to meet with greater approval than Hamish's meteorological prophecies, so Hoynes decided to say no more on the subject. 'There's little point in us all loitering here, gathering the white stuff. Look at Peeny; he's damn near a snowman as it is. We'll head up to the County and see if the auld fella will serve us a dram a wee bit before time – for medicinal use against the cold, you understand. I'm sure it's lawful for a fisherman to seek refreshment at any moment in weather like this.'

'And even if it's not, that bugger won't turn doon twelve good men and true wae a few shillings in their pockets,' Peeny remarked, as he brushed snow from his shoulders.

Like a murmuration of starlings, as one, the little band of men turned and set off up the hill to the warmth and solace of the County Hotel. For today was a day for drams and yarns beside a roaring fire, not al fresco weather-watching.

If they had been birds, they could have soared high enough to take in a scene more akin to an alpine village than a small fishing town on the west coast of Scotland. And though it bore its own beauty, it brought danger.

And still the snow fell.

2

That Hamish was out to impress was obvious to all who knew the man. For a start, the quiff of dark hair that sprung from an increasingly large expanse of forehead was oiled back to perfection. Those in the know would have instantly noted that stray ear hairs – an unfortunate family trait – had been pared back so that they couldn't be viewed when looking at his face front on.

The best indication as to his intention to impress was what he wore. He was dressed in the suit his late father had bought in 1951 for a wedding. Though it fitted him passably well – both father and son were by nature lean – his mother had taken the best part of the morning to convince him that it was still in style.

'Och, Hamish, I never took you for a gentleman o' vanity,' she chided. 'Ask Jimmy Bryson the tailor – good clothes never go out of fashion.'

But as he stared at himself in the wardrobe mirror, he saw the elderly insurance man who came to collect his mother's contributions every week, rather than the trendy man-about-town image he'd hoped to project.

'And anyway,' his mother continued, 'it's no' as though you're in the first flush of youth. If it's a wife you're trying to snag, well, you better make it quick before what hair you have is left on the pillow. Your father was the same, as was his before him. Your grandda was a right thrawn old bugger intae the bargain. Sat in the County telling his tales, waiting for someone to buy him a dram. Promise me you won't end your days like him, Hamish. It's no credit to a man.'

'You married into the family,' said Hamish, with a hint of indignation.

'Aye, well, it was between the wars, and us women in the town weren't exactly spoilt for choice. And your father was a well-doing soul . . . until the bottle became his best friend, that is.'

Hamish knew this only too well. The family had lost their fishing boat because of his father's enthusiasm for whisky. It was a hobby that killed him not long after. Had it not been for the generosity of spirit of Sandy Hoynes, who took him on as first mate, Hamish had no idea where he'd have ended up. A life down the pit at Machrie or across in the shipyard where the noise was sufficient to frighten the dead were the most likely options. It was a thought that often made him shudder.

But he felt no ill will towards his father. He knew himself the pull of a convivial dram. But he was as determined to master it as he was to make an impression this day. 'I have my sights set high, Mother. My father might be dead, and my grandfather a miserable old bugger cadging drinks in the bar at the County, but that's not me.'

'Well, I'll no' be here to find oot. But you have a look of your grandfather, and no mistake. I see it more every day as your hair falls out. It's across the eyes – there's a right slant to them.'

'Will you stop with the hair and the eyes! I'm getting one o' they complexes.'

'Don't be so dramatic. If there's one thing a woman doesn't like, it's a man with a favour for exaggeration.'

'Anyway, I never mentioned a woman.'

'Well, if you're all dressed up to meet Sandy Hoynes, I'm worried.'

'If you must know, I'm to be interviewed for the *Glasgow Times*. They're doing a piece on young fishermen from around the country.'

'And they chose you?' Hamish's mother looked momentarily taken aback.

'Well, not right at the start, no. Duncan O'May was their first choice, but he caught the chickenpox last week.'

'Oh well, that was lucky.'

'Then they went for Archie Robertson, but he's self-conscious because of that stutter.'

'But he's a fine-looking boy, great heid of hair tae, and no mistake. So you were the third choice?'

'No' exactly.' Hamish screwed up his face. 'They were keen on Alex Morrans, but he got the jail at the weekend for fighting with Bobby Johnson and he's no' out till the hearing on Friday when the Sheriff gets here.'

'Dear me, we're running out of young fishermen.' She raised her eyes to the ceiling.

'Sandy put me forward. Said it would be great to have me in the papers representing a fine craft like the *Girl Maggie*.'

'Oh aye, like the *Queen Mary*, so she is.'

'Mother, as fishing boats go, there's not a better sail in the fleet.'

'I daresay, but she looks like a tramp's underpants.'

'Sandy doesna believe in style over substance, Mother. He says it's a working vessel. We're serious fishermen, no' they day-sailors who're just after prettification.'

'Well, he's certainly succeeded in that desire. Aye, and you're starting to sound like him. I'd guard against that if I were you. For folk from Kinloch to Copenhagen know fine what a rogue the man is.'

'He is not! He's always been fair to me, and I'll not forget him for it. And I'm proud to have my photograph taken in front of his fishing boat. Proud as punch, and no mistake.'

'Aye, well, jeest don't give it any of that second-sight stuff to the reporter. That's another trait you take from your grandda.'

'Och, wheesht, Mother.' Hamish took one last look at himself in the mirror. 'Right, that's me off to meet Joe.'

'Joe who?'

'Joe Baird. He's the journalist from the *Glasgow Times*. His secretary phoned Sandy last night at his house.'

'Aye, good luck. You'll need it in all this snow.'

'Och, it'll make the pictures look fair dramatic, so it will.'

'Aye, if you say so, son.'

Hamish wished he'd worn his thick pea jacket against the elements as he took the short cut from his mother's flat in the Glebe Fields down the distillery lane. By the time he'd turned into Long Road, his feet were freezing in his good Sunday shoes, and he was huddled into the old suit that offered little protection against the heavy snow.

It didn't take him long to get to the café in the centre of

Kinloch, though on the way, even with the camouflage of a thick coating of snow, his wearing of a suit was noted and remarked upon by the locals. Jean McNaughton thought he might be heading for court, while old Peter Carmichael was sure he was after a job interview at the new clothes factory.

'Don't be so ridiculous, Peter,' said Jean indignantly. 'If it's a job at the new clothing factory he's after, he would hardly be heading there in a suit that's damn near twenty years old. What kind of impression would that make?'

Peter nodded sagely. He could see the reasoning in this. 'Wait, he's stopped.'

Despite the deepening snow, Hamish was standing in front of the florist, checking his reflection in the window; he dallied for a few moments, brushing snow from his suit and checking his quiff was still intact.

'It's a woman!' said Jean with surprise.

'No, not Hamish. If he ever had any notions of a wife, the confidence to ask a lassie oot will have been well and truly sooked out of him by that mother of his. She could turn whisky sour.'

'A shilling on it, if you're so confident.'

'Sixpence!'

'Right, you're on!' Jean rubbed her mittened hands together. 'I'll get some nice sausages from young Alastair the butcher as a treat when I win.'

'Oh aye. He might be no mair than a lad, but he's a genius wae a sausage, and no mistake.'

They looked on intently as Hamish pushed open the door to the café.

3

The gimlet-eyed proprietor of the County Hotel watched them with a furrowed brow when they arrived. But the prospect of a parcel of fishermen in funds, spending what promised to be a bad day for business in front of his fire, was a tempting one.

Soon, oilskins, bunnets and sou'westers were left hanging on the coat stand in the lobby, while the men who'd worn them sat bathing in the warmth of the coal fire in the bar.

'Aye, but is that not a fine feeling?' said Peeny, as melting snow dripped from the end of his nose. 'Whoot more is there in life but a good fire on a winter's day, fine conversation and a dram in your fist?'

'A larger dram would be an improvement,' Hoynes remarked from his seat right in front of the flames. 'But I have to say, there is a certain conviviality aboot it all, nonetheless.'

The proprietor leaned against the bar. 'Don't you all be of the notion that this is jeest a port in a storm. These seats have to be paid for. You're not all filling up places customers willing to put their hands in their pockets will be looking for come lunchtime.'

'Who do you think will brave the weather to come out on a day like this?' said McKirdy. 'They'd have to be bereft of mind.'

With that, the front door swung open, bringing with it an icy draught. Hamish stood framed in the entrance, his suit plastered in snow and his quiff white and sticking up like one of the new-fangled ice-cream cones they'd been selling at Gino's café.

'There you have it,' said McKirdy. 'I'm right. Would you look at this apparition! Fair wanting in the heid to be out in this without so much as a toorie.'

'Ach, leave the boy alone,' said Hoynes. 'Young folk these days are fair filled with ideas that oor generation canna get a handle on. I mean, who'd have thought that there'd be men walking aboot with hair the length of a lassie's, and the lassies themselves turned oot with barely a skirt on at all?'

'Aye, you're right, Sandy,' said Peeny. 'It's worse things is getting, tae. My nephew arrived hame the other night and produced one of they joints.'

McKirdy looked confused. 'Whether it was beef, lamb or pork, there's nothing to be sniffed at aboot a joint, surely?'

'Naw, not that kind of joint! The one you see these yobs wae the guitars smoking. Whoot do they call it?'

'Silly shag?' said Jim McMichael.

'Ach, away! It's the wacky baccy they're calling it. You wouldna put that stuff in a decent briar pipe,' said Hoynes.

'Well, he lit up right in front o' my sister Jean. Of course, she didna have a clue whoot was afoot, but I could smell it straightaway.'

'How do you recognise it?'

'Was I no' at that accordion and fiddle club ceilidh last month. They musicians are all at it.'

'No' wee Roger surely, he's only a boy!' said McKirdy.

'No' him. But I'm telling you, I recognise the odour; it's

'right particular, so it is.' He crossed his arms to make the point, as the rest of the assembled fishermen looked into the flames and tried to picture the members of the Kinloch and District Fiddle and Accordion club partaking in forbidden substances.

'It's this "tune in and drop out" – they're all at it. I saw it on the news. Well, I'm here to tell you, the last time I heard old McGeachy at the fiddle he might have dropped oot, but he certainly hadn't tuned in. Fair wailing, it was,' said Hoynes.

'Mind you, it's no' a patch on a good dram,' said Peeny.

'Man, you didna partake in a draw yourself, did you?'

Peeny sat back in his chair with his hands behind his head. 'Aye, well, whoot does a man's journey through life mean if he's no' willing to take a new path?'

They all turned to look at him, mouths agape.

'But it has to be said that while I got a wee sensation, it was only fleeting. After it, my mouth tasted like a Bedouin's sandal.' The thought prompted him to take his baccy from his pocket and tamp some down in the bowl of his pipe with a thumb.

'Maybe I'll gie it a go myself,' said Andy Duncan, at ninety the oldest present.

'I widna be in a rush to be doing that, Andy. I'm sure we had to get the ambulance for you last year when you had one o' they Babychams,' said Hoynes.

'It wisna that at all,' said McKirdy. 'The man drank near a bottle o' Johnnie Walker before he had a glass o' that stuff. They'd to rinse his liver oot wae a mangle.'

The old man looked McKirdy squarely in the face and raised his withered middle digit by way of a reply.

'Hamish, brush yourself doon, man. You'll catch your death encased in all that snow,' said Hoynes in an avuncular manner.

17

'And when you've done that, I'd be fair grateful for a dram. It's a skipper's privilege. One day you'll be asking the same of your crew. Just for me, mind. This parcel of rogues can dip in their ain pockets. Aye, and be sure to get yourself one while you're at it, before we need tae send for one o' they big dogs from the Alps. The creatures wae the wee barrels strung through their collars.'

'Saint Bernards,' said Hamish.

'I'm no' right sure who they belong to, but I've always fancied bumping into one,' said Hoynes. 'But if they do belong to this saint, he's got no business encouraging folk to partake in alcohol. There's nothing Christian aboot that, at all.'

'Unless you're the Reverend McSorley,' said Peeny.

'Aye, but he gets dispensation to be half cut most of the day on account of him being blown up at Monte Cassino wae the Argylls,' opined Alex Watson, who'd only just thawed out enough to be able to speak.

'Aye, he got blown up right enough. But he must have landed in a cask o' wine, for he's no' been oot his cups since,' said old Andy Duncan.

'Well, here's hoping he doesna take to the Babycham,' said Hoynes. 'The ambulance will be fair rushed off its feet.'

Amidst the laughter, and having brushed most of the snow from his suit, Hamish tapped Hoynes on the shoulder. 'Can I have a word with you, skipper?'

'There's no need tae whisper, Hamish. We're amongst friends here,' he said loudly. Then in a quieter voice: 'It's no' aboot that wee favour I did for Mrs McKay, is it?'

Hamish shook his head.

'Aye, well, spill what's on your mind, Hamish.' Hoynes was back to his ebullient self. 'Oh, and while you're at it, you can maybe tell me why you're all dressed up in your faither's suit? May he rest in peace.'

'Sure you know, I've been speaking to the *Glasgow Times*, remember?'

'Och, that's right enough,' said Hoynes, grabbing Hamish's arm. 'They've chosen oor Hamish here to represent young fishermen everywhere. The *Glasgow Times*, no less.'

'Aye, after they went round just aboot the whole fleet asking everybody else,' said McKirdy. 'And you're no spring chicken, neither, Hamish. You must be pushing thirty, if you're a day.'

'Wheesht, McKirdy,' said Hoynes. 'Let my man speak.'

'The reporter has asked us a favour, Sandy,' said Hamish.

'And what might that be?'

'Well, it's a case of wondering if we'll be heading off tae bring supplies for the toon from across on the Ayrshire coast. I let on that it sometimes happens in times of snow like this.'

'And you did right! My, tae see the *Girl Maggie* featured in the *Glasgow Times* as she braves the elements tae save Kinloch would be a fair spectacle. What do you think, men?'

'I'd gie her a lick o' paint, if I were you,' said McKirdy waspishly.

'In this weather? No' likely. The *Girl Maggie* is a working vessel, no' some pleasure cruiser. She'll be pictured as she is – a brave wee boat, working hard to save the people of Kinloch from fair starving to death. It's an honour.'

This was greeted by a disaffected murmur.

'A round of drinks for my friends to celebrate!' Hoynes smiled beatifically at his colleagues, old and young.

'Och, maybe it's not a bad thing, right enough,' said Peeny. 'A wee boost for the fleet will do it the world of good. Make mine a malt – by way of celebration, you understand.'

Hoynes gazed at him malevolently for a moment, then drew his attention back to his first mate. 'This reporter, what's his name?'

Hamish shuffled uncomfortably from foot to foot. 'Baird, the reporter's name is Baird. Aye, and here's a down payment, a kind of retainer, you understand. We'll get the full sum when the job's done.' He fished out a large white five-pound note from his pocket.

Hoynes grabbed it like a flytrap. 'Well, now, you see. Isn't that a sight to behold? A fine man this Baird must be, right enough.' He pocketed the fiver with relish.

Beside him, Hamish's face bore a pained, some might say anguished expression.

4

The snow didn't stop for the rest of that day, nor through the night. When first light dawned, the sky was bright, but to the east more ominous clouds were gathering battalions of snowflakes in good order, ready to march on Kinloch.

As predicted the previous day, the Glasgow road was snowbound, and the good people of the town were indeed cut off from the rest of civilisation. The unfortunate Reverend McNee had been forced to seek shelter from the snow halfway between Kinloch and Glasgow at Inveraray.

The town itself had taken on an altogether different aspect. Houses, once with sharply defined gabled roofs, looked more akin to bakers' loaves. Every angle had been softened under the thick snow, and if anyone acquainted with the familiar silhouettes had been presented with this new spectacle, they wouldn't have recognised the place. Fences could barely be seen. Sheep looked a dirty white against the virgin snow. The council's gritting lorry had long since given up the ghost, stuck fast as it was at the top of the Still Brae. Shops, though staying open, boasted only a trickle of customers, wrapped up in so many hoods, hats and scarves as to make them unidentifiable. This was something of a novelty for the community, where everyone knew everyone else. The new pastime of working out who was who under each great huddle of clothes was both intriguing and unsettling.

An emergency meeting of Kinloch's town council was in session in the wood-panelled chamber in the town hall. Its members sat around a huge, polished mahogany table, each face etched with concern.

'I'm minded to hold my hand out to our brave fishing community,' said Francis McMurdo, the town's provost and senior politician. 'They came through for us in nineteen forty-seven, and I'm sure they'll rise to the occasion again.'

Jessie McCorkindale looked less optimistic. 'Aye, and you'll recall the bad feeling that emerged after that. The shopkeepers gave them the bare minimum then doubled the price of everything. There was damn near a revolution!'

'Well, I have no special powers to force fishermen or shopkeepers to bend the knee to any of the ideas put in place by this council. We can only appeal to the better nature of all those involved.'

There was a general air of scepticism around the table at this remark. For memory was long in Kinloch, and an un-righted wrong was bound to have consequences even two decades on.

'I suggest we declare a state of emergency and call in the army,' said Councillor Galbraith. 'Get them on the boats at gunpoint, if necessary.'

McMurdo eyed him as he puffed on his pipe. 'There's a few flaws in that notion, Jamie. For one, if the army could get here, they'd be able to bring supplies themselves. And secondly, even if we could avail ourselves of their services, you'll remember the riots we had on our hands when they redcaps came during the war to arrest that local lad who went AWOL.'

'They flung them in the loch!' hooted Alec Macmillan, often one of the more obdurate members around the table. 'And in any case, the idea of forcing men to sea in what could be life-threatening circumstances is reckless in the extreme. You'd have a terrible load to deal with if only a fraction of the fleet returned, and no mistake.'

'The lives of the whole community will be at risk if we can't get any food from somewhere,' said the provost. 'The Co-op's running low, and the same goes for just about every shop in the town. Of course, folk are panic buying. I saw the widow Munro this very morning with a shopping basket of sugar that would have sweetened every cup of tea of a battalion on the move.'

'Could we not commandeer the boats if the fishermen don't toe the line?' said Galbraith.

'I'm glad you're not the provost, Jamie. You'd make auld Joe Stalin look like the fairy godmother,' said McMurdo.

An argument ensued, with everyone round the table talking heatedly at once.

Banging his gavel, Provost McMurdo brought the committee – with no little difficulty – to order. 'There is one ray of hope, mind you.'

The warring factions around the table ceased hostilities, as every eye turned to the man in the provost's chair.

'This came through my door this morning.' McMurdo waved a sheet of paper.

'What is it, peace in our time?' Macmillan sneered.

'No. It's a missive from Sandy Hoynes. He must have put it through my door last night, for it was on the mat first thing this morning.'

The very mention of Hoynes engendered the odd raised eyebrow and a few grunts of disaffection.

Undaunted, McMurdo continued. 'He and his boat are to be featured in the *Glasgow Times*, no less. He tells me, and I quote, "It would give me the greatest pride imaginable to be part of the effort to keep the good people of Kinloch, who are so close to my heart, fed and watered at this difficult time." I have to say I was quite moved.'

'He hasn't told you what he's after yet,' said Macmillan. 'If I know him, the price will be his own weight in whisky. And in any case, it's only one boat. That'll feed no more than a few families if we're lucky.'

'Well, I think we should accept his offer of assistance. Indeed, highlighting our plight in the *Glasgow Times* will do no harm as far as letting people know in what straitened times we find ourselves here in Kinloch. And anyway, the rest of the fleet will follow Hoynes. You know how competitive they all are.'

Despite the numerous doubts of those gathered, it was agreed that the council assist Sandy Hoynes in his endeavours with every resource at their disposal.

As McMurdo brought the meeting to a close, he thanked his fellow councillors and the proposal was passed. 'I know, while in some quarters he is considered to be—'

'Fly as buggery,' said Macmillan, finishing the provost's sentence for him.

'I would rather say . . . some remain to be convinced.' He turned to the clerk. 'Please strike Mr Macmillan's comment from the minutes, Mr McIntyre.' He stared up at the chamber windows. 'But in times like this, beggars can't be choosers.'

Outside, more fat flakes were falling on Kinloch.

5

Having managed to avail himself of the authority of the town council via a unanimous vote, Provost McMurdo was now picking his way through the snowdrift on Main Street towards the quay. He was pleased they'd managed to reach something approaching consensus. What swung it had been the intervention of the local association of innkeepers, who foretold that beer, whisky and just about every other form of alcohol would be exhausted in less than a week. It appeared that it was not only sugar that was being hoarded by the community.

McMurdo crossed the roundabout at the pierhead, almost immediately spying the rotund figure of Hoynes in his yellow oilskins aboard the *Girl Maggie*. A few stumbles and no little effort brought him athwart the vessel, where it looked as though Hoynes was busy with a paintbrush.

'Good morning, Sandy,' said McMurdo, checking his watch to ensure that noon hadn't yet turned.

'Ahoy there, provost,' said Hoynes. 'It's a lovely day, is it not? Apart from the snow, that is.'

'Aye, the sky is bright enough now, but that cloud is almost upon us, and it looks heavy-laden with snow to me.'

'Ach, jeest passing. You'll no' see any snow this day. Though it'll be blizzards up near the Rest. It could take weeks to open the road.' He sniffed the air like a dog. 'Remember, if you want to be sure o' the weather, never heed that nonsense on the wireless, just ask a fisherman. Well, one of my vast experience, at any rate.'

'I hope you're right,' said McMurdo, looking doubtfully heavenward.

'I take it you received my wee note last night?'

'Aye, I did, Sandy. A very generous offer it is, too. In fact, I've been in session with the council and the trade association since early this morning. The town clerk is negotiating an accommodation with the shopkeepers, but I think you'll find the outcome will be favourable.' He looked at the sky again. 'Of course, you'll be in receipt of a fine reward from the *Glasgow Times*, I'm quite sure, Sandy.'

'Och, not a bit of it! There's been the usual undertakings, but no hard cash has changed hands nor been agreed,' said Hoynes, ignoring the fact that the five-pound note was sitting, tightly folded, in his wallet up in the wheelhouse. 'But if it means feeding the starving and putting Kinloch on the map, who am I to say no, eh?'

McMurdo raised an eyebrow. 'I'm sure you know your own business, Sandy.'

'Aye, and fair thin times for business they are, right enough.'

'Well, we'll have an offer for you and the rest of the fleet before five o'clock. It's hoped you'll be able to put to sea tomorrow morning.'

Hoynes rubbed his chin and looked at the sky with a leery eye. 'I daresay we could do that. Mind you, I canna speak for my fellow skippers. As you're aware, they're a right thrawn outfit at the best o' times.'

'I'm sure the chance to make some money in the run-up to Christmas will be enough to change their mind. In any event, the pubs and shops are already running short of beer, whisky and the like. As you know, today is normally the brewers' delivery day. And that's not going to happen.'

'Damn me!' said Hoynes, suddenly feeling the need to reach for his pipe and baccy. 'There must be a few sore heads today if the stocks are running down so far!'

'I'm afraid some people have been stockpiling. Very selfish – human nature at its worst in a time of crisis.'

'These folk will answer for it in the next world, and that's for sure!' said Hoynes, as the wad of tobacco in the bowl of his pipe glowed red amidst the white all around.

The provost turned. A young lad was making his way through the deep snow on the pier towards them.

'Is that not young Barry Hall, the grocer's boy?'

'Aye, it kinda looks like him.' Hoynes' eyes narrowed.

Rosy-cheeked and out of breath, the boy reached the side of the *Girl Maggie*. He nodded at the provost out of deference to his office, then turned his attention to Hoynes.

'Mr Hall says he canna get his van doon the quay because of a' this bloody snow.' Young Barry rubbed his nose on his sleeve and snorted deeply.

'Oh right, young fella. In that case, tell him to leave the messages at the weigh hoose and I'll send Hamish up with a handcart tae get them when he appears.'

'Messages? It's a case o' whisky, Mr Hoynes.'

McMurdo, Hoynes and young Barry fell silent for a few seconds. Those who knew the fisherman well would have been able to discern the working of his mind.

'Damn me!' Hoynes shouted in a cloud of exhaled

pipe smoke. 'Auld Hall gets mair deaf by the day. It was only one bottle o' whisky I was after.' He shook his head.

'I'll jeest get him tae take it back then, and I'll bring doon the single bottle,' said Barry, his nose red as Rudolph's.

'No, no, I don't want a young lad like you exerting himself in this weather. No, nor Mr Hall, come tae that. Hamish will sort it oot. Sure, is that not what a first mate is for – eh, Mr McMurdo?'

'Oh, I'm sure. What on earth would you do with a whole case of whisky?' He looked sceptically at Hoynes.

'No, indeed.' Hoynes reached into the pocket of his oilskins. 'Take this for your trouble, lad. It's a penny, but all the change I have aboot me at the moment.' Hoynes flicked the coin through the air, and Barry caught it deftly.

'Thanks very much,' he said, because his mother had brought him up to be polite to his elders. However, the words 'stick the penny up your arse, you miserable auld bugger' were at the very tip of his tongue.

As Hoynes and McMurdo watched the boy wade through the snow back up the pier, they saw two other figures heading towards them.

'At last, my first mate has roused himself fae his bunk and is back in the land of the living. Young folk these days like the hammock, and no mistake.'

'I'll leave you to your day, Sandy,' said McMurdo. 'Nice to see you're applying a lick of paint to impress the newspaper.'

Momentarily Hoynes looked astonished. 'Nothing o' the kind, Mr McMurdo. This is special paint tae help stop the wood fae splitting in the snow. This is a working vessel, no' some exhibition piece.'

'I see.' McMurdo smiled to himself as a large snowflake

landed on the sleeve of his black wool coat. 'My goodness, Sandy, looks like your forecast was wrong!'

'A stray flake or two, nothing more.' He was peering at Hamish and another smaller figure as they struggled through the drifts. 'If that's the reporter Hamish has with him, he's no' a man o' great stature, that's for sure.'

As Provost McMurdo looked over in order to form an opinion, the pair were obscured by a blizzard as the heavy clouds opened over Kinloch.

'I better get back to the town hall while I still can.'

'Aye, maybe for the best,' Hoynes replied, noting with some irritation that the snow had extinguished his pipe.

'You'll hear from the council by five o'clock – you have my word, Sandy.'

'That's good enough for me, Mr McMurdo.'

The provost trudged off through the swirling snow. 'I'm not so sure I'll be coming to you for weather forecasting advice, though.'

As the dark-clad man disappeared into the whiteout, Sandy Hoynes smiled, but the words he muttered under his breath spoke of another expression altogether.

6

Though the snow was falling hard, the look of Hamish's companion intrigued Hoynes. Hard to judge the true outline of the man as he was bundled up in a thick jacket and no doubt a stout pullover or two. But to the skipper, even though this Joe was clearly of short stature, his legs looked uncommonly spindly in moleskin trousers. He had a stout toorie pulled down over his face, all but obscuring it. Hoynes wondered as to the nature of his robustness with a difficult passage to Girvan in mind. But the man was a journalist, and surely knew his own limits, he reasoned.

As they met at the side of the *Girl Maggie*, Hoynes held out his gloved hand in order to help the reporter over the gunwale. The hand offered seemed delicate, but thinking of the money, Hoynes cast aside his concerns and helped haul him aboard.

'We better go below!' shouted Hamish as he stepped nimbly from pier to boat like the well-practised mariner he was.

Hoynes nodded in agreement, lifted the hatch, and helped the guest down the short gangway into the cramped quarters below, where bunk beds sat cheek by jowl with a chart table and tiny galley. He pulled out a chair and beckoned to Mr Baird to take no weight at all off his tiny feet.

'You better take off some layers,' he said. 'I'll put them by the stove over there to dry off. I fired it up this morning. It's wee, but as Hamish will tell you, Mr Baird, there's no warmer place than down below on the *Girl Maggie* – even in weather like this.' He looked to his first mate for confirmation, but Hamish was standing in the shadows looking furtive, a nervous smile playing across his lips.

The skipper looked on, smiling proprietorially as the journalist shook the snow free from his overcoat like a dog, and removed his hat and gloves. Hoynes instantly realised why Mr Baird's hand had seemed so delicate.

'Now, I can explain,' said Hamish, holding his right hand before him in a calming gesture.

The briar pipe fell from Hoynes' mouth and landed with a clatter on the galley floor, spilling what was left of its contents, now thankfully extinguished.

Baird held out a hand to Hoynes, who took it, his eyes bulging from his head and mouth flapping like a great cod.

'It's lovely to meet you, Mr Hoynes. Hamish has told me all about you.' From under her neat fringe, Jo Baird smiled broadly. Her face was pale, but her green eyes bore a deter-mined glint.

It was one of these situations whereby had there been room in the cramped crew's quarters Hoynes may have taken his first mate aside for a quiet chat. But as they were all within a few inches of each other, that was impossible.

'Are you feeling unwell, Mr Hoynes?' The journalist looked at the fisherman, her eyes filled with mock concern. 'Or is something else troubling you?'

Hoynes sat back in his chair and finally recovered the power of speech. 'You know, Miss Baird, I've been at the fishing for over fifty years – man and boy – but this is the first time I've had such an experience.'

As Hamish retreated as far away from Hoynes as was physically possible, the journalist looked puzzled. 'And what experience would that be?' She cocked her head, awaiting a reply.

'A woman aboard a fishing boat.'

'Good grief! That's a story in itself, Mr Hoynes. I'm so glad you brought it up.' Miss Baird took a notepad and pen from a bag she'd deposited on the chart table and looked keenly at the skipper. 'Now, can you tell me just why you've never been aboard a fishing boat with a woman?'

'I will. It's well known to be bad luck, the very worst, in fact. Unless you include gentlemen of the cloth, and they all know better.'

'It's nineteen sixty-seven! Have you never heard of women's liberation?'

'Aye, they can be as liberated as they like, but they're no' doing it aboard my vessel. I'll have to ask you to leave, Miss Baird. Snow or no snow!' He turned to Hamish. 'You telt me her name was Joe.'

Before Hamish could speak, the journalist replied for him. 'Hamish was right: my name's Jo, short for Josephine.' She smiled.

'Aye, well, Joe, Davie, Jim – call yourself what you want. I'll no' have women aboard this vessel, and that's an end to it. Only the good Lord knows the brutal fortunes you brought upon us as soon as you set foot on this fine boat. I shouldna be surprised if we're sinking at this very minute.' Hoynes bent down to pick up his pipe.

'Well, I'm afraid I can't do that, Mr Hoynes. You see, you've already taken the newspaper's money, and I'm not willing to go back on the deal.'

'The money's still safe up in the wheelhouse, I'll fetch it for you directly.'

'Oh, the wheelhouse? Is that the tiny thing that looks like half a garden shed?'

'*Half a garden shed!* It's easy seen that you are not acquainted with the rules of the sea, and you know nothing about the vessels that sail upon it.' He shook his big head, jowls wobbling under his white beard. 'I'm heart sorry, for the money was most welcome. But our agreement is over, whether you want it so or not.'

Jo looked at Hamish. 'Will you tell him, or shall I?'

Hamish moved into the light of the storm lantern hanging beside the stove. 'Now, skipper, you'll understand that I had to negotiate in order to get this fine newspaper to feature us. Aye, and it wasn't easy, for as you know, though the *Girl Maggie* might have the best lines of any vessel of the fleet, she's no' the most commodious, and that's just plain-speaking fact.'

'She's the size she is so that she can ride the waves, no' plough through them like some boats I could mention. It's no' all aboot size, Hamish, and well you know it.'

Jo tried hard not to laugh, but she couldn't hide her mirth.

'It's no laughing matter. You didna see they Vikings piling intae great big ships in order to make their way across oceans. The *Girl Maggie* is no different – no different at all.'

'Not quite so sleek,' observed Jo.

'For she has a different function, that's why. If me and Hamish here were set on rape and pillage, well, we'd make sure we had a vessel tae suit. But I'm too auld for such capers, and I'm no' sure Hamish is of that persuasion, even with youth on his side.'

'So you're telling me there's nothing you'd like better than to ravish some poor helpless maidens?' Jo scribbled away with her pen.

'It's jeest an expression, nothing mair. And I've yet to set eyes on a "helpless maiden". There's none tae be found in my hoose at any rate.'

'Nonetheless, you've entered into an agreement, Mr Hoynes, and it's one you'll have to keep.'

'I hand you back the money, and the "agreement" you mention is null and void. It's the rule o' the sea, and no error.'

'Hamish, it's time to come clean.' She looked at the first mate encouragingly.

'Come clean about what, Hamish?' said Hoynes.

Hamish shuffled as much as the space would allow and delved into the pocket of his dungarees. He produced a sheet of paper that had been crumpled rather than folded and handed it to Hoynes.

The skipper reached into his oilskin pocket for his reading glasses. Soon they were perched on his nose as he read the missive in the dim light of the cabin. 'A contract, no less.' He glared at Hamish. 'What right did you have to enter intae any contractual agreement regarding this vessel?'

Hamish's mouth opened, but nothing came out.

'Hamish is your first mate, yes?'

'No' for much longer, he's no.' said Hoynes, still glaring at his charge.

'Well, as such, he's management, no question about it. As such, his word is binding on a contract regarding the vessel on which he holds this position.' Jo sat back and folded her arms, indicating the end of the discussion.

Hoynes eyed the journalist and his shipmate. He sighed

and removed the glasses from his nose and placed them carefully on the chart table. He looked again at the crumpled document, looked at both of them, and in one swift movement rolled the paper into a ball, placed it in his mouth, and after some chewing and a swig of cold tea from a tin mug before him on the table, winced and swallowed the contract whole. It was his turn to sit back and fold his arms in a gesture of triumph.

'Sandy, you're a hell o' a man,' said Hamish, looking somewhat forlornly at the journalist.

'I'll get you the fiver, and that will be the end o' the matter,' said Hoynes.

'You think?' Jo rummaged through her bag again and produced a manila file. She removed a sheet of paper and waved it in the air. 'This is a signed copy – my copy. And before you think of prising it from my hands in an attempt to consume it, you should note that a third was sent in the post this very morning to the *Glasgow Times*. You're contracted, Mr Hoynes, and that's that!'

'Ha! But you're forgetting that there's no chance the post will be heading up the road today. We're snowbound.' It was Hoynes' turn to smile. 'The postmaster owes me a favour or two. I'll soon get him to find it for me. End of story.'

'You're going to interfere with Her Majesty's Royal Mail? I believe that carries a hefty prison sentence. This story just gets better and better.' Jo scribbled some more.

'Now, jeest hold your horses. I've a duty of care to those aboard my vessel. I'm the captain, after all. In my opinion, the risk of having a wee slip of a lassie aboard on such a perilous journey would be reckless in the extreme.'

'You never read the back of the contract,' said Jo.

'Well, I canna read it now as I've swallowed it.'

'It's a disclaimer – legal and above board. I signed it. You're not responsible for my safety, Mr Hoynes.'

'In that case, I'm jeest no' going to sail, and that's an end to it.'

'Och, Sandy, consider the money. We're to get fifty pounds for our trouble, never mind the fine publicity for us and the toon. We shouldna cut off our noses tae spite oor faces. That's plain daft!' said Hamish.

'Can I have a wee word with you in private, Hamish?' said Hoynes.

The pair made their way back onto the snowy deck; Hoynes, with no little effort, struggling to extract his bulky frame from the tight space.

'Now, listen,' said Hoynes. 'I know fine you were doing what you thought was for the best for me, and for the boat. But I'll no' bring the warth o' bad luck down upon us for taking to sea with a woman. Man, it's bad enough she's aboard while we're tied up at the quay, but we might get away with that on the grounds of a technicality.'

'How so?' said Hamish.

'I brought her aboard in good faith, no' knowing for one instant she was a member of the fairer sex. No, no' even a notion.'

'We'll just have tae sit in port. She's determined, Sandy. She'll likely hold us to oor word for weeks. We'll never fish again.'

'You should keep a lid o'er that glad eye o' yours. She's bonnie enough, or she would be if she had a decent haircut. Maybe a perm like my Maggie.'

'I quite like it. It's all the rage up in Glasgow.'

'That's it, is it? Fair besotted already.' Hoynes rubbed his chin, deep in thought. 'We'll have tae take oor chances. I'm no' green enough behind the ears to know that a contract canna be broken. You take her back to her digs. We'll wait until the agreement is settled later. We should have a manifest of what we've tae pick up in Girvan by this evening. Then we'll dodge off in the middle o' the night. Sit oot at anchor in the sound, if necessary. We'll say that the weather conditions were such that we had to make a bolt for it.'

'Aye, if you're sure we won't end up in the court.'

'We? You signed the damned thing. If anyone's going to court, it'll be you, Hamish.'

Jo popped her head up through the hatch. She looked around and clicked her tongue. 'The weather's worse! Hamish, will you do me a favour, please? I'm not too keen on trudging up the quay and back to the hotel again. Would you mind picking up my stuff? The bill is on account with the paper, so no need to worry about paying. I'm quite cosy here until we sail.' With that, she disappeared back below.

Hoynes looked at his first mate and shook his head. 'We're in a right predicament now, and no mistake. Make yourself useful and away to the weigh hoose. There's a case of whisky from auld Hall sitting in there. And I need a dram!'

'Is it no' a bit early, Sandy?'

'Not a bit of it. It's never too early for a dram when a woman's taken up residence on your own vessel. I'll tell you this: we'll be fair shunned by the rest o' the fleet, and that's a fact. Mind you, it'll no' matter, for something terrible is bound to happen that will make the whole thing academic.'

Hoynes watched as Hamish tramped off up the pier in the scurrying snow.

7

After much thought, Sandy Hoynes decided he couldn't, in all conscience, leave his vessel unattended when there was a stray and unwanted female aboard. First, he considered spending the night in his bunk to ensure that this Jo Baird could get up to as little mischief as possible. But the likelihood that this would become a staple of gossip for the people of Kinloch soon dawned on him.

His wife Marjorie was an amiable enough woman. But he feared that she wouldn't take kindly when rumours of his night spent with an attractive young lady were given free flight round the town.

There was only one solution: Hamish must be a nautical chaperone.

'It widna be proper,' said his first mate desperately. 'It would add insult to injury, a single man like me, and a woman – girl – alone all night. In any case, what will my mother say?'

'First of all, it was you who took the notion to sign this damned contract. Not once, mark you, but in triplicate. Secondly, you're too old to be worrying what your mother thinks, fine woman though she is. Heavens, a man has to stand on his own two feet at some point in his life. Have you no' been reading the papers or listening to the wireless? It's the permissive society we're in noo, and no mistake. You could take up with some lassie and take it into your mind tae jump the brush.'

'Get married? There was nothing aboot that in the contract.'

'Now you're being right obdurate. When it comes to nature, there's no' a mair natural thing in the world than a red-blooded man like yourself spending the night wae a well-formed young woman, despite what auld McNee the minister would have you believe. And in any case, it'll be too cold for any carnal urges to take a hold of you.'

'I canna believe I'm hearing this,' said Hamish, sucking hard on his pipe for comfort. 'If your Marjorie could hear you now, she'd be fair dumbstruck, and no error.'

'Well, she'll no' be hearing aboot it.' Hoynes looked up into the dark grey sky. 'I'm going tae drop in at the town hall for terms and the manifest. Then I'm going home for the night. A man of my years canna take any risks in weather like this. And who knows what terror we'll face tomorrow because of your recklessness.'

'And what about Jo?'

'I'll think on that tonight.' Hoynes narrowed his eyes. 'I didna take her for a lassie before she'd her clothes off doon below.'

'No' the most fortunate o' expressions, Sandy, if you don't mind me saying.'

'Och, wheesht, man, I'm thinking. Tell me, does anyone know aboot this bargain you struck?'

Hamish thought for a moment. 'Not that I know of – unless folk in the café were taking notes.'

'You, in your suit, wae a young woman in the café? Don't be daft. The whole toon will be on aboot it.'

'My mother included?'

'Och, she'll be fair raging right at this very moment, I shouldna wonder. But she'll have tae get over it. Man, you're damn near thirty. She canna expect you to remain white as the driven snow for ever.'

'Again, the unfortunate wording, Sandy! And, in any case, how do you know what I've been up tae in my youth?'

'Because you hop from one foot to another like a man wae ants in his breeches every time a lassie so much as hoves intae view.'

Hamish puffed his pipe indignantly.

'No. If I didna recognise her when she was all dubbed up against the snow, you can bet nobody else will. None of the fleet have as keen an eye as me.'

Hamish looked doubtful. 'Aye, maybe you're right. But what aboot all this bad luck you keep banging on aboot?'

'I've been thinking aboot that, as well. When it comes tae matters like this, we have to take intae account the weel of the community. These are extenuating circumstances. Man, the way things are going with this snowfall, the road won't be clear until after Christmas. We have tae balance the good we'll do against the spirits of malevolence. But they're a tricky bunch, they spirits. I'll never forget the Sunday Tommy Meenan cut his toenails.' Hoynes shook his head ruefully.

'What happened?'

'The very next day the lifeboat was oot and hauling the crew aboard before his boat was smashed to pieces on the Barrel Rocks. I was a wean at the time, but I mind my faither put strict rules in place all about the hoose regarding toenail cutting and the like. If you so much as looked at a pair of scissors on a Sunday, you'd have the end o' his belt.'

'Och, you've got me in a right panic, skipper. What on earth am I going to be at with her all night?'

'I'm sure there's a chessboard stowed in the galley. Aye, and Scrabble tae. But you'd be well advised no' to play that with a journalist. She'd likely wipe the floor wae you in a couple o' hands, and you'd be mair miserable than you are right this moment.'

Hamish's face was etched with concern. 'I'll try my best to keep her entertained.'

'And don't let her touch anything!'

'My, Sandy, it's fair personal you are. I've no' thought of such shenanigans!'

'I mean on the boat. You know what they journalists are like, intae everything. You don't want her firing up the engine by mistake, messing wae the compass or something of that nature.'

'I never thought of such a thing.' Hamish looked earnestly at Hoynes. 'Sandy, will you do me one favour?'

'Aye, as long as it doesna involve the lending o' money. You know my opinion o' that caper.'

'No, nothing of the sort! Would you mind giving my mother a call? Jeest to set her mind at ease, you understand.'

'Aye, for who knows what she'll have heard.'

'I know you're the man to put her right, Sandy.'

'I am that.' He pulled on his oilskins. 'Right, I'm off tae see what's going on up at the town hall, then I'm for the fireside and my own bed. Marjorie likely has a right good blaze on the go. Just the ticket. Get some stores in. We canna be too sure how long this voyage intae the unknown will take.'

'Aye, lucky you, toasting your toes in front o' the fire while I'm stuck here wae madam,' said Hamish under his breath. He watched Hoynes struggling through the drifts on the pier until he became a fading yellow ball in the blizzard.

8

By his fireside, feet up, Sandy Hoynes worked his way through the manifest of goods to be picked up at Girvan. Though he never trusted the town council, even he had to admit they'd done a good job. Fine deals had been made with traders in Girvan and their counterparts in Kinloch. The fishing boats putting to sea in dangerous weather were to be aptly rewarded. If they all made it back, everyone was a winner. Hoynes lit his pipe in satisfaction.

'You're looking pleased with yourself,' said Marjorie, observing the look on her husband's face.

'Aye, for we'll make a tidy sum, as well as delivering the toon fae the perils o' starvation – and worse, the absence of drink.'

Marjorie raised her eyes. 'As long as you know what you're doing in this weather.'

'It's a straight line tae Girvan! What kind o' mariner would I be if I couldna navigate my way from A to B by just sailing forward?'

'Strange things happen at sea, Sandy. And well you know it.'

Hoynes lifted a crystal glass from the table beside his favourite chair and took a sip of the whisky it held. The phone also occupied this table, and he regarded it with trepidation.

'Why are you staring at the phone?' asked his wife, who missed very little.

'I've a bit o' a dilemma, to tell the truth, Marjorie.'

'Which is?'

'Well, tae cut a long story short, Hamish is babysitting a journalist on board the boat. She's going to cover oor trip tomorrow, for the *Glasgow Times*, no less.'

Marjorie opened her mouth, then closed it again, repeating this action three times before words would come. 'A woman, on the *Girl Maggie*?'

Hoynes waved his hand dismissively. 'Ach, tell me aboot it! She has Hamish under her spell. He signed a contract – in triplicate, mark you. We're done up like a turkey at Christmas. I've no choice other than to honour it.'

Marjorie went back to her knitting, brow furrowed. 'Your own wife and daughter have never set foot on the damned thing, but some lassie fae a newspaper can jump aboard with impunity.'

'I'd no choice. Hamish fair left me in it.'

'Aye, but you're remarkably calm. I'm thinking there's a sum o' money involved.'

Hoynes opted not to reply, as he knew well that his wife would expect a windfall from his payment from the newspaper. He'd give her something, of course, but a sum predicated on a much smaller figure than was the reality.

He reached for the phone and dialled Hamish's phone number.

'Hello, Kinloch 3550, can I help you?'

'Ethel, and how are you keeping?' said Hoynes, as evenly as he could muster. Even he could hear the smile in his voice.

In return there came a scream.

'What on earth's the matter?' Hoynes shot his wife a mystified glance.

'I knew this day would come,' Ethel wailed. 'A deid husband, and a son tae join him!'

'What are you prattling on aboot, woman? Hamish is hale and hearty – well, unless something happened tae him in the short time it took me tae walk from the quay, stop in at the County for a dram, then dive intae the toon hall for some papers.' He thought for a moment. 'Mark you, it did take me a while tae wade through the drifts tae get home. But it's good tae see they've got the miners fae Machrie helping the council boys digging trenches through the snow. Walkways. It reminds me o' my time in the first war.'

He could hear Ethel sigh.

'If I'm not mistaken, you were still at the fishing during the war. A reserved position, I recall.'

Hoynes took a sip of his whisky. 'Aye, you have the right o' it there, Ethel. But I fair kept up wae all that was going on via the newspaper, an' that. You didna have to be at the Front tae experience the fear. And, in any event, I was busy risking my life on the waves tae feed the likes o' you.'

'Aye, out on the sound when it was like a millpond. It was hardly Jason and the Argonauts, Sandy.'

'But yous all tucked into the fish we hauled in! And, anyhow, they Germans were up tae all sorts, what wae the fifth columnists, U-boats and the like. Let me tell you, every day on the sea was like an eternity.' Hoynes heard a muffled snort from Hamish's mother. 'I do have something to report, mind you.'

'I knew it! What have you done to my Hamish? If he's got the jail for the drink, you'll have me tae reckon with! He never touched a drop until he stepped aboard your boat.'

45

Hoynes frowned at the phone. 'Nothing of the kind! In fact, he's dealing with a damsel in distress.' The wily skipper had considered this problem, and reasoned that making Hamish sound heroic was the most effective way to deal with his mother.

'Well, there's a thing. I would expect nothing less from my son. A right gentleman, so he is. Jeest as I brought him up.'

'Ha! You had him as a raving dipsomaniac a second ago.'

'Sandy Hoynes, you know fine I fear he'll take the same path as his father. I was grateful to you for giving him a berth when – well, when things went wrong. But you must admit yourself, you're no stranger tae a dram, and that's a fact.'

'Hamish can hold his whisky. Aye, and he's not a man of excess neithers.' The memory of Hamish taking a well-lubricated header off the pier at Brodick passed before his mind's eye. But this wasn't the time for such revelations. And, in any case, the tide had been in, and with the help of some sturdy Arran fishermen he'd been hauled out, right as rain.

'Well, I'm glad to hear it. You've no idea how whisky frightens me, Sandy.'

'I've a notion, right enough, Ethel,' said Hoynes, taking another surreptitious sip from his glass. 'But this poor lassie, fair marooned she is, and no' a penny to her name.' Hoynes shook his head sorrowfully, while his wife rolled her eyes. 'No Christian man could turn her away in this weather. I gave her a berth on the boat and promised her passage to Ayrshire tomorrow when we're off to get supplies.'

'I have to say I admire you, Sandy. For it's long before time this nonsense aboot women and boats was put tae rest. We're travelling the world in cruise liners and the like these days. They tell me there was even a female member o' crew on the *Hindenburg*.'

'That's maybe no' the best example, Ethel. But the air and the sea are two very different elements.'

'Well, that's true. But I'm fair glad you had the decency to let me know. I'm no superstitious biddy. It's a fine and noble thing yous are doing. And if any criticism of you or my Hamish reaches my ears, you can rest assured that the appropriate answer will be forthcoming.'

'Aye, and that's right decent o' you, Ethel.' Hoynes hesitated. 'But mark you, there's a wee codicil to this tale.'

'A what?'

'Well, I couldna leave this poor lassie aboard by herself. A fishing boat is fraught wae danger, as you know. Even tied up at the quay.'

'What are you trying tae say, Sandy?'

'Well, jeest that this poor lassie – skin and bones she is, too – I had to gie her a bed for the night, wae a chaperone, you understand.'

'And?' Suspicion was audible in this one word.

'Well, Hamish is making sure she's safe and sound through the night.' Hoynes took the phone from his ear, knowing what was likely to be forthcoming.

He wasn't disappointed.

'You mean my boy is aboard a boat for the whole night – alone! – wae some lassie!'

'Aye.'

'I canna believe it, Sandy. You get doon there right this moment and haul her back onto the quay! If she needs a bed for the night, she can stay here, and Hamish can sleep on the boat. All on his own, as nature intended for a single young man.'

Hoynes grimaced. He'd expected opposition, but not solutions. 'Aye, a noble gesture on your own part, Ethel,

47

yes indeed. But the situation is more complicated than you imagine.'

'I'm no' aboot tae put words to what I'm imagining. What's tae stop this lassie coming up tae the Glebe Fields? I'll have Hamish's bed made up for her in a jiffy. Aye, and I've a fine pot o' broth on the stove, so she'll no' go hungry.'

'She's injured,' said Hoynes, uttering the first thing that came to mind.

'Injured? What kind o' injury?'

'Her leg – it's near snapped in two, so it is.'

'Heavens! The poor girl. But should she no' be in the hospital, rather than a fishing boat?'

'It's the problem o' getting her there. Doctor Duncan came doon earlier wae his Plaster o' Paris and the like. Set it for her exquisitely, if I may say so. Botticelli couldna have done a better job, himself.'

'Is he no' the wee man that has the fish and chip shop at Tarbert?'

'Might be a distant relative, I'm no' right sure. But the dilemma was simple. Wae the roads and pavements fair blocked wae snow, there was no way we could get her up tae the hospital.'

'And how did she get aboard?'

'Aye, that was the tragedy o' the whole thing, Ethel. She slipped on the gunwale as she was coming aboard. Landed wae a right clatter, so she did. That's when the leg got broken.'

'Oh, it jeest gets worse.'

'Aye, it was some performance, right enough. So you'll see, I'm obliged to her in a' sorts o' ways.'

'Could you no' make a sledge and drag her up tae the hospital?'

'I'm a fisherman, Ethel, no' an Eskimo! Anyway, whisky and Eskimos aside, you'll have no fear o' temptation getting the better o' them. The lassie's in agony. I'm sure nature's urging is well beyond her.'

'I'll get my good boots on and head down the pier myself. Hamish can go back hame.'

'Noo jeest hold your horses, Ethel. I've one woman aboard. Another would be tempting fate too far. You must understand my position.' A film of sweat had broken out across his forehead. Hoynes was sure it wasn't the whisky, and the room wasn't overly warm. 'I'm under a lot o' pressure, and that's a fact.'

'You'll be under even mair if nature takes its course. My Hamish is a fine young man – damn near a saint compared to his father. The stirring o' the loins is a force o' nature you canna mess wae.'

'You're havering. Hamish would have to be some monster to take advantage o' a lassie wae her leg in a stookie. When I left them she was fair oot o' it in her bunk. Doctor Duncan gave her a right strong sedative.'

'Well . . .' Ethel still sounded doubtful. 'It would make me much easier o' mind if you were to head down there and sit with the pair o' them. Goodness knows what my Hamish would dae if she took a turn.'

'She'll be fine. But listen, I can hear your concern. I'm just at my tea. I'll head doon the quay just as soon as possible. How does that suit, Ethel?'

Across from him, Marjorie glared.

'Aye, that puts my mind at rest. And you be sure to take care tomorrow. I'll be praying for yous all.'

'Much appreciated, Ethel. And don't worry. There's nobody that knows the way better. Not a skipper in the fleet.'

They said their goodbyes and ended the call.

'My, but you're a piece o' work, Sandy Hoynes,' said Marjorie. 'Still at your tea, indeed! You've been sitting wae a dram for the last hour and more.'

'If I was in France right now they would consider that normal. Drink is all part o' the nourishment o' the body. So, technically I was in the right.'

'Big o' you to go back to the boat, mind you.'

'Ach, I'll be there soon enough. That was a wee white lie. No' even that. I said as soon as possible. In this case, that's tomorrow morning.'

'Sandy Hoynes, one day you'll have tae answer for all the things you've done.'

'Huh, like feeding a starving town? You look to your ain misdemeanours. I've no' forgotten you using packet custard for the tart you put in for the June show and passing it off as your own.'

Marjorie dropped a stitch and rightfully blamed her husband.

9

The gull looked out over the loch from his position high on the old fort. Though the waters were as black as pitch, the town gathered around it had a luminous quality, a silvery glow, as though the place was defying night.

A catch of fishermen bustled under the bright lights of the pier. The gull cocked his head to watch as they struggled aboard their vessels, their distant voices, muffled by the snow, floating across the water and up the hill.

The ancient guardian of the town decided to fly over his charges in a spirit of goodwill. The great bird stretched his wings and called out in the still, dark morning. Then, soaring into the velvet sky, he dipped towards the little fleet of fishing boats.

Jim McMichael was sweeping away the accumulated snow from the windows of the *Evening Star*'s wheelhouse. 'Here, Willie,' he shouted to his first mate. 'Is that a new hand Hoynes has aboard? I'm sure I spied someone talking to Hamish when I arrived. By the size o' him, no more than a lad.'

Willie turned his head awkwardly. He'd lost an eye in the

war while serving with the Royal Navy, and wore a patch over the hole where his right one would have been. 'I'm no' quite sure. All I can see is Hoynes himself.'

'Ahoy, *Girl Maggie*!' shouted McMichael. 'You've a new crew member, I see!'

Under the lights of the pier, Hoynes' large, yellow-oilskinned frame was picked out. 'Sorry, my hearing's no' so good these days, Jimmy. What did you say? It's down tae too much exposure to the elements o'er a long period. If you're asking if we'll make it through, I'm sure o' it! Wae the snow being off and suchlike, it'll be plain sailing. Hamish is forecasting clear skies. And, as we all know, he has the sight. Jeest you follow my lead.'

McMichael shook his head and addressed his mate in less strident terms. 'Deaf, my arse. Likely taking advantage o' some schoolboy who's time on his hands. The lad will be getting a pittance for a rough passage and doing all the work. Aye, and Hamish wae the sight, tae – another pile o' pish.'

Before Willie could reply, the call came from the *Girl Maggie*. 'Aye, I heard you. Anyone that sets foot aboard this vessel has the best conditions on the west coast, and that's a fact! And it's been proved time an' again that Hamish is fey.'

'I thought you were deaf!' shouted McMichael.

'Sorry, I didna catch that, Jimmy. I'll need to get going. We've nae time for all this chit-chat.' With that, Hoynes disappeared into his wheelhouse.

Willie arrived by his skipper's side. 'It's funny you said that, Jimmy.'

'How so?'

'Davey fae the *Morning Sky* was having a drink up at the

County wae me last night. Swears that he saw a woman aboard the *Girl Maggie* yesterday. Smoking on the prow, so she was – according tae him, anyway.'

'Don't be ridiculous, Willie! Sandy Hoynes might be up tae many a lark, but even he's no' daft enough tae have a woman aboard. Och, you canna trust a word that comes oot o' Davey's mouth. I'm sure he telt us he'd been tae Buckingham Palace last year.'

'Technically he wisna wrong, Skipper. He was at Buckingham Palace. But it's a pub in Fulham.' Willie shrugged.

'Right, get doon below and fire up the engine. We're going tae be first oot the loch this morning.'

❄

Hoynes squeezed his way through the hatch into the cabin below. Jo was dressed in one of Hamish's thick sea jumpers, black waders and wellington boots, all of which were too large by far. Hamish was attending to some tin mugs beside a simmering kettle. The contrast in temperature was marked, the old potbellied stove doing its job well and heating up the tiny crew quarters.

'You've nae time for tea, Hamish. I'd thought we'd be first away by a long stretch, but McMichael is on the button today. Get the engine fired up and we'll beat them tae it past the island.'

'Oh, can I take some photos?' said Jo.

'You can stay right where you are until we get oot o' the loch and put some sea room between us and the rest o' the fleet. I'll let you know when it's safe to appear.'

'The Dark Ages, right enough,' she murmured to herself.

'Aye, and they'll be staying dark for you until we're in the sound.'

'Aye, aye, captain!' Jo gave a mock salute.

'I'll get the tea, Hamish,' said Hoynes.

'Nae bother. I'll get us going, jeest directly.'

When Hamish disappeared and Hoynes busied himself at the galley, Jo delved into her pocket. In her hand was a little plastic bag with three sugar lumps. She secreted them back into her pocket before Hoynes turned round.

'Do you take sugar?'

'Yes, please, just one spoonful.' She smiled innocently.

'It's lumps we have here. No time for messing aboot wae spoons when a gale's blowing.'

Jo smiled broadly. Being a free spirit, she now viewed the journey as a trip in more ways than one. It was great to be away from the smoke and noise of Glasgow. She was a country girl herself, but from a landlocked part of Stirlingshire. Though boats weren't her thing, she was sure it wouldn't be a problem. After all, she'd performed all sorts of difficult tasks for the paper, including taking photographs at an Old Firm game. No sea could present such dangers.

'Here's your tea,' said Hoynes, handing her a tin mug. 'And in that brown poke there's sugar lumps. You're on tea duties fae now on. We all have tae pull our weight in dire straits like these.'

'Don't worry. I spent my first two years at the paper making tea for those chauvinistic oafs. I'm sure I'll manage.'

'You'll find no chauvinists aboard this vessel. Equality is high on the agenda, and no mistake. Noo, I like my tea sweet – four lumps. When I call doon fae the wheelhouse, you get yourself moving quick smart, lassie.'

Jo raised her brows.

Suddenly the boat shuddered as the Gardner engine thudded into life. After a few coughs and splutters, it soon settled into a steady pulse, like an old man struggling out of bed in the morning, coughing, cursing and then hurrying off to the toilet.

'Aye, there's a fine sound, right enough. Next stop, Girvan. I better go and get us underway. You mind and stay here until I give you a shout.'

Hoynes climbed through the hatch and onto the deck, just as Hamish emerged from the engine. The skipper cast his eye about and noticed that McMichael was about to sail; first mate Willie was busy at a hawser looped over a bollard on the quayside.

'Quick, Hamish, get you up on that quay and untie us! McMichael's making a break for it. Mind, we've got the press aboard – even though she's just a slip o' a thing – and we don't want the vessel portrayed as some sluggard in a national paper. It widna be good for morale at all.'

'Whose morale?' Hamish asked.

'Mine. Noo, get a shift on.'

Hamish strode across the snowbound deck, and in one fluid movement hurdled up onto the pier. As he busied himself untying the vessel, Hoynes squeezed into the small wheelhouse and began the manoeuvre away from the quay, his eyes flicking between the loch ahead and the progress of the *Morning Star*.

Job done, Hamish leapt back aboard in his usual manner, forgetting about the snow. Luckily, he skidded into a mess of nets, only his dignity hurt.

'Serve you right!' shouted Hoynes. 'There's nae place for a' that flash stuff on a serious vessel like this.'

'It was you that wanted away quickly! The way you were turning, it would jeest have been you and Jo as a crew, for I'd have been left on the pier like a right dumpling.'

'Wheesht! I'm concentrating, man.' The tip of Hoynes' tongue was sticking out between his teeth as he made for the open water of the loch with all speed, well aware that – as things stood – he was on a collision course with the *Evening Star*.

'You're going tae see us wrecked before we even make harbour!' shouted Hamish. 'How will that look in the newspaper?'

The two fishing boats were neck and neck now. Hoynes looked to his left, only to see McMichael signalling to him with his right hand in a way that could best be described as ungentlemanly.

The *Evening Star* was a bigger boat, of more recent manufacture, but with size came a sluggishness of acceleration. Though McMichael had been first to leave the quayside, Hoynes was gaining on him as they both made for the gap between the twin piers.

'You'll need tae get a move on, Sandy!' yelled Hamish, as black smoke issued in great clouds from the wheelhouse chimney.

'I know what I'm at, Hamish.' Hoynes returned McMichael's crude gesture with gusto.

'We needna worry about beating them to the loch, Sandy. Once we're in open water, we'll gain on them.'

'I'm in command here. And we'll be first oot o' this harbour. I'll bet my life on it!'

❄

A collection of elderly fishermen had gathered on the quayside. Ostensibly they were there to wish their former colleagues godspeed, but also with an eye to any calamities or notable happenings that they could discuss over a dram later.

'Bugger me,' said Peeny. 'It's like watching two slugs racing for a plughole.'

'McMichael is a determined bugger, right enough,' said McKirdy. 'But Sandy Hoynes should know better. Whoot's the point in sinking two boats jeest tae see who can make it oot the harbour first? Aye, wae whisky supplies aboot tae run low in the whole community.'

'By the look o' that smoke piling fae the *Girl Maggie* they'll no' make it to the end of the pier, never mind Girvan,' observed Peeny.

By this time, the spectators included the crews of the other boats in the fleet. Their heads appeared through portholes, above hatches and through wheelhouse windows, as the race progressed slowly, but with no little excitement.

'McMichael's got the better o' it, and no mistake,' said Peeny. 'Hoynes is bound tae end up wae egg on his face.'

'There's been bad blood between the pair o' them since that darts match at the Douglas Arms,' said Tommy Duncan, his pyjama collar poking out the neck of his pea jacket. 'If you recall, Sandy had tae score twenty-one off three darts. Mind, he missed the board and near blinded auld Jenny. McMichael cleaned up. They County boys took it right bad, so they did.'

Both fishing boats were now nearing the gap between the two piers, the *Evening Star* ahead by a nose. Those on the quay and on the remaining boats considered the race was won – until something extraordinary happened.

A head appeared from the cabin hatch of the *Girl Maggie*. McMichael was the first to spot it, and sheer shock caused him to let go of the wheel. His boat veered dangerously to the right, heading for the new quay on the other side of the harbour.

Hoynes saw his chance, cut in ahead of his rival and made it out into the open loch first. He had the time to return McMichael's earlier gesture again as he coasted past the *Evening Star*, her skipper desperately turning the wheel to avoid a collision.

The faces of those back at the quay, fishermen young and old, bore a collective look of disbelief.

'I must have had too much tae drink last night, for I could swear I jeest saw a lassie poke her heid oot o' Sandy's hatch thonder.'

'Well, I never touched a drop,' said Duncan, 'and I saw her too.'

Provost McMurdo and the town clerk appeared. 'Oh, we've missed the first boys away,' said the former, slightly bemused by the stricken looks on the faces of those before him. 'Is there something wrong?'

Peeny turned to the provost. 'Hoynes has a woman – a lassie! – aboard his boat. We all saw her.'

'Oh, well, I can't see that being a problem,' replied the provost.

The old fisherman fixed him with a steely glare. 'You're a vet tae trade, Mr McMurdo, yes?'

'Yes, what about it?'

'Well, think on. A fisherman going tae sea with a woman aboard a boat is as vexatious as a vet leaving his wallet in a barn. Do you get my point?'

'Oh dear.'

'Aye, oh dear indeed! It doesna do tae provoke the traditions of the sea – no, not at all. I'll be surprised if we set eyes on Sandy Hoynes and his boat again, and that's a fact.'

With a general murmur of agreement, those gathered on the quay shuffled off, heads down, as though they were stepping away in widow's weeds from a funeral.

10

The *Girl Maggie* forged ahead in the still waters of the loch, easily beating her rival between the two buoys that marked the channel past the island and into the sound.

When Hoynes glanced behind, the first grey light of day revealed a ragged string of fishing boats in his wake, headed by the *Evening Star*. He smiled at the thought of his fellow skipper's indignation over losing the impromptu race out of the harbour. But he was puzzled as to why McMichael had made such an elementary mistake in steering. In any event, Kinloch's fishing fleet had set sail to rescue the town from starvation. He was merely first amongst equals. He smiled at the thought. As he turned to face forwards, a large gull deposited a great mess across the wheelhouse window.

'Here, get that cleaned off, Hamish!' shouted Hoynes. 'These bloody gulls.'

In short order, Hamish appeared in front of the window and went to work with a chamois leather and bucket of soapy water, his breath clouding in front of him.

Hoynes popped his head out of the wheelhouse door and looked heavenward. Now that the first light of dawn was spreading across the eastern horizon, it revealed a great bank of cloud ahead, dark but with the pearlescent quality of snow. Though he could see the Isle of Arran to his left, the Ayrshire coast – their destination – had not emerged with the dawn.

'Your predictions are awry again, Hamish. I'm thinking you should stay clear o' weather forecasting, for that cloud is just about to dump a great blizzard upon us.'

Sure enough, as he spoke, the first flakes appeared on Hamish's Breton cap.

'And jeest where did you get that fancy bunnet?' Hoynes asked. 'You look like one o' they French matelots, no' a proper Scots fisherman.'

'Och, they're a' the rage in London. I'm sure they Beatles were wearing them no' that long ago.'

'Well, if that's no' enough to put you off such millinery, I don't know what is. There's nae room for a fashion statement aboard a vessel o' the sea. The minute you pick up the guitar, you're back ashore, and no mistake.'

Gradually, as though the emergence of the day had been merely a short respite, darkness engulfed the *Girl Maggie*. Not the pitch black of night, but an eerie grey that rendered their surroundings almost invisible. Even the water lapping at the sides of the vessel was muffled, as though they had put to sea in a small pond. Great clouds of snow began to sweep over the fishing boat.

Hamish joined Hoynes in the wheelhouse. 'My goodness, skipper. I don't think I've ever put to sea in conditions like this. It's as though we've entered another realm.'

'You have a flair for the dramatic, Hamish. Och, you get that from your mother. The hoops I'd tae go through tae stop her from heading doon the quay last night to save your virtue near turned me into a circus dog. It's time you put your foot doon and showed her who's boss. You canna go on at the beck an' call o' your mother, no' a man your age.'

'It's a' very well saying that, Sandy. But where would I go? I can rustle up some beans and bacon, but that's aboot it. And when it comes tae a' this washing and pressing o' clothes – well, that's me buggered.'

'It's a wife you're needing, plain and simple. Nature is designed wae that in mind. While we're oot braving the wild ocean, they're at home attending tae the tasks that are a mystery tae menfolk. I have these twin tubs in the kitchen now. Man, they might as well be fae outer space, for I've no idea how to use them. But Marjorie fair swings intae action. Before you know it, the scullery is filled wae steam and she's hauling wet clothes hither and thon. Quite miraculous it is tae watch.'

'My auld mother still has a mangle. She's got forearms like a miner, so she has.'

Hoynes lit his pipe thoughtfully. In truth, he'd always felt rather inferior to the opposite sex. The manner in which they dealt with everything from domestic tasks to wiping the backsides of infants had to be admired. He'd been forced to change his daughter's nappy on mercifully few occasions. Each time it had ruined his appetite for days, and the mere sight of oxtail soup set his stomach churning to this day. But Marjorie performed the task with alacrity, happily conversing as she dealt with a great deposit the size of which a carthorse would have been proud.

'You wait, Hamish. Wae this women's lib and all, there will be a woman sitting in Downing Street before you can canter.'

'Och, no.' Hamish removed his cap and slicked back his diminishing quiff with an oily hand. 'It widna be proper.'

'What do you have tae say aboot Her Majesty, in that case? Would you no' consider that she's making a fair fist o' things?'

'Aye, but she's got the royal blood, Sandy. Look at auld Victoria, for example. She was only a slip o' a lassie when she became queen and she ruled a huge empire. I'm sure your Marjorie couldna set her hands tae that. No offence, mark you.'

'Maybe no', but I think your mother would give it a go.'

Hamish nodded, a faraway look in his eyes. 'You might be right there.'

'There's a condition wae women who've lost their husbands in tragic circumstances and the like.'

'And jeest what would that be?' Hamish asked.

'Och, they become fair attached tae their sons. No' in any romantic way, you understand, but enough that they want them aboot the place. Put it like this, have you ever brought home a lassie that met with your mother's approval?'

'That's a simple question tae answer, skipper. I've never brought a lassie hame at all. My mother would just find fault.'

'Aye, an' you were close enough wae Jessie McGown for a good while.'

'I was.' Hamish lowered his head.

'You never told me why it all came tae an end.'

A look of regret passed over the first mate's face. 'My mother wisna keen. Apparently Jessie's great-grandfather had been hung by the Duke o' Argyll for poaching. You canna bring blood like that intae the family line.'

'Nonsense. I knew the man. I was only a boy, but I can see him yet. He was a shepherd doon at Pollyfergus farm in Blaan. A fine fellow. Died on the hill wae his sheep, as all men o' that trade are want tae do.'

Hamish looked momentarily bewildered. 'Are you sure?'

'I am that. Sure, he was great pals wae my own grandfaither. He was a man o' the land. On my mother's side, you understand.'

'So my mother didna have the right o' it at all?'

'No. And I'm here tae tell you that she knew fine what she was at. Jeest fair keen that you stayed by her fireside.'

'I can hardly believe it.'

'I'm telling you, Hamish. You need tae get yourself sorted wae a nice lassie, quick smart. I know you're proud o' thon coo's lick o' yours. But, man, that'll no' last for ever. And once you're bald, you've nae chance finding a wife.'

'In that event I'll jeest keep my bunnet on, Sandy.'

'Ach, you're havering. You'll pardon me for the descriptive nature of what I'm aboot tae say. You'd be a bonny sight, fair caught up in the throes o' passion in your marriage bed, and you wae your bunnet on. Man, you might as well have your pipe clenched between your teeth intae the bargain.'

It was hard to gauge what Hamish thought of this. His expression went from one of abject horror to an embarrassed red hue. Almost as though the mere contemplation of the carnal act minus pipe and bunnet may well be a sin against all that was holy.

The snow was now falling like feathers from a burst pillow. 'I hope my calculations are right,' said Hoynes, 'or we'll fair batter intae the Cock o' Arran. For I don't know aboot you, but I canna see much beyond the prow.'

'I'm getting a bad feeling, Sandy.'

'Again? My, but you're a right doom-monger. You'll need tae brighten up your act. No woman wants to be wed tae some prophet o' doom.' With that, Hoynes sounded the ship's horn in the unlikely event that some other vessel was in the vicinity. For it had to be said, only the bravest or most foolish of mariners would have put to sea this day. Though it all depended on your perspective.

11

Down below, things on the *Girl Maggie* had taken a turn for the worse, as far as Jo was concerned. She'd stuck her head above the cabin hatch for just a moment as they were leaving the harbour. But even in those calm waters, just a glimpse of the houses on the north shore of the loch swaying to and fro was enough to set her stomach churning.

She'd consulted the large stained chart that sat before her on the table. Though she knew next to nothing about the ways of the sea, she calculated that the alarming change in circumstances aboard coincided with their emergence into the sound. It was plain enough on the chart.

The *Girl Maggie* lurched in the swell, and with it the journalist's stomach. She tried to focus on a little copper cooking pot that hung from a nail over the stove, reasoning that orientating herself within the cabin may ease her plight. But this had the opposite effect, and she felt the bile rise in her throat. Thankfully, there was an old bucket close at hand, into which she vomited copiously.

Believing that her symptoms would now ease, she rested her head on the chart table. Unfortunately, this only made matters worse, and in a few moments she was retching again into the bucket.

She remembered a story she'd read about Admiral Lord Nelson. As a young midshipman he'd suffered terrible seasickness, making his first three years or so aboard a man-of-war hell. Miserably, Jo tried to console herself that this was a relatively short journey, or so Hoynes had assured her.

Hamish stuck his head through the hatch, his Breton cap defying gravity and remaining attached firmly to his head. 'How are you faring down below?' he asked.

Through her misery, Jo managed a retort. 'That's a very personal question to ask a young lady.'

Hamish looked startled. 'Och, I meant . . . I meant no offence. Jeest wondered how you were managing, and the like,' he stammered, face bright red.

'It wouldn't be polite to give a truthful answer.' Again Jo bent over the bucket.

'Oh dear!' Hamish eased his way through the hatch and into the cabin. 'It'll be the seasickness you have.'

'I kinda worked that out for myself.'

'Och, not tae worry. There's barely a man – or woman – at sea who takes to it right away. Though, mark you, they say they do. I myself was right seasick when I first landed aboard a vessel. But it soon passed.'

'How long did it take?' Jo asked quickly before heaving again.

'No time at all. Less than a year, at any rate.'

'Let me die now,' she groaned, laying her head back on the chart table.

'I know fine what you require: a nice mug o' tea. My mother swears by it, a cure-all suitable for every occasion. Personally, I prefer a dram myself, but I do believe women are of a different construction.'

'So you've just noticed?'

Ignoring the barb, Hamish set to and hung the iron kettle above the stove. 'I'll make you a brew.'

As her head lolled from side to side on the chart table, the thought of a cup of tea only made Jo feel worse.

Then she had an idea. 'Thank you, Hamish. I'd love some tea, please.'

'It'll set your stomach to rights in no time.'

But just as he was preparing three tin mugs, a loud voice sounded through the speaking tube from the wheelhouse above.

'Get your backside up here, Hamish. I canna see a thing. We'll have tae take it slow and check depths.'

'I'll need to go back on deck. My goodness, that's a call dreaded aboard any vessel. It usually only happens in the worst fog. But this snow has the same effect. I'll be back down directly and make you some tea. But colliding wae the Cock o' Arran would do us no favours at all.'

'The cock of who?' said Jo groggily.

'Never you mind.'

As his wellington boots disappeared through the hatch, Jo's heart sank. The prospect of a mug of tea had suddenly become an attractive one, but not perhaps for the reasons Hamish assumed. She laid her head back on the table and tried to will herself not to be sick again.

Hamish whirled the line with the brass end through the air, as though he was about to lasso a horse. At exactly the right moment he let it go, and just like a cast from an expert fly fisherman it disappeared through the heavy snow and landed well to the port side of the *Girl Maggie* with a thick plop in the unseen swell.

It was eerie, with not a seabird to be heard, or sight of land or sky. The deck of the boat was now garnished with a thick icing of snow. Hoynes peered out from the wheelhouse through a window frosted like a shop from a Dickensian Christmas scene. 'How's she looking?' he shouted to Hamish as he hauled in the line.

'Aye, we're okay, Sandy. We'll have to take it steady, mind. When did you get your last bearing?'

'Jeest after we passed the island, Hamish. I'm pretty sure we're on course, but cocooned like this it's hard to tell if it's New Year or New York!'

'I'll fling the line every few minutes, just to make sure.'

'Aye, we'll come across the seabed long before we hit the rocks. But I'm convinced we're on the mark, tae. Mind you, I'll take her down to a crawl, jeest in case.' The tone of the engine lowered as the skipper slowed the craft.

'It's jeest like being Jonah – you know, stuck in the belly o' the whale,' said Hamish.

'Damn me, it wisna snowing in there tae, was it?'

'I'm wondering. Would it no' be safer to turn roon and go back the way we came? You surely weren't expecting a blizzard like this when we set off, Sandy?'

'I listened to two sources of information: the shipping forecast and your predictions. It would appear that both were sadly lacking. As far as turning round, what good would that do us? We could go clattering intae the rest o' the fleet. I don't want to be the man responsible for scuppering this emergency mission.'

Hamish nodded sagely at this reasoning.

'I'm like a block o' ice, Hamish. You take the wheel a while. Keep her on the current heading unless you have a notion we're nearing the rocks. I'll away and warm my backside at the stove and get a mug o' tea. How's the lassie doing, by the way?'

'Och, no' good at all, Sandy. She's seasick.'

'You canna expect much else fae a lassie. It'll teach her tae be so forthcoming and manipulative in order tae get aboard this vessel in the first place. Right cunning, if ever I saw it.'

'Will you get her a mug, skipper? I was about to when you asked me to haul the line.'

'Hopefully that will brighten her up. There's nothing like tea for altering your outlook on life – aside fae a dram, that is. It's no' quite the time tae splice the main brace yet.' He squinted at the sky. 'Though that time might come before we get back hame.'

Hoynes left the wheelhouse, to be replaced by Hamish. The skipper held out his gloved hand and almost immediately it gathered a covering of snow. He shook his head and made for the hatch.

12

Jo had managed to make it to the stove. She'd set herself a mug and poured some water into the tin teapot, to which Hamish had already added some tea leaves. She reached into her pocket and found the small packet containing the sugar lumps. She'd have been tempted to forgo the tea and just dissolve one on her tongue, but the thought of it made her stomach churn. She was also bitterly cold, so the warm beverage would be most welcome.

Jo was just about to place the sugar lump in her mug when Hoynes burst through the hatch like a cork fired from a gun. He landed on his feet with a thud, hard enough that he had to bend his knees in order to absorb the impact. Startled, Jo dropped the sugar lump not in her mug, but in the open packet used by the crew.

Hoynes eyed the hatch with disdain. 'Man, I'll need tae get that widened. The wood has fair contracted over the years. It's the effects of salt water, you understand.'

Though the cognitive part of Jo's brain registered this as nonsense, and it was obvious that, on the contrary, Sandy Hoynes' waistline had burgeoned, she didn't have the energy to contradict him. She slumped at the side of the galley, the cabin spinning as though she was on a merry-go-round.

'Here now, this won't do, no, not all.' He caught her under the arms and hefted the seasick journalist into the bottom bunk, normally reserved for his own use. 'Why don't you have a wee lie doon and I'll fetch you some tea. This isn't quite the jolly you imagined it would be, eh?'

Jo now felt so miserable she could barely muster a reply. She grunted and turned over on her side to see if it would banish her nausea.

Hoynes made for the galley, the curtain that separated it from the rest of the cabin already pulled aside. He placed the kettle back on the hook and soon heard it bubble to the boil. He prepared two mugs, noticing that the young journalist had already laid one out for herself. 'How many sugars?' he asked her.

'Just one, please,' she replied weakly.

'This will sort you out. If it doesna, the only place for you is up on deck. You need tae catch sight o' the horizon. Mind you, right at the moment there's no horizon tae be seen.' He reached for the sugar and put four lumps in his own mug, then two for Hamish and one for his stricken passenger. Hoynes stirred the leaves in the tin pot sitting snugly in its little guard nest on the stove.

As he waited for the tea to brew, he reached for the speaking tube. 'How are we looking, Hamish?'

'So far, so good,' came the muffled reply from the wheelhouse. 'But if anything, the snow's heavier than it was just a couple o' minutes ago when you went below.'

He shook his head. 'I've never seen the like. I'll give you a shout when the tea's brewed. I'll hand it up through the hatch.'

Satisfied that the brew was sufficiently infused, Hoynes poured the tea into each mug. The sound of tea pouring was always a comfort, the ritual of making it almost as satisfying as the beverage itself. He gave each mug a stir, added some milk from the bottle kept in an ice bucket he'd purloined from the County Hotel, and took a sip from his own mug to make sure all was well.

He tapped Jo on the shoulder. 'Here, get this doon you, lassie. I hope the next time you're sitting in your fancy office in Glasgow you'll take note o' the desperate conditions us fishermen have to endure. Man o' man, the whole profession is fair heroic, and no mistake.'

She turned round in the bunk and accepted the mug of tea with trembling hands.

'I canna see you being in any condition to take photographs and write your piece. Wae this snow, there's no' so much tae photograph at the moment.' He took a sip of his tea thoughtfully. 'Would you like me tae jot down a few o' my musings? Jeest tae give you a hand, what wae you in your current plight an' all.'

'I don't mind,' replied Jo wearily. 'I just want to feel better again.'

'And you will, you will. I better get Hamish his tea. He's a right bugger if it gets cold. Fair pampered by that mother o' his.' Hoynes had another thought. 'You're a single lassie yourself, are you not?'

'What? Oh, yes.'

'Aye, well, you could do worse than a fisherman. Oor Hamish is a fine man. Good family – well, apart from his faither, and that was a weakness for the bottle, nothing mair.'

Jo ignored Hoynes' attempts at matchmaking. The thought of becoming romantically involved with the man in the ancient suit, receding hairline and weird eyes was enough to send her stomach churning again. 'Could you please pass me that bucket?'

Hoynes pushed the bucket across the cabin with the toe of his sea boot. 'I see it's no' your first visit tae it, neither.' He gave Hamish a shout through the speaking tube. His first mate came to the hatch and took the two mugs of tea handed to him.

As Hoynes began his squeeze through the hatch back to the deck, he heard Jo mumble. 'What's that, lassie?' Hoynes leaned his head back into the cabin.

'Don't drink the tea.' Her voice was slurred now. Plainly she was suffering.

'Don't you worry. Jeest you concentrate on getting better.'

With that, he was back on the snowy deck.

Hoynes gave the wheelhouse window another rub before joining Hamish in the cramped space. The blizzard was so heavy now that it was hard to see the bow of the *Girl Maggie*. The skipper sipped his hot tea thoughtfully.

'This isna the kind o' trip we envisaged, skipper. No, not at all,' said Hamish as he peered into the snow, ship's wheel in his brawny hands.

'No. I wished we'd jeest turned doon the offer. Though it would've been a miserable time for the folk in Kinloch if we hadn't volunteered. I daresay a few would have resorted tae cannibalism when the food became scarce.'

'I know just who, tae.' Hamish shook his head.

'We can only pray that things improve.'

'Aye, you're right there.'

13

On board the *Evening Star*, McMichael was becoming increasingly concerned by the turn of the weather. Unlike Hoynes – who thought such a thing an unnecessary indulgence, not to mention an unthinkable expense – he had a radio.

'*Evening Star* to the Kinloch fleet, come in, over.' He waited for a few moments, but there was nothing but static on the crackling line. McMichael was about to give up when a faint voice sounded through the wooden speaker above his head. 'Aye, Jim, it's Davie here.'

'Davie who?'

'Davie Robertson, who do you think?'

'You're supposed tae say, "Roger, the *Black Isle* receiving, over."'

'Och, I canna get tae grips wae this radio stuff at all. You knew fine who it was as soon as I opened my mouth. You only saw me this morning.'

'That's no' the point. We should be observing the correct protocol on the wireless. You never know who's listening.'

'It's hardly Radio Caroline, Jim.'

'Clyde Coastguard, they'll have their lugs roon this, and no mistake.'

'You're worried about who's listening to your radio protocol when we're out here about tae crash intae Arran in a blizzard. You're a brave man, right enough, McMichael, but I'm no' so sure about your priorities.'

'It's why we're speaking! I think we should turn roon and make back for Kinloch.'

Apart from the crackle of static, there was silence on the other end of the line. 'Davie, are you there?'

'You're supposed tae say, "Come in, *Black Isle*"!'

'Well, what dae you think?'

'Roger. I've been conversing wae the crew, and we're o' the same mind as yourself, over.'

'And you're certain sure, Davie?'

'I'm in no hurry tae land on the Cock o' Arran. We'll make oor way back hame. I'll pass it doon the fleet.'

'What about Hoynes?'

'No' even a radio on board, has he?'

'No, nor a glimmer o' one. The man's too tight.'

'It's for the good o' the many. He'll have tae take his chances. In this, who knows if any of us will make it back.'

'Aye, you're right. I'll try and get the Coastguard and tell them he's out there somewhere.' McMichael squinted into the gloom. He'd never been the best of friends with Sandy Hoynes – the man was overbearing at the best of times; still, he wished him no harm. He lifted the radio to his mouth again and called Clyde Coastguard.

Hoynes enjoyed his mug of tea. A great wave of warmth had spread into his belly. And now, despite the weather, he found himself quite relaxed in the wheelhouse.

Idly, he watched Hamish swirl the line yet again. The whole process became strangely fascinating. The brass end seemed to be drawing shapes in the snowy sky. At first they were random, then he began to notice more discernible patterns.

'You're the clever one wae that line, Hamish,' he said to his first mate. 'I'm sure I can see my grandmother.'

'You can what?'

Hamish let the line go, and Hoynes watched it arc away until it disappeared into the blizzard. He rubbed his eyes. It was as though a rainbow had appeared where the line had landed. It was a tiny rainbow, but a rainbow nonetheless.

'Well, in all my days, I've never seen the like. Have you, Hamish?'

'No, this snow's as thick as she comes.'

'No, the rainbow, Hamish. You've got to say, that's a phenomenon, if ever there was such a thing.'

Hamish said nothing as he hauled at the rope, thinking that Hoynes was having him on. It wouldn't be the first time the wily old skipper had set him up for some prank or other.

Hoynes gasped as Hamish pulled the line back over the side. 'Now, what's the chances o' that, eh?'

'Of what?' said Hamish, still unwilling to be taken in.

'I've never seen it done before, man o' man! It's the biggest lobster I've ever set eyes on, and no mistake. Here, I'll help you get they claws under control. A thing that bloody size could have your heid off, Hamish.' Hoynes was framed in the door of the wheelhouse with a heavy spanner.

'Right, what's the joke? Are you sure this is the right time to be messing aboot, skipper?'

'It'll be no joke when that lobster has you in its clutches. You stand still, and I'll whack it wae this.' Hoynes edged wards Hamish on tiptoes across the snowy deck, the spanner clasped in his right fist.

'You're going to dae yourself a mischief. Whatever you're playing at, well, it's no' funny!' Hamish edged away from Hoynes.

Without warning, Hoynes lunged forward, brandishing the spanner. Briefly he flew through the air until both he and the spanner landed with a crash on the deck. Thankfully, the deep snow broke his fall, though he cursed as he struggled on the deck.

'What on earth are you at, Sandy? You damn near broke your neck.'

Hoynes staggered back to his feet, seemingly no worse for his leap through the air. He looked about anxiously, as though he was frightened something would come out of the shifting curtains of snow and do him harm. 'Would you believe it? How on earth did the big bugger get up there?'

'What big bugger?'

'The bloody lobster! It's taken a fair jump tae get on top o' the wheelhouse.' He took off his bunnet and scratched his head for a moment. 'Come tae think o' it, I've never seen such a creature jump. Have you, Hamish?'

'Sandy, you're starting tae worry me.' Hamish bit his lip. 'I've heard o' people seeing strange apparitions in the desert. Hallucinating water and palm trees where there's none at all.'

Hoynes looked at him in disbelief. 'You might no' have noticed, but we're most certainly not in the desert. This is a blizzard, Hamish!'

The first mate sighed with relief. 'Och, you've been winding me up, Sandy. You had me worried for a while, there.'

'Ach, you're never done worrying. You check the line while I work out what we'll do.'

'I will. So you're still of a mind tae turn back, skipper?'

'Not in the slightest!'

Hamish looked confused. 'Well, what are you planning to do?'

'I'm going tae get that huge bloody lobster doon off that wheelhouse, that's what I'm going to do.'

'Now, wait a minute, Sandy. I'm concerned, and that's for sure. What did you have for your tea last night? It wisna shellfish, by any chance? A bad clam or a mussel can fair set a man's heid awry.'

Hoynes was now studying the wheelhouse like a mountaineer might Ben Nevis. 'You'll need tae gie me a hunker up, Hamish. Better still, get doon below and grab that set o' ladders. I'll catch the bugger yet!'

'Get back in and steer the boat, Sandy. Less o' the messing about!'

'Aye, good idea. I'll keep us on the straight and narrow while you get they steps.' He entered the wheelhouse. 'Man, you should hear the racket the damn thing's making on this roof. Mind, it'll fetch a pretty penny.'

Hamish hesitated, then darted down the hatch to the cabin below.

14

Hamish stood by the stove in the small cabin wringing his hands. He'd seen his skipper drunk on many occasions. At such times, he was prone to bouts of immodesty, and could even become argumentative. But Hamish had never known him to have hallucinations. And, in any case, Hoynes hadn't touched a drop.

'What's up with you?' said Jo, stirring in the bunk and giving Hamish a fright. In his puzzlement about Hoynes, he'd forgotten all about the reporter.

'The skipper's behaving in a very strange fashion. I canna fathom it at all.'

'What's he doing?'

'Och, I won't burden you with it, you being so seasick and all.'

Jo looked wary. 'I'm feeling a bit better, actually. The lie down must have done me some good.' She looked at Hamish from the corner of her eye. 'Just what do you mean by "behaving in a very strange fashion"?'

'He's no' himself, that's all.'

'If you don't mind me saying, he seemed a bit odd to me from the start.'

'In what way?'

'A wee bit eccentric, perhaps?'

'Not at all, he's the most practical man I know.'

'So what's changed?'

'If I tell you, you've got tae promise you won't put it in the paper.'

'Don't be daft.' Though she was trying to sound upbeat, Jo felt her heart sink. Suddenly, her seasickness was the last thing on her mind.

'Well . . .' began Hamish hesitantly, 'he's seeing things.'

'Oh, what kind of things?'

'Tae put it plainly, he thinks there's a giant lobster atop the wheelhouse.' Hamish looked at Jo with a desperate look etched across his face.

'I see.' She bit her lip.

'You don't look very surprised. I can assure you, this is far from the normal turn o' events on a vessel like this. I'm worried he could be ill. My granny had a stroke and didna know who anybody was, even her own daughter.' He thought for a moment. 'Well, apart fae auld Joe Kennedy the undertaker, but apparently they'd been close years before. You can imagine how upset my poor mother felt.'

'Right.' Jo was sitting up now, biting her lip. 'Hamish, I have a confession to make.'

'For all that's holy, you're no' seeing things as well, are you?'

'No, but I think I know what's wrong with Mr Hoynes.'

'You dae?'

'You'll have heard of LSD, Hamish.'

'Pounds, shillings and pence? Of course I've heard of it. I'm no' some daftie!'

'I mean the other LSD. You know – drugs. I assume that

Kinloch isn't so isolated that some notion of the swinging sixties hasn't reached the place.'

Hamish looked alarmed. 'You mean like they Trolling Stones? No, Sandy widna have any truck wae that carry-on. In any case, Marjorie would make his life a misery if he was at such nonsense.'

'No, you're not getting this. Let me explain.' Jo went on to tell the distressed mariner just how a sugar lump impregnated with LSD had landed in Hoynes' mug of tea.

It took Hamish a while to digest this information. He stood with his mouth open for a while, making to speak, but not quite managing it. Eventually he found his voice. 'And jeest how long does this last, this LSD?'

Jo shrugged. 'It's hard to tell. Everyone reacts differently. It's really interesting, sets your mind free.'

'I'm quite happy wae my mind staying exactly where it is, thank you. I canna see any joy in conjuring up images of giant shellfish, or the like. What have you done?'

'It's okay, calm down.' Jo made to lift herself out of the bunk, but a wave of nausea swept over her and she was forced to fall back on the old blankets.

'Calm? How can any soul stay calm in these circumstances? We're lost in a blizzard at sea, and the skipper's turned intae a cabbage!'

'But you can steer the boat, yes?'

'Oh aye, I can steer the boat under normal circumstances. We call it navigation in the trade. But these are no' normal circumstances, no' by a long chalk. I've never sailed in such weather conditions.'

'Oh, come on, Hamish! Where's your confidence? It's time to step up, show what you're made of.'

'I'll tell you where my confidence is, up on top o' the wheelhouse wae that great lobster. Sandy plays the fool fae time tae time, o' that there's no doubt. But there's no' a finer sailor on the west coast.'

'Go up and see what's happening. It shouldn't be too hard to reason with him. Folk are usually quite placid under the influence.'

'I widna say he was placid. No' by a long shot. He's determined tae beat the brains oot o' this poor lobster. I mean, he's no' normally a cruel man.'

'For a start, Hamish, there's no lobster, so he can't be cruel to it. Secondly, the worst thing that can happen is he falls overboard.'

'I never thought o' that.' Hamish narrowed his eyes at the reporter.

'Look, I've taken it a few times and there's nothing wrong with me.'

'That's a matter o' debate. Tae poison the skipper o' a vessel when it's lost in a blizzard isna normal behaviour as far as I'm concerned. You should be ashamed of yourself!' With that he disappeared back through the hatch.

When Hamish first scanned the snowy deck, his heart sank, for he could see no sign of Hoynes. It was only when he glimpsed the end of a long boat hook appearing above the wheelhouse did he realise that, far from falling overboard, Hoynes was still pursuing the lobster.

Hamish hurried round the back of the wheelhouse and, sure enough, there he was, brandishing the boat hook wildly, as snow gathered on top of his bunnet.

'Right,' said Hamish, sensing that it was time to take direct action. 'I've a plan.'

Hoynes looked him up and down. 'Why are you dressed in your faither's suit?'

'What? Oh, aye,' said Hamish, playing along. 'Nice day to gie it an airing.'

'I know what you're at. Trying tae impress that wee lassie instead o' helping me subdue this monster. It's already had a couple o' goes at me wae they claws, but I managed tae evade them. Jeest in the nick o' time, though.' He gave Hamish a wild-eyed look.

'I've had an idea, Sandy. Why don't you head down below? This beast's intentions are clearly malign, so he'll likely chase you – and when he does I'll whack it o'er the heid wae something substantial.'

Hoynes looked at him as though working out a complex calculation in his head. His forefinger darted to and fro as the choreography of Hamish's plan played out across his mind's eye.

'What dae you think?'

'I reckon your plan might jeest work, Hamish,' Hoynes whispered.

'Why are you whispering?'

'Are you daft? He can hear us! That bloody thing's as fluent as you. It must have been brought up in the sea at Firdale, for he has a fair twang.'

'You've spoken tae him?'

'Och, we passed the time o' day and the like. He's never seen weather like this, neither. Quite cordial, he was, but I sense it's jeest an act.' He lowered his voice further. 'On the count o' three I'll make a break for the hatch.'

'Right you are, skipper,' said Hamish, with an enthusiasm he didn't feel.

Without counting to three, Hoynes suddenly threw the boat hook to the deck and scurried off towards the cabin hatch. But instead of lowering himself feet first, Hoynes clasped his hands together as though in prayer and dived, head first, through the opening. For a moment, his girth held him fast in its narrow confines. But gravity soon did its work and, before Hamish could grab his legs, his skipper tumbled into the cabin.

'What happened?' shouted Jo.

'I dread tae think,' said Hamish, lowering himself down beside his skipper.

15

The old quay in Kinloch harbour was thronged with people. Constable Mann was there, so was the senior fire officer, Andy Semple. Doctor Fraser's face bore a grave expression, as he puffed on his Woodbine. Peter Mitchell, the harbour master, who was staring desperately out over the loch, shook his head, as the snow piled up on the pier.

Provost McMurdo, too, looked concerned, for such snowfall had rarely been seen on the peninsula. He turned to Mitchell. 'And conditions are worse out in the sound, apparently?'

'Aye, ten times worse. I've just had Davie Robertson on the radio. The signal is terrible because of the snow. But he and the rest of the fleet have turned round.'

'All apart from Hoynes, that is?'

'Aye. That thrawn old bugger refuses to carry a radio aboard. He says it upsets the fish.'

'Well, he's more than fish to worry him now.' The provost lowered his head.

Senga Murray, the matron of the cottage hospital, sighed. 'Would you look at you all! Job's comforters, and no mistake. Sandy Hoynes might not have a radio, but he's the best sailor for miles around. There's no' an inch o' that coast he's no' acquainted with, and you know it. If any man can bring us supplies, it'll be him.'

The provost, the doctor, the police constable, harbour master and fire officer looked at each other, their faces all bearing doubtful expressions.

'My goodness, men are big on drama, and that's a fact,' declared Matron Murray. 'It's the same in the hospital. You get a man in wae a skelf in his finger and you'd think a tree had fallen on his head, while a woman will drag the thing oot wae a pair o' tweezers while engaging in some healthy gossip on the phone.'

'God willing, the rest of the boys will make it back. As soon as the weather clears, we'll get them and the lifeboat out and look for poor Hoynes. It's all we can do,' said the harbour master.

'We should sing a hymn,' said the town clerk, who was a pious man.

'For any sake,' muttered the matron. 'Should we no' jeest go the whole hog and start flinging flowers into the loch?'

'No' a bad idea,' said Semple, whose wife owned the florist.

'Wait!' shouted Mitchell. 'I see a boat coming past the island. I think it's the *Dark Isle*.'

The little crowd squinted into the snow, as the shape of one fishing boat then another emerged from the blizzard. One by one, Kinloch's fishing fleet straggled back into the loch to a hearty cheer from all those looking on. All except for the *Girl Maggie*, that is.

❄

At the head of the quay, sheltered beneath the eaves of the Mission, gathered the old fishermen. Though not in direct contact with the great and the good of the community further down the pier, they knew the score.

Peeny stroked his chin, as the fishing boats tied up. 'Och, I knew fine this was an ill-conceived idea, right fae the start.'

'And right you were,' said Malcolm Connelly. 'You canna trust a forecast these days. Och, it's one o' they once-in-a-lifetime events. We've all seen them before.'

'If we've seen them before they can hardly be once in a lifetime,' quipped Peeny, who hid a tendency for pedantry under a façade of bonhomie.

'Hoynes will be ploughing on regardless,' said McKirdy. 'I canna blame him for no' wanting to have a radio aboard. We all know fine it's jeest another ploy so the fishery officer can keep tabs on you. They buggers would stalk their ain granny if they thought she was wandering oot the chip shop wae an understated quantity o' fish in her supper.'

Peeny sighed. 'Sandy won't be fazed by the snow. He's the last o' the true fishermen, and that's a fact. He could get you fae here to New York and no' consult a chart at all.'

'He'd need a fair stock o' whisky for that passage, mind you,' said Connelly.

'I can jeest picture the scene aboard the *Girl Maggie* now,' said McKirdy. 'Big Sandy staring intae the blizzard using all his senses tae overcome the worst that nature can throw at him. He'll put the likes o' McMichael – who's no' half the fisherman his faither was – and wee Robertson tae shame.'

There was a general murmur of consensus, before the collective decision was made to decamp to the County and ponder on Hoynes' route to Girvan.

❄

Aboard the *Girl Maggie*, though, things could not have been less like the imaginings of the old seadogs back in Kinloch. It was Hamish who stood in the wheelhouse squinting into the snow. Despite the bitter cold, a bead of sweat made its way down his forehead from under his cap.

That he knew the sea and the ways of navigation, there was no doubt. But he'd no experience sailing in heavy snow. He knew he should trust in the compass, but it was only as good as Hoynes' last reading, and that had been right at the very beginning of their journey and was hardly ideal. He couldn't see the sun behind the blanket of snow. Everything was just . . . white.

In ordinary conditions, he'd have been busy keeping the lines and deck clear of snow. But with Hoynes incapacitated in the cabin, the white stuff was piling up so quickly it was hard to determine the shape of the boat at all. The *Girl Maggie* was beginning to look like a floating snowball.

Hamish was also fretting over something else. Hoynes' vessel was sturdy, well designed for its fishing duties, but it most certainly was not built for speed. Most of Kinloch's fleet was made up of newer, faster boats. They were slow to start, but once they made their way into open water Hamish calculated that they should have caught up with the *Girl Maggie* long ago. He'd called them repeatedly through the loud hailer, but to no avail, and the silence only multiplied his woes.

Hamish brushed the sweat from his forehead and reached for the speaking tube. He'd instructed Jo to keep an eye on Hoynes. To the best of his ability, he'd made sure his stricken skipper had no broken bones, and managed – with no little effort, it had to be said – to manhandle the older man's bulky frame into the bottom bunk where Jo had been trying to shake off her seasickness. She was now slumped near the other end of the speaking tube, keeping an eye on Hoynes.

'Has he moved yet?' Hamish shouted into the mouthpiece.

It took a few moments for her to master the basic technology, but soon her voice sounded weakly in the wheelhouse. 'No change, he's just lying there. His eye twitched a couple of times, but that's all.'

'Well, at least he's no' deid,' said Hamish. 'Is this what normally happens wae folk that's taken this DSL?'

'It's LSD! And people react in different ways. I'm no expert, I've only taken it a couple of times myself.'

'And what happened tae you?'

'It was . . .'

'What?'

'Kind of – sexual.'

'I never heard such talk! I'm sure the skipper isn't experiencing anything o' the kind. Wherever this poison has taken him, it'll be wholesome, I can assure you o' that!'

'And how do you know he's out cold because of LSD? It could just as easily be down to the fall. He took a right thump.'

'My, but you're a cheery soul, right enough. As if I hadna enough tae worry me up here.'

'Surely we've passed Arran by now?'

'I would hope so. Now all we have to worry aboot is crashing intae Ayrshire. Do you think you're fit tae come up on deck for a while?'

'To do what?'

'Man the wheel while I check on Sandy.'

'I'd be womaning the wheel. And even if I could make it, I've never steered a boat in my life.'

'There's nothing to it at all – well, unless we hit something. I'll only be away for a couple o' minutes.'

'I'll try. But I can't promise not to be sick all over your wheelhouse.'

Hamish replaced the speaking tube on its hook and squinted into the blizzard. Their only chance of salvation now was the Girvan lighthouse.

16

An impromptu emergency meeting was taking place in the bar at the County Hotel. It consisted of the harbour master, the provost, the town clerk and fishermen young and old. The fire was blazing, and each man had a large dram before him, but the mood was one of gloomy resignation.

The phone at the bar rang.

'It's for you, Peter,' said the barman.

Mitchell got to his feet and had to lean across the bar, as the flex on the phone was rather too short for purpose. He frowned as he listened intently to what was being said. By turns, he nodded, shook his head, pursed his lips, rubbed his temples and grimaced. 'Thank you, Wattie. Just keep looking. We'd be most obliged.'

He turned to the gathering. 'It was the Coastguard at Girvan. They've sent some boats out as far as they dare, sounding their horns, making enough noise to raise the dead. But not a peep from Hoynes.'

'He'd no' be the length o' Girvan yet. No' in this weather. He'll have tae take it slow.'

'But even saying he is, he should be in the vicinity of the search vessels and the lifeboat soon.'

Peeny looked at the clock above the bar. 'I would gie them

another hour. Hoynes is a cautious man, for all his bluster. He'll be taking it sure and steady. Dae we have any word on the weather, Peter?'

'According tae the Met Office, it's in for the day, aye, and most o' the night.'

'If it gets dark, Hoynes will surely weigh anchor if he hasn't hit land?' said McMichael.

'"Hit" being the operative word. He could easily jeest sail intae they rocks at Culzean, or anywhere. If I were him I'd be at anchor right noo, trying tae sit this out.'

'Wait!' exclaimed Davie Robertson. 'They might no' have a radio aboard, but they have a wireless.'

'And what difference will that make?' asked Mitchell.

'We could get a message tae them – over the air, so tae speak.'

All eyes turned to Provost McMurdo. He looked back at them through sad, rheumy eyes. 'What do you want me to do?'

'Get a haud o' they radio folk. Get them tae tell Hoynes tae stay at anchor until this clears – if the idea hasn't crossed his mind yet.'

'That's all very well. But what station does he listen to?'

'Och, it'll be the Home Service. Every fisherman listens tae that for the shipping forecasts,' said Peeny.

'It's got a new-fangled name now,' said McMichael. 'A number. Mind they changed it all earlier this year.'

'Right enough. So all they weans can listen tae that racket. No' a decent accordion or fiddle to be heard,' said McKirdy.

'That'll be Radio One,' observed Peeny, to the surprise of everyone. 'I'm quite partial tae thon Seekers. Right good harmonies, so they have.'

A moment's hush fell over the room, as those gathered took stock of this unexpected piece of information.

'So you want me to phone the BBC and get them to broadcast a distress call?' said McMurdo.

'That should suffice. I mean, surely Hoynes has had the wireless on, monitoring the forecast anyway,' said Mitchell. 'A wee prompt would do no harm.'

'Right. I'll get back to my office and see what I can do.' The provost hurried from the bar, closely followed by the town clerk.

'Ach, we've likely saved the day,' said McKirdy. 'They call it a brains trust.'

Harbour Master Peter Mitchell looked about those assembled. 'Aye, something like that,' he said, with little conviction.

❄

Hamish was now in the cabin, his hand on Sandy Hoynes' forehead, checking to see if he was feverish. It felt fine to the fisherman, but he wasn't sure he had sufficient experience in medical care to make an informed diagnosis. Certainly, the skipper looked peaceful enough; as Jo had mentioned, his left eye was twitching from time to time, so at least he was still alive.

Hamish knew he couldn't leave Jo at the wheel for long. Desperately, he racked his brain to think of something to do that might ease their plight. He nudged Hoynes a couple of times, but no response was forthcoming.

Then something dawned on him: Hoynes loved music. If anything was likely to bring him round, surely a good tune would be the very thing. He jumped from his skipper's side and was up and through the hatch with a fluidity of movement that would have done a pole vaulter credit.

Crumping through the snow, he was dismayed to see Jo slumped over the wheel. 'My goodness, lassie! Have you been like this the whole time I've been below?'

She shook her head. 'No, but it's worse up here. We're rolling about in nothingness. It's like some nightmare.'

'Have you set eyes on anything? The Girvan light, for example?'

'No, just snow.'

Hamish reached behind her and grabbed the dilapidated transistor radio from a shelf in the wheelhouse. 'I'm going to play some music tae Sandy. He's fair fond o' a tune. It might be the very thing tae bring him round. I've seen it done wae folk in a coma at the pictures. You'll have tae hang on for a couple mair minutes.'

She nodded feebly as Hamish once more disappeared through the hatch.

17

Back at the town hall, Provost McMurdo was looking at a large map of Kintyre, and the route they all hoped Hoynes was taking to the Ayrshire coast. To his untrained eye it all looked really simple – almost a straight line, in fact. But as the seamen had reminded him, there were many hidden obstacles and dangers lurking in the wide expanse of blue that appeared so benign on the map. And that was without factoring in the driving snow.

He looked outside just as old Mr Henderson took an impromptu dive outside Morrison's the barber. Thankfully, the gentleman's fall was broken by the great accumulation on Main Street. As Henderson brushed himself down, he must have sensed McMurdo's eyes on him. He glared up at the provost, and McMurdo waved at him by way of consolation. In return, Henderson raised two fingers and shuffled off down the street, though in a more tentative manner.

McMurdo shook his head. He wasn't native to Kinloch, having arrived forty years before as a keen young veterinarian. Now retired, he sometimes wondered why he'd taken to local politics. There was little doubt that it was an often thankless task. The burdens and irritations of the office were many. But now he felt as though he had the people's lives on his conscience, and that was not a happy place in which to dwell.

The phone on his desk rang twice, indicating an internal call. 'Yes, please go ahead.'

'I have a producer from the BBC on the line for you,' announced the town clerk.

'Good. What's his name?'

'I'm rather surprised to say that it's a young lady, a Miss Thomson.'

'Why are you surprised?'

'Och, I don't know. You just imagine a man in a responsible job like that.'

'I have to say, it's high time you altered your attitude. One of these days we'll have a female provost – maybe even a prime minister.' He heard the town clerk snort with derision. 'Put her through. And try to drag yourself into this decade, man!'

There followed a click or two, then Miss Thomson introduced herself in clipped tones that made McMurdo instinctively sit up straight in his high-backed chair.

'I understand you have an emergency you would like us to help with, Mr McMurdo?'

'Yes, we do have a bit of a situation on the go. One of our fishing vessels is somewhere between here and Girvan in a blizzard. They have no radio, but they do have a wireless. We were thinking that perhaps you could pass on a message over the airwaves, so to speak.'

'I believe the weather with you is somewhat inclement. Strange time to go fishing.'

'Yes, it's dire, in fact. That's the real problem. They're not out fishing, but on a mercy mission of sorts.'

'A mercy mission? Do tell.'

'I'm not sure how well acquainted you are with the

geography here. But we're rather out on a limb. With the level of snowfall, the peninsula could be cut off for weeks. Mr Hoynes and his crew, along with the rest of the fishing fleet, volunteered to sail to the Ayrshire coast to bring back much-needed supplies. Hoynes aside, they all turned back because of the weather, but the *Girl Maggie* is still out there.'

There was silence on the other end of the phone for a few moments, then Thomson spoke. 'So what you're telling me is that these men are heroes.'

'Well, yes, I suppose I am.'

'Now that's a real story! Leave this with me, Mr McMurdo. I'll be back with you within the hour.'

'Oh, right,' said McMurdo, slightly taken aback. 'I'll await your call.'

He put the phone down and glanced out the window. Snow was still falling thick and fast. He took a cigar from the box hidden in a drawer, lit it and puffed it into life. Outside in the community, McMurdo always smoked a pipe. But in the privacy of his office or at home, he secretly enjoyed a cigar much more. Unfortunately, those in Kinloch whom he served would have considered such a habit unforgivably bourgeois, so, in public, it was pipe only.

As he watched the cloud of smoke curl round the room, he considered the conversation he'd just had with the BBC radio producer. Then he pictured Sandy Hoynes and his reputation for skulduggery, not to mention his fondness for strong drink. Though he was desperate to see the *Girl Maggie* safely back in port, the thought of her skipper becoming the face of the town in the national media was not a welcome one.

He reached into another drawer and produced a bottle of whisky and a glass. He poured himself a large measure and silently wished he'd listened to his wife and retired to a holiday home in France rather than become Kinloch's political master. For in reality, nobody could master this place.

❄

Hoynes lay in his bunk in the cabin of the *Girl Maggie*, the sublime strains of Mozart sounding incongruously grand in such a small, dishevelled space.

At the chart table, Jo had perked up a little. Her trip up on deck had made her feel distinctly worse, but back in the cabin, nursing a mug of Hamish's strong tea, she felt herself a little restored. As she looked at Hoynes' recumbent figure, she observed no change. He lay stock still, apart from a flickering left eyelid.

Now, though she'd been aware of it all the time but too squeamish to care, their perilous situation dawned on her. Here they were on a tiny fishing boat, with no real clue as to their position. Not only that, the captain of the vessel was indisposed by ingestion of a hallucinogenic and an unfortunate plummet through the hatch. Though Hamish made reassuring noises, she could tell by his worried expression that he was less than confident of his ability to bring them safely to port, never mind find it.

The radio, though, was soothing. Jo closed her eyes and let the music wash over her. It had been an early start, and her eyes were heavy from lack of sleep and the draining effect of seasickness. Her head was drooping forwards when what she heard over the radio brought her back to full wakefulness.

'*And this is a message to the fishing boat* Girl Maggie *and her crew. From all of us here at the BBC, and I daresay the whole nation, we wish you well. The advice from the harbour master at Kinloch is to weigh anchor and ride out the storm. And from us to you, on this brave mercy mission to feed the good people of Kintyre, here is the organist and choir from King's College, Cambridge, with that wonderful hymn to mariners everywhere, "For Those In Peril On the Sea". May God bless you and bring you back safely to port.'*

At first Jo couldn't believe her ears. Perhaps it was exhaustion – or the realisation of their desperate plight – that had led her to imagine such a message echoing from the wireless. But the hymn was still playing through the crackle of static.

She reached for the speaking tube and hailed Hamish.

'Is he awake?' asked the first mate hopefully.

'No, but I've just heard a message from the harbour master at Kinloch on the radio. You've to weigh anchor and ride out the storm.'

'Have you been at the drugs, tae? Am I the only sane person aboard this vessel?'

'No, honestly, I heard it!'

Hamish was about to reply when he heard a commotion from the cabin below. It came in the form of a scream that would curdle the blood. 'What on earth is happening down there?'

'It's Mr Hoynes. He's sitting up in the bunk and staring at his hands.'

18

When Hoynes first became aware of the music, he shot up in his bunk. Everything seemed familiar. He was fully aware that he was aboard the *Girl Maggie*, though his memory was hazy as to why he was in the cabin. He had a thumping pain in his head, and felt the need to rub his temples with thumb and forefinger, a trick of headache relief his grandmother had shown him, and by which he swore.

But when he removed his right hand from under the dun woollen blanket his eyes widened in horror. For this was no hand – no human hand, at least. It was a gigantic lobster claw at the end of his arm. For a split second he was paralysed by fear, then he screamed, hearing his own voice echo round the tiny cabin. As he did so, he saw the lobster claw flex in a snapping motion.

He stopped screaming and made to move his other arm. But a figure appearing before him made him freeze.

'Sandy, thank the Lord you're okay!' Hamish stared down at his skipper with a benign expression.

Hoynes gazed at the apparition in front of him. Though strangely familiar, the vision of the deformed face was hideous. The sallow face with the slanting eyes was plain enough, but instead of hair, two curling horns like that of a seasoned ram emerged from the top of his head. To top off this terrifying spectacle, the man with the horns, who stood only feet away from him now, was dressed in the full garb of a man of the cloth. He wore a dark grey suit, under which was a black shirt with a white dog collar.

'Jeest you stay where you are!' screamed Hoynes, thrusting his large claw out before him for protection against this foul apparition.

'It's me, Hamish – your first mate, skipper.'

Hoynes saw the creature's lips move, but all he heard was a jumble of sounds that made no sense. He backed as far away as the cramped space of his bunk would allow, making sure he held out his claw before him, snapping it at the horned minister to discourage him from coming any nearer. He heard himself scream again, so loudly that the sound made his eyes vibrate and the vision before him shimmer in the gloom.

Hamish looked at Jo. 'What on earth is wrong wae the skipper?' He stared back at the man he knew so well. Hoynes' face bore an expression of abject terror, his fingers snapping together like a puppeteer with his hand in a sock.

The commotion had done enough to banish Jo's nausea and the journalist in her began to kick in. 'He's having a bad trip, Hamish.'

'It's no' been a joyride for me either.'

'No. I mean the drug. He's probably hallucinating.'

'The poor bugger has taken leave o' his senses, that's mair like it. What have you done to him?'

Hoynes screamed again, this time grabbing the old blanket

and pulling it over his face to banish the vision of horror before him. But his hand still snapped at the edge of the blanket, and his sea boots now protruded from beneath it at the bottom end of the bunk.

'It'll wear off. Try not to worry.'

'Try not to worry! My skipper's turned intae a raving imbecile and we're lost at sea in a blizzard. I would say I've every right tae be worried, wouldn't you?'

Jo ignored Hamish and edged towards her bag, where her notepad, pens and camera were kept.

'What are you at?'

'I'm going to get a picture of this. I'm sure the paper can use it in some way or other.'

But before she could get to the bag, Hamish lurched forwards and grabbed it from her by the strap.

'You're responsible for this predicament. You'll no' be taking any pictures o' my skipper while he's no' in his right mind.'

Jo shot from her sea chair and began tussling with Hamish over the tools of her trade.

❄

Hoynes could hear a commotion of sorts, though what was being said was still just an incomprehensible jumble. He made sure that, even though his head was beneath the blanket, his claw was flicking to and fro above his head to deter the fiendish minister.

But despite his fear and disorientation, he couldn't resist having a look over the edge of the blanket. He could see two figures wrestling with each other. The man appeared to be holding a baby, while an elderly woman was trying to drag it from his grasp.

The more he stared, the more he recognised the slight figure. It was his mother! It was then the thought crossed his mind. His poor mother was fighting to save her child from the beast with the horns. And something in him understood that the babe in arms was none other than himself. He had to help her!

Hoynes was about to force himself from the bed when his gaze landed on something else. At the bottom of the bunk where his feet should have been was a massive lobster tail. When he tried to move, the tail jolted up and down as though he was trying to scuttle away on a sandy seabed.

He opened his mouth and screamed again.

Hamish was hauling at the strap, but Jo had a firm grip of her bag. She was surprisingly strong for a slip of a lassie, he thought. But just as he was gaining ground, Hoynes, hitherto silent in the bunk apart from his flicking hand, let out a yell that, if anything, was louder and even more blood-curdling than the last.

The sudden scream made Jo let go of the bag, and the surprise of this caught Hamish unawares. Suddenly pulling against fresh air, he toppled backwards and hit his head off the stove.

Jo looked from one fisherman to the other. Hoynes was back under his blanket, fingers snapping frantically in the air, while Hamish was out cold, motionless beside the stove.

'Shit!' she said loudly, making Hoynes retreat further into the safety of his bunk.

She knelt over Hamish, first of all checking his pulse to

make sure the blow hadn't been fatal. Thankfully, his heartbeat was strong, though he was unconscious. It was then that the full horror of her predicament dawned. She was aboard a boat, sailing through a blizzard, with both captain and first mate incapacitated.

Jo tried speaking into Hamish's left ear, but no response was forthcoming. Gently, she slid her hand under his head, mercifully not encountering the wet stickiness of warm blood she'd expected.

As a keen Girl Guide, she knew some basic survival techniques. Carefully, recalling her first aid badge, she rolled Hamish over on his side, making sure that if he was sick he wouldn't choke. Examining the back of his head once more, she was further relieved that there appeared to be no sign of blood. Though an egg-shaped lump was plain under his thinning hair.

She spoke to the fisherman once more, gave him a gentle shake, but there was no response.

Jo felt her stomach lurch, as though she was on a roller-coaster or in a rapidly descending lift. She thought at first it was just a nervous reaction to her situation, but when a tin mug was dislodged from its hook, she realised that the boat itself had began to move most alarmingly.

Making one last attempt to rouse Hamish, and failing, she looked across at the mound under the woollen blanket that was Sandy Hoynes. His hand still grabbed at the air, and she could see his legs were trembling.

Realising there was no other option, she made for the hatch and, with the help of a chair, managed to haul herself through it.

19

Back in Kinloch, the snow was still falling.

In the town hall, Provost McMurdo had long since stopped taking calls. Since the plight of the *Girl Maggie* had been aired on national radio, it appeared as though Hoynes had become a hero the length and breadth of the country. He'd had calls from newspapers, television companies, even *Fisherman's Weekly*, all wanting to know more of the plight of what was now Kinloch's most famous vessel.

He heard the phone ring again in the town clerk's office and sighed. He'd spent much of the afternoon speaking to the Coastguard, the RNLI and even the Minister of Agriculture and Fisheries. The general consensus was that nothing could be done now that darkness had descended upon the town. They had reached the conclusion that come the morning – in the hope that the snow would have stopped, or at least lessened – a search for the *Girl Maggie* would begin. Two Royal Navy helicopters had been promised, should visibility be suitable, and the town's fishing fleet, alongside the lifeboat and their opposite numbers in Girvan, would all put to sea in an attempt to trace the missing vessel. There was even a destroyer steaming towards the area, though like the rest of the rescue party they wouldn't be able to search in earnest until first light.

It appeared that even radar wasn't working properly in these extreme weather conditions.

Burdened by guilt, McMurdo tried to console himself that he'd tried his best to mitigate the situation. But still the feeling that he was responsible for Hoynes' plight gnawed away at him.

Though he was no career politician, he realised the last thing he should do was hide away in the town hall. So McMurdo made the decision to head to the heart of the fishing community – doubtless next door in the County Hotel, he reckoned. He pulled his heavy overcoat from its hook and placed his trilby firmly on his head. Checking himself in the mirror, he made sure that his tie was straight under his starched collar, and again noticed the resemblance many had commented on over the years between himself and Neville Chamberlain. It was part of the reason he'd entered local politics in the first place.

Right now, he wished he looked more like Frankie Howerd.

He leaned his head into the town clerk's office. 'I'm going out for a short while.'

'Are you going to be some time?' replied his junior, casting a look at the big flakes falling under the glow of the streetlights.

'Very funny. If I'm Captain Oates, just work out who you are in the story.'

Without further comment, McMurdo took to the stairs. He'd never liked his assistant, who was a civil servant rather than an elected politician. Though he had the power of the local council, the town clerk had a healthy salary, and a decent pension to look forward to. McMurdo felt that this, and the fact that his post was permanent, made him feel superior to the provost. In any event, he made sure that the town clerk was kept on his toes, and there was little doubt he had to work hard for his money.

Outside on Main Street, even the path dug through the snow by the Machrie miners would have been barely visible had it not been for the massive heaps of the white stuff on each of its sides. He felt strange walking past the ground-floor windows of the town hall. It was as though he had become taller and was looking at a smaller building altogether. The fact was, a good few feet of it were now under the tightly packed snow.

The County Hotel was only a few yards away, but McMurdo took this short journey steadily, anxious not to fall and hurt himself. The town needed its leader at this time, of that he was in no doubt.

He hadn't known quite what to expect when he entered the bar, but still he was surprised by how empty it was. Normally in times of crisis locals flocked to the town's pubs for news and to have a good gossip as to the likely outcome of this or that. Of course, the opinions agreed upon were usually of the gloomy variety, but such was the temper of a small community.

Only two men sat at the bar, Peeny and McKirdy. Though they differed in appearance – McKirdy being tall and broad, Peeny slight, with a pinched face – they were easily marked out as part of the fishing community by virtue of their weathered faces and deliberate manner. Most fishermen seemed to weigh their words before they spoke, seemingly swirling them round their mind like a connoisseur might savour a fine brandy before swallowing. He supposed this came of so much time spent at sea alone with their thoughts.

'Gentlemen,' said McMurdo, brushing the snow from his

coat to the floor and engendering a glower from the barman. 'I hope I can buy you a drink?'

'Your hope is not in vain, Mr McMurdo. We'll take as much drink as you can afford, for this is a black day for Kinloch's fishing fleet,' said Peeny with a sigh and a shake of the head.

'Mair like a white day, I'd say,' said McKirdy. 'I've never seen snow like it. No' here, at any rate.'

'Aye, it's the kind o' scenario you might encounter up the Matterhorn, or the likes. But no' here at Kinloch. It's jeest no' natural at all.'

'But you surely believe that Mr Hoynes will have taken the appropriate steps. After all, he's a very experienced mariner.'

Peeny stroked his stubbly chin. 'Aye, but he's an impetuous man. You jeest had tae see that race he had wae McMichael this morning tae know that. A man o' his age should be taking his time, no' rushing off like Francis Chichester.'

'Maybe if he'd been one o' the slower boats oot o' the loch, he might no' be in the predicament in which he finds himself now – fair afloat on a dark ocean, wae the burden o' snow all around. A man can make mistakes in weather like that – aye, even an experienced one.'

'Plus he and Hamish will be drunk as lords by now,' added Peeny.

'Surely you don't think they'll have partaken in strong drink, not in the danger they're in?' McMurdo was beginning to wish he'd stayed in his office. These gloomy predictions were doing nothing for his feelings of guilt.

'It'll be like this, Mr McMurdo. Hoynes will easily see the hopelessness o' his situation and have cracked open a bottle as soon as it got dark. He'll be anchored – if he can, that is.

And that's when hope begins tae drift.' McKirdy nodded his head mournfully.

McMurdo knocked back the whisky he'd just been given and held out his glass for a refill. One thing was certain, he needed something to bolster his morale.

'Of course, they may well have made land,' said McKirdy.

'Oh well, that would be good.' Suddenly McMurdo felt a surge of confidence.

'No' if land is a great sheet o' rocks or a length o' shingle under some great cliff.'

'What would happen then?'

'If they survived the impact, they're likely out cold on a beach burning the boat for warmth tae try and attract some attention.'

'Hang on, McKirdy,' said Peeny. 'That's a right doleful thought.'

McMurdo breathed a sigh of relief at this.

'They could jeest as easy be clinging on tae some rock face for dear life. Or perhaps they've constructed one o' they igloos. I'm sure Sandy will be acquainted wae the mechanics involved. After all, he knows about every other bloody thing!'

'Come, gentlemen, I'm sure things can't be as black as you paint them.'

'Och, that's no' half as black as they could get. Man, they could collide wae some great cargo vessel and cause an international incident, or one o' they oil tankers. The loch would be pure oil, if that happened.' Peeny nodded sagely.

McMurdo threw another large measure down his throat. He had an analytical mind, and it didn't take much mental effort to realise that if such a calamity did occur, the blame would be placed firmly at his door. How he wished he'd never encouraged the fleet to take to sea. The town could easily have survived a while longer. His actions had been impetuous.

He felt he had to try to change the subject, so looking around the room he commented on the absence of customers.

McKirdy looked at him as though he was mad. 'You canna expect folk tae come rushing oot in weather like this, Mr McMurdo!'

'Well, you're both here.'

'Aye, that's fair. But I live across the street and Peeny's flat's at the back o' the car park. The place is on oor doorsteps.' Both he and Peeny shook their heads at the provost's lack of common sense.

Being assured now that the County had little to offer in terms of succour or respite, McMurdo walked to the stand and hefted his coat back on. The snow that had gathered on it had melted in the warmth of the bar, and it was now unpleasantly damp. 'I'll bid you a good evening, gents,' he said, with a tip of his trilby. 'Another two large measures for my friends, please.' He passed the requisite money across the bar and made for the door, and onwards to his office in the gloomy town hall.

'Aye, but you're a fine man, Mr McMurdo,' said Peeny.

'Jeest the best!' opined McKirdy.

They craned their necks through the serving hatch into the hotel lobby to make sure the town's provost was leaving the premises.

'Aye, a right useless bugger, he is,' said McKirdy.

'A waste o' space, to be sure. It's no' a man like that you need in times o' a crisis. They tell me young Charlie Murray the joiner has his eyes on the job.'

'He's hardly mair than a boy.'

111

'Think o' Pitt the Younger, McKirdy. He was a wean when he became prime minister o' the country, so they say.'

McKirdy considered this. 'Aye, but that's an easy job compared wae being the provost o' Kinloch. We both know it.'

The pair nodded in silent agreement and, as though choreographed, knocked back the whiskies bought by the man they'd just derided, in absolute unison.

20

Jo had done her best to make Hamish comfortable by placing a pillow under his head. She was glad to hear him groan and mutter as she did this, and hoped beyond hope that he would regain his senses before long. As for Hoynes, he was clearly conscious, but still not in his right mind.

She remembered that they'd said on the wireless that the vessel should weigh anchor. She guessed this meant chucking a large cast-iron implement overboard, but reasoned that there was no way she could lift it. And, in any case, it was nowhere to be seen under the deep snow on deck.

When first she ventured up, following Hamish's accident, she noticed the heavy swell was making the wheel swing to and fro, as if by its own accord. Jo had been taking driving lessons recently and, even though she was in a boat, rather than a Hillman Imp, she realised that this likely meant that the craft was describing a meandering path over the waves.

It was time to make a decision.

She knew enough to work out that an unanchored vessel would drift in any direction that took the tide's fancy. This meant they could be dashed against rocks, sandbanks or the other hazards she'd heard mentioned during her short time at sea.

Jo thought hard about what the driving instructor back in Glasgow had taught her. If you wanted to turn in a circle, the wheel should be turned to its full extent, one way or the other. She grabbed the wheel in the small cabin and swung the wheel to her left. Yes, she could feel the direction of the vessel change!

Finally, after many more turns than it would take the steering wheel of a car to reach its full extent, it stopped. Jo could now picture the *Girl Maggie* travelling in circles on the dark sea. This wasn't ideal, she knew, but at least it reduced the chance of drifting or ploughing into something while travelling forwards.

She tethered the wheel to a hook on the wheelhouse window with a length of old rope she found in the cabin, and then pulled back on the handle she'd seen both Hoynes and Hamish use to alter the speed. Sure enough, Jo heard the tone of the engine drop and the vessel slowed down.

Confident she'd done the best she could, Jo checked that the lights were still showing fore and aft, and, shivering in the cold, returned to the cabin and the indisposed crew. She was still worried that another vessel could collide with the *Girl Maggie*, but surely no sailors would be abroad on such a night.

Jo huddled by the stove, after piling in more coal. She was hungry, thirsty, miserable and scared. But then she heard something.

In the gloom she saw a shape emerge from the bottom bunk.

'Mr Hoynes, are you okay?'

Silence.

'Mr Hoynes, it's okay to come and sit over here.' She hoped gentle encouragement would help the skipper to calm down.

Hoynes' figure remained stock still for a few moments, then slowly he eased himself off the bunk.

'Is that you, Mother?'

Jo sighed. She'd hoped he'd have regained his senses. 'No, it's me, Jo Baird from the *Glasgow Times*, do you remember?'

A pause. 'Aye, of course I remember. The wee lassie. A right scunner you are, too. Man, but I've been having such dreams. How long have I been asleep?'

'It's a long story, Mr Hoynes.'

The skipper appeared in the dim light of the oil lamp hanging above the stove. 'What on earth is Hamish doing doon there?'

'He fell and hit his head. I'm quite worried about him.'

Hoynes knelt over his shipmate. 'Well, he's still breathing, at least.' He nudged Hamish with the toe of his boot. The younger man stirred, mumbled something incoherent, and was again still. 'How long has he been like this?'

'I don't know, an hour – hour and a half, maybe?'

Hoynes raised his head, a puzzled look on his face. 'And tell me something else. Why are we going round in circles?'

'You can tell?' Jo was impressed. 'Ah, now you'll have to let me explain.'

Hoynes listened with mounting alarm as Jo described the last few hours. Though she skirted over the real reasons for his temporary incapacitation, blaming it on the fall, the real danger they were in quickly dawned on the skipper.

'You stay here with Hamish and I'll get up there and weigh the anchor.'

'How will you manage? I couldn't even see it under all that snow.'

'Don't worry aboot that. I've been a long time at this, you know.' With that he squeezed through the hatch.

As Jo looked on, she doubted she'd been as relieved by

115

anything in her life. She stared at Hamish, who looked pale in the gloom. Now all she had to do was reinvigorate him and her job here would be done. She switched on the wireless just as the shipping forecast began its ritualised meander around the nation's coast.

Then she remembered the job she'd been sent here to do. Clearly, there were things she couldn't put in print, but she was in no doubt – redacted as it would have to be – that this would make a fantastic story. Especially now they had been on the wireless. She reached into her bag for her notepad.

Hoynes stared through the dark and the snow at the deck of the fishing boat he knew so well, illuminated only by a single storm lantern. Had a photograph of this been presented to him, he would have been hard pressed to identify it as a seagoing vessel, never mind his own.

His thoughts were still rather jumbled, and for some reason he couldn't stop thinking about lobsters, but their current predicament was foremost in his mind. Jo had told him about the messages broadcast on the wireless, and while he felt a certain pride in this he was amazed they'd made it as far as they had without calamity.

It was cold, but Hoynes was sure the anchor would still work. Its weight would be sufficient to dislodge the snow, and it was unlikely to be frozen. He stopped the engine, then hauled on the handle to release the anchor. At first his heart missed a beat, but after a few moments the familiar sound of the chain releasing the robust anchor from the bow could be heard, snow muffling the usual clanking.

He had no idea where they were. Yes, he could see the compass, but that only spoke of which way they were now pointing. He'd no notion of how far they'd sailed, or in which direction. In normal circumstances, even below, he'd have been able to tell by virtue of instinct and experience whether or not the boat had drifted off course. But as he'd been unconscious, or at least not in his right mind, he'd been deprived of this sixth sense. He was still unsure quite why he'd suffered such an affliction, and vowed to press Jo on it when they were safely in port, as her explanation had been sketchy to say the least.

Hoynes leaned on the ledge beside the ship's wheel, still jury-rigged by the rope his passenger had used to make them sail in circles. Aye, he thought. She may have no experience of the sea, but there was nothing wrong with her reasoning.

His choices were limited. They could try to plough on when the day dawned, but if the snow continued like this, there was little point. He'd have to sit at anchor until either the weather improved, or rescue was at hand. The former, he supposed, was the only real prospect; only the foolhardy would advocate initiating a search in such conditions.

Sandy Hoynes, still trying to recover himself, reached into the bib of his dungarees and fished out his pipe and tobacco. Soon the wheelhouse was clouded by pungent smoke as he puffed away.

He was just beginning to feel at peace when a flash of something to port was caught in the light of the sea lantern.

21

Kinloch's town hall was thronged with people. Provost McMurdo stood on the dais, held out his hands and called to quieten the loud chatter. Gradually, the din diminished to a low murmur. He looked around the townsfolk who had gathered at this early hour to work out just what was to be done to find the *Girl Maggie*. Many of them had been listening to the wireless appeals, and they were now anxious for news.

'Ladies and gentlemen,' began McMurdo, 'I know how worried you are about our missing friends. But rest assured that all that is humanly possible is being done to locate them.'

'The lifeboat's still at the new quay. They'll no' find them there,' scoffed Peeny, a look of disgust on his face.

'In all conscience – and after discussion with the crew and the Coastguard – I cannot ask the lifeboat to take to sea in these conditions.'

'But you didna bother aboot sending the fleet oot in it yesterday,' an elderly woman shouted from the back of the hall. She was wrapped in an ancient greatcoat, brandishing a cigarette like a rapier in front of her as she spoke.

'We had no idea how long this would last. The forecast was for the snow to clear. But as you can all see, it hasn't.' McMurdo nodded across to the arched windows through which the snow could be viewed still falling heavily under the pale glow of the street lamps.

'Huh!' replied the woman with disgust. 'It's easy seen you're a man. If I was tae hang oot my washing every time the weather forecast tells me things are improving, there'd no' be a stitch o' dry clothes in the hoose!' This garnered general agreement.

An old man in a wheelchair raised a withered, bony finger and directed it towards McMurdo. 'You've sent fine men tae their maker. The blame is yours and nobody else's. It's a fact for which there is no excuse.'

'Aye, the blood's soaked right intae your simmet,' said McKirdy with a shake of the head. 'There's no' a mair respected man than Sandy Hoynes.'

At this a hush descended on the hall.

'Well, I widna quite say that,' said Jim McCahill. 'He sails right close tae the wind at the best o' times.'

'Aye, but we've a' cut corners here and there,' said McKirdy.

'He sold me a set o' nets that weren't fit for burning,' piped up a young man in a sou'wester.

'And they say he filled a box of fish wae sand to up the weight,' shouted another. 'Right doon the gobs o' the poor creatures, tae. It's a sin tae treat a fish like that – deid, or no'.'

'He telt me he'd seen a mermaid sunning herself on the barrel rocks,' shouted a cross-eyed man. 'Even telt me she had blue hair and a fine bust – if yous don't mind me bringing up such a thing.'

'You canna blame a man for taking the rise oot o' you, Peter,' said Peeny. 'Who on earth would believe that?'

'Me!' replied Peter indignantly.

'I heard he's got a woman on board!' shouted a man in a thick blue sweater.

'Aye, I heard that,' said McKirdy.

'Likely he's floatin' aboot wae a harem. I mean, that would explain why Hamish has no lassie in tow. All sorts could be going on when he goes tae sea that we've no notion of.'

McMurdo held out his hands again like a minister about to lead his congregation in prayer. 'Come, ladies and gentlemen, let's not turn this into a forum for idle gossip. The lives of men are at stake here.'

'Aye, and a woman by the sound o' it,' said McKirdy.

'To the matter in hand.' McMurdo decided it was time to bring the meeting to order. 'It will be light in a couple of hours. Our friends in the Coastguard and the Royal Navy will guide us as to when it's best to begin a proper search. In the meantime, we should all think of those aboard the *Girl Maggie* and pray to God that Sandy Hoynes knows his stuff.'

Everyone nodded, and the hall fell silent.

❄

For a few moments, time seemed to stop in the wheelhouse of the *Girl Maggie*. Hoynes was holding the pipe in one hand, his mouth agape. He could see more of the vessel now that it was athwart his port side. She was long and sleek, with a square-rigged sail. He was mesmerised, taking in the beauty of her sweeping lines through the darkness and heavy snow.

Two large sconces at either end of the craft blazed with bright flames that silhouetted those aboard. He could see that they were broad, well-built men, and counted at least twenty, peering at him as he stared at them.

Hoynes slowly emerged from the wheelhouse. For some

reason, he felt the need to raise his hands, as though in surrender. He removed the sea lantern from its hook and stared across the few feet of waves at the sleek ship shimmering in the dancing flames.

It was then that the light from his lantern caught the face of one of those on the vessel. The man was leaning on one leg, which rested on the low gunwale, a broad smile on his face. Though it was too dark to see what he was wearing, Hoynes caught the sheen of leather from his breeches and jacket, but they were of a design he had never seen.

'We are lost, you and I,' said the man casually. His voice was deep, and seemed to fluctuate in the still air. Though they were at sea, they could easily have been on a pond such was the uncanny silence.

'Aye, I'd say that few seafarers would be able to navigate through this,' Hoynes replied.

'But I think I have the advantage. Where I am from, this weather can happen in any winter.'

Hoynes was about to reply when the light from his lantern caught something else. From the curved prow of the boat, a great wooden serpent swept into the darkness. He could just about make out its pointed head, and the intricate carvings on its flanks.

'You like my boat, I can tell,' said the stranger.

'Aye. She's beautiful. Built for speed, I reckon.'

'Yes, she is fast. Her name is *Sea Storm*. She moves through the waves as no other vessel can, propelled by the greatest waves. And we sail far and wide. She is our home, our fortress – our lover. I'm sure you feel the same way about your own craft.'

Hoynes considered this. 'Aye, well, something like that, right enough.'

His opposite number spoke quickly, using words he didn't understand, and a burst of coarse laughter came from the silhouetted crew. 'I apologise. My men have an odd sense of humour.'

'The same has been said aboot mysel' right enough.' Slowly Hoynes placed his hands at his sides. He knew he should be frightened, that something here wasn't right, but he sensed no measure of threat from the men in the beautiful boat – the reverse, in fact.

'Are you willing to take advice from one man of the sea to another?'

'Aye, I am. There's an old saying where I come from: when you're lost in a storm, take any help that's forthcoming. My faither was never done saying it.'

'Then your father was a very wise man.' The man smiled and nodded, the light of Hoynes' lantern catching the gleam of his swept-back flaxen hair and the braids of his beard.

'I hope you don't mind me saying, but that's a fine set of whiskers you have, right enough. My beard's a bit on the unruly side.'

'Thank you. My wife plaits and oils it for me before each journey.'

'My wife makes me sandwiches and a flask of tea.'

The man in dark leather threw back his head and laughed heartily at this. When he recovered he stared at Hoynes, his black eyes piercing in the snow-speckled night. 'You know that it is fate that brings us together, yes?'

'I'm prepared tae believe that.'

'A great chasm of time separates us, and yet here we are. But like seeing the coast of a distant shore in the haze of a summer's day, we too can glance through time.'

'I've heard o' such a thing. There was an old fisherman I sailed with many a year ago who swore that he saw the coast o' Buenos Aires when he was on the east side o' Islay. Mind you, he took a good drink, but he was right convincing when it came tae this. Quite fractious he'd get if anyone tried tae gainsay him. Something to dae with refraction, so they say.'

'And he was right! None of us really know what is in store. We think we are clever; we master the sea, the land – maybe even the sky one day – but to those who watch over us, we are mere playthings. It is something we should never forget. For there will come a day when man believes himself to be a god, and on that day there will be nowhere for us to go. We will cease to exit and all that will remain will be Valhalla.'

Hoynes knew he'd heard that name before. After brief consideration he reckoned it was a pub in Oban. But as he kept his visits to that place as short as he possibly could, there was no telling if his memory was playing him false. All the same, he felt it only polite to nod and smile in agreement. Though he did feel slightly disappointed that the only remnant of humanity was likely to be some run-down bar in Oban.

'I must sail on, my friend. But first I tell you this. This snow will last until the sun is high. But if you turn your vessel right round, you will be safe when it shines through the clouds. Look for a guide – a bird will point the way.'

The beautiful boat began to fade into the snowy darkness. Hoynes held the lantern higher, but it caught only ghostly shadows. 'Thank you!' he called. 'I don't even know your name.'

'My name? You know it already, I think. The part of you

that sees what can't be seen and feels what can't be felt does. Odin is with you always.' The swirling voice was distant now. 'My name is Hona, and we will meet again one day, of that you can be assured.'

Hoynes tried to speak, but no words would come.

22

Though dawn had broken over Kinloch it was a thin, miserable affair. The sky was still heavy with clouds, and snow fell without pause or hindrance on the town.

The Machrie miners had been back, digging deep trenches where once there had been roads and pavements. And a few hardy souls were battling through this new white-walled landscape to buy much needed groceries or just meet up for a chat in a pub or café with their fellow townsfolk. The main points of discussion were inevitably the unusual weather and the plight of the *Girl Maggie*.

The aromas of sausages cooking in Alistair the butcher's shop, hot coffee from the Italian delicatessen and warm bread being baked by Michael Kerr wafted through the passages: all overlaid, as ever, by the tang of the sea. From Kinloch's many watering holes, the mellow scent of whisky and tobacco drifted. Astute publicans, more than aware that the local police had enough to deal with, opened early, so by mid-morning the likes of the Douglas Arms and the County Hotel were thronged with customers eager for news of recent developments.

Provost McMurdo stood at his office window two floors above Main Street. To him the white pathways through the snow looked like the mazes contrived from great hedges at stately homes. He looked on as Andy Galbraith paused to remove his bunnet and scratch his head, wondering just where he was going. McMurdo had a mind to tap the window and guide him from above, but realised that, with Hoynes still missing, his standing with the local population was pretty low. There was no doubt that his idea to send the fishing fleet to Ayrshire in the midst of a blizzard was widely viewed as reckless, to say the least. The old man sensed his gaze and looked up at the office window. McMurdo could only smile politely and pretend he hadn't noticed the baleful expression on the face of Andy Galbraith.

He'd been in touch with the Royal Navy, the Coastguard and the harbour masters in both Kinloch and Girvan. The feeling was unanimous: no search could be mounted until the weather eased, and even the forecasters were unsure as to when that might be.

Miserably, he returned to his desk and took a cigar from a drawer. He knew that someone might arrive and witness his clandestine habit, but he was past caring. He was exhausted, guilt-ridden and at the end of his tether. Having been up all night, with only weak tea as a roborative, his stamina was sorely stretched.

Though he'd been brought up as a strict Presbyterian, once free from the influence of his overbearing father, in adulthood he'd let religion slide somewhat. But now, in desperation, he bowed his head and prayed that the weather would turn and Hoynes, his boat and crew would be found hale and hearty.

In the middle of his plea to the heavens, the phone on his desk burst into life. 'Hello, Provost McMurdo,' he said wearily.

'It's Donald Fletcher here. I'm the duty harbour master at Girvan.'

McMurdo sat straighter in his chair. Could this be the good news he was so desperate to hear? 'Yes, Mr Fletcher, what can I do for you? What we're looking for, I hope?'

'Well, I have to be honest, Mr McMurdo. Initially we thought it was the worst news possible.'

'Oh dear!'

'Please, stay calm while I tell you the details.'

Heart in mouth, McMurdo listened, lighting his cigar as a salve against what might come.

'About two hours ago, a gentleman reported wreckage on a beach just outside Girvan.'

McMurdo held his head in his hands.

'The timbers were definitely from a boat, but there was something unusual about their construction. They were very black. At first I thought the timbers were fire damaged, but on examination that didn't appear to be the case.'

'Well, what then?'

'We've had Mr Hart the county archaeologist take a look. He's just called me from a phone box. You'll remember we had storms a couple of weeks ago. Well, he reckons that these fragments could be hundreds of years old. The theory is they've been dislodged from the silt that preserved them by heavy seas. Had it not been for the beach being covered in snow, we may have missed them altogether. Mr Hart thinks he has part of a Viking longship – even part of the prow!'

'Well, yes, that's very exciting, but it doesn't help our missing fishing boat, does it?'

'No, I understand that. But the press have a hold of this already, and I didn't want you coming across tales of wreckage in some misleading report, if you know what I mean?'

'Ah, I see. Very considerate, thank you.'

'But there is a bit of good news, Mr McMurdo. The snow has stopped here, and the sky's clearing. We'll begin our search from this end shortly. Shouldn't be surprised if things will improve in Kintyre quite soon.'

McMurdo expressed his gratitude and ended the call. At least this was something positive. Though the story about the Viking wreckage he could have done without.

When he looked out of his office window, Kinloch's provost was sure that the falling snow looked lighter, the flakes a little smaller and less frequent. He took a deep puff on his cigar and hoped for the best.

Hamish was now in the bottom bunk where not long ago Sandy Hoynes had thought himself to be a lobster. His head was aching, and he was still slightly disoriented. But Jo was clucking over him like a mother hen, supplying him with tea and even a large chunk of cheese with bread.

'You don't have tae fuss,' said Hamish. 'I've a hard heid, you know.'

'I'll be the judge of that. Now drink your tea while it's hot,' replied Jo.

'For the life of me, I canna remember how I fell. I'm usually quite sure-footed.'

As it was clear Hamish had no memory of falling due to their tussle over her bag, Jo felt it prudent not to enlighten him. 'Don't fret about it. Just rest and get yourself back together.'

'I'm fretting o'er Sandy. Are you sure he's fit to be up in the wheelhouse?'

'He's fine, quite back to normal.'

'And he doesna think he's a lobster – or any other crustacean, come to that?'

'No, he's right as rain.'

With that, Hoynes boots appeared through the hatch, shortly followed by their owner.

'Skipper! How are you faring?'

'Aye, I'm fine.'

'No notions o' shellfish at all?'

'Eh?' Hoynes looked bewildered.

'Och, never mind. It's good to see you back at the helm.' Hamish paused. 'The weather must have improved. We've got a fair shake on, by the sound o' they engines.'

'It's light, at least, but still snowing.'

'But you're ploughing on?' Hamish looked at Jo with a worried expression.

'I canna spend much time chewing the fat o'er this. But suffice it tae say I had an encounter with another mariner just before dawn. He put me right in terms of direction and the like.'

'No doubt he had radar or some such contraption?'

Hoynes inclined his head in thought. 'No, I don't think so.'

'So how did he know what directions tae gie you? Maybe news from the Coastguard on the radio?'

'Och, Hamish, man. You took a right dunt on the heid, for certain sure. He was a Viking. Men like that don't need the likes o' radio and radar. They could navigate all the way tae Greenland wae jeest a glance at the sky, and perhaps identify a bird or two on the way.' Hoynes shook his head. 'I'll need tae get back tae the wheelhouse. Just checking you were still in the land o' the living.' With that, he forced himself through the hatch and disappeared back on deck.

'Help me up!' wailed Hamish.

'You should stay where you are!' said Jo.

'The skipper's been talking tae Vikings. I'll have tae get up there and talk sense intae him!'

Jo helped Hamish to his feet and, with his arm over her shoulder, they staggered to the hatch.

'If I can get up on that chair, I'll make it.'

'Are you sure?'

'It's that or a watery grave. Which dae you fancy?'

Jo rushed to get the chair.

23

With Jo's help, Hamish managed to manoeuvre himself through the hatch and onto the deck. The snow was deeper than ever, reaching almost halfway up his wellington boots, but he reckoned that even though the visibility was still awful, at least the flakes had reduced in size. For Hamish, this was a sure sign that the general situation was improving. Though he was dismayed to note that the *Girl Maggie* was hammering on at not far off her top speed. A great plume of black smoke belching from the thin funnel attached to the side of the wheelhouse bore testament to this.

Hoynes was at the wheel, pipe gripped between his teeth, staring grimly into the white wall of falling snow.

Though his head was thumping, Hamish realised that it was prudent to take a circuitous route in terms of expressing any concerns about their present rate of travel. Hoynes, at the best of times, was a man over-proud of his skills as a mariner. But Hamish wasn't convinced that the advice of a passing Viking should be followed under these circumstances – or any circumstances, come to that.

'You've got a fair head o' steam on, skipper. Man, we must be hitting near ten knots.'

'Aye, despite the snow, the boat's sailing like a dream. A wee bit low in the water, mind you, but that's tae be expected, what wae a' this weight we're carrying. Heavier than a hold filled tae the brim wae fish, Hamish.'

Hamish swallowed hard before making a suggestion. 'Sandy, dae you no' think we should haul her back a fraction? It's hellish hard tae see anything. Visibility must be only a few yards, and that's no' telling you o'er much.'

Hoynes removed the pipe from between his teeth and addressed his first mate in a restrained, but determined manner. 'I've been set a course by a man who knew fine what he was at. I've nae reason at all tae doubt the information. My, if you'd seen him yourself, you'd be fair ploughing on like I am.'

Hamish cleared his throat. 'Sandy, you've no' been yourself in the last wee while.'

'No' myself? What on earth are you blethering aboot?'

'It kind o' began when you saw fit tae chase thon giant lobster aboot the deck wae a boat hook. Something wisnae jeest quite right, you understand.'

'And what did I do then? Maybe a pirouette roon the stern?'

'No, no' quite, Sandy. In fact, you ended up thinking you were a lobster yourself. Fair snapping your fingers together like claws, you were. I managed tae get a few words from you aboot it all, but maybe we should consign that to the past.'

Hoynes looked at Hamish in disbelief. 'I can see a lump the size o' a duck egg emerging through what's left o' your hair. You need to get yourself back doon intae the warmth o' that bunk.'

'There's no need tae be so personal,' said Hamish, who was most self-conscious that his hair wasn't as lustrous as it once had been.

'I've been on the water since I was a babe in arms. When the old king was no more than a midshipman. Aye, and I've sailed under some o' the best skippers there's ever been. Not tae mention my own late lamented faither. He could navigate his way tae Mars if the equipment was available tae perform such a journey.'

They were both startled by the sound of a massive gull squawking loudly as it swept over the vessel.

'That must be the biggest seagull I've yet tae set eyes on,' said Hamish. 'A junior albatross, I shouldna be surprised.'

'No such thing. An albatross has an altogether different cant tae its wings, and an entirely different beak. Man, Hamish, your ornithological observation leaves a lot tae be desired, and you a man o' the sea. I'll tell you what it is.'

'What?'

'It's a sign. My Viking friend telt me that it would arrive in good time.'

The gull was now flying a few feet above and to the front of the *Girl Maggie*. It wheeled in the air and Sandy Hoynes spun the wheel to follow its course.

'There we are. Good as gold. Och, we'll be in Girvan before you can say, "Old McKirdy's a right miserable bugger."'

'Sandy, as first mate of this vessel, I must register my opposition to your present course o' action!'

Hoynes pursed his lips and glared at Hamish. 'You try any o' that Fletcher Christian stuff and I'll gie you another dunt on the heid wae this boat hook. I'm the captain o' this vessel. No jeest that, I'm its owner intae the bargain. One day you'll have your own boat to command. In the meantime, pipe doon and away and get me a hot mug o' tea. Fair parched, I am.'

Hamish shrugged and made his way back through the hatch and into the cabin.

'Any luck?' said Jo.

133

'Are you a religious person at all?' asked Hamish.

'No, not particularly. Why?'

'Well, if I was you, I'd try to find some o' it as quick as you can muster. For not only are we following the nautical suggestions o' a Viking, we're now taking the navigational advice o' a gull.'

'That's not good, is it?'

'Aye, you could put it in those terms. Then again, you could be much mair strident.'

'So what do we do?'

'We get some life jackets on, go up on deck, brace ourselves and hope for the best.'

❄

First of all, the skies over Kinloch brightened slightly, although the snow still fell. But soon it began to slow, and before long only the odd small flake added to the great mounds of white that covered the place.

In his office, McMurdo looked to the sky, relief spread across his face. He knew that they were a long way from finding the *Girl Maggie* and her crew, but at least this was a start. Soon, perhaps, they could launch a search in earnest.

He was about to call the harbour master when a tiny square of blue sky appeared through the snow clouds. It sent a shaft of light onto the street below that would have looked heavenly had it not been for the fact that it landed on the town clerk as he made his way back from Michael Kerr's with some bacon rolls.

Within the space of a quarter of an hour, phone calls were made, and McMurdo sat back at his desk with a strong cup of tea, savouring the taste and smell of crispy bacon. Lifeboats from Kinloch and Girvan had been launched, and a Royal Navy destroyer was steaming down the Clyde to assist with the search.

Kinloch's provost closed his eyes in a silent prayer. Hoynes was a rather prickly man to deal with, and a highly vocal member of the community who often disagreed with the decisions of the town council, but at this very moment there was no other face he'd rather see.

24

Hamish and Jo were now huddled on deck in stout yellow lifejackets. Hoynes stared at them from the wheelhouse with barely disguised contempt. 'For the life o' me, I canna understand why two almost sensible folk would choose tae shiver on deck when there's a nice warm cabin below.'

'Because we want tae be ready tae dive intae the sea if you hit they rocks,' said Hamish, quite mutinous now. He was, though, slightly taken aback by the big gull. It had held its position above the bow and was flapping as determinedly as ever, with what seemed to Hamish like clear intent. But such was the mood of the *Girl Maggie*'s first mate at this time of great anxiety that he saw the intent as malign, perhaps even murderous in nature.

Jo, who'd been watching him stare at the bird, cocked her head. 'They say that animals and birds have a sixth sense that we don't have.'

'Fish don't. They're right stupid creatures,' Hamish replied.

'But that's not a flying fish, it's a gull. Looks to me as though it knows what it's about.'

Hamish looked taken aback. 'I'm no' quite sure jeest what has got into you and the skipper. But whatever it is, I wish it would desist.'

'No, honestly, you read about these things all the time. In fact we covered a story in the paper last year. A man out swimming somewhere off Mull got out of his depth. He was tiring, trying to make for the shore with the tide against him. Out of nowhere this pod of dolphins surrounded him and pushed him to the shore. You know, like a strong wind.'

'Sounds mair to me like strong drink was involved, if you don't mind me saying. I read the other day that they'd have men walking on the moon before the decade is oot. Sheer nonsense! Look at the state *we're* in, and that's on account of a bit of snow between Kinloch and Girvan. Imagine the horrors they'd encounter on the way tae the moon.'

'They'll make it, don't you worry.'

'Aye, they'll make it up, likely. Some clever studio in Hollywood will pitch in and make gullible folk believe anything. It's all jeest one-upmanship wae they Russians.'

Jo grabbed Hamish's arm. 'Look!' she said, pointing upwards.

Sure enough, a small patch of blue had appeared amongst the snow clouds. It was tiny, but seemed to be growing. The snow, too, was turning into nothing more than a flurry.

'Sandy!' shouted Hamish. 'The weather's clearing.'

Hoynes stuck his head from the wheelhouse and stared at the patch of blue. 'Aye, and you wae no faith in Vikings – or gulls, come tae that.'

With that, the gull soared away and was soon lost in what was left of the cloud.

'Bugger,' said Hoynes under his breath.

'Land ahoy!' shouted Hamish. He was sharper-eyed than Hoynes, for soon a great white loom that definitely wasn't sea or sky began to appear through the tiny specks of snow.

'Ach,' said Hoynes, 'there we are. That's the hill that over-looks Girvan harbour, if I'm no' much mistaken.'

A shaft of bright sunlight suddenly broke through the clouds, illuminating the ghostly land like some huge spot-light.

'Never mind the hill at Girvan, Sandy. We're at the mouth o' the loch.'

'Which loch?' Hoynes looked on with a puzzled expression.

'Our ain – Kinloch – can you no' see it, man?'

As Hoynes stared, his eyes widened. Sure enough, the island at the head of the loch was to his left, the red and green buoys marking the channel into the their home port.

'Wow!' said Jo.

'It's a miracle,' Hamish remarked.

'It's no surprise tae me at all,' said Hoynes. He slowed the *Girl Maggie* and made his way confidently between the buoys, taking time to tamp some tobacco into his pipe and puff it into life with two flaring matches.

'What dae you mean, "no surprise"? You thought we were just about tae make port at Girvan!' said Hamish.

'I was just having you on. Man, you're a serious cove, right enough. It would be madness to have stayed on course for Girvan. Jeest ask Hona.'

'Who?'

'Hona the Viking. I'm sure I told you all about it.'

As the crew of the *Girl Maggie* argued back and forth, Jo disappeared. A few minutes later, she popped back up through the hatch, this time with her camera. It looked huge in her small hands as she framed shots and snapped away. 'What a story this is going to make!' she exclaimed, as Kinloch came into view at the end of the bay.

'Aye, but me and you will have tae have a word aboot that,' said Hoynes.

❄

McMurdo's phone rang. He picked it up quickly, anxious for news. Kinloch was now bathed in bright winter sunshine, making the snow that had fallen on the town sparkle like a glittering Christmas card.

'They're sailing into the loch,' said Mitchell, the harbour master.

'Who, Hoynes?' McMurdo could hardly believe his ears.

'Aye, plain as day. The lifeboat must have passed them in the snow. For they've not seen head nor tail of them since they ventured out earlier. I'm away to bring them back in.'

'Excellent! Thank you, Mr Mitchell.' Before he heard a reply, McMurdo slammed the phone back into its cradle and pulled on his overcoat. Soon he was making his way towards the quay, and although he slipped and fell a couple of times, the ache in his knee and loss of pride barely registered, as the vista opened out by the head of the loch.

Sure enough, only a hundred or so yards from the harbour mouth the *Girl Maggie* could be seen, black smoke issuing from her funnel.

McMurdo came to a halt beside Peeny and McKirdy.

'I knew fine he would make it,' said Peeny. 'The man's a genius wae navigation and the like.'

'Aye, through one o' the worst snow storms in history tae,' said McKirdy. He looked at Kinloch's provost, who was now wearing a broad smile under his trilby. 'You'll be mighty relieved, I'm thinking, eh?'

'Of course,' said McMurdo.

'Aye, they'd likely have burned you at the stake if she'd been lost at sea.'

'A tragic thought, but thankfully avoided. Don't you think you're being a touch melodramatic, McKirdy?'

'This is Kinloch. You should know that by now.' At his side, Peeny nodded his head.

On the pier, a huge cheer broke out from those who had been keeping up a silent vigil for the return of Hoynes and his vessel.

❄

On board the *Girl Maggie*, Jo had been ordered below, much against her will, it had to be said. Hoynes was more than aware that the presence of a woman on his boat would be seen as the tempting of fate that precipitated near calamity.

He stood in the wheelhouse, ready to bask in the best wishes of his townsfolk. 'Get down below and make sure young Jo knows what she's aboot, Hamish,' said Hoynes.

'Tell me again, skipper.'

'We'll tie up at the pier. While they're securing the ropes, I'll engage everyone with tales of our deliverance fae certain disaster.'

'You're no' going tae mention the Viking, are you – nor the gull?' Hamish blinked at his skipper.

For some reason, as the sky had cleared, so had the fog that clouded Hoynes' mind. He remembered being utterly convinced that he'd seen and spoken to the Viking. But now it was like a dream. 'I think we'll no' say much aboot that at the moment. Maybe jeest touch on my skills at navigation. As for the gull, well, there's nothing wrong wae that. He jeest happened to be heading in the same direction as ourselves. The creature likely recognised my determination, hence he took oor lead towards home.'

'Aye, but he was taking the lead, Sandy.'

'But I saw him looking back oot the corner o' his eye tae see where I was at. Clever creatures, they gulls. If I'd steered a degree away, that bird would have altered his course.'

'If you'd steered away, we'd have been on the rocks at the island, Sandy.'

'Well, I didna. Now, make sure your wee friend gets kitted oot in a bunnet and dungarees that'll make her look sufficiently like a cabin boy. When I alight on the pier, I'll lead everyone up tae the County. No doubt there will be the usual questions and wonder at oor skill in making port in such conditions. When the coast is clear, you and Jo can make a break for it. She's crafty enough, o' that there's no' much doubt.'

'And if she's no' of a mind tae align wae your thinking, Sandy?'

'That's what first mates are for, Hamish. I've every faith you'll use your charm to persuade her that this is the only sensible course o' action. After all, she'll have surely taken a fancy to such a well set-up chap like yourself. Fair heroic you are now, intae the bargain.'

As Hoynes watched Hamish head back to the cabin below, he was sure he'd flattered his first mate sufficiently to ensure he'd get the job done.

Expertly he slowed the *Girl Maggie* to a stop by the pier, and the fleet-footed harbour master jumped aboard with a rope to secure her to the quayside.

High above them in the clear blue sky, a gull circled, one eye cocked with interest on the events unfolding in the harbour below.

25

Hoynes was amidst a gaggle of folk, all interested to hear about his deliverance from the blizzard that should have made navigation – especially without the aid of radio and radar – impossible.

Hoynes stood, his boots planted firmly in the snow, smoke from his pipe billowing over the crowd. 'Well, you see, after a number of years on the great ocean, a mariner gets a notion – an instinct, if you fancy – aboot jeest where he is in the world. For myself, I think it's a skill bred intae us seamen, the same as it is wae salmon, pigeons and the like.'

'A lot o' pish,' said McKirdy under his breath.

'Moreover, when danger beckons, the sea looks after those who looked after it. Mother Nature's no' wanting the likes o' radar and such contraptions upsetting the balance o' things. It's all mair a cock o' the heid here and a sniff o' the wind there. I'm sure you all know what I mean.'

'I'm sniffing plenty wind right at the moment,' whispered Peeny.

'So, Mr Hoynes, would you say you were guided by the spirits of the sea?' This from McMahon, the young reporter from the *Kinloch Herald* whose prominent front teeth always made him look inquisitive.

'You could say that. Alternatively, you could say that a higher hand guided me through the perils o' the last few hours o' great darkness and despair.'

At this point, raised voices could be heard from the *Girl Maggie*. As Hoynes extolled the virtue of good seamanship in tandem with heavenly intervention, they became more pronounced.

'Is there a problem on the boat?' asked McMurdo.

'Och no, it's jeest Hamish letting off steam. You know the perilous state o' young folk these days. All kinds o' nonsense spinning aboot their heids.'

'I can hear two voices,' said McKirdy, a knowing look on his face.

'Me tae,' agreed Peeny.

'He does that sometimes,' said Hoynes. 'A hell of a man for the impersonations. He does a great Harold McMillan, though his Andy Stewart could do wae a bit o' work, right enough.'

As the voices on Hoynes' vessel became louder, everyone's attention was now diverted.

'Let's leave Hamish tae his nonsense and head up for a cosy dram and a chat in the County. I'm fair gasping for a glass o' whisky after all these trials and tribulations, no doubt about it.'

At that, a figure emerged through the hatch of the *Girl Maggie*. At first, with a greasy bunnet pulled down over the face, it looked for all the world like a small boy. But as a hand appeared and grabbed at the boy's ankle the bunnet was dislodged, revealing a young woman with a fashionably bobbed haircut.

'Just let me go, Hamish!' shouted Jo, as a collective gasp issued from those on the pier.

'Aye,' said McKirdy. 'I knew it fine. A woman, plain as day. No wonder you were lost at sea, Sandy Hoynes!'

'Och, I can explain,' said Hoynes, as Hamish emerged looking fretful.

'I'll explain, if someone will help me off this bloody tub!' Jo exclaimed.

Willing hands breached the space between the vessel and the pier, gently hauling the young woman in the ill-fitting dungarees up from the *Girl Maggie*, as Hoynes looked on, a resigned look on his face.

'I'm a reporter from the *Glasgow Times*,' said Jo. 'Mr Hoynes entered into a bona fide contract with the paper, so that we might cover his mercy mission to feed the stranded community here in Kinloch. But he took the money before he realised I was a woman.'

Another gasp from those gathered.

'I was fair conned intae it. Aye, and Hamish here is by no means without blame,' Hoynes remonstrated.

'Hold on, skipper,' said Hamish. 'You jeest misunderstood what was happening.'

A woman's voice piped up, this time from the back of the assembly. 'You telt me this lassie had a broken leg, Sandy Hoynes!'

'Mother!' Hamish wailed. 'What are you doing here?'

'What kind o' a mother would I be if I didna come to greet my own son, saved from a watery grave? But you'll wish you were in one if I hear there's been any shenanigans aboard that vessel.'

'Shenanigans!' said Hoynes. 'I'll have you know that no such things took place on the *Girl Maggie*.'

'Too right,' said Jo. 'Hamish is a nice enough man, but he's not my type.'

144

'I telt you he'd missed the boat as far as a wife was concerned,' said McKirdy.

Hoynes called for order. 'I'll admit I was mistaken in taking the young lassie aboard. But, as I say, I was misled.'

'Tell them how I saved your precious boat,' said Jo.

'You jeest get back to your work. You'll have plenty tae type up, and no mistake,' said Hoynes, in an effort to silence the reporter.

'I'll not be hushed up like some child. The truth is that both Mr Hoynes and Hamish were indisposed. It was up to me in the middle of the night to save the vessel.'

'Huh! As we thought, the pair of them fair steaming, thinking they had nothing to lose. Shame on you, Sandy Hoynes,' said Peeny.

'I'll have you know I was not drunk. I was rendered insensible by a hallucinogenic!'

This statement silenced everyone present.

'He thought he was a lobster,' said Hamish from the deck of the *Girl Maggie*.

'I think we've heard enough,' said McMurdo. 'I'm sure the harbour master will enquire further as to what happened aboard your vessel, Mr Hoynes. It all sounds most irregular to me. I'm quite sure a number of breaches of maritime law have been committed.'

'Off his heid on the drugs! Aye, the whole town will be a laughing stock when this emerges,' said McKirdy.

'Let me explain!' Hoynes shouted, but to no avail.

In dribs and drabs, the impromptu welcoming committee made their way back to the snowy town, many shaking their heads at the shame of it all.

'Well, thank you very much,' said Hoynes to Jo.

'Stop your grumbling. We'd be at the bottom of the sea – and you know it – had I not tied that wheel to make the boat turn in circles.'

'And whose fault was that?'

'You put the sugar lump in your own tea,' said Jo. 'Anyway, don't worry about that. I'll say in my report that you ate some dodgy shellfish.'

'No' lobster, mind,' said Hamish.

Shaking his head, Hoynes turned on his heel and marched up the pier, only to slip outside the weigh house and collide with a bollard. Despite this setback, he picked himself up, dusted himself down, and was soon lost in the snow-packed trenches that were the streets of Kinloch.

Epilogue

In the days that followed, outrage subsided when Jo Baird's article appeared in the *Glasgow Times*. The people of Kinloch read it a day late, the papers and vital supplies having to be brought aboard a MacBrayne's ferry.

Though Peeny and McKirdy swore that Hoynes was a martyr to narcotics, most settled for Jo's explanation that he'd been poisoned by shellfish. She was unrepentant as to the role she'd played in saving the vessel, and soon the general feeling was that it was high time the ridiculous superstition that women had no place on boats be crushed once and for all.

After many trials, Hamish succeeded in convincing his mother that nothing untoward had passed between him and the pretty young reporter. Soon, the events of the blizzard melted away with the snow that had isolated the town.

Sandy Hoynes, though, was still troubled. The nagging memory of the Viking who had been their salvation lingered on his mind. But he managed to persuade himself that it had merely been his subconscious dealing with matters in hand while still under the influence.

When Christmas and New Year were past, and strong gales were battering Kinloch, looking for a diversion before the County Hotel opened, Hoynes made his way to the local library.

'I'm wondering,' he enquired of Mrs Duncan the librarian. 'Have you anything on Vikings – particularly any known to have frequented our own coastline?'

'I can find you some good books on the subject, Mr Hoynes. But, as it happens, I have always had an interest in the Northmen myself. In fact, we had our very own Viking lord. He died at the Battle of Largs, but by all accounts – and one has to take them with a pinch of salt, of course – he was a bit of a character. Had land up near Firdale. Hona was his name, though his nickname was The Serpent. Apparently the prow of his boat was carved into a likeness of the creature. Lovely story, but likely just myth.' She smiled. 'In fact, if you give me a moment, I have a wee pamphlet I wrote on the subject. The engraving on the cover was taken from a woodcut found at Edail Abbey. But, like the story, possibly a construction of many years later.'

Hoynes stared at the book, wide-eyed. Though crudely drawn, there was the man who'd pointed his way to salvation in the snow. The sleeked-back flaxen hair, the clothes – everything was as Hoynes remembered. 'In my opinion, Mrs Duncan, no myth.' He turned round slowly and walked away. 'I'll come back for the books tomorrow.'

Hoynes paused outside the library and stared across the loch, the wind tugging at his pea jacket. 'More things in heaven and earth, right enough,' he muttered to himself before shuffling away, quite bemused.

＊

High above the town, where the ramparts of the old hill fort had once stood, sat the gull, the soul of Kinloch. Head to one side, he watched the distant figure of Hoynes as he made his way along the esplanade.

With a loud squawk, he spread his great wings and soon was soaring on the strong wind above the old town, over which he'd watched for so long.

A Toast *to*
The Old Stones

For my old pal Davie Robertson

He's danc'd awa, he's danc'd awa,
He's danc'd awa wi' the Exciseman.

Robert Burns

Prologue

There are places all over the world that elicit strange feelings of ancient things on the edge of consciousness. Lofty cathedrals, holy spaces and sacred isles possess an ambience of mystery and otherness which pervades the very air.

But the modern world has almost obliterated this otherworldly sense. Gadgets guide the way where once the stars, the sun and signs in nature did the job. Instead of sniffing the air, staring at the sky or observing the behaviour of the creatures who live all around us, radio weather forecasters do the job, announcing with calm, efficient authority that it will be showery – as if this is to be taken as unimpeachable fact by all those who listen through the crackle of static. Even though its veracity may be questionable.

Such is the vanity that has developed within our species, the very idea of knowing without proof, believing without seeing and feeling without touch has become the preserve of the 'mad' or 'unbalanced'. These arcane skills that marked out humanity for millennia have been all but lost.

Yet, when in the dark of night old rafters creek like the rigging of square-rigged schooners, or a barely perceived movement at the corner of the eye – just out of sight – grips a chilled heart, or the call of creatures of the night keeps us from sleep, we are touching the part of our minds that was once as unremarkable as a child's adoration or the embrace of a loved one. None of us can explain a tug on the heartstrings, yet our race could never exist without love, for which there is no rhyme or reason. There is still to be discovered a white-coated scientist who can explain why Joan makes John feel as though he's walking on air; it's just accepted as fact, and that's that.

Deep within every man, woman and child lurks the ability to experience much more than can ever be explained.

How many times do we think of someone then turn a corner only to find them striding towards us? How often does the sinking feeling in the pit of the stomach presage the very worst events in our lives?

Trust it or reject it, there exists the ability to see and feel beyond ourselves, our realm, our mundane reality. It harries the primal part of our minds, as it has done since our time began. Especially when we find ourselves in a place where past and present meet, where time, it seems, stands still.

On the fertile east coast of Kintyre such a place exists.

On a small rise in splendid isolation stand two stones. One is rough and squat, less than the span of three hands in height, the other, slightly taller, is slender and smooth to the touch.

When first encountered, these stones can easily be mistaken for random outcrops of gneiss deposited by the tumults that have shaped our Earth for billions of years. There is little remarkable about them, apart from their resemblance to a short, fat man standing beside a tall, elegant woman.

But take a closer look, and something else may touch your soul. At the top of the smaller rock there is a dip, almost like a bowl. Within, lie the red-rusted remnants of old pins left by farmers in recent centuries. For this has long been a place where 'votive offerings', as archaeologists call them, were deposited. On the other stone, there are marks, writing perhaps – almost weathered away – but not in any hand we now recognise.

But the stones – 'The Couple', the Vikings called them – are now hard to find. Yes, they still stand on the little rise that once afforded them views across the sound. But the only sight they now enjoy is that of tightly spaced fir trees that encase them in a dark forest where neither beast nor man stirs; from where sunlight is banished by the intertwined canopies of pine needles. They exist in silence, with neither tribute nor adoration – well, much of the time, that is.

The time passed a long, long time ago when those who erected these little stones lived. With them they took their meaning. But others, unburdened by the certainties of this age, felt their power.

Over thousands of years, no one has passed by without paying their respects. This, for no other reason than they felt the need to acknowledge the stirring of their souls, for it was known that the Auld Man and Woman, as they came to be known in the modern day, could usher in a fine harvest, bring back the deer that life so depended on in their crude settlements, or some good fortune that everyone still requires.

No sleek dragon boat passed by without leaving a memento of its visit, by way of gold or an engraved ship's name or that of a leader. The weather has worn down these messages, heartfelt offerings of those who came before us, and upon whose shoulders we stand. They are now little more than shadows.

But while trees can last an age, stones are eternal, even when forgotten. And as the tall pines grew all around them, soon came the day when men cut down the wood. Once more the stones stared across the slow waters of the sound and felt the heat of the sun.

And there they remain – and always will, no matter how many new trees grow. For they have the power of the Thin Places.

Kinloch, July 1912

The sky above the small town was deep, deep blue, a hue that only the most glorious of summers could conjure up. The loch glinted like a sea of precious stones, and the big houses on the hill shimmered in the haze. Heading for the remains of the old fort, a gull flapped lazily in the air, its screech echoing across the bay.

And it had been a good summer for fishing, too. Kinloch's fleet of little ring-net boats had chased plentiful shoals of herring and mackerel until their nets all but burst. Fishermen were in funds, and consequently so was every other business in the place, whether they be butchers, bakers or even candlestick makers. Though it had to be said that Tam Douglas, proprietor of the hostelry that bore his name, smiled broader than most.

When the fishing was good and the sun shone, Kinloch was one of the best places in the world. Only in the long dark winter, or a bad season, were pennies counted; then, anxious shopkeepers looked up and down the windswept streets for their next customer, and the menfolk would gaze out at a sea seemingly bereft of marine life. Meanwhile, always at the very heart of family life, women worked harder than ever to make do the best they could to feed their children.

But today, these times seemed like a distant memory.

The boy watched as his father's nimble hands worked at the net, the bodkin flashing in the bright sunlight with every turn of his fist. He marvelled at the dexterity; how his father could take in the activity around the harbour, have conversations as he puffed on the pipe clamped in his mouth, and repair the net, all at the same time. It was as though his hands were possessed of their own will, the product of many years' practice.

Alastair Hoynes decided to take a break. He got to his feet, stretched and yawned. The crew of the *Red Dawn* were busy resetting a mast, while Archie Robertson – never the most industrious fisherman – lay aboard the *Raven* on a pile of nets soaking up the heat, his flat cap pulled down over his eyes. On the road between the twin piers, ranks of barrels stood to attention, waiting for the women to pack them with fish and salt. Hands red raw, hair pushed under scarfs or pinned back in neat buns, their songs and chatter drifted across the harbour.

The boy cocked his head, keen to make out a song or a scatter of words. 'I canna make out the tune, Faither.'

Alastair inclined his head. 'No, nor me, son. I think it's fair tae say that there are few Mod gold medals to be found amongst that lot. Och, but it keeps them happy at their toil, so there's no harm in it at all, Sandy.'

The boy with hair turned golden blond by the salt sea and summer sun nodded sagely. 'Mother says they're all torn-faced auld scunners.'

His father eyed him keenly. 'Your mother has a habit o' finding scunners where none are to be had. I'm sure she was only speaking in jest.'

'She said you were a miserable bugger on Saturday night when she was at her purse.'

Alastair nodded. 'Aye, I daresay. But her bark is worse than her bite. And you shouldna be telling tales behind her back – she's the only mother you'll ever have, and you'll miss her when she's gone. I miss mine to this very day, and she died afore the century turned, God bless her.'

Sandy felt ashamed. His father's rebuke was mild, but he wished he hadn't opened his mouth. While his mother's admonishments were as sharp as the carpet beater with which she caught him on the back of his legs by way of punishment, his father was a more subtle disciplinarian. Sandy had never heard him raise his voice, much less engage in the idle gossip that seemed to be the pastime of just about everyone else he knew – including his mother. He studied the man, imagining himself standing tall, a lick of grey at the temples of his otherwise golden hair, face tanned under the heat of many summers accentuating his bright blue eyes.

'What are you staring at?' Alastair regarded his son over the briar pipe as he tamped in more tobacco.

'Why do we have such blond hair, Faither?'

Alastair puffed his pipe back into life. 'Now, you've fair hit upon an interesting question there, Sandy.'

'How so?'

'My auld grandfaither told a tale about the men fae the north.'

'Glasgow?'

'No, son, much further north than that. At least, that's from where they hailed originally.'

Sandy puzzled upon this for a moment or two, closing one eye against the sun's reflection on the clear water of the loch. 'I'm no' getting you at all.' He stared back up at his father.

'Do they teach you nothing at thon school?'

'Aye, but it's all that arithmetic and English. Mrs Henderson says if you've no' got your letters and numbers you might as well stick your heid in a pail and walk aboot wearing it for the rest o' your days.'

'And she has the right o' it, too. You'll no' go far if you canna tally up the fish you've caught or write a note or two, and that's a fact. But is that all they teach you?'

'How tae sit up straight and the like. But other than that it's reading and counting all day long.' Sandy sighed at the thought of returning to school in a few short weeks.

'Did she never tell you o' the Vikings?'

'No, no' a word. Maybe that's for next year.'

'Well, I'll give you a head start. Here, take a seat on these nets and I'll enlighten you.'

The boy listened to his father intently as he told tales of the men from the north. They were a frightening bunch, that was for sure. He fretted at the stories for a moment, picturing the dragon boats of which his father spoke sailing into the loch and putting men to the sword and ravishing the women. But when he found out how they'd settled the land and made it their own, and what fine fishermen and boat builders they were, Sandy became more amicably disposed towards the Vikings.

Instinctively, like the schoolboy he was, he held up his hand to ask a question.

'Aye, what dae you want to know?'

'What's "ravishing", Faither?'

Alastair cleared his throat, took a long draw of his pipe and stared out to sea. 'Och, it's too hard to explain everything right now. But you'll learn aboot it in time, I'm quite sure.'

'Do you ravish Mother every noo and then?'

Alastair raised an eyebrow. 'Nah, son. If there's any ravishing tae be done in oor hoose, it's your mother that does it. But don't worry aboot that aspect just this minute. There's mair to this tale.'

Sandy detected a flush of red under his father's tanned cheeks but put the whole thing down to the heat of the day. 'So they came and made us all slaves, or the like?'

'Aye, there was slavery that went on, that's for sure. A damnable thing that they canna be very proud o' if they look back on it now.'

'Where are they now?'

Alastair took to his feet again and stood tall, raising his head proudly like some of the heroes Sandy read about in his comic books. He had a distant look in his blue eyes. 'You're looking at one right this very minute.'

Sandy was confused. He keeked past his father, fearful that he was missing something. Or that, in the worst case, he had a squint like poor wee Donnie MacKay and his father had assumed he was looking at something else entirely.

'No, it's me, you dolt – aye, and you!'

'Eh?'

'We're off the Vikings. That's where oor blond hair comes fae. Remember, they were fine seafarers, and so are we. It's been passed down through the generations. In the blood, if you like.'

'So they were a thirsty lot too, then?'

'Why do you say that, son?'

'Because mother says you've got a fair drouth.'

'What did I tell you about telling tales?'

'Sorry.' Sandy's mind was a tumble of ideas. He couldn't picture himself cutting anyone down with an axe or a sword

162

– far less his father or grandfather being about such wicked business. Perhaps their side of the family had been part of a much less bloodthirsty lot.

'I have a book in the house. I'll let you read it if you help me get these nets back aboard.'

So, under the bright summer sun of the late afternoon, father and son readied their neat little boat for dawn the next day, and another trip out to catch the fruits of the sea.

For young Sandy, however, he would never think of himself again the same way. He was from the cold north, where men wore helmets adorned with bull horns and pleated their long fair locks and beards before jumping into boats, all set for a day of fighting and ravishing – whatever that was. He resolved to ask Ranald Kelly the next day, if he could. Ranald, being a bit older than Sandy, was a fount of knowledge. If anyone knew about ravishing, it would be him.

As they stepped back onto the pier, Alastair took his son by the hand and turned him to face Kinloch's fleet of fishing boats, sitting in the crowded harbour like the herrings being packed into barrels of salt on the pier opposite. 'Take a look at the line of the craft – their shape, Sandy.'

The boy cast his eye proudly over *Maggie*, his father's vessel. 'Aye, right bonnie, Faither.'

'Aye, bonnie they are, son. But like us they have their roots wae the Vikings. Sure, they're only dragon boats cut down to size a wee bit. I tell you, Sandy, when we're back out to sea tomorrow, just close your eyes and you'll feel your ancestors in your bones. There's a place up near Firdale where they had their great hall. Aye, they'd head there on a cold night for feasts and a good few tankards o' ale. I'll show you where it is, though there's no' much to see now, apart fae the stones.'

Together they walked back up the pier. Secretly, Sandy was pleased that the Vikings enjoyed their tankards of ale. It meant they must have had a drouth, right enough. So, his mother wasn't always wrong.

1

The paralysing snows at the end of the old year had given way to miserable, wet and windy weather. Engorged burns frothed down the hills and glens, turning the loch a peaty brown. Mrs Longmuir's dress shop experienced a flash flood, her latest batch of miniskirts ruined in the process. A gaggle of young women, who had waited for weeks to purchase the latest fashion from Carnaby Street, turned on their high heels and, disappointed, tripped back home with nothing new to wear.

Hogmanay had been a miserable affair. Only the hardiest revellers scuttled from house to house clutching bottles, lumps of coal and black buns. For old habits died hard in Kinloch. Tradition here held fast, where it had fallen away in many other parts of Scotland. Those with red hair stood forlornly in doorways until a suitably tall and dark individual arrived to be First Foot, thereby affording much needed shelter from the elements for all concerned.

This tradition went back to the days when to find anyone without the dark hair and the sallow skin of the area's original inhabitants on the threshold of one's home was to stare death in the face. But Picts, Celts and Norsemen had long mingled to live in relative peace and contentment in Kinloch, the wrongdoing of the ages forgotten.

Sandy Hoynes glowered through the wheelhouse at the rain that was beating like a thousand tiny drums on the *Girl Maggie*. With both he and Hamish in such an enclosed space, each puffing away at their pipes, the atmosphere was, to say the least, thick.

'Man, the third of January. A mair miserable day in the year canna be found,' declared Hoynes.

'Aye, Hogmanay seems like a lifetime ago, and it's only a couple o' nights back,' agreed Hamish.

Hoynes turned a leary eye on his first mate. 'You fairly made the most of it, right enough. Fair puggled you were, like auld Jock Mackenzie at the head o' the pipe band wae a half-bottle sticking oot his jacket pocket. Drunk as a skunk, you were. And let me tell you, if you have any ambitions as a singer, you can just forget them. You fair murdered "My Granny's Heilan' Hame" in oor hoose. Peeny tells me you were shouting aboot free love by the time you made it to his place.'

'It was "All You Need Is Love". The Beatles sang it in front o' the whole world last year.'

'That's as maybe. But if you've any ambition to turn yourself into one o' these hippies, just rein it in. For a start, you haven't got the hair for it, and you'll have to find another berth. There's been enough calamity on this vessel wae narcotics without you embracing them on a permanent basis.' Hoynes drew deeply on his pipe and remembered his fevered lobster dreams while under the influence of a mistakenly administered hallucinogenic. He shivered. 'From now on, the only intoxicant that will be tolerated on this vessel is good old-fashioned whisky.'

Hamish ran his hand through his thinning hair. The fact that his skipper could always find a way of bringing his encroaching baldness into the conversation was a regular irritant. In any case, from what he could remember, Hoynes's accusations were wildly exaggerated. Yes, he'd enjoyed the New Year celebrations to the full, but so had his various hosts; this meant that he wasn't in the slightest ashamed. The dark days of midwinter were brightened up by Hogmanay, and that was a fact – it was the whole point of the thing. With the notion of Christmas still a relatively new concept in the West of Scotland, the old ways still held sway.

Hoynes cleared his throat, frequently a precursor to a portentous statement. 'I have something to tell you, Hamish.'

'A cold hand grabbed Hamish's heart. His mother had been in fine fettle when he'd left her early that morning. In any event, he'd been with Hoynes the whole day, so if anything had happened to her, he'd have found out at the same time as his skipper. Mind working overtime, his next thought was as to the future of his employment. 'You're no' retiring, are you?'

'Retiring? Wae my lassie stepping out wae a police sergeant and a wedding in the offing – no' to mention my wife's insatiable appetite for spending money. I'll no' be able to retire until 1999!'

'That's an ambitious statement, skipper. Man, you'll be kicking a hundred by then.'

'When I was a boy there were fishermen working well into their eighties, and that's a fact. Wae all this modern medicine and the like, folk will soon be looking at a hundred years old like we do turning twenty-one these days. I was up at the clinic wae my bunions the other day. You should see the contraptions they have up there now. I wouldn't have been surprised if Frankenstein's monster had come lumbering oot the surgery. Gravediggers must be fair fearing for their jobs.' He nodded his head in self-confirmation of this reasoning.

'So what is it you have to tell me?'

Hoynes stroked his bushy white beard, a further indication of something monumentous. 'You're no boy any more, Hamish. Man, every time I look at your hairline that very thought strikes me.'

Hamish sighed, but thought it better to keep quiet lest whatever it was Hoynes had to say be further delayed.

'You'll be aware of the tradition we fishermen have around this time o' year.'

'Getting drunk and moaning aboot the weather?'

'No such thing! I'm talking aboot our trip to celebrate the Auld New Year. As you know, it's a privilege only afforded to the senior mariners in the fleet. A rare honour it is to be invited, that's for sure.'

Hamish ruminated upon this 'honour'. As far as he was aware, a group of old-timers took off to take in the old New Year on the twelfth of January each year at a tumbledown hut on the east coast of the peninsula. This was in commemoration of the turn of the date before the Gregorian calendar took over from its Julian predecessor. It was a regular habit of certain Kintyre menfolk to take off to various places on the coast in the summer. To facilitate this pastime, old huts had been thrown together from driftwood and anything else that came to hand. There, they would drink and tell tall tales over a weekend, getting back to nature and enjoying male companionship, away from their wives, who, with very few exceptions, ruled every roost.

The fishing community had taken this idea one step further. But a night spent in a dilapidated old hut with equally old men in order to celebrate the old New Year filled Hamish with horror. The word 'old' turned over in his mind. However, he knew that an arcane honour was being bestowed upon him, and as his father had never received the invitation, he realised this turn of events would please his mother greatly.

'I can tell you're thinking,' said Hoynes. 'Your mouth's hanging open like a beached cod.'

'I'm just surprised, that's all. My faither never got to go.'

Hoynes pursed his lips. 'Well, your faither could be right argumentative after a few drams. As you know, he'd more than a passing fondness for the water o' life.'

'Water o' death, in his case.'

'Aye, sad indeed. For when he wasn't in his cups, he was a fine man.'

Hamish nodded meekly at this. There was no doubt that his father's monumental whisky consumption had hastened his premature demise – though many of his maritime colleagues were of the opinion that his drinking was the product of an unhappy marriage, rather than any weakness of character. After all, whisky was like food, a fundamental sustenance. Any overindulgence was surely a reflection of the unfortunate course of one's life, not an addiction. Hamish had never been taken in by this reasoning.

'So, we set off early on the twelfth. You'll note I had to pull plenty strings to get you there. Make sure you don't affront yourself wae any o' this free love business. My reputation is at stake here, and you know how much store I place on that.'

Hamish nodded in solemn agreement. Many occasions where his skipper's reputation had been brought into question paraded themselves before his mind's eye. But, all in all, it was nice to be appreciated by his more senior peers, and by his reckoning, he'd be by far the youngest present.

'I'll be there, skipper. And thank you.'

'Och, your mother will likely cook up a storm tonight in celebration. A nice stew, I'm thinking.'

'It's fish pie tonight.'

'And a more nourishing dish you canna consume.' Satisfied that he'd done his good deed for the day, Hoynes tamped some more baccy into his pipe and puffed vigorously, a look of great contentment spreading across his face.

Hamish looked out the wheelhouse window as curtains of rain swept across the harbour and dearly hoped that the weather would improve in the next few days.

2

Hamish and his mother were in the kitchen of the Glebe Fields flat they shared – though the elder of the two always referred to it as the scullery. An old black range sat at one end of the room beside a deep Belfast sink. A pitted oak table dominated the space. It was around this very piece of furniture that many of the momentous events in the lives of Hamish's family and their antecedents had been discussed. At this moment, Hamish sat at the head of the table in the chair his father had once occupied.

As always, his mother had excelled herself with the fish pie. But while it was one of Hamish's favourite dishes, he longed to see a plump roast chicken, or a succulent joint of beef. However, Kinloch's fishing community looked after its own. Widows of lost fishermen and their families benefited from a generous supply of free fish. While it was a touching gesture, the tradition did lead to a somewhat limited menu.

'Get that down you,' said his mother. 'In weather like this a man needs as much nourishment as he can get.' She stood over Hamish, hands crossed over her blue apron, making sure he left a clean plate. 'You'll be for a second helping?'

'Aye, that would be grand, Mother.'

'Well, you canna have it.'

'Why not? You just offered.'

'You know I'm not long for this world, Hamish. Goodness knows how few years we've left together before you have to lower me into to the ground down at Kilgreggan.'

'No' again,' muttered Hamish.

'Don't mumble. It's right bad manners. Your faither was a terrible man for the mumbling.'

'Och, he was likely just thinking aloud.'

'No, he was likely just drunk. But, whatever his reasons, I don't want you slipping into the habit.' She leaned over her son and removed his plate from the table.

'So, no second helpings, then?'

'As I say, I could drop deid at any time – I'm of the age. You need to snare a wife to look after you in my place.'

'You're only fifty-eight, Mother.' Hamish shook his head at this regular prophesy of imminent demise.

'It's no' just that, son. Being a woman myself, I'm more than well aware of what the fairer sex looks for in a potential husband.'

'Oh aye?'

'It's a fact. And one thing I can tell you for certain sure is that the combination of a receding hairline coupled wae a burgeoning belly isn't something likely to turn a girl's head. The reverse, in fact – more likely to turn her stomach.'

'There's barely a picking on me!' Hamish was indignant.

'Aye, but once you're by thirty the least morsel can add the weight. So, no more fish pie for you this night. You can chew on a carrot if you feel peckish.'

Hamish looked on forlornly as his mother brandished said carrot in front of him, for all the world like Boudicca with her sword. 'I'm actually quite full anyway.'

'That's the spirit, son.'

'I've got some good news.' Hamish had decided to keep his invitation to the Auld New Year celebrations until after dinner.

'Is it a lassie?' She adopted a stern expression. 'Mind, as keen as I am to see you settled and happy wae a nice girl who'll meet all your requirements, you canna hitch your wagon tae the first pony that trots by.'

'Requirements?'

'You know fine what I mean. A man needs more than just a plateful o' fish pie. I'll no' go into details. You canna just spread your seed wae careless abandon.'

'Mother, we've been through this! I value your opinion, but when I meet a lassie I want to wed, it'll be my own choice. We're no' going to wade through the last six generations of her family and look for phantom murderers, smugglers or sneak thieves, like we did the last time.'

'Sandy Hoynes was talking nonsense. That lassie was off a bad lot, no doubt about it. If you'd any sense, you'd have realised yourself just by the look o' her.'

Hamish brushed this notion aside with a dismissive wave of his hand. 'Can you sit down, Mother, please. I've something important to tell you.'

'She's in the family way! Some vixen has lured you wae the turn of her ankle – I knew it. Your father had a weakness for that kind o' thing. As well as the drink, obviously.'

'I'm unlikely to be lured by an ankle, Mother. Anyway, it has nothing to dae with women.'

Hamish's mother stared blankly at him for a few moments. She held her head in her hands and sighed loudly.

'Whatever is the matter wae you now?'

'I know that it's all the rage now. I was reading the paper

the other day. But tell me at least that it's no' Sandy Hoynes.'

Hamish was puzzled. 'Is what no' Sandy Hoynes?'

'I realise we live in a different world. And I know what you were trumpeting when you were steaming drunk the other night – all aboot this free love and other such horrors.'

'I was singing a Beatles song.'

'Oh aye?'

'Yes! Och, you're just as bad as the skipper.'

'You'll no' be able to stay in Kinloch. These tendencies might be tolerated where they Beatles come fae, but the folk here won't look at you favourably if you're stepping oot wae another man – especially one near auld enough to be your grandfaither.'

'Heavens, how have we got to this? The working o' your mind's a mystery to me, Mother.'

Drying her eyes with the hem of her apron, Hamish's mother regarded him warily. 'So you're no' that way inclined?'

'No, I'm not. And even if I was, Sandy Hoynes wouldn't be the object of my affections.'

'So, it's plain that you've thought about it.'

'Honestly, Mother! All the dreadful things going on in the world and you perplex yourself with issues that are private between folk. You need to find some kind o' interest to keep your mind occupied.'

'I beg your pardon! It's a full-time job making sure you're fed, watered and have clean clothes to put on your back. Do you think this hoose runs itself? I'm telling you, don't expect Sandy Hoynes to run after you the way I do. You'll be pressed into service domestically in that relationship, make no mistake.'

'I'm no' *taking up* with Sandy, Mother. I've been invited to the Auld New Year celebrations. You know, up near Firdale.'

The expression on his mother's face transformed. Then she looked suspiciously at her son. 'You're just pulling my leg.'

'No, Sandy imparted the news to me this very afternoon.'

Her expression was suddenly doubtful. 'Did he . . .'

'Don't you dare! It's got nothing to dae wae that, Mother. It's a grand tradition in the fishing community, as you know. I'm privileged to be asked.'

'Aye, you are that. Your faither never sniffed it. But we all know why that was.'

'Time to put that behind us. Poor faither was his own worst enemy. It's best to let it lie.'

Without taking time to reply, Hamish's mother bustled away from the table.

'Where are you off to now?'

'I'm phoning my friends, Hamish. What do you think I'm doing?' She hesitated for a minute. 'Right enough, I don't need to go to the expense o' phoning them all. Wae Hilda on the exchange the whole o' Kinloch will know in jig time.' She hurried into the hall where the phone resided in splendid isolation on a scalloped table. It was her only indulgence.

Hamish sat back in his chair. He was going to an old hut with some even older fishermen to drink whisky and celebrate the old New Year. Judging by his mother's reaction, you'd think he was taking up a seat in the House of Lords. The young fisherman was convinced he'd never learn the ways of the older generation. These people were an impenetrable mystery to him – especially his mother.

Hearing her excited voice in the hall, he grabbed a spoon, made for the oven and helped himself to a large dollop of fish pie.

3

Being the tenth of January, it was now only two days until the exclusive celebrations of the Auld New Year. Thankfully, the rain had abated. A light grey sky settled over Kinloch as the *Girl Maggie* sailed past the island and towards the harbour. Though a few streetlights were popping into life along the esplanade, given the time of year, there was still a couple of hours of light left in the day. But judging by the flurry of black smoke issuing from the metal chimney that ran up the side of the wheelhouse, and the look on Sandy Hoynes's face, he was in a hurry to reach port.

'You're fair hammering the old girl,' Hamish observed as he took in his skipper's countenance; there was a steely-eyed, pipe-clenched determination he rarely witnessed.

Hoynes nodded grimly. 'All day the day I've been thinking it was the ninth. It's my wife's fault.'

'How so?'

'She has me fair bamboozled wae a new calendar in the kitchen. Aye, plenty o' admirable photographs, but the dates are too small. I'll have to see if Mr Keith at the newsagents has some 1968 ones left, because if we carry on this way I'll be heading for my Christmas dinner a week late. It's called style o'er substance, Hamish. A thing to avoid at all costs. A bit like that revolving door they installed at the King's Hotel last year.'

Hamish thought for a moment. 'I canna say I hold that in any regard. Wae doors generally, there should be no necessity to pause and think before you use them – in my opinion, at least. Man, but that one at the King's Hotel is an article to beware of, and no mistake.'

'As poor Connie MacCallum found to her cost just a fortnight ago.' Hoynes shook his head. 'A fine wedding day fair ruined.'

'What happened?'

'Och, nothing more than a simple case o' mistiming. You know how it is wae thon door. You've got to judge your moment before committing yourself. They tell me poor Jock Tolly was stood out in the pouring rain for near half an hour, feart to put as much as a toe in the thing.'

Hamish nodded in agreement. 'The bugger caught me a right dunt on the knee just after Christmas. Then it had the cheek to fling me into the lobby like a gutted herring. It's only because I battered into big Robbie McQuilkin that I was able to keep my feet.'

'You'd have been carrying a fair cargo o' whisky if your antics at Hogmanay were anything to go by, eh?'

Hamish chose to ignore this barb. 'You've no' told me what happened at the wedding.'

'Oh aye.' Hoynes cleared his throat. 'It being her big day, Connie was dressed up to the nines. A white wedding dress wae one o' they trains.' Hoynes turned to Hamish with a knowing look.

'White?'

'Aye, did you ever? But that means nothing these days. It's all this free love that you're never done wae that's to blame.'

'It was a song!'

'Indeed, just as you say. Anyhow, the bonnie bride gets oot o' the taxi wae the help o' the bridesmaids. Just as pretty as a picture, she was. They'd managed to cover up her acne really well wae a hefty dab o' makeup.'

'The poor lassie's fair afflicted wae the plooks, right enough.'

'In any event, her being all jangled wae the excitement o' the day and all, she made straight for thon revolving door as though she was walking into her own front room.'

'A mistake, no doubt about it!'

'A mistake! She managed to get herself into the wee wedge, right enough. But then the husband pushed his way in beside her. Of course, as you know, there's only room for one body in any part o' that thing.'

'And Tommy Shaw is a big lump o' a lad.'

'He is that. I'd been fair dragged doon to see the bride by my good lady. It never ceases to amaze me how women get themselves so worked up at the sight o' a wedding. It's the same wae babies. One glimpse o' a cot and they're blubbering like a man aboot to be hanged.'

'That's a hellish thing, too.'

'We've seen the last o' that in this country. Don't you worry, when you get up to no good full o' narcotics and free love, the most you'll get is a few years behind bars.'

Hamish chose not to take the bait. 'You're losing the place, Sandy.'

'Aye, just so. So, there's the happy couple crammed into the same compartment of the door. Her face was fair pressed up against the glass. Man, you could see right up her nose. No' a bonnie sight, Hamish. Especially for a lassie on her wedding day. Well, anxious to free him and his new wife,

178

Tommy gives the door a right shove. But he's never realised his own strength. Before you know it, the bloody thing's away like a merry-go-round at the fair. There they are spinning aboot in the revolving door, feet going like the clappers, fair terrified to make a wrong move in case a limb is lost, or the like.'

'Heavens! That sounds dire, right enough.' Hamish took a comforting draw on his pipe.

'But there's worse to come. You see, all the time they're rotating in the door, her train is wrapping itself round the mechanism in the middle o' the damned thing. Suddenly, without any warning, it comes to a standstill, the pair o' them neither in nor oot.'

'Imagine!'

Hoynes held up a chubby forefinger. 'But in the process o' the door coming to a sudden halt, poor Connie fair rattles her hooter off the glass. Och, there was blood everywhere. She's greeting, all the women are greeting, and big Tommy's looking as though he wished he'd stayed at his mother's hoose and enjoyed a dram or two in front o' the wireless instead o' all this marriage lark.'

'What a shame. Did they carry on with the proceedings?'

'Not at all. It took young Charlie Murray the joiner near an hour to free them. By the time Connie was liberated they'd to rush her up to the cottage hospital wae her nose. Bent as a question mark, it was. Man, has she no' been cutting aboot like a panda for the last couple o' weeks. A finer pair o' black eyes I've yet to see.'

'And what aboot Tommy?'

'He was that shaken they had to help him into the bar.' Hoynes took another puff on his pipe. 'Mind you, they'd to help him back oot four hours later. He had a fair swallow, by all accounts. But who can blame the man? Starts off the day wae thoughts o' the marital bed and ends up getting assaulted by a door and flung oot o' the hospital when he goes to visit his new wife because he's fair steaming. And all of it down to that damned door.'

As Hoynes was relating the sad tale of Connie MacCallum's wedding, they were nearing the harbour. Hamish squinted in the fading light at an unusual vehicle parked at the head of the new quay. The grey Bedford van looked perfectly normal apart from what appeared to be the installation of a small shed where the roof should have been.

'What on earth is that?' said Hamish.

'Ah, good!' Hoynes peered out of the wheelhouse window. 'That's Donnie Robertson fae Wellside distillery.'

'And what's he about, skipper?'

'Knowing fine we were heading up the east road in a couple o' days, he asked me if I could deliver a few cases of whisky – for the laird, you understand. He doesna like taking the van up that way as she's a wee bit top-heavy, and you know the twists and turns involved.'

'You can say that again,' said Hamish. 'But it looks like he's built his hoose on the back there.'

'He's no' much o' a coachbuilder, right enough – no, nor timekeeper neither.'

'How so?'

'He wisna due on the pier until after dark.' Hoynes adopted a demure butter-wouldn't-melt expression. 'Och, we'll maybe just have to sample a dram or two while we wait for sunset. It wouldn't be right to send the Laird o' Firdale inferior whisky, would it?'

Hamish shook his head.

4

By the time the sun had set, Hoynes, Hamish and Donnie had passed the whisky as being suitable for consumption. So, under the scythe of a waning winter moon, with the help of the winch, six cases of the finest Wellside malt whisky were hauled aboard and stowed in the hold under a stout tarpaulin.

Hoynes tied up at the very end of the new quay, an unusual berth for the *Girl Maggie*. Only a curious cat watched them from within a tumble of old nets. The harbour was as quiet as the town itself, for it took the good people of Kinloch a few days to get properly back into the swing of things after the New Year.

Donnie drained the tin mug of whisky and eyed the skipper under his brows. 'Have you decided if you're available for that other wee favour we spoke about?' he said, his bright red hair doing its best to escape from the flat cap that was pushed back on his head and now at a jaunty angle.

Hoynes swirled the remnants of the whisky round in his mug, brows furrowed. 'Aye, well that depends, Donnie. As you know, we're heading up for a celebration that night, plus we'll have guests on board. It would have to be worthwhile to take on such a – well, *delicate* mission under those circumstances.'

Donnie nodded solemnly. 'I reckon such difficulties could be taken into account if you were willing to consider it.'

Hamish looked between the pair, his mind working overtime. He was well aware that his skipper was happy to bend the rules here and there if it meant an extra few bob. However, he got the impression that the deal that was being discussed, though tangentially, was of greater import than anything he'd witnessed in his time as first mate. Hoynes had adopted the expression of a sheriff about to hand down his judgment on some wrongdoer.

'How many cases?' Hoynes asked.

'Maybe thirty,' replied Donnie. 'Mind you, we started out wae thirty-five. But, och, there was some natural wastage and breakages to be considered.'

'To be expected wae such a delicate cargo, right enough.'

Donnie, a tall man, put his arm round Sandy Hoynes's shoulder and led him further down the deck, their conversation now out of Hamish's hearing.

The first mate looked on as Donnie whispered into Hoynes's ear. The old skipper stroked his beard, then muttered something in a low voice. The two men looked out across the loch, still and striped with the bright glimmer of streetlights.

Suddenly, hands were outstretched, and the pair smiled convivially at each other.

'A fine piece o' business, right enough,' Hoynes declared in his normal voice.

'Just perfect,' said Donnie.

Hoynes turned to Hamish. 'Are you up for a wee bit overtime the night? I'll make it worth your while.'

'What's to be done?'

'A deed o' mercy,' said Donnie.

'Aye, Donnie has the right o' it, Hamish. You'll be aware o' the price they're charging for a dram at the Firdale hotel?'

Hamish shook his head.

'Well, all I'll say is that it's in excess o' extortionate. Man, it's like the profiteering experienced during the war. Poor men – aye, and a fair portion o' women – are right thirsting for a small libation, but no' willing to sell their own weans for the privilege. As is only right,' he added through a cloud of pipe smoke.

'It canna be as bad as that, Sandy?'

'Every bit! Auld Jamieson that has the hotel up there is as grasping a man as you'll meet. I wouldn't be surprised at all if he was descended fae the moneylenders at the temple. You'll remember their fate, for I know you're well acquainted wae the Scriptures, a must for any man, never mind a fisherman.'

Hamish mulled this information over. For some reason, injustice made his blood boil. He supposed that this emotion stemmed from the way his father had been dispossessed of the family fishing boat as he descended further into the bottle. But in any event, the thought of the poor people of Firdale being extorted by the wicked hotel proprietor was enough to make up his mind. 'I'm your man, Sandy,' he said, the gleam of the righteous in his eyes.

With the three of them crammed into the cab of the distinctively modified Bedford van, Donnie drove out of the town then took the road to Blaan. There was little in the way of moonlight and only a feeble glow from the headlights, so

Hamish had to squint to make out where they were headed. Nonetheless, Donnie appeared untroubled, the cigarette dangling from his mouth tipped by a long curl of ash that, seemingly defying the laws of gravity, remained in place despite his puffing and the bumpy progress of the vehicle.

Hoynes also appeared undaunted by the chancy driving conditions. He sat contentedly in the middle of the three, busy at his pipe and merrily humming reels and jigs to himself – something to which he was prone after the consumption of a few drams.

'So, what are we about?' asked Hamish.

'We're just collecting a few things from Ballywilline farm.'

Hamish thought for a moment. 'Is that no' in the middle o' nowhere?' While he knew most of the farms in the area by name, he was hazy as to their actual whereabouts.

'Och, nothing more than a wee jaunt up a few farm tracks and we'll be there in a jiffy,' said Hoynes.

This information proved to be less than accurate, as they left the main road and seemed to spend an eternity rattling along narrow, rutted lanes that Hamish hadn't known existed. Mercifully, just as he was beginning to regret the whisky he'd consumed and the cheese sandwich he'd had for lunch, they came to a halt at a farm. A solitary light shone from the farmhouse window. The lowing of cattle emanated from an outbuilding.

'I don't know how farmers can live wae the smell,' said Hamish as he alighted from the van into the cool night air.

'They think the very same o' us and the odour o' fish, Hamish. It's a case o' each to their ain. I'm sure if you lived on a dung heap for long enough it would smell as sweet as one o' they French perfumes.'

A thin, sharp-featured man appeared in the farmyard, his way illuminated by a flickering oil lamp. 'Is that you, Donnie?' he said in a loud whisper.

'Who else were you expecting in a van o' this manufacture, Jock?' said Hoynes.

'And no need to ask who you are, Sandy Hoynes, and no mistake! Well, there's a thing. I canna remember the last time I set eyes on you, and us living barely ten miles apart.'

'It's a long time since oor schooldays, Jock.'

'That's for certain sure. Right, we better be about oor business before Jessie is finished her baking. You know fine her opinion o' this lark.'

Jock turned on his heels and headed across the yard towards a shed that loomed before them in the darkness.

5

If it's true what they say about everything being connected, and time working in an infinite, ceaseless wheel, then maybe the events that night, unseen by everyone apart from Gilbert MacIntosh, could have been explained away as fact. But in the cold January darkness of hushing surf and the whispering of branches called into life by a swirling wind, rationale and reason could easily have been distorted into something other.

MacIntosh, a Firdale man by birth and inclination, had spent most of his life as a gamekeeper. Though he'd plied his trade over the course of almost forty years and for a number of masters, he had been happily employed by the Absdale Estate for the last five seasons. His main tasks were to make sure that all was well with the estate's livestock, especially the hens, which produced eggs famous for their taste, quality and size up and down the West Coast.

Tales of persons of ill-intent from Glasgow were hot gossip in the area. Indeed, six of the Semples' best ewes had been wrangled from the farm that skirted Absdale only the previous night. So, fears for the prize hens were at an all-time high.

It is easy to wonder why these precious birds were only contained within their coops in the hours of darkness. But the laird – a free-thinking libertarian – felt strongly that every bird had the right to roam. Indeed, it was posited that this very unusual husbandry was the main reason the end product tasted so good. You didn't need salt on an Absdale egg; with a diet of seaweed they were salty enough. It was said, though not all agreed, that within their creamy, deep yellow yolks, a distinct hint of green could be detected. If eating eggs with a green hue was initially unpalatable to some, once tasted, customers returned again and again to repeat the experience, the consumption of all other eggs foresworn.

However, many other producers in the area disputed this tale. The very idea of hens with a taste for seaweed was, to say the least, daft. But when their profits failed to match those of Absdale Estate, they, too, decided to try a similar method. None had succeeded. Meanwhile, every day without fail, the dutiful Absdale hens, bred to do so over generations, returned to their coops as the sun set. So, as a reward for their faithfulness, their accommodation was guarded as though it contained the most precious of jewels.

Gilbert had been responsible for a wide range of creatures, from pheasants to prize heifers. But when he took on the position of gamekeeper, he was the first to admit that the tutelage of poultry was a novelty. Though, all this time later, here he was, under an overcast sky with only a glimmer of a crescent moon with which to see, making sure that none of his flock came to any harm. With his shotgun broken in the crook of his arm, he was equally ready for fox, fiend or poacher. And though some birds were inevitably lost to predatory creatures during the day, it was his job to guard the hens at night. It was a task he took most seriously.

Gilbert took a long draw on his cigarette: pipes were all very well for those with the time and light to fill them, but his business was done in darkness, so a packet of Woodbines and a box of Swan Vestas were much more convenient.

He sat on a surprisingly comfortable jut of rock studying the dark spread of the Kilbrannan Sound before him, for poachers in this part of the world often went about their clandestine criminality in boats. He could just about make out the loom of the Isle of Arran, but without stars and a full moon, Ailsa Craig and the Ayrshire coast were invisible in the velvet darkness. Even the billions of stars that adorned the heavens were obscured by high cloud. At night, the tang of the sea being subdued, he could smell burning coal from the distant fires of the castle on the other side of the wood beyond the shore. But all was still, with only a gently swirling breeze carrying the smoke from his cigarette to the nor'west.

The first thing he heard over the soothing slip and slide of the tide was the unmistakable sweep of oars as they propelled an unseen vessel forward. Gilbert's heart began to race. It made sense that the men from Glasgow would appear by such means; any kind of engine would instantly attract attention.

Quietly, he edged back into the hedges that bordered the beach, watching, waiting.

The sweep of the oars grew louder, and with it, an unusual feeling of dread filled Gilbert's breast. He'd faced down poachers many times, but something deep inside told him to flee this place, for reasons he could not explain.

But he was a steadfast, conscientious man, and whatever was causing this foreboding, he was determined to carry out his job to the best of his ability.

A shadow of flame appeared on the water. He took a deep breath, ready to move at a moment's notice. But what he saw rooted him to the spot. The fire came from a brazier at the prow of a vessel. It illuminated a large, coiled snake's head and the sweep of a beautifully wrought bow.

Gilbert looked on from the safety of the bushes as the sleek craft passed by only yards from the shore. He could clearly hear voices but couldn't discern what was being said. The words sounded garbled, foreign to his ears. But he stared on, transfixed by the apparition.

He could make out the shapes of men on the craft, all of them in shadow; some were rowing, others stood or lounged in the gunwales.

All bar one.

At the stern of the boat, another brazier flamed in the dark night. A tall man dressed in black stood underneath it, the flickering shadows of flames shining from his leather tunic and breeches. His hair was blond, pulled back in thick pleated knots, his oiled beard long and glistening.

As Gilbert fought to hold his breath, the man turned, looking directly at the bushes where he was hiding.

'A fine night to you!' called the apparition. 'The moon is just right for dark business, yes?' The voice was accented, but plain.

Gilbert fell backwards, gasped for breath, then took off up the short rise and into the trees. His face was slashed and harried by thorn and briar, but he didn't care. His only thought was to escape this vision – this man from another realm, from another time.

6

Hamish rubbed the sweat from his brow under the light of three oil lamps hung about the barn. They had just stowed twenty hay bales into the back of Donnie's van. Well, he and Donnie had done most of the work, while Hoynes and Jock the farmer cackled over old times and cracked even older jokes.

At first, Hamish wondered why on earth they were moving bales of hay until Donnie tripped on the rough earthen floor and a lemonade bottle tumbled onto it. The bottle didn't break; rather it rolled towards Hoynes, who picked it up, a frown on his face.

'Damn me, I might as well have had two o' Jock's coos load the lorry. Hooves would be handier than your slippery mitts.'

Hamish delved into the bale he was carrying. It didn't take long for him to find another lemonade bottle. He unscrewed the cap and inhaled the contents of the bottle. 'I might have known – whisky! Why on earth would you fill old lemonade bottles wae whisky then hide them in hay?'

Hoynes, standing directly under a lamp, shook his head as the blue smoke from his pipe drifted up into the rafters. 'Och, it's plain that you have little understanding of how to carry bottles safely. Man, if they weren't fair encased in the hay, they'd rattle aboot like nobody's business in the back o'

Donnie's van. You know how irregular the road surface is on the way back to the main road.'

Jock's thin face was a mask of concern as he flicked Hoynes an anxious look.

'Now look, you've fair put Jock on edge. It's no' healthy for men o' oor age to be shocked in any fashion. I wouldn't be at all surprised if Jock here went to his bed the night and never woke up again, what wae the trauma o' the whole proceedings.'

Jock looked even more worried. 'Surely you don't think so, Sandy? I keep myself fit, you know.'

'And eat like a sparrow, by the look o' things. You need tae get a bit o' fat aboot you. You'd hardly expect to sell a beef coo in such a pallid, emaciated condition, would you?'

'But nobody's taking me in wae thoughts o' their Sunday lunch, Sandy.'

'These days, wae hippies and the like, you never know just what's in store. The world's fair going off the rails, and that's a fact. Even Hamish is into thon free love now.'

Jock and Donnie gawped at the younger fisherman. But rather than defend this wholly erroneous statement for the umpteenth time, Hamish was inclined to discover more about the contents of the hay bales.

'I'll give you the packaging theory, skipper. But how do you explain the fact that the whisky isn't in whisky bottles?'

'Dae you never read the papers? Sure, there's a glass shortage that would frighten any glazier wae half a brain. Right across Europe, too – something up wae the sand an' all that pollution fae oil tankers you hear aboot on the wireless. It's right wasteful to discard anything when it's perfectly functional. Easy seen you never lived through two World Wars. You'd have taken a dram oot o' a dirty pail, such were the shortages. Am I right, Jock?'

The farmer nodded his head, unconvincingly. 'To be sure, young man. A right hard time it was for one an' all. You couldna even buy a bag o' sweets in Effric's sweet shop in Kinloch. I'd to resort to dunking rhubarb in sugar, just to get the sensation o' a poke o' sweets.'

'Right enough, you've always had a sweet tooth, Jock. You were the same in school. I don't think I ever saw you without a sherbet dab poking oot o' your gob.'

Hamish narrowed his eyes. 'My mother warned me aboot this kind o' caper. She said you were always at some devilment, Sandy.'

'Your mother has a right fertile imagination, so she does. But there's nae harm in her.' Satisfied that he'd offered up a sufficiently feasible explanation as to why lemonade bottles filled with whisky were concealed within hay bales, he cleared his throat. 'Right! Less o' this banter. I'm fair needing my bed. And it must be well past the time you should be oot searching for some o' that free love, Hamish.' He winked at Jock, opened the lemonade bottle and took a swig of its contents before handing it to the farmer. 'My, it's good to note that the whisky has been improved by resting in the hay, Jock. Likely there will be distillers across the country getting up to the same process as soon as they're able.'

'Aye, and their customers will get money back on the bottle when they've finished their dram,' said Hamish with a knowing look.

'Again, you have the right o' it, Hamish. I knew I'd picked the perfect man to be my first mate – despite your hair falling oot wae free abandon. But nobody's perfect. Now, let's get a shift on!'

It took another twenty minutes to stow the van safely with the bales of whisky. Donnie made for the cab with Hamish, as Hoynes wished his old friend goodbye.

Just as they were parting company, though, an apparition in tartan slippers, quilted dressing gown and hair tightly bound up in curlers appeared in the broad doorway of the barn.

'What's all this?' said Jessie as she took in the house on wheels, the two men in the cab and her husband standing beside an instantly familiar figure.

'My, Jessie,' purred Hoynes. 'But you look as good as you did when you were sweet sixteen.' He smiled broadly. 'If it wasn't for the charms o' Jock here, I'd have fair lured you away tae be a fisherman's wife and no' a farmer's, make no mistake.'

'Aye, and I'd have jumped in the loch at the first opportunity to be free o' you. Just what is it you have my poor husband inveigled in?'

'I was just dropping by to say hello, Jessie. Fair missing my auld school chum, right enough.'

'So, you arrived here under the cover of darkness wae a hoose on board a lorry, and this pair o' ruffians just to pass the time o' day wae my husband? You must think I came doon in the last shower, Sandy Hoynes.'

'And a right heavy shower it would have been,' muttered Hoynes under his breath, eliciting a snort of laughter from Jock.

'Well, you've seen him now, you can be on your way. Decent folk should be in their beds by this hour.'

Hoynes produced his pocket watch and squinted at it. 'Man, it's barely seven o'clock. What on earth dae you get up to in bed all that time? It must be a good book you're reading.'

On hearing this, Jock chortled again. But noting that his wife was advancing into the barn, his expression soon changed to one of concern. 'Quick, Sandy, get yourself back in the lorry. She's a fair temper, as well you know!'

For a man of his size and vintage, Sandy Hoynes was remarkably fleet of foot when the occasion demanded. So much so that he covered the distance between Jock and the van with admirable speed, all the time clutching a lemonade bottle of depleted contents. He hoisted himself into the cab. 'Right, Donnie, it's time we were taking oor leave.' As the engine fired into life and the van pulled slowly out of the barn, Hoynes glanced in the wing mirror just in time to see Jessie administer a sharp clip round her husband's ear.

'You're a right man for the flattery, Sandy,' said Hamish.

'In what way?' Hoynes replied, only slightly out of breath.

'Telling the woman she looked as good as she did when she was sixteen. What a plaster you are.'

Hoynes inclined his head towards the wing mirror once more, but Jock and Jessie were out of sight. 'I was speaking nothing but the truth, Hamish. She was never a bonnie lassie and she's just the same to this day.'

Soon, they were rattling their way down the farm track and back to Kinloch, the bottles of whisky safely encased in hay.

7

The morning of the eleventh of January dawned bright, but cold. Had it not been for the gnarled fingers of trees and a brush of frost on the hills, anyone seeing a photograph of the loch and the harbour of bobbing fishing boats would have assumed it was high summer.

A low winter sun shone on a small huddle of men gathered beside the *Girl Maggie* on the pier. They stamped their feet and clapped gloved hands to keep warm, while their frozen breath mixed with the smoke from pipes and cigarettes.

'Just like Sandy to be late,' opined Peeny, his sharp face screwed up in disgruntlement.

Jim McMichael nodded in agreement. 'We should have taken my boat. Man, we'd have been there by now. I hate wallowing in this old tub.'

Malcolm Connelly looked unimpressed by this comment, as he stroked his beard thoughtfully. 'Mind, this auld tub fair beat you out into the loch just a week or two ago.'

'Only because I was distracted when I saw that lassie's heid popping through the hatch like some apparition. I wouldn't be surprised if the boat's fair stowed wae women and ministers. Hoynes likes to chance his luck. And as we all know, that's tempting providence.'

'Aye, I canna say I was convinced by the story o' the gull that was supposed to have guided them back in the snow,' said Donald McKirdy. 'It all sounded a bit far-fetched to me. He's a slippery bugger. Who's to know that he didn't hold up in some wee inlet, watch us all sail by in the blizzard, and wait to return the conquering hero, escaping death by a whisker. He didna take long to get a story out, did he? Everyone had him down wae the best o' us, but he came back wae nothing but the clothes he was standing in – bugger all good to anyone.'

Peeny sniffed his agreement in the cold air.

Andy Duncan, the oldest fisherman present by some margin, smiled broadly. 'You have to admire his brio, mind you.'

'His what?' said Connelly.

'He always comes oot smelling o' roses. He was the same when he was a boy – never got caught, despite all his schemes.'

'The luck o' twenty men, so he has. And he's always at something.' Malcolm Connelly looked sour. 'We all knew Hamish's faither well. The last thing he'd have wanted would have been to see his only son learning every bad habit there is to be had from the likes o' Sandy Hoynes.'

'To be fair, they had little choice. There wasn't a berth to be had in the fleet and they'd lost their own vessel to the money changers at the bank. A damned shame,' said Andy Duncan, the process of age having mellowed his outlook.

'Still, Hamish is working under a right rogue, and no mistake. Only the good Lord knows if we'll make it to the bothy at Absdale. But it was Hoynes's turn, and that's a fact, bad apple or not,' said Peeny.

A cloud of freezing breath rose into the air as the little group murmured in agreement.

'It's a fine day, right enough,' declared Hoynes, appearing as if from nowhere, Hamish at his heel.

'It's yourself, Sandy. Aye, and in good time as always,' said Peeny.

'We were just commenting on how lucky we were to have you at the wheel, what wae the navigational skills you showed getting back through thon blizzard. Man, that was a feat and no mistake. I was reading aboot it in the papers for days. You're a credit to the fleet,' said McKirdy.

'Very kind of you to say so, Donald. At least we have the right weather for our wee jaunt. I expected a right dreich affair, the way it's been the last few days.' Sandy Hoynes looked about with satisfaction at the cold but otherwise benign conditions.

It was Jim McMichael's turn to speak. 'I was just telling the boys how lucky we are to be making passage in the *Girl Maggie*. My boat's built for speed, but you canna beat a vessel broader in the beam for comfort, and that's for sure.'

'And she can get a fair turn o' speed under stern when required. Say, if you were fair rushing oot into the loch, for example.' Hoynes winked at the assembled fishermen, old and young, retired or still on the water.

'Right enough, Sandy, right enough.' McMichael smiled with every part of his face but his eyes, as the rest of the company chortled at the observation.

'Right, let's be aboot it, lads. I don't need to show you how,' said Hoynes.

One by one, the party stepped off the pier and over the side of the *Girl Maggie* across the lapping gap of water as though it was of no consequence. Each man was an experienced fisherman, even young Danny O'May, who at the tender age of twenty-three still had eight years before the mast under his belt, even if he did make Hamish look like a veteran.

It was to this end that Hamish caught the ear of his skipper. 'You never telt me that O'May was part o' all this. I thought I was to be the youngest here – "a rare honour", you said, Sandy.'

'Och, what are you worried aboot? Are you no' just after winning fisherman of the year?'

'Aye, only 'cause he was doon wae the chickenpox.'

'You've no confidence in your own abilities, Hamish. I blame that mother of yours. Fair undermining, she is. But it's my job to make sure that you feel you can take on the world. So, to that end, you'll skipper this fine craft during the entirety of the trip. Young Danny O'May will be your first mate. How does that sound, eh?'

At first, Hamish felt great pride in being trusted – not only with the *Girl Maggie*, but with the responsibility of sailing the most esteemed fishermen in Kinloch to their destination. He also fancied the idea of lording it over young Danny, which made the prospect all the more satisfying.

Hoynes patted him on the shoulder as he passed by. 'I better get oor guests settled. You make ready to put to sea.'

It was only then that something troubling crossed Hamish's mind. 'Does this mean that I've tae stay sober, Sandy? Yous can get fair puggled while I'm at the helm.' He'd reached the conclusion that, along with Danny, his job was to ferry the collected revellers to and from their Auld New Year celebrations. In fact, the invitation was not the honour that his skipper had made it out to be; rather it was a duty to be carried out in strict sobriety. He was a mere functionary, nothing else.

'Man, but you're the most cynical body I know. Of course that's not what I had in mind.'

'Oh, just thought I'd ask,' said Hamish, much relieved.

'Mind you, you'll no' be partaking while sailing there and back, and it wouldn't do to get too tight the night either, just in case the fishery officer is abroad when we're on our way back. Other than that, just you have a good time like the rest of us intend to do.' Hoynes thought for a moment. 'Though, maybe best no' to mention the inclination for thon free love you're so taken wae, eh?'

Hamish didn't bother to argue the point. He knew he could sail back and forth to Absdale in his sleep. And in any case, as his skipper often said, 'The fish guts roll downhill.' So, he would instil a great sense of duty and responsibility into Danny O'May, his junior by seven years, but still more than capable of navigating their way back to Kinloch the next day. In any case, Hoynes and the rest of the more venerable passengers would be in no state to wonder at his level of sobriety. He had the advantage of resilient youth. This thought cheered him as he called for Danny to cast off.

'That's a right pile o' straw you've accumulated aboard, Sandy,' remarked Peeny, examining the deck. 'I hope we're no' sharing quarters wae a coo?'

'Just a wee favour I'm doing. I can guarantee that there's no livestock aboard.' Hoynes glanced around the harbour. There was no sign of the fishery officer or the harbour master. He smiled contentedly as he settled his passengers aboard and Hamish went about the business of setting sail for Absdale.

It was a fine day, right enough.

8

Customs House, Glasgow

Alan Marshall had been surprised by a message left by an anonymous caller. The call had been made prior to his arrival in the office, but his secretary, Blanche Dunlop, had taken the content down verbatim using her formidable shorthand skills.

'Let's go over it again, Blanche,' said Marshall, sitting in his wood-panelled office in Glasgow's India Street. The building's antiquated heating had yet again failed to keep up with the sudden change of weather, and he was glad he'd chosen to wear a pullover beneath his suit to take the chill off the day. As always, the air was thick with tobacco smoke. Marshall sucked on a pen as, once more, he scanned the neatly typed transcript of the call.

'The phone rang, Mr Marshall. I answered in the normal fashion,' said Blanche, her shorthand notebook poised in her hands.

'I think we can take that as read. Let's get into what was said, shall we?'

'Well, just as you see it, sir. I took notes as she was speaking. I think you'll find they're accurate.'

'I don't doubt it, Blanche – no, not for one minute.

I'm more interested in the tone of the call, the person with whom you conversed. What did she sound like?'

Blanche, in her early twenties and already marked out for better things, thought for a moment. Her tongue tipped her front teeth as she went over the conversation in her head. 'She reminded me a bit of my Auntie Amy, I suppose.'

'A Glasgow woman?'

'No, she lives in Ayr – why do you ask?'

'I'm trying to establish her accent, Blanche.'

'I was meaning that she sounded like my Auntie Amy because she was old – maybe in her fifties, or something like that.'

Marshall, who was fifty-two, was yet again reminded how young people perceived age. It was clear that anyone above the age of thirty was considered positively ancient, even though he felt every bit the same as he had in his twenties. Blanche would experience this same cruel deception that life was certain to play, so he decided to say nothing of it. 'Right, a middle-aged woman, then?'

'I'd say old – fifties is old, isn't it? Maybe even a bit older.'

'So, not a young woman. I think we've established that. What about an accent? You mention here that she refused to give any clue as to her own whereabouts but wanted to report happenings in Kinloch, am I right?'

'Yes, though she didn't sound like anyone I know from that neck of the woods, sir.'

'Oh, so you know people from Kinloch?'

'Well, I went to typing school with a lassie from Skye, sir. Kinloch is up that way, isn't it?'

Marshall screwed up his face. He had learned not to be surprised how little the people of Glasgow knew about any part of Scotland beyond the boundaries of their city. He walked over to a large map of Scotland that hung on the wall behind his desk. Pointing to the Isle of Skye then down to the long Kintyre peninsula that jutted out towards Ireland, he addressed Blanche in schoolmasterly tones. 'Actually, it's not up that way at all. While Skye is well to the north of Glasgow, Kinloch is well to the south – do you see?'

'I'd always thought it was up north. Isn't that strange?'

'A common mistake. The people of Kinloch have a distinct tongue – long vowels, odd words and the like. For instance, she might have said "aye" in this fashion.' Marshall's mimicking of the Kinloch accent was accurate. He'd spent two years in the Customs office in the town when he'd first joined up. Though he'd grown to like the place, he was the first to admit that there were few communities like Kinloch – unusual, to say the least.

'Yes, that's it!' exclaimed Blanche, her eyes wide with the intrigue and excitement of it all. 'You are clever, sir.'

Rather pleased with himself, Marshall addressed the rest of the transcript. 'Says here that a vessel called the *Girl Maggie* is involved in the clandestine transportation of illicit spirits – in this case, whisky.' He looked at Blanche levelly. 'Would you say this person was telling the truth? We do get a lot of malicious calls, you know, from people seeking revenge and the like.'

'I'd say she sounded angry, sir – furious, in fact. She mentioned that her husband had been an unwitting party to this, as you can see. I suppose she's just standing up for him.'

'Yes, very interesting,' said Marshall. 'Did you notice anything else during the call – in her tone, I mean?'

'A cow, sir.'

'Now, now, Blanche. There's no need to get personal about this woman. Let's stick to the facts, please.'

'No. What I mean is that I heard a cow, sir. You know that mooing sound they make.' Blanche puffed out her cheeks and executed what could only be described as a reasonably accomplished effort at the imitation of a cow.

Marshall raised his brows and reached for his pipe. 'Very impressive, Blanche. If you find you don't like it here, you can always get a job on the wireless with your impersonations, eh?'

The young secretary was momentarily taken aback. 'Oh no, sir. I don't think I'd like that at all.'

'I was only kidding,' said Marshall as he tamped down the tobacco in his pipe. 'You've been most helpful. I'll take things forward from here.'

Blanche executed what could best be described as cross between a bow and a curtsey before turning on her heels and leaving the office.

Marshall walked to a wall of files set in a metal frame that filled most of one wall in his office. He peered along the rows until he came to 'K' for Kinloch and pulled out a heavy file for further examination.

Sitting behind his ample desk, Marshall flicked through various incidents that had attracted the attention of Her Majesty's Customs and Excise over the years. Most were related to the town's distilleries or the odd individual who had appeared on a vessel looking to flee their home from behind the Iron Curtain and relocate to Great Britain. But these were few and far between, and the majority of cases involving the distilleries amounted to little more than minor pilfering, for which the trader was inevitably punished with a disproportionally high fine.

Having spent half an hour working his way through the

records, he decided to flick to the end of the file, typically where notes of the local collector were appended.

Marshall scanned a few paragraphs of leader prose until he reached the subheading PERSONS OF INTEREST.

He ran his finger down a list until he came to a name strangely familiar from his time in Kinloch: one Alexander Hoynes, skipper of the *Girl Maggie*.

'Well, well, Mr Hoynes, there you are, after all this time,' he whispered to himself as he read a catalogue of crimes and misdemeanours to which the fisherman had seemingly been connected, but without sufficient proof to bring him to book.

Marshall puffed on his pipe and thought back to his two years in Kinloch. The image of a thickset man with fading blond hair and a patchy beard crossed his mind. Yes, he was sure this was the same Sandy Hoynes in which the present senior officer in Kinloch seemed to be so interested.

Marshall reached for the phone on his desk.

9

Though the sail to the destination on the north-east end of the Kintyre peninsula was not a long one, at around the halfway point, conditions in the small cabin below deck were becoming difficult. With every man smoking either pipes or cigarettes, many of the venerable mariners were now coughing and spluttering, their eyes watering.

Even though the whisky bottle was in liberal use, disgruntlement was setting in.

'I'm buggered if I can see the hand in front o' my ain face,' said McKirdy irritably.

'It's like being back in the war,' said Peeny. 'They had me aboard a tug in the Clyde. Man, what a smoky bloody thing it was. But it was like standing on top of a Swiss Alp breathing in sweet fresh air compared wae these hellish conditions. Can you no' do something, Sandy?'

'Och, I had the hatch open a while ago and yous were all complaining it was too cold.'

'You've fair gone up in my estimation,' remarked Andy Duncan, a thin roll-up poking from the corner of his mouth. 'It's many years since I had to endure such an environment at sea. I'm quite sure the galley slaves you hear all about thousands of years ago enjoyed better working conditions than this.

It's a credit to your powers of endurance, Sandy, and no mistake.'

'You'll note there's only one or two o' us in here at any one time under normal circumstances. The human cargo is a great deal larger than I'd normally countenance,' replied Hoynes indignantly.

'I'm just waiting for a lassie to appear fae nowhere,' opined Jim McMichael, engendering a throaty chuckle from the other fishermen.

It was Malcolm Connelly's turn to make a comment. 'Aye, or a Robertson. Man, it must be one o' the few times in all my years there's no' been one o' that clan on this trip.'

'Wee Davie's fair entangled playing wae his banjo. They've a new band on the go – the Vaccineers, would you believe.'

'I heard them at a wedding in November. It's jeest a' wailing and laments. Fair dirges from start to finish,' said McKirdy. 'I was forced to take refuge in the bar downstairs in the County for maist o' the night, their repertoire was leaving me that melancholy. No' a decent reel or jig to be had. Some tale o' a soldier at Culloden and his sweetheart.'

'I was there too, mind.' Peeny thought back to the night in question.

'Aye. She was feart that he'd be killed, so she went in his place.'

'You're right, Donald – cut her hair, the lot. But when she gets back fae the thick o' the battle, she finds him wae another lassie, kilt round his ankles, I don't doubt.'

'Right depressing stuff. He can keep thon banjo, as far as I'm concerned ... much as I like the man.' McKirdy polished off the last dregs of his whisky. 'I'll have another, if you don't mind, Sandy.'

Hoynes leaned over with the whisky bottle he'd led Hamish to believe was intended for the Laird of Firdale, and poured his demanding guest a bumper. 'You've no heart, that's your problem. There was a tear in my eye when I heard that ballad.'

'Ach, away, man. The only time there's a tear in your eye is when you get a shilling less on a box fae the fish buyer,' said Malcolm Connelly.

Suddenly, Hamish's head appeared though the hatch. 'Skipper, it's thon radio. Fair burst into life just there a minute ago.'

'Did you answer?' said Hoynes.

'No, I got a right fright. By the time I'd recovered, it was too late. You know fine I'm no' acquainted wae the bloody thing yet.'

'This'll be the radio the harbour master forced on you after your meanderings in the blizzards, Sandy?' said Peeny. The rest of the company bowed their heads to disguise their mirth. 'Man, they tell me you and Hamish got that lost in Glasgow when you were buying it, you had to walk into a polis station to ask directions. Country comes tae town, right enough.'

Leaving his mocking companions behind, Hoynes hoisted himself through the hatch to find out what the radio message was all about.

'It's like watching a ewe give birth,' said McKirdy in his wake.

On deck, Hoynes made for the wheelhouse and the 'contraption' – as he'd christened the new radio.

'You're no' covering yoursel' in glory, Hamish.' Hoynes studied the device. He turned a large knob on a panel, grabbed the mouthpiece and spoke loudly and slowly, as was the habit of any man of his nationality and generation when encountering someone from another land. 'The *Girl Maggie* here. Come on, if you would, please.'

'I think you just have to say "come *in*", Sandy,' said Hamish.

'Listen tae you. You took fright as soon as the damn thing came on. Don't lecture me as to its operation.'

'I think it was the harbour master, Mr Hoynes,' said Danny.

'And how do you know that, young man?'

'We've had a radio for years on oor boat. I can get him, if you want?'

'You're a clever lad, right enough. Stand aside, Hamish. It's clear you have none o' the skills necessary for this task. Och, I'm black affronted.'

'We've only had it for three weeks, Sandy. Be fair!'

'You should have picked it up by now.'

'You said no' tae touch it!'

'Have you never heard of initiative? Peer through the window, and fair take in what young Danny's at.'

Reluctantly, Hamish and Danny swapped places, the latter squeezing into the small wheelhouse alongside the ample skipper.

'Right, Mr Hoynes, you just turn this dial to the right number.' Danny did this and picked up the mouthpiece. 'The *Girl Maggie* to Kinloch harbour master, over. Come in, Kinloch harbour master.'

Hoynes looked at Hamish through the murky window. 'See that? Sharp lad this is, right enough. You'll need to watch your back, Hamish.'

Before the first mate could reply, the radio burst into life. Mitchell the harbour master's voice was loud, if somewhat distorted through the round speaker. 'Receiving you, *Girl Maggie*. Go ahead, over.'

Hoynes grabbed the handset from Danny. 'It's Sandy here, you called us, eh?'

There was silence from the speaker.

'You've no' said "over",' said Danny.

'Damn me, whoot a carry on. You don't say "over" when you're on the telephone, so why on here?'

Danny shrugged as Hoynes shouted 'over' as loud as he could into the mouthpiece.

'Sandy, I was just passing on a point o' interest – nothing more, you understand, over.'

'You're a terrible man for the gossip, Mitchell. I didna think that's what this contraption was all aboot . . . *over*.'

Mitchell was silent for a moment. He was an old lobster fisherman himself, and always tried to make sure his former colleagues were as well informed as possible. 'Sandy, I've just had word that the Customs cutter is on her way. She'll be berthed in Kinloch tonight. Just for your information, over.'

What could be seen of Hoynes's face above his beard turned white. 'Here, son,' he said handing the mouthpiece to Danny. 'You tell the harbour master I've a sudden call o' nature.'

As Danny ended the communication with Kinloch, Hoynes rushed from the wheelhouse. 'Right, Hamish. Get back in there and give it all she's got.'

'There's no rush, is there?' replied the bemused first mate.

'Och, the boys are getting right restless below. We'll need to get to oor destination as quickly as we can. Give me a shout when we're close. It can be a tricky wee bay to negotiate.'

Hamish watched Hoynes hurry off, wondering what was in fact the real reason behind the sudden haste. But as his skipper had requested, he grabbed the wheel then throttled the *Girl Maggie* forward. Soon she was making nine knots.

'Is that it?' said Danny, unimpressed by the slight increase in speed.

'Och no, we'll get a knot or two mair once she's got going. Given a fair wind, that is.' Hamish stared out over the calm sea as black smoke belched from the tiny funnel, praying the engine would take the strain.

'I better lash myself to the mast, then.' Danny grinned.

10

A gathering of bemused seals looked on as the *Girl Maggie*, a very small wave at her prow and a very large column of black smoke behind her, slowly turned into the bay. Their heads poked up from the still waters as they looked at each other in silent communion before, as one, disappearing back to the depths. It was clear that these creatures of the sea did not like the look of the fishing boat.

Hoynes, as though by some sixth sense, forced himself through the hatch and made his way to the wheelhouse.

'I'll take over from here, Hamish. We need to get ashore and up to the bothy before sunset. There's nothing worse than a shoal of inebriated fishermen trying to find their wae aboot on land in the dark. A recipe for disaster, and no mistake.'

He took the wheel, pulled back the vessel's modest speed and made a wide sweep across the bay before turning the *Girl Maggie* towards the shore.

'You're no' going to beach her, are you, Sandy?' Hamish looked worried.

'Indeed I am not. But there's a nasty wee set o' rocks at the head o' the bay thonder. Aye, many a mariner has come to grief at this very point. Why dae you think it's called the Smuggler's Hole?'

'I'd no idea that's what it was called.'

'There, you see. The ignorance o' the young. Many a time in decades gone by, fine seamen would put in here when being pursued by the authorities.' Hoynes slowed the vessel to a crawl. 'Just ahead is a convenient sandbank. We'll glide into that, fair brushing it like a feather. Then we need to make our way over the side, and Bob's your uncle.'

Hamish thought for a moment. 'We'll get soaked!'

'You're mother should have called you Thomas. The name would have served you well. Have I ever let you down in matters nautical?'

Hamish bit his lip at this question, recalling several times when the skipper's nautical theories had in fact been somewhat open to question, as the *Girl Maggie*, her engine now disengaged, bumped softly to a stop.

'There, you see. Like powdering a wean's backside.'

'What would you know aboot such things, Sandy?'

'I'm a father of many year's standing. There's nothing Dr Spock can teach me aboot weans, and that's a fact.'

Hamish, clueless, shook his head. He looked over the side into the clear water below.

'You'll be seeing the sandbank now?'

'Aye, but thon water looks cold.'

'You'll have to toughen up, young man. You'll witness these old seadogs fair throwing themselves o'er the side wae gay abandon. The water's no more than a foot deep, and we've all got our seaboots on. Sometimes I wonder if you shouldna be behind a plough rather than a ship's wheel.'

One by one, Hoynes watched his passengers emerge through the hatch, all with less difficulty than himself, he noted with dismay. Yet again, he resolved to have the offending hatch widened at the earliest opportunity. He wasn't remotely concerned that he'd put on a few pounds. Most of the poor souls he visited at Kinloch's cottage hospital were pinched-faced, emaciated souls heading for the unknown waters of oblivion. To Hoynes, an ample girth was a sign of rude health, despite his doctor's advice. What did he know? The man smoked cigarettes by the dozen, and every fool knew that while a pipe was a healthy aid to meditation, cigarettes were lung-choking offences to nature.

Peeny looked over the side. 'Aye, you made a grand job o' that, Sandy. I couldna have done better myself. You just kissed the sandbank like a fair maiden's cheek.'

'If he was going round kissing fair maidens, I'm sure the constabulary would be involved,' said McKirdy, somewhat uncharitably.

'Sheer jealousy,' said Hoynes. 'The time we came here on your old tub we damn near ended up in the trees thonder, such was the rate you ploughed into the bay. It was like watching wee Jackie Stewart take a bend, so it was. My neck was sore for a fortnight.'

As the gloaming began to settle over Absdale Bay, fishermen young and old gathered their possessions – mainly fresh underpants and whisky – and made their way nimbly over the side of the *Girl Maggie*.

Peeny was the first to set foot on the sandbank, having made his way down the narrow rope ladder, kitbag slung over his shoulder. Despite his small stature, as Hoynes had predicted, the water was just below the top of his seaboots. He waded along the sandbank and onto the shingle shore as Hoynes lowered the anchor with a splash.

As, one by one, the seasoned mariners went over the side,

very soon, only Hamish and Hoynes were left aboard.

'Make sure you've switched off that contraption, Hamish. We don't want the damned thing self-combusting in the middle o' the night and leaving us wae only charred timbers instead o' the fine vessel that got us here. I'll get myself onto the sandbank and wait for you.'

Hamish looked on as, not without a little difficulty, Hoynes made his way onto the rope ladder and, red-faced, struggled down onto the sandbank. The first mate made sure that everything was secure and in order aboard, before hauling himself over the side. Though he'd used the rope ladder on many occasions, the passage of seaboots had made the rope slick, and just as he reached the penultimate rung, his foot slipped. Hamish, his kitbag pulling him backwards, fell into the shallow water, right at Hoynes's feet.

The skipper cursed as he brushed the splash of seawater from his beige duffel coat. 'Man, but you're like an elephant on a tightrope, Hamish. All these old boys doon here as lithe as you like, and you taking a dive like an arthritic dolphin. I'm right ashamed, for you've besmirched the good name o' oor vessel.' He waded off along the sandbank in high dudgeon, leaving his first mate, dripping wet, to get back to his feet. The sound of laughter echoed round the small bay as, muttering under his breath, Hamish followed his companions onto the shore.

The little party threaded its way up the beach and into a covering of fir trees. They followed a path which meandered its way up a low rise that became steeper as they progressed. Fortunately, the passage of time and many booted feet had dug little footholds into the bank, so the going wasn't as hard as it might have been. However, bringing up the rear and still shivering following his immersion, Hamish grew increasingly miserable and began to doubt the wisdom of his participation in this trip.

But, as he reached the top of the steep rise, his spirits were lifted by the site of a small wooden construction in a clearing. He turned to look back through the trees and could see the *Girl Maggie* resting safely at anchor below. It was then he realised how well named Smuggler's Hole was. From his position, he could see out into the sound, but any vessel passing by would be unable to see into the sheltering bay. Undoubtably, any craft berthed there was, in effect, invisible. And with the bothy blending in with the trees all around, the place made for the perfect lookout.

The old hut was musty and rustic, but cosy in its own way. Three sets of double bunks adorned by lumpy mattresses and woollen sea blankets were placed along the walls. Three iron camp beds – no doubt liberated at the end of the war – stood against a wall, ready to accommodate surplus guests. At the far corner was a fireplace, already filled with peat, sea coal and logs. Beside it sat two scuttles bearing more fuel and kindling. A few wooden chairs were scattered around.

'Munro's as good as his word, as always,' said Malcolm Connelly. 'Always makes sure we have a fire set for oor arrival and aired blankets.'

'Never misses a year, and him retired from the fishing near as long as you, Andy,' said Hoynes.

'No' quite,' said Andy Duncan. 'But he's always been a fine fellow, and what a man for finding fish! I hear he still goes out from time to time when the fleet at Firdale is struggling for a catch.'

'Somebody better light the damned thing before young

Hamish shivers tae death,' said McKirdy.

Sure enough, in the corner of the room, Hamish's face had taken on a particularly blue hue.

While Danny got busy with the fire, Peeny set a match to the oil lantern that hung in the small-paned window. In minutes the gloomy room was illuminated by jumping flames and the bright flicker of the lantern.

Hamish made for the fire and soon its warmth made him feel more human. Indeed, he felt as though the whole evening was looking up.

Feeling slightly guilty for admonishing his first mate after his fall, Hoynes handed Hamish a tin mug, half-filled with whisky. 'There, get that doon you. I've a spare pair o' dungarees rolled up in my kitbag. They'll no' be neat on you, but they'll do while your own gear dries.'

Hamish smiled. 'Thanks, skipper. Much appreciated. I'm fair looking forward to the night. It'll be time for yarns and a convivial dram or two, I've no doubt.'

Hoynes hesitated. 'Aye, first we've to do that favour. You know, the bales from our friend the farmer.' He winked at Hamish in the firelight.

'You mean, we go back out?'

'Aye, just me and you. Och, it'll take minutes. Once your clothes are dry, we'll be about it.'

'I'll no' manage all those bales myself, Sandy.' Hamish sounded alarmed, recalling his efforts at the farm and back at the *Girl Maggie*.

'You're a right worrier. It's all taken care of, trust me.'

As the fire warmed his backside, a chill ran down Hamish's spine. For when Sandy Hoynes said 'trust me', rarely did it bode well.

11

Collector Alan Marshall looked from the wheelhouse of the cutter *Diane*, as the sun set in cold hues of purple, green and fading gold. Their sail down the Firth of Clyde had been as splendid as it had been speedy. The twin-engine vessel had made short work of the journey from Glasgow on a glorious winter's day, the white-capped hills of Argyll making for a spectacular backdrop.

He cast his binoculars around their new anchorage with an inquisitive, practised eye, aware of the light tread of his second-in-command, John 'Jocky' Cummings behind him. A veteran of this coast, having served for many years in one of the steam puffers that had plied their trade for so long amongst the islands and peninsulas of the West Coast, before opting for a more predictable income, he was a solid, dependable and wise colleague.

'Excuse me, sir, but I'm a wee bit confused,' said Cummings as he stroked his well-trimmed beard.

'Are you, indeed? Why so?' replied Marshall, not taking the binoculars from his eyes.

'Well, it's just that you had me plot the passage to Kinloch. I even informed the harbour master there that we would be seeking a berth on our arrival. But you seem happy to be anchored here in Lochranza, sir.'

Marshall let the binoculars hang by the leather strap round his neck. He took a deep breath of sea air as he regarded the castle on the point of the small jutting headland within the bay. 'I've always liked it here on Arran. Scotland in miniature, they say, and an honest, hard-working populace into the bargain.'

'You'll be meaning unlike the parcel o' rogues in Kinloch?'

'Aye, something like that, Jocky. But isn't it grand to be back at sea? I spend far too much time these days stuck at my desk. It's not a healthy life.'

'But a productive one, sir. If we weren't here to keep tabs on some of the freebooters that sail these waters, the Revenue would suffer the consequences, and no mistake.'

'You've answered your own question.'

'How so, sir?'

'Well, I told you about the tip-off we had first thing this morning. Having you book us a berth at Kinloch was no more than a *ruse de guerre*.'

Getting his superior's intention without necessarily picking up on the French, Cummings nodded sagely. 'I see, sir. You're quite right, of course. You can't trust a body down in Kinloch not to broadcast the slightest detail of anything going on.'

'Including the harbour master.'

'Most definitely. I remember I fell into the hold when we were hauling coal onto the quay at Bowmore on Islay – I was eighteen. Broke my wrist, so I did, though the doctor there did a passable job at setting it.' Cummings flexed his left wrist to prove the statement. 'That was late afternoon on a Tuesday. We sailed for Kinloch first thing the next morning. Man, every bugger and his friend knew what had happened to me – the circumstances, treatment and even the name of the doctor who attended me – by the time we tied up at the pier.'

'I don't doubt it. I worked there for two years. It only took them a matter of days to find out where I was from, what church I attended and my wife's maiden name. I'm quite sure they knew more than me about her antecedence, and that's a fact.'

'If ever there was a place where a local newspaper was surplus to requirements, it's Kinloch, and no mistake. I still can't work out how they do it.'

'Ah, but such free-flowing knowledge can work both ways, Jocky. It's easy to throw a spanner in the works of a good tale.' Marshall reached for his pipe. 'Our quarry will have heard of our imminent arrival at Kinloch. Had they not heard this, the grubby transaction I reckon is about to take place would have been risked in daylight. But now, knowing we're abroad, our perpetrators will no doubt seek the cover of darkness.'

'True, sir, very true.'

'But as we know, nothing can be done in the dark without recourse to lights of some kind. During the day, we could sit off the peninsula and easily miss wrongdoers. But a clandestine light is easily spotted at night, wouldn't you say?'

'Oh, I agree wholeheartedly, sir.'

'So, that's what we're going to do. We'll stay here until dark then make way into the sound. With the radar at our disposal, we'll be fine to leave off our own lights. A few good men with binoculars is all that's required. We'll have a great vantage point to see almost from Firdale to the head of the loch. At the first sign of any unusual, suspicious light, we'll make for its source at full speed.'

'Very cunning, sir, if I may say so.'

'You have to be cunning to catch whisky smugglers, Jocky. And from what I hear, this won't be an insignificant haul.

Plus, we'll bring a man to justice who has been a thorn in our side for many years.'

Cummings mulled over this for a moment as the light leached from the sky over the line of houses, the hotel and shops of Lochranza. 'Would you mind if I ventured a guess at the name of your quarry, sir?'

Marshall turned to his number two with a curious expression. 'Be my guest. I'll be interested to hear if you get it right. In fact, a dram for you on me when we bring the bugger to book.'

'It'll be Sandy Hoynes, I'm thinking.'

'Ha!' Marshall clapped Cummings on the shoulder. 'That's a large whisky I owe you, Jocky!'

'He's a slippery one, sir. I've known him since I was no more than a lad. I think his record is as clean as the driven snow.'

'By tomorrow it'll be well tainted, Jocky. You have my word.'

12

A sickle moon shone brightly before a carpet of stars, the sweep of the Milky Way silhouetting the bothy amongst the fir trees, as the world turned. Only the pale flicker of the oil lamp in the window spilled yellow light onto the path as the revellers, set to bring in the Auld New Year, warmed themselves up with stories and the tinny sound of fiddle music from an old wireless. The bothy was warm now, notes of burning peat adding to the heady tang of the whisky with which each man nurtured his soul.

Hoynes, quieter than was his habit, reached for his pocket watch. With the hour nearing seven, he calculated what was to be done. He reckoned that if he and Hamish went about their business in half an hour or so, they should be able to return to the festivities well before ten of the clock.

Peeny was busy with a shaggy dog's tale of a man from Tarbert who'd eaten a whole bicycle for a bet. Hoynes had heard the story before, but its delivery was nonetheless entertaining.

'The last bit he'd to swallow was the bell,' said Peeny, as the company looked on, enthralled.

'A hellish mouthful,' opined Connelly.

'He'd just eaten the frame, wheels and the handlebar,' replied the storyteller indignantly. 'The bell presented no obstacle. But there was a catch, mind you.'

'Isn't there always? I've never known anyone in Tarbert go about anything in a straightforward manner.' There was a mumble of agreement from the gathered Kinloch fishermen, who, to a man, regarded the fishing port at the northernmost end of the Kintyre peninsula with the utmost suspicion.

'Aye, every time he moved, from that day on, you can hear the bell ring as though it was still attached to the bike. Ding-ding, all day every day. Can you imagine?'

'Ach, wheesht, man. I've never heard the like,' said Andy Duncan.

'I tell you, it's true!' Peeny thumped the bowl of his briar pipe on the arm of his chair by way of affirmation. 'The whole escapade cost him dear, for though he won the bet, he suffered terribly. For a start, his wife couldna bear all that ringing when they were going about their conjugal procedures. It fair put her off the notion, right enough. She ended up running off wae a man travelling in fancy goods fae Paisley. Aye, and that wasn't the worst o' it.'

'You don't say,' said McKirdy.

'No, not by a long chalk. He lost his berth at the fishing – understandably, you'll agree. Who'd want a man aboard that rings wae every step? Even if you could thole it, the fish would take fair exception to the racket.' He paused for effect as everyone considered this. 'In any event, he took to a life o' crime in order to keep body and soul together. Och, it was petty stuff at first, a bit o' shoplifting and the likes. He was helped by the fact that every time he dinged, the shopkeeper looked to the door, and oor man was free to fill his pockets. But it soon got worse. His career as a criminal ended up at a bank somewhere in Glasgow. Armed robbery, no less.'

'For any's sake,' said Danny, his mouth agape.

'Aye, he and this other bloke were caught in the act. The Tarbert fella made a bolt for it up a close. But you know fine how sharp the polis in Glasgow are. They'd clocked the ringing. So, two stout bobbies just hung aboot in the shadows until oor man decided the coast was clear. He was no sooner oot into the street before half the polis in the city descended on him. The poor bugger got eight years for his troubles.'

Those taken with the story shook their heads at the plight of their fellow fisherman, while the more sceptical – including Hoynes – merely raised their eyes to the ceiling and took another sip of whisky.

'He was back oot in five for good behaviour,' said Peeny. 'Man, I was up in Tarbert when I saw him last. The poor soul had aged twenty years.'

'How did you recognise him?' enquired young Danny.

'His face was wrinkled and drawn, hair sparse and grey. But the fact he was ringing all the way down the street fair gave him away.' Peeny winked at the older and wiser members of the company, as the more gullible wondered at this sorry tale. 'They tell me he passed away not long ago. No doubt the result o' all that time spent in the jail, no' to mention the unhealthy aftermath o' eating a whole bicycle.'

'Poor bugger,' said Danny with a shake of the head.

'Mind you, they say his son's a dead ringer for him.' Peeny managed to keep his face straight as he finished his tale.

The laughter that filled the bothy was halted by a sharp knock at the door.

Hoynes was first to his feet. 'That sounds right official, does it no'?'

'Like the polis,' whispered McMichael.

'Or worse still, the fishery officer,' croaked Andy Duncan.

Hoynes straightened up and headed for the door, his heart thudding in his chest at the thought of the cargo in the hold of the *Girl Maggie*.

'Who's there abroad at this time o' night?' he called.

'It's me,' came a muffled voice from behind the door.

'That's all very well, but I'm no' right sure who "me" is,' replied Hoynes.

'Munro!'

The sing-song Highland voice of the Firdale fisherman put Hoynes at his ease. Recovering from his palpitations, he opened the door wide for the man who'd left them peat, coal, logs and fresh bedding. 'Come in, come in,' said Hoynes. 'We owe you a few bumpers and a bite to eat at the very least for your kindness.'

Munro appeared from the shadows of night into the flickering warmth of the bothy.

'You're as pale as a ghost,' said Connelly, staring at their guest, a small, spare man with unruly grey hair sticking up from his round head.

'I'm sorry to be a nuisance, lads. I know this is a Kinloch thing, but I've just had a bad experience.'

Hamish, still clad in Hoynes's more than ample dungarees, ushered Munro into the chair he'd been occupying.

The Firdale man smelled strongly of the cold outdoors from which he'd just emerged. 'Thank you, son, much appreciated.'

'Here,' said Hoynes, pushing a large glass of whisky into their unexpected visitor's trembling hand. 'That should warm the cockles nicely.'

'Kind of you, Sandy, most kind, indeed. Man, what a fright I've had. I'll no' forget this night in a hurry.'

'Don't leave us wondering, Mr Munro,' said Hamish.

'Well, this morning I had a visit from MacIntosh, the gamekeeper. Yous will likely know who I mean?' Munro looked around to nods of recognition. 'He's babysitting they hens for the Absdale Estate.'

'A finer egg canna be consumed,' said Hoynes. 'The creamiest yolk you'll ever sample – even if they do have a tint o' green aboot them, which is unfortunate.'

'You're right, Sandy. But that's no' the gist o' the story.' He took a gulp of whisky. 'MacIntosh telt me aboot an experience he had last night. There's been poachers aboot, you see. He had his eyes and ears fair peeled in case they tried to make away wae the hens, for there's folk far and wide would like to set hands on them.'

'I'm no' so sure you can peel your ain ears, Munro,' said Hoynes thoughtfully. 'But carry on while I ponder on the matter.'

'You'll no' be worried aboot what can or can't be done wae ears when you hear this, Sandy. Anyhow, MacIntosh thought he heard the drip o' oars. As yous will know, these poachers are fly buggers and they make sure their rowlocks are muffled when they're about their business.'

'You canna trust a man wae muffled rowlocks, and no error,' said McKirdy, caught up with the serious nature of this news.

'MacIntosh cracks together his gun, ready for action, and he hides in the bushes beyond the beach. He's a fearless man, and I'm sure he'd no' hesitate to shoot anyone aboot to interfere with his birds.'

'Aye, and quite right,' observed Andy Duncan.

Munro took another draw at his whisky. His face, flushed by the heat in the room and the spirit, became suddenly pale.

'Well, as it turns out, he was right aboot the oars. But these were no poachers.'

'It surely wasn't the Kilmartin rowing club at that time o' night?' said Hoynes.

'Was it the fishery officer?' said McKirdy, the remark predicated upon the notion that the appearance of said official could be the only reason behind the fearful look on the Firdale fisherman's face.

'No fishery officer nor rowing club. It was a Viking longship – men at the oars, fire burning fore and aft from braziers, and a menacing figure at the prow. Like a nightmare.' Munro stared into the fire. 'Damn me, but did this bugger no' call oot to MacIntosh, and him concealed behind a bush.'

'What kind o' bush?' asked Peeny.

'Och, that's irrelevant, man' said Munro. 'Let me get on wae the tale, will you?'

Hoynes drained his glass and all but fell into a chair. Hamish noticed this with puzzlement, that and his skipper's unusual reticence on the subject. For, as the first mate had experienced, Sandy Hoynes was not a man who kept his opinions to himself – under normal circumstances, at least.

'This MacIntosh must tell a fine tale, eh? The colour of you sitting there, a body would swear you'd seen this ghostly vessel yourself,' said Peeny.

The older man looked blankly into his face and raised a bony finger. 'That's the thing. I've just witnessed the very same apparition. I was heading here to make sure all was well, rounded the point on the path and was making my way up the wee hill . . .' His eyes widened. 'I don't know what it was that made me turn – perhaps the hairs on the back o' my neck, perhaps another sense o' which I'm no' aware – I canna be sure. But turn I did. Down in the bay, just yards away from Sandy's boat, there it was. Long, sleek, the figure of a snake picked out by firelight at the prow.'

A disconcerted mumble passed its way amongst the Kinloch company. For, to a man, they were creatures of the sea. And every one of them knew that the laws of nature enjoyed by the land-bound didn't apply to those who took to the ocean for a living. In a storm, in dead calm or a sea mist, they had all experienced things that rarely formed part of the yarns for which fishermen are rightly famous. Things so troubling they were beyond frivolity. Each of them had felt a chill hand on the heart, but more often than not, such events were more a sensation, a feeling, rather than the full-blown experience that Munro had just described. All the same, these occurrences were best not discussed, fishing being a dangerous enough occupation without the addition of the supernatural.

Peeny pursed his lips. In Kinloch, such a story would be banished to whispers and nights when whisky flowed all too freely. Kinloch fishermen, regardless of the contents of their hearts, were practical men, not given to fancy – not in public, at any rate. 'You boys fae Firdale are always prone to the wind-up. Many a tall tale I've heard at the hotel in the village. If you've come to spook us, you'll find a poor audience.' He laughed, but there was something hollow in the sound that made it somehow disingenuous.

'Aye, come on, Munro. We're no' a parcel o' daft wee boys – well, apart fae Hamish and young Danny o'er there,' said McKirdy.

'I'm near thirty!' Hamish protested.

'But that mother of yours would still have you in short trousers if they made them in a suitable size,' said Peeny.

He'd hoped to engender some humour back into the proceedings, but with Munro looking pale and greatly unsettled, the response was a thin snigger rather than the belly laugh for which he'd hoped.

It took Hoynes to break the spell. 'Right, Vikings or no', me and Hamish have a wee errand to be getting on with. It shouldna take us more than an hour or so. I'll leave you to tales o' the Norsemen.' He nodded to his first mate. 'Your gear will be dry by now. You better get oot o' they dungarees o' mine and get yoursel' shipshape.' Hoynes lit his pipe as Hamish sloped off into the shadows to change his clothes.

'And what are you at, eh?' said Andy Duncan, his weatherbeaten face sombre after the tale they'd just been told.

'Nothing at all. A wee favour for a friend o' mine just up the coast a bit. His auld auntie died a month back. She left him a fine piece of furniture. I think they call them Welsh dressers – a grand thing it is, at any rate. I said I'd drop it off earlier, but damn me, did it no' just slip my mind, what wae all the excitement at being abroad wae all you fine fellows.'

Peeny stroked his stubbly chin. 'I had a notion the *Girl Maggie* was sitting low in the water. Had I not known better I'd have thought that you'd a fair catch aboard.'

Hoynes brushed this aside with a wave of his pipe. 'You're forgetting I'd passengers. And some o' you aren't at your fighting weight, I think it's fair to say.'

As Peeny raised his brow, Munro looked up from the flames of the fire, his expression still haunted. 'You're no' taking to the water after what I've just told you, surely, Sandy?'

'I'm a man o' little fear, as you all know fine. And, to be fair, I'd rather meet up wae a Viking than the fishery officer any day of the week.' Hoynes laughed heartily at his own observation. But when he turned away from the little huddle of fishermen, his face, shadowed in the dancing flames of the fire, took on a deadly serious expression.

13

Now out in the sound, Marshall, Cummings and the three crewmembers of the Revenue cutter had their eyes focused on the length of the east Kintyre coast. Each man was searching for the tiniest glimmer of light from the many bays and inlets that dotted the peninsula. Though Marshall's memory of the area had diminished with the years, he knew Cummings had every part of the place off by heart. In short, with a powerful engine and the inside knowledge that had sparked the mission from the outset, they were well placed to bring wrongdoers to justice.

The night, though, was still. The stars arched over the sound in a magnificent display, but the only other lights to be seen were those of the lighthouses on the Cock of Arran and the distant Ayrshire coast.

'Nothing yet, sir,' said Cummings, his duffel coat buttoned up tight at his throat and a stout scarf wound about his neck.

'There's time aplenty,' replied Marshall. 'Hoynes will appear when we least expect it, you'll see. From what I remember, and the reports I've been reading today, the man has a talent for surprise.'

'There can be little doubt about that, sir. A wilier mariner there has never been – with the exception of that Raleigh fella, pirates and the like. And they've no' set sail for a goodly number of years.'

'I can just see Hoynes at the helm of a privateer. He has the looks for it.'

'He was more akin to Father Christmas the last time I saw him, right enough. He's carrying a fair cargo o' timber round the belly these days. Aye, and his beard's as white as his hair.'

Marshall took his eyes from his binoculars, surprised by this information. It was strange how people changed. When one saw an individual on a regular basis physical change was so gradual it barely registered. But encountering someone for the first time in years was bound to be a surprise. Reflecting on his own appearance, he realised that the flecks of grey at his temples and the wrinkles around his eyes hadn't been there when he worked in Kinloch so long ago. In fact, he'd considered himself rather suave and sophisticated in his trench coat and trilby hat back then. But fashions had changed, and in common with most other middle-aged men, Marshall thought less of his appearance and more of comfort, as the wearing of the warm Toorie that was pulled low down over his forehead proved.

He was still ruminating on the subject of age and the changes it engendered when there was a call from one of the crew.

'Sir, look to port – I'm sure I can see lights.'

Both Marshall and Cummings swivelled their binoculars in the appropriate direction.

'Well done, Frazer. I see them,' said Marshall.

'Confirmed,' agreed Cummings.

'Right, the chase is on. Engage the engines and steer for those lights at full speed, Mr Cummings!'

The deep growl of the powerful engines banished the silence of the cold night. In a few minutes, the cutter was making her way to port, a foaming wave at her bow translucent in the darkness.

✧

Hamish followed his skipper down the narrow path towards the *Girl Maggie*, the roll neck of his thick sea jumper pulled over his chin. The air was frosty, the smell of the fire burning in the bothy overlaying the tang of the sea and the earthy notes of the land.

The younger man cast his eye first to the bay, then out into the sound. But there was no sign of a Viking longship, just the stout figure of their broad-beamed vessel nestling under the lee of the sandbank. The tide had receded now, and the sand next to which the fishing boat wallowed shone silver in the starlight, like a celestial path.

'At least you'll manage to stay dry this time,' said Hoynes, the pale smoke of his pipe billowing into the air.

'You're right sore on me, Sandy. That ladder was slick – any man could have come a cropper.'

'If you say so. But, mind, men more than twice your age navigated it with ease, Hamish.'

The first mate mumbled something under his breath then decided to change the subject. In truth, though he knew of the hay bales and the lemonade bottles filled with whisky, he'd supposed that they'd have been taken to their destination the following day. He hadn't reckoned on the convivial atmosphere of the bothy being interrupted by this covert jaunt. And though he'd always suspected that there was something 'below decks' about the whole enterprise, he was now sure that the *Girl Maggie*'s cargo was less than lawful. 'What will I be getting for my trouble this night, skipper?'

232

Hoynes stopped his progress down the bank and turned to face his first mate. 'What on earth do you mean?'

'I reckon you'll be getting a good wee cut of whatever it is we're to be up to. I should surely get my share.'

'You'll remember that you have a half share o' the working finances o' this vessel. We're merely doing a favour for the much put-upon folk o' Firdale. Every man deserves a recreational dram at a reasonable price. I thought you would realise that.'

'Even if it comes in lemonade bottles?'

'Now, I explained that to you. Not that I needed to, mind. Remember. *If I can help my fellow man along the way then my life was not in vain.* That's from the Scriptures, though just what book and verse escapes me at the moment.'

They made their way onto the sandbank. It took Hoynes a couple of goes to lift himself onto the rope ladder, but with remarkable speed he was soon over the side and back aboard the *Girl Maggie*, Hamish in his wake.

'Do you reckon she'll come off all right, Sandy?'

'Och, I daresay a day sailor would have his work cut out. But I could get us back out into the sound wae my eyes closed. You get down and fire up the engine, Hamish. The sooner we get about this mission o' mercy, the quicker we'll be back amidst the warmth and celebrations.'

'There wasna much in the way o' celebrations going on, as far as I could see. Just a parcel o' auld sea dogs blethering – aye, and Peeny's tall tales. Would we no' just as well be at the County?'

'Man, you've let the free love turn your mind, Hamish. There's mair to life than propping up the bar at the County, as you'll find out as you get older, I hope. I'd hate to picture you as one o' the old soaks that bide in there, fair shaking their empty glasses in the hope someone will be good enough to stand them a replenishment. No life at all.'

'Don't be daft. When I'm that age, I'll likely be dandling some grandweans on my knee.'

'In that case, you'd better get a shift on. You don't go straight to the grandweans – the weans come first. And if you don't mind me saying, you're no' making much progress on that front.'

Hamish looked suitably aggrieved by this comment, choosing only to grunt in response.

'Maybe the Auld Stones will put lead in your pencil. They can work all manner o' miracles.'

'The Auld Stones?'

Hoynes hurried to the wheelhouse. 'Och, I've no' the time to enlighten you at the moment. We have an errand o' mercy to be at. You'll find oot soon enough.'

'And what aboot these Vikings, Sandy?' Hamish laughed.

Hoynes spun on the heel of his seaboot. 'You'd do well not tae mock, Hamish. Aye, none o' us know what we think we know, and that's a fact.' He opened the door of the wheelhouse, and soon the lantern hanging in that small space flickered into life.

14

As anyone with the slightest knowledge of Scotland's West Coast will acknowledge, the weather can change in an instant. And this night was no different. No sooner had Marshall set off in search of his prey, than a mist began to envelop the vessel. The nearer to the coast of Kintyre they sailed, the thicker it became.

'Damn!' exclaimed Marshall. 'Where has this come from?'

'Not unheard o' in cold weather like this, sir. Och, it's likely a freezing fog. They can be damnable tricky, right enough.'

'Just as well we've the radar to rely on.' Marshall played with a toggle on his duffel coat, deep in thought. 'In fact, it may be a blessing in disguise. They'll never know where we are now, and we'll see any vessel that moves. There won't be many honest folk abroad on a night like this, eh?'

'I'd reckon not, sir. And it's the old New Year. That still holds in these parts, in certain communities, at least.'

'Good grief. The Dark Ages, to be sure.' Marshall checked the radar. By his reckoning, they were less than a mile from where the lights had been spotted, but the green sweep of the screen showed no sign of any vessel. 'Right, let's linger here a while. Cut the engine. We'll keep our eye on this.'

'It's not as though we can see much else, that's for sure.'

'You have the right of it there, Jocky. Who'd have thought this would come down so quickly?'

Hoynes eyed the sudden fog with disdain. 'Would you credit it, Hamish? The night was as clear as a bell – man, you could see Venus. Now I canna see the prow.'

'It's bad luck, right enough, Sandy. Should we leave the bay?'

'Some things have to be done, and this task won't wait.'

'Can we no' jeest drop off the cargo tomorrow? It's no' as though we'd be going far out of our way.'

'Och no, that wouldn't be a good idea at all. For a start, the fishery officer could get wind o' the whole thing and take umbrage.'

'Surely he's no' interested in hay bales.' Hamish looked for Hoynes's reaction from the corner of his eye.

'These buggers are into everything – don't ever doubt it. You could be dropping off the Queen by special appointment and the fishery officer would want her weighed, verified and accounted for, and that's a fact.'

'Anyway, we should be mair worried aboot the Ministry of Agriculture, the amount o' hay we're carrying.'

'Just you wheesht. I've tae navigate oot o' here in a pea-souper. Take note and watch an expert at his trade. It's the only way to learn.' Hoynes tugged at the wheel as the tone of the old diesel engine rose. 'You see, it's all up here.' He tapped his temple. 'When nature deprives you o' your senses, you've only your heid to do the seeing. Now, if I was just any sailor, we'd likely be—' Hoynes didn't get to finish his sentence. The *Girl Maggie* came to a sudden and unceremonious stop, throwing both of them forward in the wheelhouse. Hoynes's pipe, clenched between his teeth, was sent flying, its owner cursing.

'What happened?' said Hamish.

'You go and take a gander over the side while I find my pipe.'

Hamish did as he was told. Picking up a torch from the wheelhouse, he ventured into the mist. It was so thick that he had to shine its faded beam down at his feet, just in case he fell over a net. As he directed it over the side, he frowned at the sight. Carefully, he made his way back to Hoynes.

'Is it a stray log or the like, Hamish?'

'Man, it would have to be a fair-sized log to bring us to such a standstill, Sandy. No, it was the sandbank. You must have turned the wheel the wrong way – fair disoriented by the fog, and all.'

Hoynes thought for a moment. He smiled broadly at Hamish. 'Now, let that be a lesson to you. I was waiting for you to correct me, but you were as mute as a wooden horse. You'll need to pay more attention if you're to skipper a fine vessel like this.'

'So, the fact we went the wrong way was my fault?'

'Merely testing your faculties, Hamish. They're clearly no' up to much. Now, lesson over, I'll get us out into the sound. You could help by giving that sandbank a prod wae the boathook. Aye, this'll be a night you won't forget in a hurry.'

Hamish left the wheelhouse and raised his eyes to the heavens. He always marvelled at the elaborate excuses Hoynes could concoct to cover his deficiencies. He'd heard politicians on the wireless desperately trying to cover their tracks following some blunder or other. They should seek out my skipper for advice, he always thought.

Just as Hamish reached for the boathook, something caught his eye. For a moment, he was sure that an orange flash crossed his line of sight. He peered into the fog, but there was nothing to be seen.

Marshall stared into the radar screen. He was beginning to doubt his own reasoning now. Perhaps their quarry had given them the slip? The lights they'd seen could quite easily have been a decoy. But, he reasoned, nobody knew where they were, so why employ such tactics? Being a man confident in his own ability, he quickly dismissed the notion and squinted harder at the screen.

He was about to hand the duty over to Cummings when, sure enough, as if from nowhere, the ping of what could only be a vessel appeared, emerging from the coastline like a miracle. 'Cummings, we have them!' Marshall made a rough calculation in his head. 'Steer sixteen degrees to port!'

15

Back at the bothy, the Kinloch contingent were busy trying to console Munro, who was still spooked following his run-in with the spectral longship. Catching McKirdy's attention, Peeny gestured to the door with his pipe.

'I fancy a wee breath o' the night air,' he said. 'Though I love my baccy dearly, wae all of us smoking in such a confined space, I'm no' sure I'm smoking my pipe or McKirdy's.'

'I'll come and, eh, keep you company,' replied McKirdy awkwardly, as though he'd taken time to learn the lines.

They stepped out into the cold night and were immediately taken by the fog that had appeared so unexpectedly.

'Man, this won't help us trek up to the stones,' said Peeny.

'We've time yet. And, mind, we're waiting for Hoynes to come back after delivering his furniture.' McKirdy looked sceptical.

'Furniture! I had young Danny take a look intae the hold when Sandy was busy at one of his yarns. He telt me the boat is fair stowed to the gunnels wae hay bales. That's why she was so low in the water.'

'Hay bales? What on earth for?'

'Your guess is as good as mine. But you can be damned sure the bugger's up to something – and I'll wager it's not farming-related.'

'Och, it's none o' our business, Peeny. As long as he's back in good time for midnight, we canna make comment.'

'It would be oor business if the authorities had happened upon us on the way here, and him wae goodness knows what contraband aboard. Guilty by association, that's what the cry would have been.'

'You surely don't think he's at the smuggling?'

'You hear aboot it all the time these days. The young folk are falling o'er themselves to get a hold o' the drugs, and no mistake. It seems a good dram is of no consequence to the younger generation.'

'Heavens! I've known Sandy pull a few stunts in my time, but this isna a buckshee octopus, or a few extra pounds o' mackerel. They say his daughter is winching the police sergeant. He'll likely have one eye on the wedding. Every ha'penny is a prisoner in that hoose. The poor lassie will likely walk doon the aisle in widow's weeds.'

'Drugs is a serious matter. I've been thinking Hamish has been sampling them for a while. Look at that carry-on at New Year. Aye, and Sandy himself. I'm still no' quite sure what happened in that blizzard before Christmas. But I'd no' be surprised if he was on a trip.'

'Where tae, Peeny?'

'That's what they call it when you're away wae the fairies on the drugs. I didna mean he'd taken the weekend in Edinburgh.'

McKirdy took this in with a grave look. He pictured Sandy Hoynes partaking in the opium he'd read about in novels. But somehow, he couldn't reconcile the mental image. 'Where would he get the time? He's either out at sea at the fishing or he's in the County Hotel wae the rest o' us.'

'The man's likely up half the night abusing himself. It's Marjorie I feel sorry for.'

Again, a mental image formed in McKirdy's mind's eye. But it was so alarming he felt a change of conversation was warranted. 'What are your thoughts on Munro's ramblings? You don't reckon he's taken to the drugs and all, do you?'

'He's fae Firdale. They'll have all manner o' hallucinations in that place. Quite common, I should say. They reckon that half o' the village are by-blows o' the sailors fae the Spanish Armada. That's a trauma that would go down the centuries. It's a wonder it wisna auld King Henry he was seeing.'

'He beheaded all o' his wives.'

'Munro? The bad bugger.'

'No, auld King Henry. I'm sure you don't get off wae beheading these days – even in Firdale. But, thinking on it, I reckon that Elizabeth was on the throne at the time o' the Armada.'

Peeny looked unconvinced as he stared around in the dense mist. 'I wonder how many souls spent their days in this place, eh?'

'The village?'

'Aye. They say the last body that lived here went mad wae isolation. That was well o'er a hundred years ago. Their rough auld cottages are nothing more than a heap o' ruins now. It makes you wonder.'

'Wonder what?'

'Who'll remember us when we're gone?'

McKirdy pondered upon this as he puffed on his pipe. 'They might no' remember us, but I'm willing tae bet they remember Sandy Hoynes.'

16

Marshall could almost smell the success. The more he thought about it, the more he could remember his time in Kinloch. The image and reputation of Sandy Hoynes became clearer, the closer they came to the vessel, which was now picked out brightly on the radar screen.

'We should be in hailing distance of them within five minutes, sir,' said Cummings.

'We'll use the Tannoy. It normally scares the life out of these miscreants. That's the one good thing about this mist. They won't see us coming. I don't believe Hoynes will be equipped with radar.'

'I hear he only purchased a radio a wee while ago. The authorities forced it on him after that caper before Christmas in the blizzards. You'll remember it was in all the papers, sir.'

'That was Hoynes? My goodness, I hadn't realised.'

'Aye, he's quite the celebrity, these days – in Kinloch, at any rate.'

'We'll soon put a stop to that. Let people see the real man behind the myth, eh? Slow the engine, Cummings. We want this to be as big a surprise as possible.'

✧

Meanwhile, all was not well aboard the *Girl Maggie*. Sandy Hoynes still couldn't find his pipe, and Hamish had taken a tumble amidships and was now sporting a bruise visibly burgeoning from his forehead.

'Don't take a smoke, Hamish. It's the very worst thing you can do wae an injury such as the one you've just sustained.'

'Why so, Sandy?'

'Ach, the baccy fair aggravates the trauma. Hand me your pipe and keep a weather eye on the coast. You should see a swaying light on the shore. That's the signal.'

'Signal for what?'

'Signal for us to heave-to and get rid o' all this hay.'

'I'll be hard-pressed to see anything through this mist, Sandy. And for discussion's sake, the word "signal" has worrisome connotations.'

'It's a word – what are you worried aboot?'

'I read a fair pile o' books when I was a lad. Thon smuggler Red MacEachran was forever looking out for signals.'

'Man, you're heid is fair planted in the clouds, and no error. What do you expect them to do, wave a wee flag? You'll no' see that in the mist, that's for certain. Lights, you can see in the dark; flags are fine in the daylight, but hellish useless at night – especially in a mist. Now, get your glimmers on that shore or you'll have another bruise to match the one you've already got.'

It was at this moment that a number of things appeared to happen simultaneously. No sooner had Hamish turned his attention to the shore than he spotted a light, swaying in the mist, just as Hoynes had described. The first mate turned to his skipper, about to speak, when the silence of the night was shattered by the sudden roar of an amplified voice.

'Stop engines and drop anchor! This is her Majesty's Revenue cutter *Diane*. We intend to board. I repeat: we intend to board.'

Hoynes expressed his feelings with the use of a loud oath, as, for the second time that night, a pipe dropped from his mouth and landed on an undisclosed part of the wheelhouse floor.

'Damn me, Sandy, but we're done for!' wailed Hamish.

For Hoynes, the few split seconds that elapsed seemed like hours, as he desperately sought to find a believable response to the question of why there were a large number of hay bales cosseting lemonade bottles filled with illicit whisky in his hold. But before he could come up with anything suitable, a blazing flash of fire passed before his line of sight.

The sudden rush of flames made Marshall take a step back. 'What on earth? The bloody man has set his vessel on fire!'

Cummings rushed to his side. 'Sir, he's making a run for it. We should pursue. He'll never outrun us in that tub.'

'Yes, get after him! I'm damned if that rascal is going to outsmart us.'

The great engine of the cutter roared once more as Cummings steered towards the flickering flames, now disappearing into the mist. 'I don't know what he's at, sir. If his vessel is on fire, eventually they'll need to abandon ship. What chance will men have in the water in these conditions? They'll freeze to death before we can locate them.'

'Hoynes clearly has no regard for his own safety or that of his crew. The man's more ruthless than we imagined. Make haste, Mr Cummings. There could be lives at stake!'

Hamish looked open-mouthed at Hoynes, as the cutter disappeared back into the mist. 'What on earth happened, Sandy? How did you make that fire appear oot o' nowhere?'

'Och, think nothing of it,' muttered Hoynes. 'You've got to be on your toes for any eventuality, right enough.' Had he been in possession of a pipe on which to draw, he would surely have done so. Instead, he bit his lip as he stared back out to sea. 'We need to get into the shore as quickly as we can, Hamish. You steer to my signal. I'll make my way out on deck and guide you. But mind and keep your lugs open. One mistake and we're beached.'

As Hoynes stumbled out of the wheelhouse, his mind was a tumble of thoughts. When he'd heard the Tannoy from the cutter his blood had run cold. Though he wasn't responsible for the appropriation of the whisky he carried aboard, he'd have faced questions he'd have been unable and unwilling to answer, had the Revenue vessel not taken off after the flames. That thought took him back to only a few short weeks ago. Though his memory was still hazy, muddled by an accidental ingestion of narcotics, he could still picture the handsome longship, braziers burning bright with flame, fore and aft. But it couldn't be; that experience had been chemically induced. The whole escapade had haunted him ever since.

Then there was Munro's tale to take into account. His description of what he'd seen earlier that evening had chimed almost exactly with Hoynes's vision while under the influence.

Now, more than ever, Hoynes was convinced that what he'd seen in the heavy snow was not a drug-fuelled fever dream. But he had more pressing matters to think about now.

Troubled, yet relieved, he looked over the side of the *Girl Maggie* at the lantern swaying on the shore. 'Ahoy!' he shouted. 'Guide me in, and we'll have to get moving!'

Hoynes called to Hamish to steer slowly towards the light. As they neared the shore, the shadows of men, seemingly cut in two, with only their heads and torsos to be seen, emerged like some ghastly vision through the mist.

'What are you taking us into, Sandy?' Hamish's trembling voice issued from the wheelhouse.

'Wheesht, man, and concentrate on what you're doing. When I raise my hand, stop the engine and we'll drift into place.'

The closer the *Girl Maggie* came to the shore, the more obvious it was that the shadows of men weren't the gruesome visions that Hamish had conjured up. Indeed, not far off the beach, as the mist cleared, he could see around twenty figures wading through the waist-height water, each man wearing fishermen's waders. They were dragging something behind them through the waves – a large raft, Hamish quickly realised.

'Stop!' shouted Hoynes, waving one arm in the air to reinforce the point.

Soon, and with admirable speed, men were pouring over the side of the *Girl Maggie* and up the rope ladder like a pirate boarding party. One man whispered to Hoynes, and soon they'd formed three human chains. Men passed hay bales out of the hold and up into the arms of their companions, who then handed them over the side to men on the raft. Hamish was mesmerised by their speed and skill, remembering how long it had taken to load the vessel in the first place.

In minutes, the hay and the whisky were aboard the raft and it was slowly pushed toward the shore. Almost as quickly as they had appeared, one by one, those aboard the fishing boat had disappeared over the side and slipped into the darkness.

'Right, Hamish! Let's get back to Smuggler's Hole. There are celebrations to be had!'

Hamish stepped back to let Hoynes take over the wheel of the *Girl Maggie*. 'I don't know how you did that, Sandy. Man, it was like a military operation.'

'Thirsty men are easy to motivate, Hamish. Those poor buggers in Firdale have throats like camels' feet. Anything can be achieved if the spirit is willing – never forget that.'

'Aye, "spirit" being the operative word.' Hamish thought for a moment. 'It would be you who conjured up the fire to distract the Revenue? How did you manage it?'

Hoynes remained silent for a moment. When he did speak, his voice was almost a whisper. 'Hamish, I'm going to tell you something, but there's two things you must promise me before I do.'

'Aye, I promise.'

'For a start, you must never repeat this to a soul – not even your ain mother.'

'You have my word.'

'But before that, a more pressing task.'

'Aye – just tell me.' Hamish was anxious to hear more as he looked wide-eyed at Hoynes.

'Get yourself down on the floor and find they pipes. I'm fair gasping for a smoke.'

17

It was just after ten, and all talk in the bothy was centred around Sandy Hoynes and his whereabouts. Munro was shaking his head, prophecies of doom on his lips. Meanwhile Connelly, McMichael, McKirdy and Peeny were merely irritated by his absence.

'It's always the same,' said Peeny. 'If there's disturbance to be had, Hoynes is at the heart o' it. He was the same as a boy when he left the school for his father's boat. I'm a couple o' years older, but I remember him fine wae his blond hair and his schemes. Drove his auld fella daft, and that's the truth. Trouble has always followed Sandy like an auld dog.'

Andy Duncan was sitting by the fire, quietly contemplating the flames as they sparked and danced before his old, wrinkled face. At his great age, he had found peace from gossip and speculation, taking everything very much in his stride, approaching everyone as he found them – well, in most cases.

'You're devilish quiet, Andy,' opined McKirdy.

'I daresay. I've been pondering on much we've heard tonight from Munro here. It's brought some stories to mind. Aye, tales I'd forgotten all about – fae years back.'

Peeny looked at McKirdy, raising his eyes to the ceiling. For everyone knew – as much as they respected the man – that once Duncan embarked upon a yarn, great swathes of your life were likely to be eaten away. 'You'll need to be quick wae your story, Andy,' said Peeny. 'Hoynes or no Hoynes, we'll have to head for the stones soon to make midnight.'

'Always in a hurry, Peeny. You should slow down and smell the fish for a change.' He shifted in his chair, still staring into the flames of the fire. 'When I was a lad, I mind my faither telling me o' one night just like this. It was the Auld New Year – och, must be o'er seven decades ago.'

McKirdy leaned into Peeny's ear. 'It'll take him another seventy years tae tell the tale.'

'I can hear you, McKirdy,' said Andy Duncan. 'My eyes might no' be what they once were, but there's bugger-all wrong wae my lugs.' He coughed, indicating the story was to resume. 'This place, the auld village in which we find ourselves, has long since been abandoned. But it stood for hundreds o' years, right back to the times o' the Vikings. The very stones we're making for shortly were held in high esteem by the Northmen. So much so, that they wouldn't think o' embarkation on any kind o' caper before they left some silver at them. We don't have an abundance o' the silver, but we still toast them wae good whisky, and that's much the same thing.'

'I'd rather have a dram than silver,' said McMichael.

'Then you're a bigger fool than I took you for, Jimmy. For you can purchase a fair cargo o' whisky wae silver, but you'll get damn-all silver for a bottle o' the good stuff, and that's a fact.'

Suitably chastised, McMichael found nothing more to say.

'Now, back in my father's time, they were all gathered here as we are now. Mind you, the bothy hadn't been raised then, so they slept under canvas amongst the ruins.' He took a sip of whisky. 'This night, they were making their wae doon fae the stones, having partaken in the usual ceremonies.'

'Aye, drinking a bucketful,' said Peeny.

'The observances that we still follow to this day,' retorted Duncan sharply, somewhat piqued by yet another interruption to his story. 'Anyhow, they spied something on their way doon the wee path. It was a boat, but nothing like what was to be found at that time. Ach, my father had notions fae time to time. But he described it, and hearing Munro this night has brought the memory back to mind. Long, sleek, wae fire blazing fore and aft – just as you say.' He raised his glass to Munro. 'The theory was at the time that each Auld New Year the spirits o' the Northmen made for the stones to pay their respects.'

'See, I'm no' wrong in the heid,' said Munro.

'They canna have been much good at telling time,' said Malcolm Connelly.

'How so?' asked Duncan.

'Well, if oor boys had been up at the stones to take in the Auld New Year, the spirits o' the Vikings doon in the bay must have missed the boat – if you pardon the pun.'

'You're a right pedant, Malcolm,' said Andy Duncan. 'It's a trait I've noted in you long before now. You'll understand that the men from the north weren't in possession o' wristwatches and the like that we have now. They held their time by the moon and the stars, and such a thing isna accurate to the very second. Nor does it matter, for oor time has little consequence in the great scheme o' things.'

'We're surrounded by ghostly Vikings, then – is that what you're telling us, Andy?' said Peeny.

'This was their settlement; they founded this wee place. So I don't see why their memory o' them widna be abundant. Anyway, there's more to the story.'

'For any's sake, it's a bloody saga,' McKirdy whispered to Peeny.

'Wheesht, McKirdy, for this is the best bit.' Andy sat forward in his chair, his eyes now averted from the fire, as he glanced at them all, one by one. 'There was one Archibald MacEachran – a fine fisherman, by all accounts – in the party. As we all know, there's no' an older family in this peninsula than the MacEachrans – they were here long before the Norse arrived. Some say they became bitter enemies.'

This statement was met with nods of general agreement, it being well known that the MacEachrans were descended from 'the people of the horse' who had first inhabited Kintyre. 'I'm no' so fond o' them myself,' said Peeny. 'Right thrawn buggers, the lot o' them.'

Duncan continued unabashed, as a log spat loudly in the fireplace. 'Though they were all a bit put off by the vision in the bay, MacEachran was near demented. No doubt, his blood calling to him doon the generations, fair warning the man o' the danger o' the wild men fae the North.' Duncan paused, his wrinkled face drawn into a grimace, rheumy eyes narrowed. 'All they wanted was to be back at their camp, safe and sound wae a warming dram in their hands. But with their encampment in sight – the very ground on which we find ourselves this night – a terrible thing happened.' Andy Duncan's voice was little more than a whisper now. 'MacEachran's legs were suddenly fair rooted to the spot wae fright. Suddenly, out of nowhere, there was this mighty crack!' He made an expansive gesture with his arms. As he did so, the door swung open on its hinges, making Peeny shriek and jump from his chair, tipping a bottle of whisky to the earthen floor, where its contents glugged out until McKirdy dived to rescue what was left. As though delayed by the shock, young Danny let out a blood-curdling yell, as Andy Duncan, the storyteller himself, clasped a hand to his chest, his old heart having leapt with fright.

'Man, but yous are right jumpy,' said Hoynes, framed in the doorway, a wisp of fog trailing into the bothy from the cold night behind him.

18

The chase had taken the Customs men almost the full length of the Isle of Arran. The flickering light that looked so much like flame had always been just within sight, but just out of reach. Despite Marshall's encouragement, they seemed unable to make any ground on the vessel they assumed to be the *Girl Maggie*.

'What on earth does Hoynes have for engines? The boat's jet-propelled!' exclaimed the frustrated collector.

Cummings stroked his chin. He'd been at sea long enough to recognise the knot presently in his stomach was the intimation of an instinct that all was not well. 'It's the fire I don't understand, sir.'

'The man's clearly using it to trick us. Any sensible mariner would be showing lights fore and aft in these conditions. If Hoynes thinks he's put us off the scent by the use of fire, he's got another think coming.' He stared at the flames shimmering in the fog ahead. 'Surely we can get more from the engine? This vessel is designed to overtake lesser craft and bring them to book.'

'We're at full speed, sir. I'm as puzzled as you that we can't make any headway.'

To his right through the mist, Marshall saw lights. 'Is that Lochranza, Cummings?'

'Yes, sir. We'll soon be out in the firth. With a bit of luck, once we're past the island, this will clear and we'll be able to get a better fix on Hoynes.'

'Good. Damn the man. I don't know how he thinks he can continue to outrun us.'

'It has to be said, he's done no' too bad so far, sir.'

Marshall picked up the radio mouthpiece from its cradle. 'Her Majesty's Revenue cutter *Diane* to Clyde Coastguard. Come in, over.' As he waited for a reply he turned to Marshall. 'I'm determined to catch this rascal. We'll have another vessel head him off in the firth – the Royal Navy, if necessary. We'll cut him off!'

As Marshall called for assistance over the radio, Cummings noted the lights of Lochranza were now behind them. As he stared out, he fancied he could see the mist begin to thin as they headed for the narrow channel between Firdale and the last stretch of the Isle of Arran. 'Sir, I think I was right. The conditions seem to be improving.'

Marshall hung the mouthpiece back on its cradle. 'Let the fox see the chicken, eh? Good stuff!'

But, to the dismay of both men on the bridge, as the mist cleared to reveal again the stars under which they'd begun their journey, so any sign of the flames they'd been following all the way up the sound had disappeared.

'He's vanished, sir!' said Cummings, his mouth gaping open.

'He can't have done. I'll get a man on the searchlight. He's likely extinguished the fire when he saw the mist clear. Hoynes can't be far away.'

As Marshall ran off to supervise the searchlight, Cummings remained unconvinced. Though the moon was no more than a crescent, the night was bright with stars. From the dimly lit bridge, he could see their reflection in the dark water of the Firth of Clyde. What he couldn't see was any sign of a vessel, fire or no fire. His hands gripped the ship's wheel. 'We were following something tonight,' he muttered to himself under his breath. 'But I'm not sure it was Sandy Hoynes.'

Hamish was on his third bumper of whisky before they were all ready to head up to the stones. His skipper took him in with a leery eye.

'Man, but you've got a fair drouth the night, Hamish. We've plenty whisky to go round – don't worry. You don't have to drink it all at once.'

Hamish looked back at him with a heavy-lidded gaze. 'Sandy, I'll no' lie to you. I got a right scare tonight.' His voice was already slurred. 'I could picture me an' you standing in the dock o' the High Court in Glasgow and being dragged off to the jail. Aye, where we'd spend years.'

'Don't be daft, Hamish. There was no risk o' that. I reckon it was some prankster fae Firdale at work. You know fine what buggers they are for a wind-up, eh?' Hoynes puffed on a pipe, a spare one borrowed from Andy Duncan, his own still somewhere on the *Girl Maggie*'s wheelhouse floor. 'Besides, we'd have been tried in the Sherriff Court in Kinloch. It's no' as though we murdered anyone.'

'Och, that's a weight off my mind, Sandy,' said Hamish. 'I'm no' sure what I was worrying about at all.'

'Sarcasm isna your strong suit, son,' said Hoynes. 'I had the entire matter in hand start to finish. You saw yourself how slick the operation was wae thon raft. Man, it was like the Marine Commandos during the war. We could have stormed Greece wae such fine organisation.'

'But the Commandos weren't smuggling whisky, they were fighting Hitler. There's a big difference when you think aboot it, Sandy.'

'Who said anything aboot smuggling? We were just helping oot some dry-mouthed souls. A mission o' mercy, nothing more.'

'Whisky in old lemonade bottles. Do you think I sailed up the Clyde in a banana boat?'

'You're a right mistrustful bugger, Hamish. Aye, and insulting with it. As though I'd be up to any such caper. I've a good mind to inform your mother o' your suspicious state o' mind when we get back to Kinloch. Sheer paranoia, and that's a fact.' He lowered his voice. 'And I'll thank you no' to be making any more mention of tonight's goings-on. You know fine what a band o' auld fishwives this team are. Before you know it, we'll be the Bonnie and Clyde of Kinloch, once they start at the gossip.'

'Who are Bonnie and Clyde, Sandy?'

'A right pair o' scunners fae America. Robbers and thieves. Though if the comparison was made, I'd have tae be Bonnie, because you're no' blessed wae good looks.'

'Eh?' Hamish looked abashed.

'They funny eyes you've got – aye, and the way your hair is on the retreat. You're an oil painting, but one o' little merit.'

Hamish leaned into his skipper with a stagger. 'And what happened wae those flames, tell me that?'

Hoynes coughed. 'Flames? I'm sure I've no idea what you're on aboot!'

'I know fine you saw them, Sandy. They flashed between us and the Customs cutter. We're only at liberty because they took off after them, and you know it!'

Hoynes took another puff. 'If I was you, I'd lay off the drink. I'm sure your brain is fair addled wae it, and you no mair than a youngster.' He shook his head, but there was something about his expression that rendered this statement unconvincing.

'Come on!' shouted Peeny. 'We'll miss midnight if we're no' careful.'

One by one, the Kinloch fishermen left the warmth of the bothy and stepped out into the freezing night. Frost sparkled on the branches of the fir trees as they plodded along a narrow path in single file. There was no mist now, and the clean, fresh smell of pine was strong in the air, mixing with the tang of the restless sea far below, where the *Girl Maggie* nestled safely in the tiny cove.

Hamish and his skipper were bringing up the rear, just behind Andy Duncan – who, for his age, had a healthy stride. He stopped for a moment and beckoned Hoynes.

'A wee word, Sandy.'

Hoynes approached the older man. 'Aye, what can I help you wae, Andy?'

'I've been remembering times past, Sandy. And I should tell you that I've a right sore feeling in my heart.'

'A sore feeling? Should we call the Firdale doctor?'

Duncan stared at Hoynes, a man almost twenty years his junior. 'I'm thinking you know full well what I mean.' He turned on his heel and followed the others towards the old stones.

Now out in the broad firth, with searchlight deployed, it soon became obvious to Marshall that, somehow, Hoynes had given them the slip. He bounded back onto the bridge, his mood dark.

'This is damnable, Cummings, just damnable. The man's like a ghost.'

Cummings bowed his head.

'What on earth is the matter with you?'

'Och, nothing, sir. Just auld tales and ancient fancies. Men o' the sea like myself are prone to different ideas at times like these.'

'Such as?' replied Marshall impatiently.

'Nothing in particular. But rogues of all generations are thought to look after their own – no matter how many years have intervened.'

'Good grief, Cummings. Don't tell me you seriously thought we were following a ghost ship. I must say, this nonsense does you little credit.'

Cummings merely shrugged and looked out at distant lights on the shores of the Firth of Clyde.

'Hoynes is holed up in some bay. Arran is dotted with them. Your job is to know these waters as well as he does!'

'And that I do, sir.'

'So, your explanation is that he was rescued by some spectre dedicated to the liberty of every smuggler and rogue to be found? A kind of patron saint of thieves.'

'All I'll say is that I've seen my fair share of strange things at sea, sir.'

'I'm here to prove you wrong, man. We'll double back and run the coast of Arran close – examine every nook and cranny under the searchlight. I tell you, once Hoynes sees we're dedicated to the task, he'll have no choice other than to break for cover. My guess is, just before dawn. He won't want to be pursued in broad daylight. He won't be able to pull any of his little tricks.'

'If you say so, sir.'

'Yes, I damn well do. Get a grip, Cummings, and turn us back towards Arran.'

'Aye, aye, sir.' Grimly, the first mate turned the big wheel, and soon the *Diane* was sailing as close to the coast of the island as she could, a powerful searchlight probing every rocky beach and tiny inlet.

19

Hoynes stopped and leaned against a stout oak tree. A life at sea didn't prepare you for the rigours of traversing the land. While the skipper was more than happy to scale any mountainous wave behind the wheel of his fishing boat, he wasn't quite so comfortable on foot facing a climb. He patted his belly and took a deep breath.

'You're out of condition,' said Hamish. The cold night air appeared to have cleared his head, and he looked much less tired and emotional.

'Wae one thing and another, it's been a busy few days. You remember, I'm more than twice your age, Hamish. Though I'll be long dead, remember these words when you're in your sixties. It's a hellish thing, but, damn me, nothing works the way it once did, and that's a fact. Man, that's why I'm telling you to get a move on in the marriage stakes. There's nothing worse than a man who likes sitting by the fire wae a good dram and the newspaper married to a younger woman keen to be about the jolly old thing of an evening.'

'The "jolly old thing"?'

'Don't tell me I have to teach you aboot the birds and bees, too? I signed up for getting your navigating and fishing skills up to muster, no' matters o' an intimate nature.'

Hamish looked puzzled for a few moments, then what his skipper was saying dawned on him. 'Here, Sandy, there's no need for that. I'm perfectly aware o' my duties in that department – aye, an' more than capable o' their execution, I'll have you know.' Despite the cargo of whisky he'd consumed, the whole subject was enough to make him blush but he had to defend himself.

'Well, I'm heartily glad o' it. All you need to get on wae now is putting theory into practice. I'd a picture in my mind there o' me fairly having to lead you to the marital bed, a bit like the auld kings.'

'The auld kings? What capers were they up to?'

'There was no privacy in that job, man. You'd to get on wae it in full view o' the court. Imagine! A whole room full o' folk keeping you right at every turn, eh?'

Hamish shuddered. Though he wasn't prepared to admit it, the whole idea of an intimate interaction with a member of the opposite sex made him rather nervous. The very thought of having to share such activity under the scrutiny of his elders and betters was unimaginable.

As though he'd read his young charge's mind, Hoynes piped up. 'I know what you're thinking, Hamish. You're fair visualising Peeny and McKirdy standing over you in the throes o' passion, handing out helpful hints and tips, eh?'

'I was thinking nothing o' the kind, Sandy.'

'I widna worry too much aboot auld Andy Duncan. He's probably forgotten anything he knew aboot such things. I'm sure he'd be happier wae a good bowl o' soup than any cavorting. Come to think o' it, so would I – as long as it was a decent broth, mind you. I canna bear a weak, watery offering.'

'Can we change the subject, Sandy?'

'Of course. I was just making sure you were acquainted wae your duties as the man o' the house. It's good to know you've at least got some notion.'

'Have you drawn enough breath? We'll need to catch up with the rest.'

'There's plenty time, and in any case, we've no' far to go.'

The skipper and first mate of the *Girl Maggie* continued their slog up the winding path as an owl hooted plaintively in the woods beyond.

In a few more minutes, the path broadened out, and Hamish saw the rest of the party gathered in a small clearing, their oil lamps illuminating the scene with a warm, almost ethereal glow.

As he and Hoynes approached, Hamish could see two little stones. They were of an unusual shape – one like an oversized mushroom with a dimpled top, the other a more geometric shape, akin to a triangle. Though the latter was the bigger, neither of the tiny monuments were above knee height.

'Ah, there we are, the Auld Man and Woman – the Couple,' said Hoynes, a beatific smile spreading across his bearded face.

'They're no' exactly what I was expecting,' said Hamish.

Hoynes looked at him through narrowed eyes. 'Exactly what *were* you expecting? The Hanging Gardens o' Babylon? Stonehenge?'

'Maybe something bigger – a bit more dramatic?'

Hoynes shook his head. 'As you'll no doubt find out, size is of no consequence. These stones are older than you can even comprehend. Aye, and they have a power that is hard to explain.'

Hamish gazed at the Auld Man and Woman under the lamplight, then at his companions, who were all contemplating the stones with great reverence.

'Here,' said Peeny. 'There's something glistening on the auld fella.'

'Andy?' Danny blurted.

'Just you watch yoursel', son,' said Andy Duncan.

'No. Look.' Peeny bent over and picked an object from the smaller stone, which he examined at close quarters under the flickering light of his oil lamp. 'Damn me, I think it might be gold!'

Hoynes shouldered his way through to where Peeny was standing – the very mention of gold a magnet for his attention – and snatched the item from his companion's grasp. The object was only a few inches long, and though he'd suspected Peeny's gold was that of a fool, he soon realised his old friend was right. The thing shone in the dim light with a buttery glow that could only be that of the precious metal. Geometric shapes carved along its length looked like coiled snakes.

'Don't you have any ideas aboot pocketing that, Sandy,' said Peeny, aggrieved he'd been dispossessed of the item in such a brusque manner.

'It's a gold brooch,' declared Hoynes. He took in the swirling artistry engraved on the tiny piece of jewellery with wide eyes.

'Looks like it was only made yesterday,' said Peeny.

'That it does,' agreed Andy Duncan, now beside Hoynes and peering at the golden brooch through thick reading glasses. 'It's a right bonnie thing, so it is.'

The rest of the party huddled round, anxious to have a look at the curiosity.

'Must have been left by one of the Firdale boys. What do you think, Munro?' asked McKirdy.

'You must be doing better at the fishing in Kinloch than we are in Firdale. There's no' much gold to be had in oor village. And what there is stays firmly round the fingers o' married women.' Munro folded his arms in adamant dismissiveness.

Hoynes looked mesmerised. 'I've seen the like o' this before,' he said dreamily.

'Whereabouts? No' in the window o' Blue's jewellers in Kinloch, that's for sure. The man sells cheap tat,' said Malcolm Connelly.

'No, not at all.' Hoynes held the brooch in cupped hands to give every man a better view. 'I saw it in a book about the Vikings. I'd bet anything it's their work.'

'You'll be finished wae the fishing and getting a job at the British Museum then,' said Peeny sarcastically.

'Ow!' exclaimed Hoynes suddenly. He dropped the brooch like a hot coal.

'What on earth's wrong?' asked McKirdy.

'The damn thing burned me!' Hoynes blew on each hand to ease the pain.

'Your backside,' said Peeny. 'You should be on the stage, Sandy. Drama is never far off when you're around.' He bent forward and picked the brooch off the ground. 'See, not a problem, as cool as a cucumber . . . oh, you bugger!' He exclaimed as he, too, dropped the brooch and rubbed his hands with a grimace. 'You were right, Sandy. Hot as a fresh fish supper!'

They all regarded the golden object, now lying on the pine needles that covered the ground.

'Put it back on the stone!' said Andy Duncan in a commanding voice. 'That's where it was placed, and that's where it belongs.'

'Do it yourself. I'm no' burning my hands again,' said Peeny.

The old man knelt stiffly over the brooch, picked it up, and placed it carefully back in the bowl-like indentation on the stone. 'There, that's order restored. Now, let's be about our business, for the auld year is about to turn.'

20

Hamish was glad to have consumed a few drams as the old members of the party droned on with their toasts and mysterious incantations – mutterings that made little sense to him. He had been expecting something more raucous, more entertaining. Frankly, this was a disappointment.

He turned to young Danny. 'I was hoping for mair than this, eh?'

'You've to listen to what they're at, Hamish. My father says that we'll have to do this one day, and we should take note. He'd be up here himself if it wasn't for his hip.'

Hamish looked less than impressed by this point of view. He watched Andy Duncan, who appeared to be taking the lead in proceedings. 'Is he at the Gaelic?'

'I'm no sure,' said Danny. 'I canna understand a word o' it, to be honest.'

'We'll have a job remembering all this for when oor time comes, eh? I hope somebody has it all written down.' He shuffled from foot to foot uncomfortably. 'Here, will you hold my glass, nature is taking its course on my bladder. I'll nip into these trees for some relief.'

Handing his dram to his companion, Hamish made for the shelter of the fir trees. He reckoned that having a pee at such a sombre ceremony may be considered bad form, so he made sure he walked far enough into the forest so that he was well out of sight.

Though it was dark, and he could hear the sound of small creatures rustling through the woods, he carried on. Thankfully, the soothing balm of whisky had insulated him from the nerves he'd normally have experienced under such circumstances. He pressed on until he found a tree far enough away to be discreet. Hamish breathed a sigh as he relieved himself against the trunk. It was a damnable facet of enjoying a drink. The more you consumed, the more often you had to go.

The deed done, he was about to make his way back to the stones, when something caught his eye. Through the trees shone a light, green then red, seemingly swirling between the tall pines. Intrigued, Hamish made his way towards it.

One by one, each man pulled a half-bottle of whisky from his bag and poured it over the taller of the two stones. In the bowl of the other, on top of the gold brooch, they placed a coin.

Andy Duncan looked at Peeny with distaste as he laid down a ha'penny. 'Man, is that all you can manage? It's an insult to the auld fella, right enough.'

'I've a son still at home, if you remember. He was laid off by Martin the joiner last year, so every penny counts. It's the gesture that makes the difference, no' the sum, Andy.'

'If you say so.'

'Before the war we used to pour out a bottle, now it's a half-bottle. It's the same thing.'

'Rationing put a stop to that, Peeny. And besides, wae the price o' drink now, what wae taxes and all, I'm sure the stones are happy wae what they're given – adjusted for inflation, as they say on the wireless.'

'Good, so the same goes for currency.' Peeny smiled, happy that he'd made his point.

Young Danny made his way to the stones. With great reverence, he poured his whisky over the Auld Woman and placed a shilling in the bowl of the Auld Man.

'That's the spirit,' said Andy Duncan. 'No lack o' respect and generosity, son. It makes my heart glad.' Purposefully, he stared at Peeny.

'My faither says it's best to give what you can. The stones did him proud during his time at the fishing. He'll no' forget it, he says.'

'A grand sentiment, right enough. Your father was always a generous man – something that can't be said for every fisherman, sadly.' Andy Duncan shook his head.

Before Peeny could protest, Hoynes looked round the small party. 'Has anyone seen Hamish?'

'He left me his dram and telt me he was off for a pee, Mr Hoynes,' said Danny.

'When was this?'

'Och, a while now, come to think of it.'

It was Hoynes's turn to shake his head. 'He'll likely be lost amongst the trees. I better go and look for him. Young folk these days . . . Which way did he go?'

'Danny pointed to a break in the trees behind them.

'He can't have got far. I'll no' be long, gentlemen.'

Hoynes grabbed a rusty oil lamp and went in search of his first mate, quietly cursing as he did so.

For a while, the swirling red and green lights were elusive. But eventually, Hamish happened upon a clearing in the trees, just ahead of a point where the hill fell away. He looked to the sky in wonder. Curtains of red and green light were floating in the starry sky, changing shape and form in a mesmerising way. He'd heard tales of the Northern Lights, but apart from a green glow above Jura late one evening, he hadn't seen them – certainly not like this.

Hamish was so impressed that he decided to take a seat on the ground and study the whole phenomenon more closely. The lights in the sky were reflected in the waters of the sound, making the whole place look magical – enchanted – like a child's fairy tale. He'd been told that the Aurora Borealis was a common sight further to the north. But tonight Kintyre was being treated to the full display, as the sky above swirled and shimmered with vibrant colour.

For emergencies, he'd stashed away a hip flask of whisky in his pocket. He gulped down a dram, eyes still on the spectacle. Old fishermen chanting incantations over two wee stones was nothing compared to this.

For the first time on the trip, Hamish was glad he'd come along.

I hope Sandy's spied this, he thought to himself.

✧

Hoynes was now lost in a forest of thick, tall pines. Though the oil lamp afforded a little light in his immediate vicinity, it did nothing to aid a wider perspective. He looked above, noting no stars in the sky, and reckoned this was because the thick canopy of branches above him was obscuring any celestial light.

'Damn me, Hamish,' he swore to himself. 'I'll wring your neck when I find you.'

He stopped for a moment and considered his predicament. If he was to go on, he was sure to become hopelessly lost. In any case, he was sure even Hamish, dizzy as he was at times, wouldn't have trekked so far away from the stones just to answer the call of nature.

He turned on his heel and began to make his way back the way he was sure he'd come.

'Hamish!' he shouted at the top of his voice. But so dense was the forest, his voice seemed strangely muted –as though he was calling from under a thick blanket.

'Bugger!' he cursed again. 'You're for your jotters when we get back to Kinloch.'

Then, to his great dismay, the flame in his oil lamp began to gutter and fade. He turned the knob on the side of the lamp desperately, but nothing happened. However, touching its base, Hoynes noticed his hand was wet. The old lamp had been leaking oil. Slowly, despite his best efforts, the flame flickered once more and died.

Now he was in complete darkness.

21

Marshall had travelled the whole length of Arran, checking every nook and cranny with the cutter's powerful searchlight. They'd found nothing, apart from a young courting couple who had braved the cold night for the purposes of getting to know each other better in an old ketch. The pair looked shocked when they were illuminated by *Diane*'s bright beam. However, Cummings managed to quell their embarrassment with a quick chat about the weather and the offer of a packet of Woodbines.

'That's us by the King's Caves, sir. It looks as though Hoynes must have taken off somewhere else.' Cummings looked to his boss for further instructions.

Collector Marshall was busy staring at the sky. 'A wonderful display tonight, eh?'

'Aye, it is. I'd welcome the lights on most nights, but not so much on this one.'

'Why so?'

'Auld tales o' nonsense, I daresay. But they used to reckon that if the lights shone at Auld New Year, the laws o' nature somehow meant nothing. The dead and the living shared the same place. But you're no' a fan o' such fancies, are you, Mr Marshall.'

'Indeed I am not. I'm more a fan of catching miscreants. But, most regrettably, I think we've let one give us the slip this evening.' Thankfully, Marshall's righteous zeal had ebbed away the further down Arran's coast they had patrolled and the less likely it seemed that Hoynes was to be found. 'You don't think he made it round to the other side of the island without us noticing, do you?'

'He'd have to have had six engines to accomplish that, sir. From what I'm told, the one they have on the *Girl Maggie* isn't an up-to-date model. In fact, I'd go so far as to say that it's well past its best.'

'I just don't know.' Marshall thought back to the call he'd had the previous morning. It was after midnight now, and he'd been on the go without a break for far too long. Now that the adrenaline of the chase had dissipated, his eyes felt heavy, and he wanted nothing more than to get his head down for a few hours.

Spotting this, his first mate felt it appropriate to make a suggestion. 'Why don't you go to the cabin for a wee nap, sir? I can handle things up here. I've one notion o' a place we've no' explored.'

'Where's that?'

'A part o' the coast I heard about a long time ago when I was at the fishing. Back on the Kintyre side. They call it the Smuggler's Hole.'

'Now that's bloody appropriate. If Hoynes is anywhere, it'll be in that place. Though, for the life of me, I can't work out how he could have made it back to Kintyre with us hot on his heels.'

'These auld skippers are up to all sorts of tricks, sir. I wouldn't put anything past the man. You get below, and I'll be sure and wake you if we come up with anything.'

Yawning noisily, Marshall made his way from the bridge to seek the sanctuary of a short sleep and a break from thoughts of Sandy Hoynes.

✧

Though Sandy Hoynes wasn't a man prone to unmerited fear, he had to admit that being without a light, deep in a thick forest of trees and in a heavy frost, was something that left him rather unsettled. Not only that, he had lost all sense of direction and was worried that he'd become even more lost if he went in just about any direction.

Hoynes decided that the best course of action was to make for a gap in the pines, where at least he might be afforded a glimpse of the sky and some kind of orientation via the stars, with which he was well acquainted.

He moved slowly forward, hands held out before him, helping his navigation from tree to tree. The going was slow and hard, and his spirits were low. The enticing smell of pine resin was now overpowering, making his eyes water. His mouth – following a few whiskies – was dry. All told, he was as miserable as sin. A night of tales, drinking and old traditions ruined by his accident-prone first mate. He made a mental note to have Hamish paint the whole vessel when they returned to Kinloch. But a little voice in his head piped up with, 'If you make it back to Kinloch.'

After about twenty minutes of stumbling around in the dark, he decided to rest up. He eased his back down against a stout tree trunk and, shivering with cold, sighed deeply at his plight.

Meanwhile, with the Northern Lights having faded to little more than a fluorescent glow in the sky, their spell over Hamish weakened. He wasn't sure how long he'd been staring at the celestial display, but whatever time it was, he supposed that it was too long.

He stood up, turning his back on the sound and assessed the forest of trees through which he had come. Hamish stroked his chin, trying to decide by which route he'd arrived at this place. To aid this process, he took the flask from his pocket and took another draw of the whisky.

'I think that looks right,' he said to himself, squinting at a narrow path that disappeared into the trees.

Glad to be on the move, and buoyed by the spirit, he whistled a jaunty reel as he took off to find his companions.

Back at the stones, Andy Duncan was less than happy. Even the warmth of the whisky he'd consumed wasn't enough to keep the cold from making his old bones ache.

'We can only assume they've made their way back to bothy. Aye, and it's time we did likewise.'

There were general mutterings of agreement, for each of them was cold and wanted nothing more than to be by the warming fire of their temporary home for the night. Only young Danny demurred. 'They'll find it hard to survive the night in this cold, will they no'?'

McKirdy blew on his hands. 'None of us will survive if we don't get back into the warmth soon. Look at auld Andy. His face is blue. I swear I can see it fae here.'

'Can't we get help?' Danny was a thoughtful lad, having been brought up to look out for others by his fisherman father.

'What do you suggest? The RNLI?' Peeny sneered. 'They'll no' come trooping all the way up here. It's the sea for them, and I'm sure they've no forestry equivalent.'

'Sandy will turn up. A man like that has infinite wiles at his disposal,' said Malcolm Connelly. 'Man, he and Hamish are likely sitting by the fire in the bothy right now, wondering what's up wae us.'

'Right. So we head back,' said Andy Duncan through the chatter of his teeth.

They decision was made. With their oil lamps lighting the way, the party of fishermen headed away from the stones and back down the path, minus two of their number.

Danny caught up with Jim McMichael. 'What if the same thing that happened to thon MacEachran has befallen Mr Hoynes and Hamish?'

'Don't be daft, son. That's just a story. They'll be fine, you'll see. I've known Hoynes since I was a wean. It'll take more than a few trees and a cold night to do for him, let me assure you.'

All the same, Danny bit his lip in concern as they progressed down the hill, losing sight of the Auld Stones.

22

Collector Marshall's Dream

The gentle sway of the cutter lulled Marshall to sleep. He was stretched out along a bench seat in the small cabin below deck. As he drifted off, the irritation at not apprehending Sandy Hoynes was replaced by the muddled fancies of the world of dreams and the subconscious.

He was back on the bridge, alone, peering out into an impenetrable fog. Though no light could be seen, the intermittent drone of a fog horn could be heard, its lowing tone like some great beast lost in the darkness, warning wayward mariners off the rocks and skerries.

The vessel appeared out of the fog like a wraith. Though this craft had fine lines and looked of masterful build, it was ruined. The square sail, striped with red and white, was tattered and burned. It hung loosely in the dead calm. At the prow, a carved likeness of a snake was hanging, broken at its base. Sinews of pale, newly exposed wood cracked and creaked. A great gash in the hull was fortunately just above the waterline, though any persistent sea would surely sink her very quickly.

Fore and aft, tall braziers stood on stout poles. The fire that once blazed from them was now nothing but dying embers.

Wisps of fog clung to them like the thin fingers of a spirit intent upon pulling this fine craft into the other world, the dominion of death.

Along her side was a broken cluster of targes – round shields, split and broken, their centre bosses battered – the tattered remnants of defeat, trophies of failure.

For Marshall, the whole scene spoke of pride and power brought low, as the great buildings of the ancients were now nothing but ruins in shifting desert sands. The stench of death hung about this ghost ship like a curse.

He could see a man hanging over the side, long blond hair trailing into the water. Even in the dim light, the gash on his arm was black and livid, another on his shoulder deeper, almost severing the limb from his torso. Beside him, another man lay back at an impossible angle, a wicked sword piercing his neck from back to front, pinning him to the mast behind. His arms were spread out wide in death, as though he was imploring those who might have the power to do such things to bring him back to the life he loved.

Marshall wanted to scream, but no sound would come. He pulled at the wheel, anxious not to collide with this vision of hell and destruction. But the ruined boat seemed only to drift closer and closer.

He heard movement from behind and turned to call his first mate to his side. But the man who faced him wasn't Cummings. This dark-clad figure shimmered as though his body wasn't quite corporeal. Despite this, the black blood that ran down his face and the split in his skull looked all too real. Still, there was about him a glimmer of light, a flickering symbol of fading life.

The apparition stared at Marshall, flaxen hair streaked dark by gore. 'Why are you here?' The big man's voice was slow and accented, but Marshall could understand him well enough.

'It's you that shouldn't be here,' Marshall stammered.

The tall man bowed his head, his arms hanging loose at his side. Marshall noticed that one of his hands was missing; only the stump remained, dripping blood onto the wooden decking of the bridge. 'Then we are already passing into another realm. This is the Thin Place.' The voice was no more than a whisper, but in it was the loss of all hope. No despair, just the resignation of defeat, the surrender to the inevitable.

'Can I help you?' Marshall didn't know why he asked the question but felt compelled to do so; whether out of compassion or fear, he wasn't sure.

Black leather creaked as the apparition before him raised his head. His eyes were a piercing blue, his gaze so penetrating that Marshall held up a hand to shield his own eyes, fearing this man was looking into his soul.

'You and I are on a journey. Our paths have crossed, that is all. You find me as you find me. My journey is near its end, so I fear yours may be too. It's the only way I can explain us being together at this moment in time. Unless . . .'

Marshall gasped for air, as though he was being slowly strangled. 'I don't understand what you mean – unless what?'

His visitor laughed weakly. 'We all try to escape the end. I am lucky – I see mine coming. You, I think, do not see yours. But that is the way of things. There is nothing to fear, for nothing truly comes to an end. Life is only how we see ourselves at one point in time. There are many lives.'

He pointed a finger at Marshall. 'I have known you before, as you have known me. We will meet again, but we will never be on the same side. We will never be brothers, always enemies. Though there is more that binds us than mere enmity.'

'What – what binds us?' Marshall couldn't understand why he felt compelled to ask the things he did, but he uttered the words nonetheless.

'Eternity – eternity binds us for ever. You on one side, me on the other.'

'I've never seen you before, so how can we be bound by this *eternity*?'

'By a moment in time – by this moment – by every moment. We are of different worlds now, but those worlds are only separated by a whisper. They collide in places like this, and always do so for a reason.'

The image of the man before him was fading.

'See not only what is before you, but what lies behind and is yet to come.'

'You're talking in riddles!'

'Listen to the blood that flows through you. Because it has flowed for ever.' With that, the man disappeared like a clearing mist.

Marshall turned back to the wheel. Both vessels were about to collide. He fell to the floor and braced for the impact.

This time the scream came.

23

Hamish could smell smoke. He halted his progress through the trees and sniffed at the air like a dog. He was sure it came from the direction he'd been walking. The thought that the cosy little bothy may be nearby cheered him. His passage from the hill from which he'd watched the Northern Lights to this point had been a happy meander, whistling his favourite tunes and thinking on happy times past.

Hamish weaved his way between the pines. Then, sure enough, the trees began to thin and he found himself atop a little outcrop. Not far below, the bothy was picked out under the stars.

Hamish paused at the door and took a deep breath. The aroma of peat smoke and whisky was in the air, intermingled with pine resin and the tang of the sea. He was worried about his skipper, and how angry he'd be that his first mate had missed much of the ceremony at the Auld Stones. Being the polite man his mother had brought him up to be, he knocked on the door before throwing it open.

But the scene inside the bothy wasn't at all what he'd expected. All of the familiar faces looked grim, and all were directed at him.

'Where on earth have you been?' asked Andy Duncan, perched on a chair by the fire alongside Munro of Firdale.

'Och, I had to answer a call o' nature, but, damn me, did I no' get lost. But looking on the brighter side, I got a rare glimpse o' the Northern Lights. Just fair amazing, they were. The whole sky was dancing wae red and green. Like great curtains, it was. Just as I've heard them described. It made my night, and no mistake.' Hamish looked around for some appreciation of his tale, but there was none. Indeed, if anything, his companions bore even more disapproving expressions than they had when he'd first arrived.

'Well, I'm glad you had a good time,' said Peeny, staring at the floor.

'I'm right sorry to have missed the tribute to the stones. I know how much store yous all place upon it. But a man canna help getting lost, and that's just the fact o' it. Anyway, I'm back safe and sound, and there's bound to be many other years to be at this caper.' For the first time since entering the bothy, Hamish sensed that something was wrong. And whatever this something was, it wasn't just the matter of his missing the ceremony at the stones. 'Here, where's Sandy?' he asked, looking about the small space for his skipper.

'Man, you're quick off the mark, Hamish, eh? There you are, blethering on about lights in the sky, when all the time your skipper is missing, and only the good Lord knows where. Lost he is, off looking for you.' Andy Duncan shook his head.

'All this wae the Northern Lights. Have you been on they drugs?' Malcolm Connelly said. 'It's only a matter o' days since you were banging on aboot free love and that. I can only wonder at what your poor mother thinks of such capers.'

'But . . . where can he be?' Hamish stammered.

'Man, if we knew that, don't you think we'd be off and found him?' said Munro.

'You know this place, Mr Munro. Surely we can have a scout about and get a bearing on him?' Hamish looked desperate.

'I'm fae Firdale, that much is true. But you surely don't think I'm acquainted wae every tree and shrub in the place? Do you know much about the woodland around Kinloch? In any event, I'm a fisherman, no' a forest elf. Aye, and in case you've no' noticed, it's pitch-black outside, and damn well freezing into the bargain.'

'No man can last long in such conditions,' opined Jim McMichael. 'It's nothing short o' a miracle you made it back yourself.'

'We can't just sit here and do nothing!' wailed Hamish at the top of his voice.

'If there's no sign o' him at first light we'll fan out and search,' said Andy Duncan, clearly the self-appointed leader of the group due to his great age and the respect in which he was held. 'But I fear it's a corpse we're likely to find. There's no' a mair resourceful body than Sandy Hoynes, but even he can't defeat Mother Nature and her cold grasp.'

'We should say a few words to the Almighty,' said McKirdy. 'If this was happening at sea, we'd all be on oor knees in prayer. It's no different wae calamities on land, I'm thinking. I'm quite sure the dear Lord cares as much for those in peril in the woods as he does for those in a similar position on the waves . . . Though I know fine he's mair partial to seafarers,' he added to the general agreement of those gathered.

Solemnly, each man put down his dram and bowed his head in silent prayer for their missing companion.

Following a suitable period of silence, Andy Duncan spoke. 'It's the auld parable – *ninety and nine were safe in the fold, but one was lost in the hills* – or something o' that nature.'

'You're right, Andy,' said Munro. 'Though I canna just place what happened to the stray.'

There followed a heated discussion on biblical matters, which reached no conclusion other than no one could remember the fate of the lost sheep. McMichael had it roasted on a spit, until he was reminded that that was the fatted calf in an altogether different tale.

Hamish sat down heavily on an old chair. He remembered the time of his father's death, vividly remembering the feeling of utter despair, the ache in his heart that wouldn't go away.

Hamish reckoned that Hoynes was as close as any man could be to replacing his father, yet he felt nothing. Yes, he was worried for his skipper's wellbeing. But he had none of the gnawing sadness that had overwhelmed him before he knew his father was even ill. Hamish stood, and cleared his throat loudly, interrupting the ecumenical discussions taking place in the tiny bothy. 'He's fine, I just know he is,' he declared emphatically.

'This will be you at the second sight again?' said Peeny, an edge of sarcasm in his voice.

'It's just a notion – I have them from time to time.'

'Well, I hope it's better than your forecasting the day o' thon blizzards just before Christmas. As far as Sandy was concerned, all you predicted was a light flurry. It was the worst snow for twenty-odd years.'

'Sandy should have known better. The sight's no' designed for matters meteorological.' Hamish sighed and sat back in his chair, deep in thought.

Young Danny, feeling more empathy for his youthful colleague's plight than his elders, handed him a dram.

Hamish let the spirit warm him as he desperately hoped Sandy Hoynes would be the next to burst through the door.

24

Hoynes was chilled to the bone, miserable and – for maybe the first time in his life – losing all hope. He had wracked his brains to find a solution to his current predicament, but little had come to mind. He remembered a survival story from a book he'd read at school. The hero had found himself lost in the woods in freezing temperatures, just as he was now. But the construction of a turf shelter and the rubbing together of sticks to coax a fire into life, as good as it read on the page, seemed highly impractical when faced with the reality.

He could feel a terrible weariness settling in and recognised it for what it was. If he succumbed to sleep now, it would be a slumber from which he'd never wake.

Then, as he drew breath in through his nose one more time, he could smell it: the sea! And where the sea held dominion, no tree grew – or at least none he'd experienced in this part of the world. He would be free of the darkness, and by the light of the stars and the sickle moon make his way to safety. Hoynes forced his back off the tree trunk and sniffed at the air. The sea, he was certain, was to his left through the trees.

He moved from trunk to trunk, rough bark scraping his hands. He was aware that he was breathing heavily with excitement, so tried to measure it to slow down the thudding of his heart. The further he went, the less dark it became. Yes, he could see shadows now, the sharp outline of branches, the hulks of the trees themselves.

All of a sudden, the night opened out before him. Looking straight ahead, he took in the dark expanse of the sound, the twinkling stars above and the rippled shadow of a thin moon on the calm water.

Relief washed over him like a wave on a hot summer day. The fatigue disappeared in an instant, as, now free of the hampering pines, he took a great stride forward out of the forest's grip towards the element on which he'd spent most of his life.

But no ground met the sole of his boot. It was as though the world stopped for a moment. But that moment didn't last long. Hoynes felt the sickening pull of the abyss as he toppled forward into emptiness.

Cummings rushed into the cabin, concern etched across his face, a crew member behind him, bewildered. Marshall was curled up on one of the bench seats, screaming at the top of his voice.

'Sir! What on earth is the matter?' He placed his hand on Marshall's shoulder, but the collector brushed it away with such force that Cummings almost toppled over.

'Get away from me! Leave me alone – get back to your own world!' Marshall held his hands in front of his face like a boxer on the ropes, desperate to fend off blows from a superior opponent.

'Sir, it's me, Jocky Cummings. You must be having a nightmare.' As he said this, he was aware that crew member Jackson was gawping over his shoulder. He dismissed him without ceremony.

'What?' Marshall stared at Cummings as though he'd never seen him before, blinking in the dim light of the cabin.

'I think you've had a nightmare, sir. Nothing to worry about. We heard you screaming and feared the worst, but you're still hale and hearty.'

Marshall lifted himself off the bench and leaned against a table. He coughed and rubbed his eyes. 'Can't you smell it?'

'Smell what, sir?'

'The blood, man!' Marshall turned to face him angrily.

'There's no blood to be seen, sir. As I say, you've had a nightmare. Och, it sometimes takes a few moments to throw off the feeling. Just you sit down, and I'll get you some nice hot tea. That's bound to have you shipshape in no time.'

'Damn you and your tea and sympathy!'

'Sir?'

The look on Cummings's face was enough to bring Marshall back to something like himself. Though, in truth, he felt nothing like it. The vision of the ship and his encounter with the ghoulish apparition was all too fresh in his mind. He couldn't reconcile this experience with a dream – even a nightmare. It had all been so vivid – so real.

Marshall reached out and grabbed Cummings by the sleeve of his duffel coat. 'I'm . . . I'm sorry, Cummings. As you say, I must have drifted off and had a nightmare, eh?'

'Aye, that'll be right enough, Mr Marshall. No need to worry on my account. You sit back down. I'll have that tea with you in a jiffy.'

'Where are we?' Marshall sat back on the bench seat.

'As discussed, sir. We're not far from the Smuggler's Hole.'

'Where?'

'The place I reckon Hoynes might be hiding out. An old favourite of smugglers for hundreds of years, they say. Perfect. You can't see any boats berthed because of a big sandbar that obscures the bay. They say the Vikings built a settlement on the hill above. But I'm no' much for hill climbing, so I've never been there.'

'The Vikings, you say?' Marshall sounded suddenly anxious again.

'Aye, the very same. The Northmen settled most of Kintyre. A frightening bunch, they must have been.' Cummings immediately regretted what he'd said, as it seemed to have a most deleterious effect on the collector, who immediately held his head in his hands and groaned as though in pain. 'Sir?'

'Stay away from that bay, Cummings, do you hear me?' Marshall's voice was somehow both authoritative and uncertain at once.

'But we stand a good chance of catching Hoynes –'

'I don't care about Sandy Hoynes!' Marshall thumped the table with his fist. 'We anchor in the sound and make for Kinloch at first light.'

'I'm sorry, sir. I don't understand.'

'You don't need to understand, Cummings. Just do as you've been ordered!'

Cummings straightened up, bridling at Marshall's attitude. 'Very good, sir. We anchor off in the sound and make for Kinloch at dawn.' His voice was now clipped. The first mate turned on his heel and made to leave the cabin.

'Wait!' Marshall stopped him in his tracks.

'Yes, sir.' Cummings stood still, not turning to face his superior.

'I want to ask you something.'

'Go ahead, sir.'

'Have you ever heard of the Thin Places?'

Cummings turned slowly. Marshall was now looking at him with a pale and troubled expression. 'Indeed I have, sir.'

'What are they . . . it . . . whatever?'

'They are places where the past, present and future come close enough to touch, sir. Maybe even sometimes a bit more than that. Och, scientists and the like would have you believe that it's a lot of sheer nonsense. But I don't always hold with scientists. My guess is they'll soon work back to the way folk have thought for generations. There are many lives, many times – all within a whisper o' each other. It's what the auld folk here thought. Aye, and they knew mair than most, scientists or no scientists.'

'I see.'

'I'll away and get you that tea, sir.'

As Cummings made his way to the galley, he was sure that whatever Marshall wanted to call it, his experience hadn't been a nightmare. After all, in this place at this time of year, worlds came close. But, although he'd tried to make Marshall understand, it was a great leap of thought and reasoning for a man so steeped in logic and practicality. Still, that he'd had a taste of the Thin Places, Cummings was in no doubt.

25

Sandy Hoynes had always hidden a secret fear of falling. He supposed that, coming from a family that had spent so many generations at sea-level, it was natural to be mistrustful of heights. Yet, as these thoughts flashed through his mind, he could feel nothing beneath his feet but thin air.

He flailed desperately, trying to gain any purchase on shrub or rock to prevent his descent. He heard a roar – a cry of despair – and realised that the sound was coming from his own mouth. An image of his father, tall, strong and blond-headed. His mother's kind face smiling at him. The pet collie, Magnus, he'd had as a child, running towards him, big, wet tongue lolling. His life was passing before his eyes, just like the stories he'd heard of those nearing their end.

Time seemed to slow as he cast about wildly, trying to arrest his fall. Under the light of the stars, Hoynes saw his own arm arc above his head like the toppling of a steeple, and just as he felt his last hopes fade, he felt pressure on his right hand, then an iron grip. The next sensation was one of being pulled up, away from the abyss into which he was tumbling.

Before he knew it, Hoynes found himself lying on his back, choking and spluttering, trembling from head to toe in shock.

'You are a man who needs to be rescued often, I think.' The odd-sounding voice boomed above him.

Hoynes squinted into the darkness, still gasping for breath. 'I canna quite make you out, sir. But I'm right grateful to you. You wouldna happen to have some baccy on you, by any chance?'

A guffaw echoed above the crashing tide. The man – Hoynes's saviour – leaned down and looked him straight in the eye. 'I see you are no worse for your adventures.' The figure with the long, plaited blond hair and beard smiled. He was surrounded by a colourful glow that shimmered in the darkness like a guttering candle.

Hoynes gulped. Although the sight of the man who'd saved him brought fear to his heart, it was somehow comforting. 'It's yourself, Hona,' he replied, as though addressing one of his old cronies from the Kinloch fishing fleet.

'You remembered my name! This is very good. Though I wasn't sure I'd see you again so soon, I knew our paths were bound to cross. The connection we have is strong – even across so very many centuries.'

'I still canna understand. I know who you are – I read about you in a book from the library.' Hoynes realised how ridiculous this sounded as soon as he said it. Here he was – again – face to face with a man who died so, so long ago. But, that conundrum aside, Hona had saved his life – of that there could be no doubt.

Hona stood to his full height, towering over the recumbent Hoynes. 'I remember standing on this very spot when I saw the great silver bird in the sky.' He looked heavenward through the darkness, as though the image was above him. 'I knew it was not from my time. But then, I knew that time is nothing we can grasp or feel – it just is. It is all around us every day of our lives and beyond, yet can we hold it in our hands? No. I know in your heart that you, too, feel the pull of the Thin Places.'

Hoynes pushed himself up onto his feet. The shivering dread he'd experienced was gone now. Though the man before him was almost a foot taller than himself, he recognised the blue eyes that he'd noticed when the *Girl Maggie* was hopelessly lost in the blizzard only weeks before. 'There's so much I don't understand,' he said – meaning every word.

'It is not for us to understand, it is enough for us to be.' He looked around. 'Your little bothy is where my great hall once stood. Those nights, how I miss them.'

'So, where are you now?'

'I know not. I have passed into another realm and nothing remains the same, yet it is what is meant to be. We never disappear; our blood travels on. The blood in your veins is the same blood that is in mine. Always remember that, and never fear the end, for there is no end.'

Hoynes opened his mouth to speak, but already the image of the man clad in dark leather was fading. 'You don't hang about, eh?'

The shadow of his rescuer threw back his head and his laughter rang out once more, though it seemed more distant now, like an echo in a deep valley.

'I'm still no' sure where I'm going!' shouted Hoynes, suddenly realising that, despite his ghostly deliverance, he had no idea how to get back to the bothy. But the shadow had faded into nothing.

Hoynes stepped forward gingerly and inclined his head over the edge of the cliff. The drop was sheer and unforgiving. He swallowed hard and pictured his broken body lying on the jagged rocks far below. 'Aye, you're a lucky bugger, so you are, Sandy.' Though he wasn't sure if luck really covered what had just happened to him.

He looked left and right, puzzling on which way to go, in order to find his way back to the bothy. Behind him lay a thick pine forest.

Then, he heard the beat of wings. As he looked out over the sound, hovering in the air was a huge gull. It squawked loudly, regarding him with a beady eye, and then circled in the air, before flying straight ahead, a cry in its wake.

'Right. Good stuff. I know the score fae here. I'll just follow you.'

Being very careful where he trod, Hoynes skirted the clifftop, following the great seagull. Though it soared high above him, the bird was always close enough to see in the starlight. Its cry echoed again in the cold night air.

26

Back at the bothy, the mood was a sombre one, to say the least. Hamish had retreated to the darkest corner of the room, where he sat on the floor, hands clasped round his knees. He had neither a pipe of tobacco with which to ponder nor a glass of whisky to ease his sore heart. For there was no relief from the guilt he felt.

The older men in the party were sipping at their small glasses, huddled round the blazing fire. They knew that the revelry that had been planned was now at an end, for as soon as first light dawned, the search for Sandy Hoynes must commence.

'It's been a dark night indeed,' said old Andy Duncan, shaking his head. 'I wouldna be surprised if this is the last time anyone visits the stones to bring in the Auld New Year.'

'Why so?' asked young Danny.

'The whole experience will be forever tainted by the death o' Sandy Hoynes,' said McKirdy. 'What man could derive pleasure from this night in years to come? The thoughts will all turn to Hoynes. It'll put a right gunker on any celebration.'

'We don't know he's deid yet,' came a tremulous voice from the back of the room.

'This will be you with the sight again, eh, Hamish?' scoffed Peeny. 'As you'll hopefully come to understand with the passing years, practicality is what will keep you alive, no' some bloody nonsense that only exists in your own head.'

Hamish turned his face to the wall and said no more, though in his heart he could feel that his skipper wasn't dead. But there was no point arguing with such intransigent men as Peeny and McKirdy.

McMichael stared into the flames of the fire. '"Nearer My God To Thee", that was his favourite hymn.'

'Och no,' said Andy Duncan. 'When I was standing beside him at the Highland kirk at poor Tam Hastie's funeral he was fair belting out "Amazing Grace". Like an opera singer, he was. Well, maybe the odd waver on the higher notes noo and again, but the gusto was there, no doubt about it.'

'Nah. "Eternal Father Strong To Save," that's the one,' said McKirdy. 'No man o' the sea should be lowered doon to anything else; it stands to reason.'

'Aye, but the words are "for those in peril on the sea",' said Peeny. 'That hardly fits when you've frozen to death up in the woods, does it?'

'I've always liked "The Old Rugged Cross",' opined Malcolm Connelly. 'After all, he's likely perished on a hill far, far away.'

There seemed to be a general consensus around this choice being the most fitting. But the whole subject sickened Hamish to the stomach. 'That's it! I've had enough. I'll leave yous to get busy wae picking the floral arrangements and deciding on the purvey. I'm off to look for Sandy – dark or no dark.'

'Don't be a fool, Hamish,' said Andy Duncan. 'They trees are packed tighter than sardines. We'll be choosing hymns for you if you go out there.'

'Well, it's better than sitting here with a bunch o' auld ghouls. I'll take a stout lamp and plenty o' baccy – I'll be fine.' Then, in an afterthought: 'I'd be obliged if someone would lend me an extra coat, mind you. Two's better than one in this temperature.' Hamish jutted out his chin determinedly.

'I'll come with you,' said Danny, anxious to show some solidarity with his young companion. 'It'll be safer if one of us ends up in trouble.'

Peeny looked at McKirdy and shook his head. 'We canna let these boys go back oot in that cold alone.'

'You're right,' said McKirdy. 'Though it's a fool's errand, mark my words. Who's going to choose all our hymns? For the record, I'm in favour o' just a few sandwiches and tea. Man, you go to some funerals and it looks like a baking competition. Keep it simple, that's my motto.'

'Aye, and cheap,' said Malcolm Connelly. 'There's bound to be plenty pockets sewn into your shroud, and no mistake.'

'Well, I'm away, whatever yous think.' Hamish was searching about for another coat.

'Haud your horses, son,' said Andy Duncan. 'I'm too old for this caper, and so is Munro here. But if the rest o' you men feel that getting oot now to look for Hoynes is the right thing, then it must be done.'

'It's fine for you, Andy. Sitting beside the fire wae a dram when you know we're all risking oor lives,' said Peeny.

'If it was a man overboard in a heavy sea, you wouldna hesitate,' replied Duncan, nodding sagely.

This point was received with quiet agreement. While men of the sea would think nothing of mounting a rescue on their own element, the thought of heading into a dark, impenetrable forest was an alien concept.

'Let's get kitted out. Andy has the right o' it,' said McKirdy.

Slowly, reluctantly, the fishermen dragged themselves away from the warmth of the fireside and set to the task of filling oil lamps and shrugging on thick duffel coats and gloves. The odd glass of whisky was drained and the last puff of a pipe taken. But soon, with scarves wrapped around their faces, the attempted rescue of Sandy Hoynes was set to begin, regardless of how foolhardy the majority of those taking part thought the whole venture.

Munro and Duncan looked them up and down from their perch by the fireside.

'Aye, a right noble thing it is to see such brave men go about saving one of their own,' said Munro. 'I'll raise the Firdale men at first light, have no fear o' that.'

McKirdy swore under his breath as Hamish headed for the door. 'Here goes nothing,' he said to Peeny, who returned the sentiment with a raised eyebrow.

Hamish opened the door and took a step back, his mouth gaping open.

'What on earth is wrong wae him, noo?' said Andy Duncan, whose view of the doorway was obscured by well wrapped-up fishermen.

At that moment, a bulky figure with a blue face and frost encrusting his white beard staggered into the room.

'Sandy!' exclaimed Hamish, a broad smile on his face.

'Och, I knew he would be just fine,' said Andy Duncan levelly, taking a draw on his pipe.

'I take it there's a dram on the go?' said Hoynes through chattering teeth.

27

'I'm telling you, that's what happened,' said Hoynes, now sitting by the fireplace and wrapped up in numerous coats and scarves that made his already rotund figure look almost spherical.

'You're no' in your right mind wae the cold, Sandy,' remarked Andy Duncan. 'You take your time and sip at that hot toddy and get the warmth o' the fire. You'll soon regain your senses and wish you never came oot wae such nonsense.'

The old radio was crackling in the corner, though the music wasn't to the taste of most of those gathered, Danny having tuned it to Radio Luxembourg. To the strains of the Troggs' 'Wild Thing', Hoynes shook his head emphatically. 'Och, yous know nothing aboot it. One minute I was plunging to my death, the next I was dragged back to the land o' the living by something I'll never be able to explain.'

'I'm thinking you'll need to pay a visit to Doctor Fraser when we get back,' said Peeny. 'It might be the cold fair jumbling up your brain, but it could just as easily be the whisky.'

'What are you saying?' said Hoynes indignantly.

'We all like a wee goldie noo and again, Sandy. But you've developed a right habit o'er the last few years. We've a' noticed it.' Malcolm Connelly looked deadly serious.

'The cheek o' you! Man, it's only last year you got so drunk the polis had to take you hame. Aye, and you tried to evade justice by climbing up a lamppost on Long Road. Calling the constable every name under the sun, you were – aye, and some well beyond it, too.'

'My auntie had just died. It was all part o' the grieving process. That's what the GP said.'

'Oh aye. That could be a reasonable excuse, apart fae a couple o' wee issues,' said Hoynes. 'For one, your auntie died the year before, and you hadn't seen her since you were about three years old. Fair enough, it's bad luck to be trampled to death by a rogue herd of kangaroos, but the woman did move to Australia. She knew the risk. Spiders coming shooting oot o' the toilet when you're about your business. The place is fair stowed wae the deadliest o' beasts.'

Those gathered ruminated on this horror for a moment.

'Och, the whole tragedy o' it all just hit me that night.'

'Sure it did.' Hoynes took another sip of his toddy. 'But if every time a body who lost a relative in tragic circumstances took off up a lamppost, where would we be, eh? Man, the polis would have to be on it full-time. Criminals would be running amok.'

Andy Duncan piped up. 'I think it's fair to say, Malcolm, that the day you took to the drink was when big Campbell the lawyer telt you that instead o' the fortune you were hoping for in the poor woman's will, all you got was a painting o' Canberra and an ornamental boomerang. Is that no' right?'

Connelly looked mildly put-out by this. 'It was a bit o' a surprise, I'll admit. We'd all thought she'd done well for herself doon under. Though, I'd say the most disappointing aspect o' the whole thing was the only time I threw the bloody thing it near knocked Michael Kerr's heid off and flew oot over the loch. The bugger made no attempt to come back.'

This revelation was again met with a contemplative silence for a few moments.

McKirdy, being the diplomat he wasn't, decided to pour oil on troubled waters. 'Well, we all have problems in life. Sandy might think he's been rescued by Thor, and you've hellish problems wae boomerangs, but everyone is in one piece. We should be thankful.'

Both Hoynes and Connelly glared at McKirdy.

'Here, I'm no' so sure it's a "herd" o' kangaroos. That's surely reserved for coos, sheep and the like, is it no'?' said Hamish thoughtfully.

As a grey dawn broke over the sound, the Revenue cutter made for port at Kinloch in order to refuel.

Marshall, having spent much of what was left of the dark hours of night fretting in the cabin below decks, was now back on the bridge. Clean-shaven, straight and tall in his uniform, he was an altogether different specimen from the one who'd screamed and raved in his sleep only a few hours before.

'No' so bonnie today, sir,' said Cummings, manning the wheel as they sailed past the island and into the loch. The sky was heavy with cloud.

'Indeed not. We'll berth here until tomorrow – let the lads have some rest. It was a long night, Mr Cummings, was it not?'

'Aye, sir, it was that.' Cummings eyed his superior intently. 'And how are you feeling this morning, sir?'

'Never better. Tip-top, in fact.' He moved closer to his second-in-command. 'I trust we can keep my little nightmare between ourselves?'

'I've forgotten all about it already, sir.' Cummings looked straight ahead, his manner steadfast and reassuring. 'Mind, the lads could maybe do wae a bit R&R when we get to Kinloch, sir.'

'Yes, yes, of course.' Marshall coughed with embarrassment, realising that his odd behaviour had been witnessed by other members of the crew. He delved into his pocket and produced a wallet, from which he extracted a large, white five-pound note. 'They should be able to dine well on that, and enjoy a few libations into the bargain, eh, Jocky?'

'The very thing, right enough, sir. I'll make sure they know where it came from.'

'Excellent. Well, as soon as we tie up at the pier at Kinloch, I'll pay a visit to my old colleagues at Customs House. They tell me old McGregor is still in post, though he must be nearing retirement by now.'

'He is that, sir. A gentleman, too, I must say. Always a good bottle in his drawer, if you know what I mean?'

'Oh yes, that much I do remember.' Marshall nodded in agreement as they neared the twin piers at Kinloch.

28

It would be fair to say that those gathered in the bothy slept through much more of the morning than was their habit. But, being the fishermen they were, and despite some sore heads and dry mouths, by nine o'clock, one by one, they began to wake – apart from Andy Duncan who, the years and whisky having taken their toll, slumbered on, head tipped back and mouth gaping on his chair.

Hamish leaned across to Hoynes, who was drinking his habitual pint of morning coffee. 'Here, dae you think auld Andy is still in the land o' the living? He's no' moved for ages, and I canna even see any sign o' him breathing. I've been taking note this wee while.'

Hoynes, still wrapped up in several coats and a blanket, made his way between his companions, all in various stages of wakefulness, and stood over Andy Duncan. 'Man, it's hard to tell, right enough. What a tragedy that would be, eh? This trip has been ill-fated fae the start. The last thing we need is the auld fella hauling in his last net.'

Hamish and Hoynes's interest in Duncan prompted Peeny and McKirdy to sidle over to investigate.

'What's up?' said Peeny, stifling a yawn.

'It's Andy. He's no' moving. Aye, and I'm no' sure I like the colour o' him, neither. His face is as pale as the driven snow.'

'You're right,' said McKirdy. 'What a time this would be to lose a man like himself.'

Hoynes stroked his white beard for inspiration. 'This needs careful handling. Any sudden shock could be enough to stop his heart, a man o' his age.'

'You're right, Sandy,' said Peeny. 'You'll need to be right gentle, but we canna all stand here wondering if the poor bugger is deid or no.'

'You're no' often right, but you are on this occasion, Peeny. Leave this to me.' Hoynes leaned into Andy Duncan's ear, ready to whisper a gentle wake-up call.

'He's no' going to kiss him, is he?' whispered McKirdy.

Hoynes turned to face him, his expression showing little amusement. He quickly turned his attention back to Duncan, his mouth only an inch or so away from the older man's ear.

'Mind, he's quite deaf noo, Sandy. You'll need to give it a wee bit o' vent or we'll be none the wiser.'

This time, Hoynes decided not to turn round. He opened his mouth and was about to whisper into Andy Duncan's hairy left ear, when the old man's eyes shot open and he turned to face Hoynes with a blood-curdling scream.

Hoynes took two steps back, stumbling over Peeny and McKirdy's feet. 'Bugger me, Andy. You near gave me apoplexy!' Hoynes wiped his brow free of cold sweat with the back of his hand.

Duncan was breathing heavily, glaring at the figures standing over him. 'It's like a night oot wae the Munsters. What on earth were you trying to do, kill me? What poor soul wants to wake up wae your big coupon inches fae his face?

You look like Santa wae malicious intent.' Duncan held his hand to his chest as he tried to slow his breathing.

'Hang on, we might no' be out o' the woods yet,' said Peeny, taking in the pale-faced, gasping older man.

Duncan's reply was as unrestrained as it was curt.

Soon the company, amidst cups of tea and black coffee, were getting their kit together, ready to leave the Auld Stones for another year.

Young Danny was tasked with cleaning out the fireplace, while Hamish was set to work with a broom on the wooden floor. In no time at all, the bothy looked spick and span, and the weary mariners were ready to make their way back to the *Girl Maggie* and sail to Kinloch.

'That's a year we'll no' forget in a hurry,' said McKirdy as they made their way in single file down the steep path towards the Smuggler's Hole.

'Sandy won't forget it, anyway,' replied Peeny. 'Will you have us all rowing back hame? I know they Vikings liked a set of oars.' He winked at McKirdy.

Though Hoynes chose not to reply, he did address Hamish in quiet tones. 'Don't you be falling flat on your face like you did on the way here. This mob are on our tail wae their poor attempts at humour.'

They made their way along the sandbank and, with the rope ladder deployed over the side of the *Girl Maggie*, were all quickly aboard.

The grey water stirred as Hamish coaxed the engine into life, and Hoynes expertly steered his vessel out of the sheltered bay and into the sound.

✧

Marshall's visit to Kinloch's Customs House hadn't been the nostalgic return he'd hoped for. McGregor, the local officer and once his superior, was old and jaded, more than ready for retirement. Marshall could sense that his old mentor resented his visitor's rank, and the reception was polite but frosty. The 'good bottle' that Cummings had mentioned was not forthcoming.

'You were after Hoynes, I hear,' said McGregor, nursing a cup of tea.

'Well, we had information that proved to be inaccurate, to be exact.'

'Aye, I daresay. You have to be up early to catch the tide before Hoynes does. But, mind, he can be careless. When you keep getting away wae it, well, it makes you a bit complacent. Well worthwhile having a look at the boat before you go.'

'I've no idea when he'll be back. We're staying in port today. But duty calls, back in Glasgow.'

McGregor leaned back in his chair, looking across the green and the harbour beyond. 'I'd say that was the *Girl Maggie* at the pier now.'

Marshall bounced to his feet and rushed to the window. 'You're right! You'll have to excuse me. I want to have a little chat with Mr Hoynes.'

Without taking the time to look round the office where his career had begun, Marshall shot out of the room and quickly strode across the harbour green, the pier in his sights.

Their short journey had been uneventful and, with a fishing boat full of tired revellers, the banter conspicuous by its absence.

'No' so smart wae their tongues right noo,' said Hoynes from the wheelhouse to Hamish at his side. He was watching Peeny and McKirdy gather up their belongings, ready to disembark. 'It'll be dark early in their hooses, of that I'm sure.' Hoynes turned the wheel, coaxing his vessel next to the pier. 'You jump-to and tie her up, Hamish. I want to see if I can find my pipe.'

Hamish was over the side and securing a sturdy hawser round a bollard when he became aware of a pair of feet beside him.

'You – are you a member of the crew of this vessel?' The man in the distinctive Customs uniform addressed Hamish sharply.

'I am the first mate, sir. Can I help you at all?'

'You can indeed, young man. I want to have a look at your hold.'

Hamish felt a momentary twinge of terror quickly followed by relief at the thought of the cargo they'd carried away from Kinloch the previous day. 'I'll give the skipper a shout.'

'Never mind that. I don't need your skipper's permission to examine this vessel. Her Majesty's writ is long, you know. Please move aside while I board.'

Doing as he was told, Hamish stood back as Marshall deftly boarded the *Girl Maggie*.

The boat's passengers looked on with distaste as the collector hurried to the hold. Though he glanced at the wheelhouse, there was no sign of Sandy Hoynes.

By the time Hamish boarded the vessel and got to the wheelhouse, Marshall had opened the hatch and was making his way into the hold down a steep ladder.

'Sandy, the Revenue is aboard. He's away into the hold!' Hamish was breathless.

Hoynes shrugged his shoulders. 'If he's looking for fish, he'll no' find many.'

'It's no' fish he's after, skipper. You know fine what he'll want. We had a narrow escape last night – don't ask me how – but he's back on oor tail.'

'Good luck to the man. Now let me find my pipe!'

Hoynes's attitude calmed Hamish. But soon that calm turned into terror as Peeny called out from the prow, 'Sandy! Hamish! Your man's found something in the hold. He's examining it on the port side. Looks like a lemonade bottle.'

Hoynes shot up from the deck of the wheelhouse like a Jack-in-the-box. 'Make way, Hamish. This could mean trouble. It was dark when we were about oor business last night. I should have checked the hold for strays.'

A small crowd had gathered round Marshall as he examined the bottle under the grey sky.

'What's the meaning of this?' said Hoynes. 'You have no right to board a man's boat without the courtesy of informing the skipper.'

Without taking his eyes from the lemonade bottle full of whisky, Marshall replied, 'On the contrary, I have the right to do what I want.' He unscrewed the top of the bottle and sniffed at its contents. 'A good malt whisky, I'd say. The lab in Glasgow will confirm that, I'm sure. Any idea what it's doing in a lemonade bottle?'

By this time, Hoynes had made his way through the gathering and was standing next to the collector. 'Och, just an accident wae the proper bottle. I decanted it into that one. It's a sin to waste good whisky, so it is.'

For the first time, Marshall removed his gaze from the bottle and looked into Hoynes's face. He was about to open

306

his mouth to speak when he caught sight of the skipper's piercing blue eyes. He tottered backwards. 'It can't be ... no, it's not possible!' He backed away from Hoynes as though he'd set eyes on the Devil himself.

'The man's notorious, right enough. What have I been telling you all these years?' said Peeny. 'Aye, you've got to have some reputation to put the wind up a Revenue officer like that.'

'I can explain,' said Hoynes. He reached out for the bottle, but Marshall backed away.

'Leave me alone. I'll call the constable – I mean it!' There was a genuine look of panic in his eyes.

'Now, wait a minute. If you're no' careful, you'll ...' It was too late. Marshall had retreated at such a rate that he collided with the port side of the *Girl Maggie*. He teetered for a while, desperately trying to regain his balance, but it was not to be. The collector fell backwards over the side, still clutching the lemonade bottle full of whisky.

29

Without a thought, Danny O'May dived over the side and, after a few seconds submerged under the cold oily waters of the loch, reappeared holding the collector by the collar of his sodden duffel coat. Peeny, just as quick to the task at hand, threw a lifebelt into the loch, while Hamish brought the rope ladder and extended it down the side of the *Girl Maggie*. He leaned over and, with the help of McMichael and a boathook, hauled both Marshall and O'May aboard.

Hoynes eyed the collector as various members of the party fussed over him. 'You seem to have lost your bottle, sir.'

Marshall looked back at him fearfully. 'Keep away from me!'

'Och, he's no' that bad – you get used to him,' said McKirdy.

'Can't you see his eyes, man – pure evil! I've seen those eyes before!'

'He can be a bit o' a scunner, I agree,' said Andy Duncan. 'But I wouldna go so far as to say he was evil.'

'The man's suffering from concussion,' said Hoynes. 'Hamish, you get over to the harbour master's office and phone an ambulance. A doctor is required, and no mistake.'

Making sure there were bodies between himself and Hoynes, Marshall began to wail. 'You've two hands!'

'Aye, I've always had the two hands, right enough,' Hoynes replied.

Marshall looked around the gathering. 'I want you all to see justice done here! That bottle must be retrieved, and this man must be brought to justice.'

'I'm thinking that won't stand up in court,' said Hoynes with a beatific smile. 'You'd have to dredge the loch. And in any case, there will be bottles o' all descriptions under there. You'll be hard pressed to identify the one you found on my vessel.'

The fishermen looked on as Marshall was stretchered into an ambulance, still raving and wailing in equal measure.

The excitement over, but not without reference to Hoynes's luck, the men who'd been to the Auld Stones drifted away, leaving only Hamish and Hoynes on the *Girl Maggie*.

'What on earth do you think was wrong with him?' said Hamish.

'Looked to me like one o' they nervous breakdowns. These high-flyers are prone tae such events, so I'm told. All that success goes to your head.'

'Aye, but we were lucky, eh?'

'Luck had nothing to do wae it. We were just bringing thirsty men a drink, as I've told you all along. Anyway, Hamish, you better get home. No doubt you'll have some free love to be at.'

Not willing to enter into another debate on the subject, Hamish made his way onto the pier and headed into town.

Hoynes, still determined to find his pipe, lit a match and knelt down on the wooden decking of the wheelhouse.

He cursed as, one by one, the matches burned down to his fingers and he had to light another one.

Just when he was down to his last match and about to give up, the flickering light caught something small and shiny.

'Aye, just the ticket. I knew I'd find it,' Hoynes said to himself.

But it was no briar pipe that Hoynes trawled from the deck. He stood up and examined the item. Nestled in his palm was the same brooch he'd seen at the Auld Stones. On that occasion it had burned his hand. This time, it was cool to the touch. He looked closer, admiring the swirling design of a longship with a snake's head, swirls and swords engraved expertly into the beautiful buttery gold.

'Thank you, Hona,' he said, grasping the small piece of jewellery in his meaty fist. 'I hope to see you again soon.'

From the leaden sky, a huge gull swooped over the *Girl Maggie* then circled back to head for the hills beyond, its cry echoing around the masts and hulls of the fishing boats nestling in Kinloch harbour.

Epilogue

1912

The boy panted as he tried to keep up with his father's long stride. The hill was steep, and the footholds that had been worn into it over the years were too far apart to be of use to his little legs.

Finally, his father stopped, held out a hand and pulled his son up the last part of the hill.

'That's us, son. Now follow me.' The man walked towards two small stones sitting in splendid isolation on the bare hillside.

'Is that the Auld Man and Woman, Father?' the little boy asked, his flaxen hair bright in the summer sun.

'Aye, there you are. This is them, right enough.'

Young Sandy Hoynes took in the objects with interest. 'They're no' very big, eh?'

'Don't worry aboot the size, son. Just you do what we said.'

Sandy thrust his hand into the pocket of his shorts and produced a silver pin.

'That's it, you know what to be at.'

The boy approached the stones and, in the one with the bowl-like depression, he carefully placed the pin.

311

'There, you see. You look after these stones, and they'll look after you. They've watched o'er oor family for generations – longer than anyone can remember. Aye, and mind how I showed you how to sail safely into the wee bay? It'll see you right one day.'

Young Sandy Hoynes smiled up at his father and followed his line of sight out across the sound. He felt warm inside, for there was something about this place that felt like home.

Ghosts *in* The Gloaming

In memory of every soul who set sail never to return.

Every new beginning comes from some other beginning's end.

Seneca

Prologue

Kinloch, June 1920

The morning had dawned bright and warm. After the unremitting hell of the war years, the place was finally getting back to the old, much-loved traditions, resurrected and ready to be enjoyed by the good folk of the town.

Young Sandy Hoynes, flushed with success following his successful navigation exam at the Ministry of Agriculture and Fisheries, stood on the pier. He couldn't wait for the fancy certificate to arrive, so that he could frame it on the living-room wall at his parents' home. A pair of stout oars were cradled in the crook of his right arm. The sun shone on his golden hair, as the summer breeze tugged a strand across his tanned face. For the sixteen-year-old boy life was good – very good. He took in the scene before him through blue, blue eyes, smiling benignly at all around.

It was nearly midday, and hundreds of grinning, laughing, happy people thronged the harbour, awaiting the fun and frolics the day was sure to provide. For Kinloch stayed true to its seafaring traditions. Elsewhere, there were Highland games, with hammer throwing, caber tossing, tug o' war and the like. But this community enjoyed its sport on the blue waters of the loch. For them, there was no challenge like a maritime one. The air was heavy with the smell of beer, whisky and tobacco smoke, and the enticing aroma of sweetmeats being sold from stalls drifted along the promenade. After such dark days, and so many lost souls, this was akin to rebirth.

'That tub won't make it to the island and back,' said a dour-faced lad. He nodded to the rowing boat that Sandy and his father had built with such love, care and pride over the last two years.

'Your backside, Dreich MacCallum,' Sandy replied, eyeing his critic with a flashing dislike. Though the lad – a year older than Sandy – stood tall, he was painfully thin. He was known to everyone as 'Dreich', after the good old Scots word for grey, rainy, miserable weather, and suited the moniker perfectly. He had little to say that wasn't fault-finding or dismissive of others, and Sandy couldn't remember ever seeing him smile.

'My faither says that you and your old man can't mend a net, never mind build a boat,' Dreich continued.

'Does he now? But you think that leaky old sieve of yours will stay afloat until we're out of the harbour? Man, it looks as though it's leaning to port, as it is,' said Sandy. Sure enough, the venerable rowing boat that Dreich MacCallum was to use in the race to the island and back appeared to have a distinct list to starboard.

'I'll bet you tuppence it does!'

'You're on.' Sandy spat on his hand, and the pair shook on it. 'Mind you, if you do win, it'll be consolation for failing your navigation exam – again.' Sandy grinned at Dreich, taking him in from the corner of his eye.

'I did not fail!'

'Auld Watson the clerk said you did. He told my father.

Man, they were having a right good laugh aboot it at the Douglas Arms just last night, apparently. You'll be thirty before you pass, so they're saying.'

It was true to say there were challenges surrounding the award of a navigation certificate in Kinloch. Only five such qualifications were handed out per year, based on the top papers returned. It was also true to say that, if one was fortunate enough to sit the exam during a dearth of sufficiently bright mariners, the chances of being successful rose exponentially. But that was just the way it was.

Dreich furrowed his brow, a wicked sneer playing across his lips. 'Och, we'll just need to wait and see, Sandy Hoynes. I hear the certificates will be out soon.'

Just as Sandy was about to reply with a witty remark, a whistle blew, and the competitors were called to their positions. The rules were simple: when the starting pistol sounded, each lad, oars in hand, had to race down the steps at the corner of the harbour, get into their rowing boat, and set off. The winner would be the first oarsman who managed to round the buoy near the island at the head of the loch and make it back across the finishing line, a notional one between Kinloch's two piers.

'Good luck to you all!' shouted harbour master Johnson. He hefted the starting pistol in the air. There followed a tantalising wait before a sharp report sounded, the crowd cheered, and ten young men pelted down the slick steps, then waded out to their boats.

Young Billy Duncan was unlucky straight away. He took a tumble and emerged from the still waters of the loch with a bloody gash to his right elbow. The rest, however, made it safely into their boats, and with much plunging of oars, jostling, and one or two oaths, set off like a small flotilla in the foaming water.

Beyond the protective arms of the harbour, the going became more troublesome. The sea was choppy despite the light breeze. The churning produced by so many sets of oars working away in such close proximity ensured that each young man must pay close attention, lest a collision occur. This wasn't just a battle of strength but one of skill, judgement and seamanship.

Two leaders emerged. Sandy Hoynes and Dreich MacCallum were neck and neck as they neared the buoy, placed just before the causeway to the island. Not far away, a fishing boat bobbed with two umpires aboard, there to make sure each craft followed the rules and no corners were cut.

Sandy was narrowly in the lead as he and Dreich turned towards the buoy in order to navigate their way around it. But young Sandy was unlucky; a rogue wave caught him amidships just as he executed his turn. His rowing boat wallowed alarmingly, drifting away from the obstacle and allowing Dreich to cut inside to the shorter line.

Undaunted, Sandy bent his back into the oars and pushed on. In a few seconds, the boats were level again.

'You'll be down tuppence!' shouted Sandy as he looked across at Dreich's boat. The rest of the field were only just rounding the buoy, carefully scrutinised by the umpires.

Without warning, Dreich angled his little rowing boat to port, and headed straight for Sandy. Though the latter tried his best to avoid it, their oars entwined. Before he knew it, and with surprising strength considering his slender frame, Dreich caught Sandy by surprise. He wound his oar a few times like someone churning butter, and thrust his competitor's oar into the air. Sandy felt it slip from his hands, and despite his best efforts he lost his grip. The oar slid through the rowlock and, propelled by the churned-up water between the pair, drifted away from the boat.

'I'll be waiting for you on the pier. Be ready wae your money!' shouted Dreich, working hard and pulling away from the stricken Sandy.

Forced to pursue his lost oar, Sandy looked on with dismay as the rest of the field sailed past him. By the time he managed to retrieve it, Sandy was in last place, with no chance of winning. Though he managed to pass a couple of stragglers, by the time he reached the finishing line, Dreich was being cheered to the echo as he mounted the steps and set foot back on dry land, arms aloft in triumph.

Sandy's father was standing at the top of the steps as his son secured his boat and struggled back onto the pier. He was holding a piece of paper in one hand, a grim look on his face.

'Did she no' sail well, Sandy?'

'No, she sailed just fine. Dreich caught my oar with his, and it ended up in the water.'

'Aye, such things can happen in a close contest. There's always next year, son.'

'He did it on purpose, Faither. He's a bloody cheat!'

'Now, you watch your language, Alexander.' His father only used his proper name when his son had done something wrong.

Back on the pier, Sandy apologised. The race run, crowds now thronged the stalls, so they were on their own at the steps. Sandy looked at the paper his father held in his great paw. There was something odd about him, a shuffling from foot to foot. Sandy had rarely seen him look awkward – nervous, even.

'Is there something the matter, Faither? Apart fae losing the race, I mean.'

The big man handed his son the paper. It was a letter from the Ministry of Agriculture and Fisheries.

'My certificate!' Sandy grabbed the letter and unfolded it.

> *Dear Master Hoynes,*
>
> *I regret to inform that you failed to reach the standard required to award our Standard Navigation Certificate. I enclose an application form for next year's exam, should it be required.*
>
> *Yours sincerely,*
> *Thos. MacFarlane*
> *Senior Clerk*

Sandy read the letter again, just in case he'd misunderstood. But on second inspection – if anything – the words appeared even starker than before.

'I'm sorry, son. We'll get into the books before you sit it again next year.'

'But auld Wattie told you I'd passed. He marked the paper, didn't he?'

'Aye, he did. Och, he must have got it wrong, Sandy. It's fair to say he'd had a drink or two when he imparted that information to me, right enough.' Sandy's father cleared his throat. 'Anyway, I better get back to your mother before she buys any more tat from these stalls.' He smiled at his son. 'Try not to be too disappointed, Sandy. What's for you won't go by you. Remember that.' He walked back to the promenade and soon vanished into the crowd.

Despite his father's encouragement, though, Sandy couldn't help feeling utterly miserable. He'd been cheated out of the race and, worse still, had failed his navigation exam. The day just couldn't get worse, as far as he was concerned.

Sandy felt a tap on his shoulder. 'Dreich, if you've come for your tuppence, you'll have to wait. My money's at home. I'll give it to you this afternoon.' He paused. 'Even though you cheated.'

The reply surprised him.

'Take your time. I'll no' have time to get the money from you this afternoon. My faither's taking us out for high tea at the County Hotel.'

'Wonderful. Have a great time.'

Dreich delved into the pocket of his short trousers and produced a folded piece of paper. 'You see, we're celebrating.' He waved the letter in Sandy's face. 'This is from the Ministry. I passed my exam after all.'

'Eh?'

'Aye, no more worries about navigation for me.' He looked slyly at the younger man. 'Of course, you'll have yours, too. Are you away out for high tea?'

Sandy bunched his fist. 'I don't know how you did it, Dreich. But you know as well as I do you failed that paper.'

Dreich, perhaps for the first time in his life, smiled broadly. He took a step towards Sandy and lowered his voice. 'Of course I did. But my faither's great friends with the Fisheries Officer. Do you understand?'

Sandy was aghast. 'I understand you're a liar and a cheat, Dreich MacCallum!'

'It's sad. But someone had to miss out this year. There can only be five passes, you know.'

Still brooding on his disappointments, Sandy hadn't fully taken in what Dreich had said. But now the truth dawned on him. Not only had he been cheated out of the race, he'd also been cheated out of his navigation certificate. Without thought, Sandy tightened his balled fist and swung it into the face of his tormentor.

1

Kinloch, December 1968

Though the weather was miserable, at least there was no sign of the blizzards that Kinloch had encountered in the lead-up to the previous year's festive season. Just the same, Hamish huddled into his pea jacket against the cold, while clamping his Breton cap on his head to prevent the strong wind from carrying it off. He shivered as he turned into Sandy Hoynes's street. The scheme sat on a hill overlooking the town, a bracing five-minute walk in good weather but a real trudge in conditions like this.

But Hamish was answering a call for help and felt duty-bound to answer that call.

He plodded along the street just as the rain began to pelt down. He stopped, pushed at the garden gate, and was soon on the steps of number 76, where he knocked on the door and waited. Sure enough, a light appeared behind the frosted glass, and a figure could be seen making its way down the hall.

'Hamish, you're a sight for sore eyes,' said Marjorie Hoynes. She was pulling a long Aran cardigan close to her ample frame in order to keep out the cold. 'It's a terrible night. Come in, lad.'

Hamish wiped his feet on the doormat and stepped into the Hoynes's hallway.

'Come and get a heat at the fire,' said Mrs Hoynes, ushering the young fisherman into the cosy living room. The place was neat and tidy, with a fine fire in the hearth and an artificial Christmas tree standing on the sideboard. Festive cards were dotted about the place, some on a string above the fireplace. 'You take Sandy's seat beside the hearth, Hamish. Get yourself warmed up. Can I get you a cup of tea – a dram, maybe?'

Though Hamish was sorely tempted to accept the offer of a restorative whisky, he opted for tea for politeness's sake. He watched the flames dance in the grate, warming his hands against it, as Mrs Hoynes went about the business of making tea.

She returned to the room with a tray, on which sat two cups and saucers, a plate of shortbread, a red teapot, sugar bowl and small jug of milk.

'You take sugar, don't you?'

'Aye, three spoons, if you don't mind, Mrs Hoynes.'

'You're nearly as bad as Sandy wae his sweet tooth.'

'He takes four. Many a cup of tea I've made him, right enough. He says the stuff's pure poison wae no sugar on board, so to speak.'

'Aye, that sounds like oor Sandy.' Mrs Hoynes poured Hamish's tea, added a drop of milk and three spoons of sugar. She handed it to him. 'Help yourself to shortbread, Hamish. I made it today.'

Remembering how tasty Mrs Hoynes's shortbread was, Hamish was tempted to take two pieces, but decency forced his hand and he only availed himself of the one.

'You'll have had a lean time, what wae the boat up on

Galbraith's slip,' said Mrs Hoynes. The *Girl Maggie* had been out of the water for three weeks because of a problem with her Gardiner engine. The wait was on for a part from Glasgow. It was of such a specific nature that one day had rolled into another, and still there was no sign.

'Aye, the days have been quite long. But it's nice to have a wee holiday,' said Hamish.

'And Christmas and the New Year will tide you over. I'm sure the boat will be back in the water by the first week in January.'

It was only now that Hamish noticed how worn-out she looked. Mrs Hoynes's face was pale and there were large bags under her eyes she'd done her best to hide with powder.

'How is he today?'

'Och, Hamish. I've never seen Sandy like this. Not in all the years I've been married to him. It's like living with a stranger, so it is. He's just fair scunnered at everything. I took him a plate o' mince earlier – didna eat half o' it.'

'And he fair likes his mince and tatties.'

'There's no' a body that enjoys them more.'

'Is he taking a refreshment?'

'Whisky?'

Hamish nodded.

'He's no' touched a drop since he arrived back from the County that night. Och, it must be near enough two weeks ago.'

Hamish frowned. Mince and tatties were one thing, but whisky was another matter altogether. The man he knew enjoyed a moderate drink every day – sometimes not that moderate. To have been two weeks without a drop was surely some kind of record.

'We should maybe call the Guinness people. You know, them wae the book,' said Hamish, by way of lightening the mood.

Mrs Hoynes looked confused. 'If he'll no' take a dram, I doubt he'll want a pint o' Guinness. He's never been that fond of the stuff, Hamish.' She shook her head. 'Can I ask you, did anything happen that night? Anything untoward, I mean.'

Hamish had pondered this himself. Though, if he was honest, that particular evening was quite disjointed in his memory.

'We'd a good night, Mrs H. Sandy seemed full o' the joys. An old friend of his arrived in the County. Man, they were fair reminiscing, the pair o' them. Och, the drams were flying. You know how it is.'

Hamish looked on as his host's face changed. Suddenly Mrs Hoynes's expression altered from one of concern to downright panic.

'We didna have too many drams. I'm sure Sandy had only maybe three or four,' said Hamish, wishing he'd kept quiet on the subject of alcohol.

'This friend. Can you remember his name?'

The young fisherman's mind was a blank. Hamish had never been good at names, and faced with a crisis, the likelihood of him remembering someone he'd only met once in a haze of whisky was remote.

'You know, I canna, Mrs H. I get fair confused with names. I just canna mind, at all.'

'Did this man have a nickname?'

Ah, now that did ring a bell. He racked his brain, desperately trying to remember what it was. He was convinced that the nickname was an unusual one. But still it wouldn't come.

'Could it have been Dreich, by any chance?' said Mrs Hoynes.

Hamish pulled off his cap, revealing his alarmingly retreating hairline. 'Man, you've got it! That's just who the gentleman was. If I have it right, he's in Kinloch until the middle of January. He's a sea captain on one of these luxury cruise liners. You know, like the *Queen Mary* – though it canna be her as she's retired.'

'Oh, goodness me.' Mrs Hoynes worked a handkerchief between her hands.

'Do you no' like this Dreich fella, Mrs H?'

'I can barely remember him, if I'm honest. But if there's one man in the world who Sandy despises, it's Dreich MacCallum.'

'Aye, that's it! Dreich MacCallum. A right odd nickname, if you ask me. He's got a good pouring arm, mind – very generous. I canna think why the skipper dislikes him so much. They seemed to be getting on like a house on fire, and that's a fact.'

'It's a long story, Hamish. Oh, I know Sandy wouldn't let on in public. But there's bad blood between those two that goes back decades. That's what Sandy says, at least. He mentions him now and again, but mostly when he's drunk or in a bad mood. Though he's never once said what happened.'

Hamish frowned. 'This Dreich bloke wisna the one who borrowed all that money then ran off to Australia, was it?'

Mrs Hoynes shook her head. 'No, that was Scunner Boyd.'

'Right. What about the swine who sold him the stolen car?'

'Doddie McGarry.'

'Oh aye. I remember the name now.' Hamish sighed. 'Do

you mind the time he was reported for being drunk in charge of his bike? Man, he wasn't pleased about that at all.'

'No, it all goes back long before any of that, Hamish.' Mrs Hoynes shook her head and dabbed a tear from her eye. 'Would you mind taking the stairs and having a word with him?'

'Of course.'

'You're a good lad – a credit to your mother, right enough. How is she, by the way?'

Hamish sighed. 'Just the same, Mrs H. We're off to her cousin Mary's for Christmas dinner this year. I'm sure my mother's no' happy aboot it.'

'All this fuss. When I was a girl, folk used to go to the church on Christmas Day, if they had a mind. But it was a day like most others. We had our presents at New Year, such as they were. I can see a day coming when Hogmanay will be a thing of the past, the way things are going.'

'No first footing? No, that'll never happen. It's the best bit o' the holiday. Folk getting together to celebrate another year. That'll last for ever.'

Mrs Hoynes shrugged. 'Would you like to go up now, Hamish?'

'No bother. Will I take him some tea?'

'Aye, but he'll only take it in a certain way, as you know.'

Mrs Hoynes disappeared into the kitchen and returned holding a chipped enamel mug with a blue rim. 'I'm right embarrassed when anyone sees this. But you know fine what he's like.'

'Aye, he has one like it on the boat.'

'When we went for a trip to Edinburgh, he took it with him. There he was in the hotel dining room wae this damned thing. Folk were fair gawping at us.'

Mrs Hoynes poured tea into the old mug, added four heaped teaspoons of sugar, a splash of milk and stirred.

Mug in hand, Hamish ascended the stairs to see his ailing skipper.

2

Though the carpet on the stairs was thick, the wood underneath protested at Hamish's tread. He wasn't quite sure in which room he would find his skipper, but his first guess proved to be right. On opening the door at the end of the landing, he was greeted by a wall of tobacco smoke. Sandy Hoynes might have foresworn alcohol, but he hadn't set his pipe aside; that much was obvious.

The bedroom was in darkness, save for a chink of light coming through a gap in the curtains from the streetlamps outside. Hamish could hear the rain battering off the window and shuddered at the thought of facing the elements again on his way home.

'Who's that?' said Hoynes, his voice cracked and weak.

'It's me, Hamish. I've brought you some tea, skipper.'

Hoynes was just a dark huddle in the bed. 'Don't put that big light on – I'm no' decent.'

'Are you in the scud?' Hamish blanched at the thought.

'No, I've no' got my bunnet on. Wait till I find the bloody thing.'

Bunnet found, Hoynes struggled onto one side and switched on a small bedside light. Though this did illuminate the room to some extent, it was with a pale sepia glow.

Hoynes propped himself up on a cascade of pillows, his striped flannelette pyjama top just visible above the faded red of the candlewick bedspread, and adjusted his fisherman's cap over his tousled grey locks.

He was a sorry sight. For a start, Hamish had rarely seen his skipper out of his sea jumper. Only at weddings and funerals did Hoynes deign to wear anything else, and even then, it was under protest. And there was a bleakness about him; with the pale face and sunken eyes, he almost looked like a stranger.

'Here's your tea, Sandy.'

Hoynes took the mug and slurped at the beverage. 'Man, it's fair stewed! How long did it take you to get up those stairs?'

'It was fae the pot me and your good lady shared. I can go and get you a fresh one, if you like.'

'No, son. It's no' worth it. I think my tea-drinking days are coming to an end, and that's a fact.'

'Are you moving onto the coffee?'

'Hamish, you're no' a man for subtlety, are you?'

'How so?'

'For when a body declares their tea-drinking days to be over, it's an intimation that they're not long for this world.'

'Don't say that!'

'It's nothing but the truth. When you get to my age, you can feel yourself running down like an old engine out of oil. It's the way the Good Lord intended, and there's nothing to lament aboot – that's a fact.'

'I think it's a trip to the surgery you're needing, Sandy.'

'There's no doctor can save me. And anyway, you'll have heard about Dr McMurdo and his brother?'

'No, I canna say I have, to be honest.'

Hoynes cleared his throat and sat up in bed. 'You'll know that one brother – Kenny – is the doctor, and the other, his twin – Ross – is a lawyer?'

'Aye, I know the pair of them. Snooty buggers, if you ask me.'

'That aside, they've much to hide, I'll tell you.'

'Eh?'

'Kenny likes a refreshment, as you know. In fact, I think it's fair to say he's one of the most refreshed men I know.'

'Aye, he takes a good bucket, and that's for sure.'

Hoynes beckoned Hamish to come nearer to the bed. He lowered his voice. 'The tale I'm hearing is that, on a number of occasions recently, Kenny has been too far gone to conduct his business.'

'You mean he's still drunk?'

'Just that, Hamish.'

'Good grief, and the surgery left without a doctor. There's only the one most days.'

Hoynes tapped his nose with the stem of his pipe. 'That's where you'd be wrong.'

'How so?'

'For, knowing his brother would be in trouble with the health board and he'd likely lose his job, Ross – the lawyer, mind – put on the white coat and filled his place.'

It took Hamish a few moments to come to terms with this information. But when he did, a look of alarm crossed his face. 'You're saying that Ross is posing as the doctor?'

'Aye, you're quick, right enough. That's just what I'm saying.'

'My mother was at the surgery the day before last. You don't

334

think she had a consultation wae the lawyer instead and never knew anything aboot it?'

'Aye, that's exactly the case, Hamish.' Hoynes took a contemplative puff on his pipe and eyed his crewmate grimly. 'I hope your mother's ailment wasn't of a *personal* nature?'

'What dae you mean?'

Hoynes raised an eyebrow and said no more.

'Oh, right. I get you, skipper.' Hamish's face reddened. 'Man, it was of a very personal nature, now you come to mention it.'

Hoynes shook his head. 'I'm sorry to hear it, Hamish. To be honest, I think it's a case of letting sleeping dogs lie. There's no need to worry the woman unnecessarily.' He took another puff. 'Though she'll be fair affronted when she finds oot. Goodness knows what your poor mother exposed to that imposter, all the time thinking he was a legitimate man o' medicine.'

'She'd to take off her stockings and put her leg up in a contraption, I know that much.' Hamish's face was pale.

'For any's sake. Say no more, Hamish, for I get the picture more than adequately. Just stop there, man.'

'Under the circumstances, she should have been saying that to McMurdo – whichever one it was.'

'You have the right o' it there, right enough.'

'She's had this problem for a good while now. It's that bad she walks wae a limp sometimes.'

'She does? The poor soul.' Hoynes looked surprised.

'Aye. She says the doctor gave her cream. You know, to soften it up before he tries to cut it oot.'

'Damn it, Hamish! I'm feeling quite bilious. You can spare me any further details.'

'She had me rubbing it wae a warm cloth the other night. You know, to ease the pain and that.'

Hoynes's concerned expression had now morphed into one of genuine shock. 'Now, son, I know you wear your heart on your sleeve, but what goes on in your ain hoose is a matter for you both. My advice is not to mention this to another soul, you hear me?'

'Och, it was fair throbbing, so in the end I sprayed it wae some disinfectant and wrapped a plaster roon it.'

Hoynes turned a whiter shade of pale. 'You know, Hamish, I confess I've taken a right notion for a dram after hearing your tale of woe.'

'It shows the quality o' man you are, Sandy.'

'How so?'

'Just the thought o' one woman's suffering wae an ingrown toenail is enough to stop you feeling sorry for yourself and get you back on the straight and narrow.'

'An ingrown toenail, you say?'

'Aye, it's fair been giving her gyp this last wee while.'

Breathing a sigh of relief, Hoynes struck a match and put the flame to the bowl of his pipe, which had extinguished itself during Hamish's torrid tale.

'Still, I'm no' happy about the McMurdo twins. They're professional men. Surely they should know better. Who told you about this caper, Sandy?'

'It was Nessie Watson that spotted something was awry. She was at school wae the pair o' them. Twins might be identical by definition, but when you see them every day throughout your time in education, well, you get to recognise certain individual traits, mannerisms and the like. She was fair adamant aboot the whole thing.'

At this point, Hamish was ready to comment that Nessie Watson had glasses as thick as milk bottles. In his opinion, at least, he felt it unlikely she'd be able to spot a trait or mannerism at a distance of two inches. Still, the whole subject seemed to have reinvigorated Hoynes, so he thought the better of any further comment.

'Anyway, it's good to see you, Hamish.'

'And you, Sandy. I've been down to Galbraith's slip every morning, just like you asked. Still no sign of that part.'

'It's just damnable, that's what it is. What's auld Galbraith got to say for himself?'

'The usual stuff about it being a bad time o' year, what wae the post being busy and all.'

'Typical of the man. He has the best collection of excuses under the sun.'

'He did mention that a fella had been admiring the *Girl Maggie*. Said he'd buy her in a trice. The bloke has plenty coin, by the sound o' things.'

'What bloke?'

'Galbraith didna say, and I didna ask.'

Hoynes sat bolt upright in his bed. 'I know fine who it will have been!' He stroked his ample beard. 'Right. Tomorrow morning at nine, meet me at Galbraith's slip.'

Thankfully, the next morning when Hamish opened his bedroom curtains, the rain had gone. In fact, the sun was out, and he could see a layer of frost sparkling on grass, walls and trees. He selected a warm knitted scarf to wear for his trip to Galbraith's slip.

In the kitchen, as was her morning habit, his mother was busy at the stove.

'Good morning, son. And what are you aboot today?'

'I'm meeting Sandy at the slip. He's no' happy about the time it's taking to fix the boat's engine.'

'And that's no' all he'll be unhappy about, I venture.'

'What dae you mean?'

'I hobbled down the street yesterday – wae my stick, you understand.'

'Aye.'

'I was in the greengrocer's when I saw a man that I'd forgotten existed.'

Hamish thought on this for a moment. He'd read in the *Fishing News* about elderly people losing their faculties. In the case of the article he'd perused, an old skipper had set out alone on his lobster boat and completely forgotten where his creels were or how to get back home. Being a worrier, Hamish was concerned that his mother's absentmindedness may be the first sign of something similar.

'Who was this body, mother?'

'I knew him in school. He was a couple of years ahead of me, but he fair turned heads wherever he went.'

'A looker, eh?'

'No such thing. He was a long streak o' misery back in those days. Mind you, when I saw him in the shop, he was smiling like the Cheshire cat.'

'Dreich MacCallum, I'll wager,' said Hamish instantly.

His mother frowned. 'How on earth would you know the man? He left the town when I was a lassie. As far as I know, this is his first time back in . . . och, it must be fifty years.'

'Sandy has himself in a state about him.'

It was his mother's turn to think. She stirred a pot of porridge absently until realisation dawned on her. 'There was an incident between that pair just before Dreich left Kinloch. I've been trying to remember what happened. I'd go so far as to say that Hoynes frightened the poor lad into exile.'

'Don't be daft. This is Sandy we're talking about.'

She ladled some porridge into a bowl, stirred in a teaspoonful of salt and placed it in front of Hamish on the table. 'You're too young to realise, but some folk change as they get older. Sandy Hoynes is a fine example.'

'I'm no' stupid enough to believe that he was born wae a pot belly and a big grey beard, if that's what you mean, Mother.'

'That's no' it at all, son. Sandy's no' the man you see today. Oh aye, he was every bit the rogue then as he is now. But your skipper was quite fiery as a lad.'

'Temper, you mean?'

'Just so, Hamish. Man, he'd a right quick temper. Accused

Dreich o' all sorts. The poor lad was fair affronted. It likely drove him away.'

'What kind of thing did he accuse him of – Sandy, I mean?'

She thought for a moment. 'Well, there was the boat race. It must have been after the Great War. We'd lost so many men, and those that were left were either old or too tired out wae fighting and the miseries o' conflict to be worried about a daft wee boat race. So they made it the preserve of youth. Young lads competed.'

'Aye, go on. What happened?'

'I canna mind the details at such a distance now. But it's fair to say that your skipper lost to Dreich MacCallum. He made such a fuss, accused Dreich o' cheating – the whole thing went on and on. To be honest, Sandy Hoynes couldna bear to be beaten fair and square. His mother and father were affronted at his carry-on. But there was worse to come.'

'There was?'

'Aye, there was. In those days, they handed out the seamanship certificates – I canna mind what they called them – to five young lads every year. They had to sit exams and the like.'

Hamish thought on this and considered himself lucky that such a restrictive practice was no longer in place. If it had been, the added element of competition, as well as the pressure of the exam hall, would have prevented his passing any nautical exams – ever. 'Go on, Mother. You're dreadful for heading off on a tangent when telling a tale. Aye, and you rarely reach your destination.'

'Listen tae you! I can just picture you in fifty years' time, sitting in that County Hotel spinning yarns for drams, just the way your auld grandfaither did.'

'I'll have grandweans to dandle on my knee, never mind yarns and drams.'

Hamish's mother cast him a baleful glance. She worried that he hadn't settled down. What lonely life was ahead of her only son, whiling away the hours all alone? She wouldn't last for ever. And the trials of life were best faced with a companion.

'I know what you're thinking,' said Hamish. 'I'll find the right girl, just you wait.'

'You'll no' find her in the County wae Hoynes, Peeny and the likes. You'll be an old man before your time.'

'Don't you worry about that. I have a plan.' Though he did his best to sound confident, Hamish felt anything but. There seemed to be a distinct lack of young ladies willing to walk out with him. This, plus his diminishing hairline, made him wonder that he may just not be the marrying type. 'Anyway, get on wae the tale, woman.'

She sighed. 'Well, as I remember it, Sandy failed miserably and concocted this great tale about the fishery officer conspiring to award the certificate to Dreich and no' himself. There was a right stink about it all. Hoynes was a laughing stock, and that's a fact.'

Hamish was loyal to his skipper. After all, had it not been for the offer of a berth on the *Girl Maggie* when his own father had been forced to sell his boat, Hamish wasn't sure there'd have been a place at the fishing with his name on it. Yes, Hoynes ribbed him about this and that, but he had a great affection for the man, considering him something of a surrogate father. The thought that his skipper had tried to cheat his way into a seamanship certificate, or whatever it was, left him strangely disappointed. And though he tried to mark the whole thing down to youthful indiscretion, he didn't manage to convince himself.

Whatever the truth, he had to meet Hoynes at Galbraith's slip in half an hour. After another helping of porridge and a second cup of tea, Hamish was ready to face the day. But, he mused, he wasn't entirely sure he was quite so prepared to face his skipper.

4

Hamish crossed the roundabout at the bottom of Main Street, passed the Weigh House, and made his way along the promenade to the slip. He was glad of the scarf he'd wrapped round his neck, for it was bitterly cold. Still, the loch was as deep a blue as the sky, in which gulls wheeled and called, and Hamish drew deeply at the smell of the sea. There was nothing like it for clearing the head. And mixed with the frosty air, he felt invigorated as he neared the *Girl Maggie*. He always thought of her as a fine vessel. But now, even he had to admit that, removed from her natural element, sitting on rails on the slip, she did look rather odd, even on the tubby side.

At first, he thought he was alone, until he heard voices coming from the other side of the fishing boat and spotted a tell-tale cloud of smoke appearing over the vessel's prow: Sandy Hoynes's pipe, to be sure.

As he rounded the prow, Hamish saw Galbraith and Hoynes in a heated discussion amidships. Galbraith was pointing up through the bottom of the boat, clearly indicating his displeasure.

'I don't know how you've kept her afloat all these years, Sandy,' said Galbraith, a man of average height with similar features.

'I beg your pardon,' Hoynes replied indignantly. 'This is one of the soundest vessels in the fleet, and no error.'

'You're deluded, man. All I can say is that I've kept your pumps in good order. They must be working harder than the engine, the bilge you're carrying.'

'It's merely ballast. She doesn't sit right in the water unless she's carrying some weight. A boat like this is fine-tuned to a high degree.' Hoynes took an extra-long draw of his pipe.

'What about this, then?' Galbraith reached above his head and poked his right index finger between two planks on the underside of the boat. 'Man, you can near get your fist in there, such is the gap. It's my assessment these planks are rotten.'

'I plug that wae oakum. There's no' a vessel afloat in which oakum doesna play a vital role.'

'True, Sandy, very true. But everybody else uses it for lining the decking, no' plugging great holes. Man, I'd love to see the ball o' the stuff this requires. It must be the size o' a melon!'

'Listen,' Hoynes pointed the stem of his pipe in Galbraith's direction, 'I'm paying you to fix the engine. If I wanted the advice of a shipwright, I'd ask one.'

'Fine.' Galbraith bent his knees and picked up a piece of rusted metal from the ground beside him. 'What would you say this was, Sandy?'

'You're the mechanic, you tell me.'

'Well, in all my thirty years o' being around engines in fishing boats, cars, lorries, motorbikes and the like, I've never seen anything like it.'

'Where did you find it?' Hoynes was pleased that this mystery was distracting the engineer from the poor state of the *Girl Maggie*'s superstructure.

'From the floor of your engine room, Sandy. It was in three inches o' water, so likely you missed it.'

'Is that the thing I've been tripping over the last couple o' years?' said Hamish.

Hoynes shot him a wicked glare.

'This'll be it, Hamish. I don't suppose you have any idea what it is?' said Galbraith, holding the metal up like a trophy.

'I'm no' just sure, I have to admit.'

'I think the mair worrying thing here is that you don't know what it is, Angus.' Hoynes shook his head. 'After all, there's no' a creature that comes oot o' the sea that I canna recognise. Is that no' right, Hamish?'

'There was that thing we hauled up in oor nets just off Plada, Sandy. You telt me you'd bugger-all clue what it was.'

'It was a rotting sheep, Hamish. Don't be daft.'

'It had two heids!'

'You're a terrible man for exaggeration.' Hoynes tamped more tobacco into the bowl of his pipe. 'It just looked as though it had two heids. In actual fact, it just had the one, rotted away a bit.'

'How come it had four eyes, then?' said Hamish, eager to defend himself.

'I've no' got the time to stand here talking aboot the flights o' fancy you pair have out at sea,' protested Galbraith. 'The mind boggles. I've got cars to fix back at the garage.'

As the argument continued, Hamish spotted a smart holiday cruiser tied up at the New Quay. Though she was around the same length as the *Girl Maggie,* her sweeping white lines made her look like something out of the space comics Hamish read. If this was the future of sailing, Hamish liked what he saw.

'I see you taking in that cabin cruiser, Hamish,' said Galbraith during a cessation of hostilities.

'She's a beauty, and no mistake.'

'All skim and bluster,' said Hoynes sourly. 'Underneath it'll be as fragile as a newborn. No' fit to face a decent wave, I'll venture.'

'Not true, Sandy. Not true at all. The owner let me aboard to see her engines yesterday. Engineered in Italy, would you believe? He says she can reach near thirty knots.'

'Man, if we stoated aboot at that speed, we'd frighten off every fish left in the sea. It's stealth we're after in our business.' Hoynes clamped the pipe between his teeth and put a match to the bowl. After a few puffs he saw fit to comment further. 'Mind you, I wouldn't say no to a leaf out o' the bank book o' the owner. Likely mair money than sense. One o' they pop stars that Hamish goes on aboot when he's in his free love moments, likely.'

'Not at all,' said Galbraith. 'In fact, she's owned by a local man – albeit he's been away from Kinloch for years. Nice chap – a ship's captain, no less.'

There followed the kind of pause Hamish had read about in books. Everyone stood stock-still: Galbraith awaiting a response, while Hoynes appeared to be chewing his pipe stem, jaws working furiously.

'You look as though you're about to blow a gasket, Sandy,' said Galbraith.

'The man you speak of – he's the one you were showing round my vessel the other day?'

'I was hardly showing him round. We were passing the time o' day. That's all.'

'I'm no' paying you to pass the time o' day, Angus. I'm

losing money hand over fist every day my boat is up here like some great exhibition. Maybe you should charge folk to come and have a gander, eh?'

Through the cool morning air, the tinkling of a bell could be heard. Wattie the postman was on his bike, heading towards them at speed, waving one arm. There was a parcel wedged into the basket on the handlebars.

'Mr Galbraith, here's the thing you've been waiting on,' said Wattie as he dismounted the bike. Helpfully, Hamish held it upright as the postman grabbed the parcel and handed it to the engineer.

Galbraith went about the package with a penknife he produced from the pocket of his boiler suit. It proved to be a metallic object about a foot in length with a spring at one end, tapering to a point at the other.

'Is that what's been holding us up? said Hoynes.

'The very thing.' Galbraith examined the engine part with a nod of satisfaction. 'I can have it fitted in a couple of hours, but you'll need to give me peace.'

'At your earliest convenience,' said Hoynes. 'Hamish and I can go and take the air while you're about it. When d'you think she'll be back in the water?'

Galbraith looked at the watch on his grubby, oil-stained wrist. 'Around lunchtime, I'd say. But remember, this isna an exact science.'

'Given the amount of time I've been waiting, I'm sure you'll do your best. We'll leave you to it,' said Hoynes.

Hamish watched Wattie the postman cycle off at speed. It was the kind of job he might have fancied, had he not managed to continue with his maritime career. Though he'd always worried about finding the correct addresses. It was a strange phenomenon, but at sea, he instinctively knew where he was going. On land, the whole process seemed more difficult. He comforted himself in the knowledge that Sandy Hoynes suffered in a similar manner. In fact, he recalled Mrs Hoynes saying that her husband could find his way from the house to the boat and back again, via the County Hotel, and that was about it. Hamish felt sure that this disparity between land and sea must be as the Good Lord intended. He and Hoynes took to the promenade and strode back into the town.

'I'm no' too sure about this "taking the air" business, Sandy,' said Hamish. 'It's on the cold side for traipsing about the streets.'

'I'm sure you've never learned a thing from me, Hamish. It's ten o'clock – we'll be sure to get an early dram in the County.'

'Man, you've fair bounced back after two weeks in your bed, skipper.'

'Maybe I was just needing some rest and recuperation. Have you ever thought o' that?'

'Nothing to do wae Dreich MacCallum, then?'

Hoynes took a couple of puffs of his pipe. 'I'd thank you not to mention that name again, Hamish. I'm sick o' hearing it. The sooner he returns to wherever he came from, the happier I'll be.'

The pair turned the corner and strolled on towards the County Hotel.

5

A small parade of guests were gathered at the County's reception desk, ready to check out. A large man with a pendulous belly was first in the queue, checking his watch with an impatient shake of his head.

'Good morning to you all,' said Hoynes, with what could best be described as a disarticulated bow.

The man waiting at the reception desk eyed him with contempt.

'My name is Waring – Geoffrey Waring. Are you the owner of this establishment?'

Hoynes looked about in faux confusion. 'Are you talking to me?'

'Well, I'm not talking to that gormless lad tagging along behind you, am I?' Mr Waring was an outspoken Yorkshireman, judging by his accent.

'I'll have you know that my first mate is one of the finest young fishermen on the West Coast, sir.'

'In that case, he cheats his appearance. Either that, or the rest of them leave a great deal to be desired. And I note that you haven't answered my question. Are you responsible for this . . . place?'

'I believe the word "gormless" refers to a person lacking

in sense or initiative. A foolish man, perhaps. Would you agree?'

'Though I'm surprised to say it, you're right.'

Hoynes tamped down some tobacco into his pipe. 'In that case, do you think I look like the owner of the hotel? I mean, a stout jumper, Breton cap and these yellow Wellington boots are hardly the garb of a man who runs such an establishment, wouldn't you say?'

'A smart arse. Just the thing I didn't want.'

'What did you expect?'

'An explanation as to why my bed sagged in the middle and my breakfast wasn't fit to feed a sparrow.'

'Och, you'll no' be needing the owner of the hotel to answer that.' Hoynes puffed yet another pipe into life.

'Why so?'

'Because any bugger can see that with the girth you're carrying, only a bed made of concrete would fail to sag in the middle. That aside, the paucity of your breakfast – if that was indeed the case – likely saved you from a coronary. Good day to you, Mr Gormless.'

A young woman in the queue giggled as Hoynes and Hamish made for the bar, while Waring spluttered and failed to find a suitable retort.

'You didna miss him, Sandy.'

'I canna stand such an attitude. And in any case, you're no' gormless, Hamish. Slow is a much more appropriate description.'

As Hoynes pushed the door to the bar open, Hamish smiled. The smile continued until he thought a bit longer about what Hoynes had just said. His expression turned into a frown.

In keeping with the time of day, the place was quiet. An elderly couple sat at a table at the back of the room, sharing a pot of tea. At the bar, almost as though they were fixtures, stood Peeny and Malcolm Connelly.

'Dear me,' said Connelly. 'It's the dry-land sailors.' The pair of them chuckled.

'Just ignore them, Hamish. Any man that thinks it fine to indulge in strong drink at this time of day isna worth listening to.'

'In that case, you'll be having tea, Sandy?' said Peeny.

'I'll have you know I've barely touched a drop o' the hard stuff in the last fortnight, Peeny.'

'Doctor's orders, I take it? The poor bugger will have to wring your liver oot wae a mangle.'

'Nothing o' the kind. And anyway, I've lost my faith in the local medical profession, given that you're more likely to encounter a lawyer than a doctor.'

This engendered a consensus amongst those gathered. Sandy and Hamish found a seat at a table as the elderly manager arrived behind the bar and took them in balefully.

'Man, the fleet's thirsty this morning, eh?'

'Fishing is a thirsty business. Hamish and I will have a dram each, when you've had your fill of ridiculous observations, thank you.'

And so, an interlude in the County began in much the same way that it always did. Peeny and Connelly wondered about Hoynes's absence and the wellbeing of the *Girl Maggie*, while the vexed subject of the McMurdo twins and their lack of professional ethics proved to be one upon which everyone could agree.

When they'd exhausted the many and varied ways a lawyer

performing the tasks of a clinician could lead to almost certain death, Peeny eyed Connelly with a wink.

'You were saying you've just been down the quay, Sandy?'

'That I have, and fair bracing it was. The weather's turning more seasonal, for sure.'

'You'll have seen that beautiful cabin cruiser at the pier, eh?' Peeny smiled guilelessly.

Hoynes took another sip of his dram. 'I'm sure I don't know what you mean. I was there to check on the progress o' my own vessel, no' worry aboot everyone else's.'

'Bonnie she is, right enough,' said Connelly. 'They say she can do near thirty knots. Can you imagine?'

'I'd like to see her hauling in a good catch, right enough,' said Hoynes. 'Man, she'd be low in the water wae a couple o' herrings and a lobster creel, I reckon.'

'You're no' purchasing a boat like that to go fishing, I don't think, Sandy,' said Hamish.

Hoynes kicked his second-in-command under the table. 'Man, I'm reconsidering my definition o' the word gormless, Hamish. Right now, I reckon it could mean a balding fisherman in his thirties, with grim career and life prospects into the bargain.'

'Let the lad speak, Sandy,' said Peeny. 'He has the right of it. I remember Dreich MacCallum just as well as you. And without taking into account the situation between him and your good self, I'd like to say a dourer boy never left this toon.'

'Aye, like a night oot wae the Grim Reaper,' said Malcolm Connelly in agreement. 'I wouldna fret on his massive success and riches, if I were you.'

Hoynes leaned back in his chair. 'Maybe it's time to let

sleeping dogs lie. I hadn't thought about the man for fifty years until he appeared in here a couple o' weeks ago.'

'Mrs H says you only speak about him when you're in a bad mood or drunk,' said Hamish.

Peeny and Connelly were doing their best to keep a straight face. They resorted to the old trick of holding their glasses to their mouths pretending to drink in order to cover their mirth.

'You pair would find a deid haddock amusing,' said Hoynes. 'I may be prepared to leave the past in the past, but I'll never forget what that imposter did. He set me back two years. I didna have the heart to sit the navigation exam the following year. After all, it had been stolen from me in a most wicked way.'

'No' to mention the race, eh?' said Connelly.

'It was a fine pointer to what a rascal we had in our midst. Goodness knows what he'd have been up to if he'd stayed in Kinloch. We were better rid of him, and no mistake,' said Peeny.

The door to the bar swung open once more. Framed in it was a tall, cadaverous man, with a shock of grey hair. His expensive brogues, well-cut sports jacket and tanned face were enough to identify him as comfortably-off. He stood before the gathered drinkers for a while, his expression a mask of abject misery.

'Dreich,' said Peeny. 'Man, I knew you were back in town, but it's still a surprise to see you.'

Dreich nodded solemnly, then did something few of them expected. A huge smile broke out on his face, and by the time he'd reached the bar he was beaming from ear to ear.

'A drink for my good friends,' he said in a heavily anglicised accent with only the merest trace of his hometown. He looked round the room. 'Sandy, I'm glad to see you're up and about again. We enjoyed a few drams the night I arrived, right enough. It's a shame you don't have the stomach for it. But I note it's doing its best to rise to the occasion.' He nodded to Hoynes's ample belly.

'Man, you've found your wit,' said Connelly, in truth rather amazed by the transformation in the man he'd known as a dour schoolboy.

'When you're the captain of a top-of-the-line cruise ship, a certain amount of bonhomie is expected.'

'Is that what you're at these days?'

'Forty years before the mast, Peeny. I missed this old place for a while, but I soon realised that leaving was the best thing I'd ever done. I worked my way up from deck boy. In seventeen years, I was a captain. And that's what I've done ever since. But I thought Sandy would have filled you in with all this, given he was here the night I arrived.'

Hoynes sipped his dram. 'Och, as you say, I've been a bit poorly the last couple of weeks. But I thought you'd have met up wae these rascals before now.'

'This isn't just a nostalgic trip, Sandy. I've been busy.'

'Busy at what?'

Dreich tapped his long nose. 'You'll see. But it might help bring this rundown old town into the twentieth century.'

'Are we going to get traffic lights?' said Connelly.

'Sorry?'

'You know, for the traffic in Main Street. Man, it's a nightmare trying to get out of Long Road.'

'The man's just telt you he's the captain o' a cruise liner. Why on earth would he be doon here to oversee the installation of traffic lights, Malcolm?' said Hoynes.

Connelly shrugged. 'Well, you never know.'

'No, I'm thinking that Captain MacCallum is here on matters o' a maritime nature. Would that be right, Dreich?'

'You are absolutely correct, Sandy. I can't say too much about it right now. But it will change this place for ever. You won't need to rely on the fishing. That'll soon be a thing of the past.'

There developed what could only be described as a chilly silence. The prospect of their beloved fishing being rendered obsolete by whatever Dreich MacCallum had up his sleeve was too much for the gathered mariners.

'There will always be fishing in Kinloch,' said Hamish eventually.

'No need for a young man like yourself to be worried, Seamus. You'll be much better off working for me. And anyway, fish stocks won't last for ever, not the way you're all plundering the sea.'

'The lad's name is Hamish,' said Sandy. 'And he works for me.'

'And how long will you carry on in the wheelhouse, Sandy? Peeny and Malcolm here have already hung up their nets. You should follow suit. A man in your condition won't last for ever.'

The collective intake of breath made the elderly couple drinking their pot of tea look up. Peeny stared at Connelly, Hamish glared at Dreich, and Connelly blew out his cheeks as he waited for a response from Hoynes.

'I'll have you know that I'm in fine physical condition. You canna face the ocean in all her many moods every day o' life without being ready for the challenge.'

Dreich smiled again, an unpleasant thing that didn't suit

his dolorous features one bit. 'It's a couple of pillows hidden up your jumper, then?'

'I'm heavy-boned, MacCallum. And unless you want a repeat o' what happened all these years ago, you'll shut your face.'

Hamish was surprised. He'd seen his skipper in many states of agitation, but never had he witnessed him threaten anyone with violence, if indeed that's what he'd just done. The atmosphere remained tense as Dreich stood at the bar and tossed back his dram with no comment. The whole scene reminded Hamish of a western he'd seen at the pictures a few weeks before – the gunslinger, a stranger, silent but menacing, finishing his drink before shooting up the bar.

Dreich put down his empty glass deliberately. He turned to address Hoynes. 'I'll tell you what, Sandy. Talking of old times, and if you're so hale and hearty, why don't we repeat our race?'

'You mean row to the island and back?'

'Yes. But let's make it more interesting. How about we race to Kilconnan rock and back. After all, we were just wee boys way back then. Now we're men, we can surely row a bit further.'

Hamish whispered to Hoynes under his breath. 'Sandy, that's a round trip of about five miles. You'll never manage to row a distance like that.' He was about to remind his skipper that the last time they'd been in charge of a rowing boat was when they'd been ashore at Lochranza. Hamish being rather in his cups, Hoynes had taken it upon himself to row back to the boat anchored out in the bay, just past the castle. By the time they got back to the *Girl Maggie*, Hoynes was so out of breath he had to wait for half an hour before he attempted to take the rope ladder up the side.

'Sorry, but you're not on, Dreich. I have to say, I'm surprised that a man like you – a ship's captain – would countenance such a ridiculous notion. We may have been wee boys back then, but now we're old men.'

'Oh, well, that's a pity. You may be happy to sink into old age . . . I'm not,' said Dreich.

'Madness, sheer madness. You've done the right thing, Sandy. A younger man would find it chore enough rowing that distance against wind and tide,' said Peeny.

'I'll be right busy over the festive period. My boat's about to go back in the water. I've no time for frolics of such a frivolous nature,' said Sandy.

'You've made your point, Hoynes. Just a pity we'll not have that rematch.' Dreich winked at Sandy.

'Aye, you're a wise man, right enough, Sandy,' said Connelly. 'It's fine enough today, if bitterly cold. But as yous all know, at this time o' year, the weather can turn on a sixpence.'

'There's such a thing as the shipping forecast. Or are you gentlemen still licking your finger and holding it in the air to predict the weather?'

'Ach, I've made my decision, and that's that,' said Hoynes. 'Let's get onto more important subjects.'

'Enough's enough, eh?' said Dreich. 'Oh, well, after that disappointment, who wants to come down to the pier and have a turn round the loch in my cabin cruiser? My wife Tabby is on her way from London today. I want to make sure it's shipshape for her. She likes her boats like she does her men: sleek, powerful and fast. Get my drift, Hamish?'

The young first mate blushed and said nothing.

'I've to go down and supervise Galbraith,' said Hoynes.

'Ah, your boat, Sandy. I had a look at her the other day.

I might make you an offer. She could be useful for my project.'

'No sale, MacCallum. She's a working vessel. But you're welcome aboard to see what good form she's in.'

That agreed, it was Hoynes's turn to buy another round. As he stood at the bar, Hamish studied Hoynes and MacCallum. Dreich was taller by a good four inches, but Hoynes was the wider. The *Girl Maggie*'s first mate was glad his skipper had made the right choice. Frankly, Hoynes was in no shape to be rowing anywhere.

6

The full round of drams had to be taken, each man buying the other a drink. So, it was a good while later that Hoynes, Dreich and the rest of the early morning drinkers made their way, somewhat haltingly, back to the harbour. This process was further delayed when Peeny slipped on black ice just outside Michael Kerr's bakery and had to be manhandled back to his feet.

As they turned onto the promenade, Hoynes was surprised to discover that not only was work on the *Girl Maggie* complete, but she was also being towed by an old tractor down Galbraith's slip ready to be moored against the pier.

'It's a fine sight to see, a proud vessel being restored to her natural element,' said Hoynes.

'It reminds me of the time I saw a dead whale being dragged off the beach in Newfoundland,' said Dreich.

Peeny looked at Connelly with an expression that indicated, *trouble ahead.*

By the time they'd walked to the slip, the *Girl Maggie* was afloat, Galbraith himself securing her to a stout bollard.

'Man, but that was quick, Angus,' said Hoynes.

'It took me near three hours. But I suppose time flies when you're having fun,' said the engineer. Judging by the all-pervasive aroma of whisky, this gaggle of mariners hadn't stinted on a dram or two.

Galbraith tugged at his oily cap and greeted Dreich. 'It's good to see you again, Mr MacCallum. Though I see you're not choosy when it comes to the company you keep.'

'Old pals, from way back in time,' Dreich replied.

'I think his memory is fair addled, Hamish. For none of us were his *pals* – the bugger never had any,' said Hoynes in a whisper. Then to Galbraith, 'If all is in order, I'm going to set her to the loch straight away by means of a sea trial.'

'As long as you pay me by the end of the week, you can take her to Australia for all I care.'

'You'll get your money. In the thirty years you and I have been doing business, have I ever let you down in matters o' a fiscal nature?'

The engineer rubbed his chin. 'No, I must say that you've paid every penny due.' And in a lower tone, 'Though "eventually" should be deployed in that sentence somewhere.'

Hoynes led the little party down the quayside and took to the ladder to access his fishing boat.

'It reminds me of that sea-clock at Greenwich,' said Dreich.

'What dae you mean?' said Hamish.

'It's a great ball that goes up and down a pole on the hour, and suchlike. I can't put my finger on it, but Sandy puts it in mind.' He grinned at Peeny.

Now on the deck of the *Girl Maggie,* Hoynes was back in his element. He beamed as he caressed the wooden frame of the wheelhouse. 'It's good to be back on board, old girl,' he said lovingly.

Though they'd all had a drink, one by one, the seafarers

took the ladder expertly. After all, for them, it was second nature.

Galbraith shouted down from the pier, 'Sandy, make sure and no' push her too hard. They didna send the right housing for that part that came wae the post. I had to fashion one on the fly, so to speak. She'll likely be fine, but take it easy at the start, just to be on the safe side.'

'He means don't go at your full pelt of three knots,' said Dreich with a laugh.

'He's fair changed, eh, Malcolm?' said Peeny. 'You couldna get as much as a giggle oot o' the bugger when we were young. Now it's like a Royal Command Performance.'

Connelly nodded his head. 'Some folk are like that. Look at my Margaret. She was a barrel o' laughs when I met her at first. Now, she's a right misery.'

'Aye, but staying wae you all these years is enough to silence anyone. Man, I get fair depressed just having a dram wae you.'

Connelly was about to reply when Dreich appeared at their side. 'Isn't she a beauty?' He pointed to his cabin cruiser tied to the pier opposite. 'Took her down to the South of France last year. It was like sailing with your slippers on. Just wait until you see inside, boys. You'll be fair wishing you abandoned the fishing and made something of yourselves like me.'

'No doubt,' said Peeny, not meaning it at all.

'I just wish I was you,' said Malcolm Connelly. 'The very thought of my many failings in life is sufficient to have me tying bricks to my ankles and jumping overboard. It would be a precious release.'

'You can scoff, Malcolm. But you'll eat your words when you're aboard. I even have a bar, you know.' Dreich marched off to torment Hoynes.

'You may well have a bar on your fancy cruiser, but you're still nothing but a scunner,' said Peeny. 'You'll no' have had the many rewards oor families and friends have bestowed on us.'

'Not sure that his family or friends have bestowed many rewards on him at all.'

Sandy Hoynes's head and shoulders were hanging out of the wheelhouse window. He was barking orders to Hamish, whose own head appeared now and again through the engine-room hatch further down the deck. 'Be sure and check the oil pressure, then we'll fire her up,' said Hoynes.

Dreich appeared below the window. 'It'll be a slow boat to China getting this old tub out of the harbour, Sandy.'

'There's many that think that, Dreich. But they're all wrong. It was only last year that I won a race oot into the loch wae a boat half her years in age.'

That unpleasant smile broke out across Dreich's face again. 'I remain to be convinced.'

'That's her ready, skipper. All in order in the engine room,' said Hamish, his oil-stained face emerging through the hatch.

'Leave that hatch open, Hamish. If I know Galbraith, there will be a surfeit o' lubrication oil to burn off. Better to let it vent.'

Hamish did as he was told then joined Dreich under the wheelhouse window.

'Is she shipshape, Seamus?'

'Aye, she's that and more.'

There was a chug, followed by a thud or two. Then something akin to a small explosion issued from the engine, sending a great cloud of black smoke through the hatch and the little chimney that abutted the wheelhouse.

'I knew it!' shouted Hoynes above the din. 'It's always the same when Galbraith has had his mitts on an engine.'

Though smoke still bellowed from the engine room through the open hatch, its colour became more grey than black. Shortly, the thudding and banging modulated into the gentler putt-putt of an engine in reasonable trim.

'Sweet as a nut,' said Hoynes, with no little pleasure. 'Untie her, Hamish, and we'll be off!'

The first mate dashed over the side, removed the rope from the bollard, and jumped back aboard the *Girl Maggie* with the grace of a ballerina.

'That's her ready for the off, skipper.'

Hoynes steered the vessel carefully away from the pier, pointed the prow roughly in the direction he intended to leave the harbour by, paused for a moment and pushed the throttle forward.

At first, nothing happened. But soon the gentle putt-putting increased in volume and frequency, as the *Girl Maggie* under Hoynes's command made for the gap between Kinloch's twin piers.

'Now we're talking, Dreich,' said Hoynes, his head poking back out of the wheelhouse.

'It's hardly Sterling Moss, is it?'

'Och, that's a different thing all together. You canna expect the same thing from a fishing boat that you can from a racing car.'

Dreich shrugged, though the shadow of a smile crossed his lips at Hoynes's efforts to impress him.

Galbraith looked on from the pier. He turned to Archie, the tractor driver. 'What on earth does he think he's doing? I telt him no' to push her until that new part settled in.'

'You know fine what he's like,' said Archie. 'The man's a bloody show-off.'

Despite this dismissive remark, Galbraith was chewing his lip as, in a flurry of smoke and thudding engine, the *Girl Maggie* approached the harbour mouth.

But just as Hoynes's attention was on the wheel, something odd happened. He felt the vessel shudder beneath him. There was a screaming noise, like the song of a steel hawser about to snap. The *Girl Maggie* appeared as though she had stopped in mid-stride. And though the engine was clearly in the process of slowing, the screeching noise continued. In fact, it grew to such a pitch that those aboard put fingers in ears to block it out.

Just as Hoynes was puzzling over what on earth was happening, there was a loud crack. A slim black object shot from the engine-room hatch like a bullet from a gun and soared into the clear blue sky.

'What's that?' said Peeny as he watched it gain height, causing seagulls to squawk and dive out of its way.

'It puts me in mind o' what might have happened in Cuba, had everyone no' seen sense,' said Malcolm, shading his eyes with one hand in order to follow its progress.

'What on earth happened, skipper?' said Hamish, visibly alarmed as he tumbled into the wheelhouse.

Hoynes had his field glasses trained on the unexpected projectile that had issued from his engine room. It was rapidly becoming a black speck in the blue, frosty sky.

'I'm no' right sure, Hamish. But there's something far wrong, that's certain.'

All aboard the *Girl Maggie* eyed its flight path. The object had almost disappeared, but, through his binoculars, Hoynes was first to notice its change of altitude. The projectile's progress slowed, it arced in the air as though caught by an invisible hand, and what had been an upward trajectory now reversed, as the forces of gravity came into play.

'What now, Sandy?'

'It's the old story, Hamish. What goes up must come doon!' Hoynes thrust his head from the wheelhouse. 'Take cover, everybody!'

As those present scattered about the fishing boat's deck, Hoynes, still peering through the binoculars, noticed that whatever had fired itself from his engine room had altered its angle of return. 'I think we're going to be fine. By the looks o' things it's going to land in the loch!'

Peeny was first to take note of this advice. The projectile was, once more, visible, and it appeared to be accompanied by a shrill whistling that was growing in intensity the nearer it came. 'It sounds like a Stuka!'

'Aye, but it's no' going to hit us, Peeny,' said Connelly. 'It's fair veered to the left. Hoynes may be right – it might come doon in the loch.'

'Aye, and it might no'.'

'Any chance o' the bloody thing hitting the fishery office?'

But just as the words left Connelly's mouth, the whistling noise became a scream and the impromptu missile appeared to accelerate through the thin winter air. Instinctively, everyone dropped to the deck. There was a large bang, followed by a crunching noise and the shattering of glass.

Hoynes got to his feet. His prediction had been wrong. Whether caught by the wind or simply propelled by the laws of physics, whatever had shot from the *Girl Maggie*'s engine room had landed on Dreich MacCallum's cabin cruiser with such force that it ploughed straight through, broke the vessel's back, and, in two perfect halves, sent it slowly sinking into the oily waters of Kinloch harbour.

7

Those aboard the *Girl Maggie* stood stock still. The shock of it all had rendered them mute and motionless.

It was only when Hoynes looked back at Galbraith's slip that he saw the engineer throw his cap to the ground and jump up and down on it.

'Mr Galbraith's no' looking too pleased, Sandy,' said Hamish meekly.

'This is his fault! If he'd done his job properly, we'd be oot in the loch without a care in the world.'

'Instead, you've sunk Mr MacCallum's cabin cruiser.'

As though he'd heard the comment, Dreich MacCallum recovered himself enough to shout up at Hoynes from the deck. 'You wait until I get my hands on you, Sandy Hoynes. That boat's worth a small fortune. At least ten times the cost of this heap!'

'Hamish, just slip the snib down on the wheelhouse door, will you, while I have a think. If Dreich breaks through, let him have it wae that claw hammer.'

The first mate looked on in horror. 'I think things are bad enough without me knocking MacCallum over the head wae a hammer, don't you?'

'Aye. But at least they might let us share the same cell in the gaol.'

As Hoynes predicted, Dreich MacCallum began hammering the wheelhouse door with his fist. 'Let me in there, Hoynes!' he roared.

'What are we to dae, skipper?' said Hamish through the din.

'I'm no' sure, but it'll likely involve Campbell the lawyer. Man, that could have killed someone, never mind wrecking that fancy cruiser o' Dreich's. We've faced many trials, Hamish, but this might prove to be the worst yet.'

Above Dreich's tirade, another sound could be heard. The voice was harsh and metallic, but Hoynes recognised it immediately.

'Sandy Hoynes, your vessel is blocking the entrance to the harbour. I'll have the *Evening Star* tow you to a berth. Then I want to see you in my office, do you hear?' Harbour master Mitchell's voice was plain as day through the megaphone.

Mitchell, by way of the megaphone, persuaded MacCallum to cease his wailing. A tender had been sent to the side of the *Girl Maggie*, and now Hoynes was sitting across the desk from the harbour master, cap in hand.

'I don't need to tell you how serious this is, Sandy. You've destroyed an expensive vessel – that's bad enough. But you could easily have wiped out half the town. If the wind had caught that … whatever it was … we could have had folk felled all along the Main Street. And what would have happened if it had hit the fuel tanks?'

'Aye, but surely the crucial thing we should keep in mind

is that none o' these things *did* happen. Granted, Dreich's boat is at the bottom o' the sea. But he'll be insured. And to be honest wae you, I can hardly be blamed for this incident,' said Hoynes. He knew that he was stretching mitigation to breaking point. But he had to try.

'I've had to inform the Ministry. Aye, and the fishery officer.'

'Och, this had nothing in the least to dae wae fish, unless we have a shoal o' the flying variety in the loch. I'll speak to MacCallum, and we'll come to an understanding.'

'An understanding? Sandy, do you have any idea how much these cabin cruisers cost – thousands. You'll lose everything – and that's being optimistic. If the police get involved ... man, they could be carrying you off in hand-cuffs.'

'Aye, and it nearly Christmas. So much for the spirit o' joy and forgiveness.' Hoynes pulled his pipe from the depths of his pea jacket and tamped some tobacco into the bowl, a slight tremble in his hands. 'What aboot Galbraith, eh? Man, that was a shoddy job, and no mistake. I expected him to fix the engine, no' install a ballistic missile.'

'But, Sandy, you pelted away from the pier as though auld Nick was after you.' Mitchell sighed. 'And you know full well what folk are going to say, don't you?'

'Plenty, if I know this toon.'

'They'll say you did this on purpose. Everybody and their friend knows that you and Dreich MacCallum have a *past.*'

'And they'd be right! The bugger diddled me oot o' my navigation certificate and cheated in a race. It's him you should be talking to. Man, he might be sailing the world without so much as a qualification.'

'I'm sure he's faced harder tests than the one you both sat as boys.'

'But you don't know that for a fact.'

'I'll have to write a report and take some statements. You'll have all and sundry wanting to speak to you, Sandy.'

'Aye, I dare say they will.'

'My advice is to find out where you stand legally. Go and see a lawyer.'

'I'd have been with auld Campbell this minute if we weren't sitting here chewing the cud like a couple o' fishwives.'

'Sandy, you sank a boat in the harbour for which I'm responsible. You surely can't think I'm going to let this go on a nod and a wink?'

'Well, I canna say I'd be averse to the idea, right enough.'

'It was only months ago that you threw an exciseman in the loch.'

'You canna blame me for that. He fair jumped in over the side of his own accord.'

'So you said at the time.'

Hoynes filled the room with pipe smoke. 'You can do me a favour, if you will.'

'Oh, what now?' Mitchell the harbour master was a former lobster fisherman, and although he could be stern, he was always on the side of his fellow mariners.

'Can you see where Dreich is, please?'

Mitchell stepped to the window of his office. Sure enough, MacCallum and Galbraith were staring forlornly over the side of the pier at what remained of the former's vessel.

'He and Galbraith are peering into the loch where his boat should be,' said Mitchell. 'I don't know what they're planning, but if it's salvage, they can forget it.'

'Good. Well, if you wouldn't mind giving me a quick hurl up to the lawyer in that fine motor car of yours, I'd be much obliged. I'm no shrinking violet, you understand, but at this stage, I think it prudent to avoid any altercation wae Dreich.'

'His wife's on her way from London, too – to see the boat. It's only just been refitted.'

'Just make matters worse, why don't you? Come on, let's get going.'

8

There was something about Campbell's office that Hoynes didn't like. It reeked of oppression and last chances, of dwindling hope in the heart of miscreants everywhere. Not that he was, by any means, a miscreant. What had happened was an accident, plain and simple. No man could have avoided it – or so he told himself.

The place was scattered with papers. They sprouted from drawers and filing cabinets, and lay in heaps across the old oak desk, behind which sat the elderly lawyer. He had rheumy blue eyes, a crumpled face and, clamped between his teeth, a cigar from which a length of ash drooped. Though Hoynes knew the man – had done all his life – he still brought to mind a Cockney spiv rather than a man of letters and the law. He was in his late seventies and looked every year of it.

'Sit down, Mr Hoynes.' Campbell took an ample draw of his cigar. 'I don't know what I'd do without these bloody things. They get me through the day – and a wee dram, of course.'

'Mr Campbell, I'll tell you true. Add a good fillet o' fish two or three times a week and you have the recipe for eternal life. I'm sure o' it.'

'You may be right, Sandy. It seems like yesterday I was

sitting at this desk opposite your late father. He was a fine man. I fancy you sail rather closer to the wind than he did.'

'As close as the wind will allow, sir. A man has to be on his toes to make a few bob in these straitened times, and no mistake.'

'Absolutely. My race is almost done, I'm glad to say.'

'Och, don't say that, Mr Campbell. I'm sure you have a year or two left in you, right enough.'

'I was meaning that my professional race is almost done, not that I'm about to breathe my last. I'm just waiting for my son to take over. He should be in place by March next year. So, you might be my last chance for fame. The young ladies in the office tell me you nearly killed half of Kinloch with a missile.'

'As I might have expected, exaggeration oot o' all proportion. It was a mechanical failure, nothing more, Mr Campbell.'

The old lawyer sat back in his chair. 'I'm all ears, Mr Hoynes, all ears.'

The skipper went on to describe that morning's events. Campbell grunted here and there, in order to feign interest. But as Hoynes came to the part of the story where the mechanical component shot from the engine-room hatch and took to the skies, his eyes widened, and he removed the cigar from his mouth. By the time the *Girl Maggie*'s skipper finished his tale with the sinking of Dreich MacCallum's pleasure cruiser, he threw back his head and laughed heartily at it all.

'My, Sandy, but you're a tonic on a cold day. I'd forgotten the lad had that nickname. They called his father the same thing. A more twisted, untrustworthy man never lived. I daresay his son is no better.'

373

'Not one bit, Mr Campbell, I assure you.'

Campbell stubbed out his cigar and rested his head on one hand. 'Tell me, Mr Hoynes, is your insurance up to date – for the boat and operation thereof, I mean?'

'I think so. I've never quite had cause to have much to do with the insurance company. Other than make sure the premiums are paid up on time, of course,' said Hoynes hurriedly.

'And as you describe it, the whole episode appears to be an unfortunate accident. Though you may have to implicate Mr Galbraith, if you believe his work to be sub-standard. I know that will be hard, considering how close the fishing community is in Kinloch.'

'Think nothing o' it, Mr Campbell. As far as I'm concerned, he's mair to blame than me. In my books, a man should dae his work with diligence and pride. It's clear to me Galbraith just bolts one thing to the next wae very little thought whatsoever.'

'I see. Good to know that misplaced loyalty won't be a problem here.'

Hoynes adopted an angelic expression. 'I could be preventing a calamity of a much more serious nature.' He placed his right hand on his chest. 'I feel it is my duty to the public rather than friends and business acquaintances, Mr Campbell.'

'Just so, Hoynes, just so.' He rummaged around the papers on his desk, managing to extract a large leather-bound diary from under the mess. 'I'm making a note here to check on some of the more arcane elements of maritime law and how it applies to this case. I hope you have no issue with me seeking testament from your guests aboard the *Girl Maggie* and other pertinent witnesses?'

Hoynes folded his arms. 'None at all.' He scratched his beard. 'Mind you, I'd steer clear of Dreich MacCallum.'

'Obviously.'

'And Peeny canna help but spin a tall tale or two. He'd likely embellish normal events into something extraordinary. The man should write books.'

'I see.'

'And Malcolm Connelly has a miserable home life. Fair scunnered he is, and that's a fact. Man, I think he'd come oot wae any sort o' nonsense for the sake o' amusement.'

'That doesn't leave many reliable witnesses on board, Sandy.'

'Well, there's Hamish.'

'I knew his father, too. I hope he doesn't suffer from a similar affliction?'

'Now you come to mention it, Mr Campbell, he can take a fair bucket. He has a noble thirst, would be a fairer way to put it. Och, and you know fine what young folk are like these days. He'll likely be up in the air on some concoction o' drugs or another.'

'I believe the term is "high".'

'There, you have the right o' it straight away, Mr Campbell. I'm forgetting you have a young son yourself. He'll likely be fair stoating aboot on the drugs. You'll have had plenty o' experience.'

'He's forty-seven, Mr Hoynes. Rather long in the tooth for such indulgences, wouldn't you say?'

'Man, how time flies. I remember him when he was just a wee lad doon the pier wae a fishing rod. Mind, it wisna me that booted him up the arse when his line got caught in the nets.' Hoynes directed his gaze to the floor, lest his eyes give him away in this particular instance.

'Good. It sounds to me as though, judging by the unreliability of the rest of the witnesses to this incident, it's mainly your word against MacCallum's. The cause of the mechanical failure must lie with Galbraith.'

'Very much so, Mr Campbell.'

'Who would have thought little Kinloch was home to such a parcel of rogues, eh?'

Hoynes nodded in agreement. But he saw fit to raise one index finger as a troubling thought crossed his mind. 'This information – all about the witnesses, I mean. It's between you and me – confidential?'

'Of course.'

'Aye, just so, as expected.'

'Unless, in the unfortunate event of an action, they are called by the other side, and I have to make your opinions of these people known to the court.'

'A court action?'

'Hopefully, it won't come to that, Sandy. But this MacCallum sounds as though he has a bob or two. You can never be too sure with the wealthy. But if everything is as you say it is, I feel we can reach an amicable conclusion to this problem. However, there may be considerable animus, as far as our friend the captain is concerned. I'd lie low until I sort things out, Sandy.'

'You're the man for the job, right enough. I'll no' keep you back. I daresay you'll need to spend the rest o' the day getting this office shipshape. That's bound to take up a few hours o' your time. It looks like thon part fae my engine landed here.' Hoynes stood, shook the lawyer's hand enthusiastically, then took his leave.

Campbell lit a cigar as he watched the fisherman close the door behind him. 'And you're the biggest rogue of them all, Sandy Hoynes.'

9

Sandy Hoynes shivered in the December chill as he made his way down Main Street. The big tree at the bottom of the road was being adorned with lights, and with the smoke from coal fires in the cold frosty air, the place was beginning to feel festive. But what kind of Christmas and New Year would be in store for him? At best, the inadvertent sinking of Dreich's boat would cost him money, at worst there could be a higher legal price to pay.

He had the notion for a dram but knew it would be foolish. It was then that Hoynes remembered his wife had asked him to pick up a couple of things from the shops. He thrust a hand into a pocket of his dungarees and produced the shopping note she'd entrusted him with earlier that morning.

It turned out that all she needed was a loaf of bread, some turnips and a tin of shortbread. It would make for an unusual supper, he thought. But he'd never had cause to question his wife's culinary skills.

As Hoynes made his way down the street, he saw Nancy and Agnes McGowan hobbling towards him. The sisters, of a certain age, were both on sticks. They were kind, well-thought-of women in the town. Long widowed, the fisherman made sure they didn't go without a fillet of fish or two every now and again.

'Good day to you, ladies. Are you out for a bit o' shopping before Christmas?'

Nancy – the elder of the two – glared at him. 'Aye, that was the plan. But since you launched an attack doon at the pier, we're heading home in case we get caught in the crossfire.' Her sister nodded in grim-faced agreement.

'Now, come on, Nancy. You know fine what like the gossip is in this place. It was a mechanical failure, nothing more.'

'Your backside, Sandy Hoynes,' said Agnes. 'Everybody and their friends knows you bear a grudge against Dreich MacCallum. Aye, and you're like an elephant, too. Decades you've been waiting to get back at that man, and you've succeeded. Some memory!'

'And by wicked means into the bargain,' Nancy added.

'None o' this is true at all, ladies.' Though he tried, Hoynes wasn't going to get a chance to speak.

'Norman MacLay telt us that you learned your skills in the Boys' Brigade,' said Agnes.

'What skills?'

'The making of bombs and the like. Well, I'm here to tell you, you'll no' be dropping anything on oor hoose.'

'This is ridiculous. Why don't you both come with me, and we'll get a nice cup o' tea down at the Copper Kettle? I'll even indulge you in a cake or two, eh?' Hoynes smiled at the pair.

'You can stick your cake where your mother never kissed you, Sandy Hoynes,' said Nancy. 'And you needn't bother offloading your auld fish on us. The cat will miss it, but I won't. In any case, I don't want wee Magnus being fed by a scunner like you.'

'You give the best fresh fish to your cat?'

'Watch out, Agnes. He's no' happy. Best we stay in the old bomb shelter tonight in case he drops one o' his missiles on us. Do you know what folk are calling you, Sandy?'

'No, but I could have a guess.'

'Doodlebug, that's what. And, come to think o' it, you've got the build, right enough.'

'Just so, Agnes. There's no' a body in the toon feeling safe this day, and that's a fact,' said Nancy. 'And we're just two o' them.'

With that, arm in arm, they shuffled off, leaving Hoynes in the street feeling most perplexed.

The situation wasn't much better in Michael Kerr's bakery. The young woman who served him was perfectly polite but eyed Hoynes with great suspicion. To the rear of the queue, customers were talking behind their hands.

As he left the shop, Hoynes heard a man's voice say, 'Aye, cheerio, Doodlebug.' It was clear that his worst fears had been realised. The unfortunate accident that had happened earlier that day was now growing arms and legs. Sandy Hoynes was rapidly becoming a pariah in his own community.

It was with great relief that he opened the door to Gilmour's the greengrocer and was greeted with a broad grin by the proprietor.

'How are you the day, Sandy?' said Duncan Gilmour, his hand cupped to his right ear in order to hear the reply.

'I've had better days, to be honest,' said Hoynes in a loud voice. The greengrocer was notoriously hard of hearing, so everyone had to speak up.

'You'll have heard about the basking shark that sunk a boat earlier this morning, eh?'

'No.'

'It was Davie MacClement that told me. I wisna quite catching the detail o' it, but apparently the bloody thing went sailing into a posh boat at the Old Quay.'

Hoynes pleaded ignorance. At the same time, he was well aware that the shopkeeper had just misheard his tale of woe.

Gilmour thrust two large turnips into a paper bag, which he spun round in both hands to twist closed. 'They're saying there's a search on for this fish. Davie reckons they'll gut it. I'm no' for harming such beautiful creatures, but it canna go aboot sinking boats. It's better put oot o' its misery.'

By the time his shopping transactions were complete, Hoynes felt utterly miserable. No doubt, people wanted to gut him. He had to get home; he needed time to think. He'd planned to catch the local bus, but judging by his reception at the shops, the best idea was to take the quiet route up to the scheme.

Sandy Hoynes, master mariner, fishing legend and erstwhile boat sinker, cut a dejected figure as he made his way up to the road with his little bag of groceries. The joy of the festive season might be settling on all and sundry, but for him the prospects were bleak.

10

Dreich MacCallum was sitting on his own in the little reception office of the County Hotel. He'd been trying to contact his lawyer in London since the demise of his cabin cruiser. But the man was proving elusive, and rather than feed coins into the public phone box, he'd asked the hotel management if he could use their facilities, for which he'd pay. They reluctantly agreed, and here he was, waiting for the hour to turn, and to call as he'd been instructed.

With a few minutes to spare, Dreich reflected on his decision to leave Kinloch, all those many years ago. Hoynes and his father had made much of the fact that he'd cheated them out of the navigation certificate, and his father had felt it would be best for his son to spend some time elsewhere.

He remembered the day he'd landed on the docks at Glasgow. There was the promise of a job from a distant cousin, but little more. He'd felt homesick and alone. But things had gone his way. He'd been employed as a junior hand on a small merchant vessel plying her trade from Scotland to Norway. At first, the tug of Kinloch was strong. But as he met new people and saw new places, his dislocation eased, and he soon revelled in being away from the gossip and scrutiny of his hometown.

As Dreich MacCallum looked around the lobby of the County Hotel, he realised almost nothing had changed since his first visit to the place as a boy. In fact, the whole town looked almost identical to the way he remembered it. He shivered at the thought of being stuck here, in the middle of nowhere, for a lifetime. And unlike many folk from Kinloch who found themselves living in other places, he didn't consider this place as home. No, that had been a long time ago.

He checked his watch and dialled the number on the card his lawyer had given him. The phone rang and was answered by a bright female voice.

'Chetlam, Morris and Fincher, can I help you?'

'Yes, Mr Fincher, please. It's Captain James MacCallum, I've been trying to contact him for most of the day.'

'Apologies, Captain MacCallum. He's been in court. I'll put you through straight away.'

Following a click, buzz and a short period of silence, Nigel Fincher's voice boomed from the telephone.

'MacCallum! How are you, old boy? Hope you're spending Christmas on dry land this year?'

'As it turns out, that's very much the case, Nigel.'

There followed Dreich's long description of what had happened that day. Though his depiction of events was reasonably accurate, it was heavily weighted against Hoynes, whom he painted as the villain of the piece.

Once the tale was complete, Fincher hesitated for a moment. 'I must say, this Hoynes chap sounds like the very devil. You've had a lucky escape, if you ask me. My advice would be to steer as far away from him as possible, if you intend to stay in this Kinlock for much longer.'

'It's Kin-*loch*,' said Dreich, still loyal enough to his old home to make sure its name was pronounced properly.

'Damn it, man, you can't expect me to attempt that. I'd choke. I'm of the opinion that one has to be born in Scotland to get your tongue round these guttural words. The bloody Welsh are just as bad. I was drenched by a male voice choir there once. As I recall, it was in a bar in Llanfairfechan . . .'

'Nigel, what are my options?'

'Well, entirely up to you, old boy. His insurance should cover the material loss. But if this chap's the rogue you describe, then perhaps you're as well to try some more punitive civil action – you know, for emotional distress, trauma and the like. I'll have to read up on Scotch law, of course. But there must be some recourse to compensation – above and beyond the initial material payment, you understand.'

'Cash, you mean?'

'Yes, cash, of course. But failing that, well, goods, property and suchlike.'

Dreich thought for a moment. 'Would a fishing boat count in this?'

'It'll depend on the court, but I see no reason why you shouldn't seek some recompense for inconvenience to you, not to mention the shock of it all. It sounds bloody terrifying. The law is very sympathetic to frightened people – on both sides of the border.'

'Right, in that case, I'll go for his fishing boat, the *Girl Maggie*. I'll sail that bloody tub out of Kinloch harbour for the last time.'

'Worth something, is she?'

'I doubt it. Fit for scrap. But it'll ruin Hoynes, and that's what I want to do more than anything.'

'Ha! I wouldn't like to come across you in a dark alley, MacCallum. I'll be in touch. It's this County Hotel, isn't it?'

'It is indeed, Nigel.'

With that, the call ended. Dreich placed the phone on its cradle and sat back, hands behind his head. It was all he could do to keep a wide smile of satisfaction off his face. He knew he'd run into his old enemy on his visit to Kinloch. Dreich hadn't thought much about him for years, but as soon as he spied Hoynes in the bar at the County Hotel, the old feelings returned. He remembered hating him when he was young. The lad was fair-haired and good looking. He caught the eye of the lassies with his easy wit and charm.

But Dreich MacCallum had won the day all those years ago, and he'd win it again.

'Are you finished wae the phone, Mr MacCallum?' said Maureen, the young receptionist. 'It's just I need to use it.'

'Yes, I'm all done here. Thank you very much for the facility. Be sure to add it to my bill. I better get ready for my wife's arrival. She comes off the bus at six.'

Dreich MacCallum swept out of the office, a spring in his step, and disappeared up the wide staircase to his room.

Maureen sat back behind her desk. She thought for a moment or two before consulting the local phonebook. She dialled a number and waited for a reply.

'Hello, two-seven-nine, can I help you?' The woman's voice was warm and friendly, with just a touch of concern.

'It's Maureen at the County Hotel, Mrs Hoynes. Is Mr Hoynes about at all?'

11

To say that the atmosphere in the Hoynes household was tense was putting it mildly. The man of the house was chewing on his pipe, a large dram by his side. Meanwhile, his wife was grating cheese, staring into the middle distance. So distracted was she, the cheese was flowing over the rim of the bowl positioned to contain it.

'There's cheese all o'er the floor, woman,' said Hoynes before taking a fair swallow of his dram.

'Aye, and I'll be lying in amongst it, the way I feel right now, Sandy. What on earth are we going to do?'

'Och, I don't know. The whole thing's grown legs, arms – aye, and a big heid. It was an accident, plain and simple. Aye, no' to mention Galbraith's shoddy workmanship.'

'Still, it was good o' wee Maureen to let us know. Lucky she heard Dreich on the phone.'

'I'm no' sure that *lucky* is the word I'd use aboot any o' this. *Desperate* is a more apt description, I'd say.'

A knock sounded at the door, and Marjorie Hoynes hurried off to answer it, casting a worried look at her husband as she did.

'It'll be Hamish, no' the Grim Reaper. Calm yourself, dear.'

Despite his bravado, Hoynes listened carefully to hear just who was at the door. But his prediction had been correct. Hamish burst into the lounge looking pale-faced.

'Is it true, Sandy – he wants the *Girl Maggie*?'

'So it would seem, son. Here, sit yourself down, and don't be standing there like a prophecy o' doom.'

'What are we to dae, Sandy?' said Hamish, now sitting on the edge of the settee.

'I have a plan, don't worry.'

'Oh, for heaven's sake,' said Marjorie. 'I'm going to phone the doctor and get some o' they Valium folk are going on aboot. I'm a nervous wreck. If it's no' bad enough he's sinking boats, now he's got a plan.'

Hoynes shook his head. 'You needna worry. I've got auld Campbell on the case right this minute.'

'But will Dreich no' have the best lawyer money can buy? No disrespect to Mr Campbell, but he's hardly in the first flush o' youth, Sandy.'

'That he certainly isna. But wae all those accumulated years comes experience. Dreich can have as fancy a lawyer as he likes, but he'll no' have been there and done it like Campbell.'

'That's your plan, then. Put your faith in a man that's near a hundred years old,' said Marjorie. 'I canna say I'm confident.'

'It's a terrible world,' said Sandy. 'Folk think as soon as you're over sixty your race is run. Well, I'm here to tell you, that's a lot o' rubbish.' He straightened his collar. 'Look at me, for instance. Still the finest fisherman on the West Coast, and I saw sixty a good while ago.'

'They say Ronnie Hervey up in Oban has been bringing in huge catches over the last couple o' years,' Sandy,' said Hamish.

'Och, fish are more plentiful up there. Everybody and his friend knows that. It doesna make him the best fisherman.'

'And that Wilson fella on Mull goes right oot into the Atlantic. I hear he's the most formidable navigator aboot.'

'What's he after, whales? There's no point heading away oot into the ocean. Man, you can catch all manner o' strange fish. My father was on a boat once that went away oot. Near at the Azores, they were.'

Marjorie rolled her eyes.

Undaunted, Hoynes continued. 'They hauled in this great fish. As big as a basking shark, she was.'

Unlike Mrs Hoynes, Hamish was all ears. 'What kind o' fish was that, Sandy? A tunny, maybe?'

'No, nor tunny. Nobody could identify the thing. They were all standing gawping at it when the thing raised its heid. "Put me back in the sea, this minute," it said. Aye, wae some authority, too. My faither told me he near had apoplexy. There was the fish, speaking the King's English, as plain as day. If I mind right, it had a bit o' a Spanish twang. But that's to be expected when you're as close to the Azores, right enough.'

'Stuff and nonsense,' said Marjorie.

'It's true, I tell you. They were so feart, the crew did exactly as they were told and threw the damn thing back o'er the side. Did it no' thank them when it was back in its natural element.'

'You'll be telling us it waved them goodbye next,' said Marjorie.

'Don't be ridiculous, dear. Any man knows that a fish canna wave. It's just no' physically possible. But my faither fancied that it swung its tail a couple o' times by way of a "cheerio" before it disappeared.'

Hamish mulled this over for a few moments before

continuing. 'I'm hearing there's a Macleod over on Islay that's a fine fisherman. Never lost for an abundant shoal, they say.'

'Well, that's nonsense right fae the start. Everyone knows fine that there's never been a good fisherman come off that island. Och, they're too immersed in whisky o'er there to steer, never mind catch a fish.' Hoynes took another gulp of his dram. 'In any case, Hamish, you're supposed to be here for moral support. So far, you've done nothing but tell me that near every fisherman on the planet is better at the craft than me.'

'I was just passing on what folk are saying.'

'In that case, haud your wheesht while I tell you my plan.'

'Here we go,' said Marjorie. Knowing her husband as she did, she was sure that what she was about to hear would be inventive. Successful? That was another matter.

'Hamish, you know auld Willie MacEachran.'

'The lobster man that broke his leg?'

Hoynes smiled. 'Aye, you have it straight away.'

'What about him?'

'He asked me the other day if I widna mind attending to his vessel. As you know, a good boat needs much care and attention, and he's no' capable at the moment, being on crutches.'

'I canna see how looking after someone else's boat will save the day, Sandy,' said Marjorie.

'That's no' the plan at all.' Hoynes turned to his first mate. 'Hamish, I want you to be at Dalintober pier at five tomorrow morning. We'll pick up the *Golden Dawn* then.'

'*Golden Dawn* is right, Sandy. Why on earth are we going to fix up the boat that early? Man, it'll be freezing.'

'Aye, and dark, too.' Hoynes winked.

Marjorie thought for a moment. 'I know what you're going to do. And if you think you can hide out in that lobster boat, you're wrong.'

'Och, that's just sheer nonsense. Folk would know the boat was missing. The whole fleet would be out looking for me.'

'What then?' said Hamish.

'I'm taking a wee holiday. Marjorie, where's that bell tent we used to go up the hill wae?'

'That auld thing? It's in the loft, where it's been for about twenty years.'

'Good. Hamish, you can help me get it down. I'm going to go camping for a while.'

'But it's nearly Christmas, Sandy.' Marjorie adopted an incredulous look.

'I'll be back by then, don't worry.'

'It's next week!'

'Listen, I just need time for Campbell the lawyer to come up wae something. Right now, I'm a sitting duck. Forbye, you canna charge folk wae any misdemeanour when they're away working hard and can't be contacted.'

'Busy doing what?' said Hamish.

'Taking Willie's boat out on sea trials.' Hoynes drained his glass. 'I've had enough o' folk looking at me as though I'm about to eat their weans. Aye, and I have to say, I'm a bit put out that folk have mair time for Dreich MacCallum than they do for me. And him a right scunner, too.'

'It just shows you, eh?' said Hamish. 'From hero to villain in a few hours.'

'I know fine, son.'

'And what will you eat? How will you stay warm, Sandy? It's December!' Marjorie bit her lip.

'And how do you think our ancestors survived the cold night, eh? They couldna just put a few more coals on the fire.' Hoynes pondered on this for a moment. 'Well, they likely could, but I'm no' right sure they'd invented coal back then.'

'Coal's been in the ground for millions o' years, Sandy,' said Hamish.

'Aye, I daresay it has. But it's no' been in one o' MacNeally's sacks for that length o' time. Tell me, if I asked you to go and find fuel supplies, what would you do? And don't say you'd be off to the coal merchant.'

'There's the pit at Machrie.'

'Now you're just being obtuse for the sake o' it, Hamish. The answer is simple.'

'What?' said Marjorie.

'Wood. There's piles o' the stuff all around. And where I'm going there's no shortage o' the stuff at all.'

'And where are you going?' said Hamish.

'Needs to be a place I can hide if some bugger happens along. A place wae wood, aye, and plenty o' it.'

'On the coast, Sandy?'

'Aye, on the coast, Hamish. Portroy beach is where I'll hide for a while. Dreich won't take my boat off me, and that's a fact.'

Marjorie wrung her hands. 'But why Portroy?'

'Easy. There's a good forest o' trees just up from the beach. Firdale isna far away in case of emergencies, and there's plenty places to pitch my tent behind big rocks and the like. And face it, who's going to be aboot Portroy beach at this time o' year, eh?'

'Only a fool,' said Marjorie.

'You're no' to be countenanced when it comes to plans,

Marjorie. Just pure misery, every time. Hamish can keep me supplied until it's safe to come back. As far as anyone is concerned, I'm off to Glasgow on business.'

'Is that before or after the sea trials, Sandy?' said Hamish.

'You're just complicating matters wae your attempts at hilarity. I don't care what Dreich tries to do, nobody is taking the *Girl Maggie* off me, and that's a simple fact.'

Marjorie looked at the determined cast of her husband's features. She could have argued that camping out with an ancient tent in the depths of winter was a ridiculous idea. But she knew her husband. Once he'd made his mind up, that was it – for better or for worse.

12

When his alarm burst into life at a quarter past four the next morning, the last thing Hamish had in mind was getting out of bed. When he sat up and put his bedside light on, he could see a great cloud issue forth as his breath froze before him on this bitterly cold day.

But he had his instructions. And since Hoynes was determined to take the course of action upon which he'd settled, as a loyal first mate it was his duty to be of any assistance he could.

Still, as he sat in front of two buzzing bars of the electric fire in the parlour, a cup of tea clasped between both hands, he wished he'd never heard the name Dreich MacCallum. But then he remembered how his father had lost his fishing boat, and how it had cut the man to the core. So much so that the drink, for which he had always been partial, took his life as he wallowed in the misery of it all.

Though Hamish tried to picture Hoynes in this predicament, he found it hard to imagine his skipper succumbing in such a way. Hoynes – even when things were at their darkest – managed to find solace in something, usually his wit and resourcefulness. Yes, there were many great fishermen in the fleet at Kinloch, but none matched Sandy Hoynes for his guile and willingness to think his way out of any dilemma.

But were Dreich MacCallum and his sunken boat a problem too far?

Putting on a vest, two jerseys, his pea jacket, a woolly scarf and a stout pair of gloves, Hamish ventured out into the cold and headed for Dalintober pier.

The town was different in the dark hours just before dawn. The majority of Kinloch's citizens were snuggled in their beds, and there wasn't a soul to be seen. Nothing moved, there were no cars on the road, and the whole place seemed frozen under the great splash of light from a full moon. As Hamish turned a corner, the loch now in view, it cast a great shimmering ribbon across the water. Fishing boats bobbed, a crow shifted from foot to foot on the branch of a tree, its head still under its wing, and a black cat made Hamish jump as it scurried across his path.

He took to the promenade, huddling into his coat against the chill breeze blowing off the loch. The very thought of spending a night out in a tent in such weather seemed akin to madness. But faced with the same difficulties, he couldn't imagine a less dramatic, never mind more effective, course of action. Kinloch could be an unforgiving place to those perceived as wrongdoers, even though what had happened had been little more than an unfortunate accident.

By the time he reached Dalintober pier, it was just before five. He looked about, but there was no sign of Hoynes. Hamish walked along the pier, which once served a separate town. Kinloch had been split in two. But when the head of the loch had been reclaimed, the place became one. Though, even now, there were those who wouldn't live on the north side – and vice versa – not for all the tea in China.

There were three vessels at the pier. Two were fishing boats like the *Girl Maggie*. Just under a ladder sat an open craft, adorned with lobster creels and a pile of old tarpaulins to keep the rain off. Though there was, as yet, no sign of the real thing, the *Golden Dawn* looked in reasonably good shape, given that her owner had fallen out of a taxi some weeks before, following the consumption of a surfeit of whisky, and managed to break his leg.

Hamish stood for a few moments. There was still no sign of Hoynes, so he decided to make his way down the ladder and board the *Golden Dawn*. Once on the vessel, he could at least find some warmth under one of the tarpaulins while waiting for his skipper.

Hamish placed one foot carefully on the side of the boat, before stepping off the ladder and safely aboard. He made his way between some creels before reaching the tarpaulins. Just as he was about to lift one and crawl underneath, the black material stirred and, without warning, a dark figure rose from its midst, sending Hamish staggering backwards.

'Will you stop banging aboot like some bull in a china shop?' said Hoynes. 'Man, you'll wake the whole toon. I've been lying under this bloody tarpaulin for an hour. Come on, let's get underway before everyone's up and aboot.'

With Hoynes choosing to stay partially hidden, it was Hamish's job to fire up the engine, a small in-board diesel.

'That's one hell o' a racket, Hamish,' Hoynes complained as his first mate cast off from the pier.

'There's no' much I can do aboot it, Sandy. Unless you want me to row oot the loch, that is.'

Hoynes stroked his beard. 'Now there's an idea, right enough, Hamish.'

'Well, there's no oars, so you're no' on. I'll keep the revs down, and hopefully that'll keep the racket doon.'

With Hoynes concealed once more under a heap of tarpaulins, they made their way into exile to the chug of the engine. Just as they reached the head of the loch, by the island, a large gull flew low over the boat.

'Look at that great bugger o' a thing, Sandy. Between it and you jumping out the shadows, my heart's going like the clappers.'

'It's a fine beast, right enough, Hamish. Trust me, it's a good sign.' Hoynes watched the great bird soar into the air and head for the hills above Kinloch.

'It'll take us a while to get to Portroy beach. I wish I'd had some breakfast,' said Hamish.

'I thought you'd be light on victuals, what wae your mother still being asleep.' Hoynes handed Hamish a small package wrapped in a brown paper bag. 'Marjorie made them for you. The bacon's cold, but it's welcome at whatever temperature on such a morning.'

Hamish munched down on the bacon sandwich as he navigated between the two buoys that guarded the passage in and out of the loch. Soon, the stars still sparkling overhead, they were in the sound. Hamish turned the vessel north and made for their destination.

'I hope you've got all you need, Sandy. It wouldna be me, camping oot in weather like this.'

'But, remember, you've no' just sunk an expensive vessel belonging to the most vindictive man alive. It's enough to send a soul to the Antipodes wae a view to escape, so it is.'

Now out of the loch, Hoynes felt it was safe to puff a pipe into life. He drew at it lovingly, watching its smoke curl up to the stars. 'Man, we might be on the run, but sometimes it's just good to be alive. Look at the beauty o' it, Hamish.'

But Hamish's gaze wasn't set on the tumble of stars in the clear sky, but on other lights he'd spotted. 'Look, skipper, to starboard, there's a vessel heading this way!'

Hoynes's head snapped round. Sure enough, the lights of an approaching boat were clear in the cold air.

'Do you think it's the fishery officer, Sandy?'

'Don't talk daft, Hamish. He doesna get oot his bed before noon. I hope it's no' the Revenue.' He reached into his pocket and produced a hip flask from which he drew a decent enough dram. 'I'd gie you a swallow, but it's no' the right thing for the man at the tiller.'

'And the sun's no' up yet, never mind o'er the yardarm.'

'I've been under great stress, as you well know. And this isna helping.' Hoynes knocked back another dram and smacked his lips. 'Man, just the thing for this cold weather.'

Though night still reigned over the sound, Hamish had sharp eyes. He peered at the vessel as it neared theirs. 'I'd bet my last penny it's Davie Robertson in the *Sea Harvester*. It's no' like him to be out at this time o' year – or this time o' morning, come to that.'

Hoynes angled his head in the direction of the oncoming craft from under the tarpaulins. 'Worse still, he's the biggest gossip in the toon. If he sees me at this caper, the game's up.'

'Just you stay hidden under there, Sandy. I'll think o' something.'

'I'd like to say I'm convinced of your skills at such matters, but I've little choice.' Complete with his pipe, Hoynes disappeared beneath the tarpaulins.

The chug of the *Sea Harvester*'s engines rent the early

morning air. Her skipper cut them, and she drifted towards the little lobster boat.

'Ahoy there! Is that you, MacEachran?' shouted Robertson from the wheelhouse. The *Sea Harvester*, though a more modern vessel, resembled the *Girl Maggie*, if rather broader in the beam and with generally larger proportions. Having come from the same shipyard, this was no surprise. Robertson never failed to taunt Hoynes about his vessel being the newer, more commodious and of better design.

'It's me, Davie. Hamish from the *Girl Maggie*.'

There were only a few yards between them now. Robertson keened his head out of the wheelhouse. 'It's yourself, right enough. Has Hoynes got you at the boat rustling now?'

'What?' said Hamish, quite confused.

'It's the same as cattle rustling, but wae fishing boats. Man, you're no' yourself this fine morning, Hamish. No' sharp at all.'

'Sandy promised to take auld Willie's boat a run – keep her ticking o'er, so to speak.' The conceit of it all was making the first mate nervous.

'Aye, I see the sense in that. But could you no' do it during the day?'

'I've things to attend to. You know, what wae the *Girl Maggie* being back on the slip.'

'Are they training you how to launch missiles? I've been o'er on Arran playing a couple o' Christmas functions. The whole island is on aboot it. An old boy asked me if Hoynes had any intention of coming to Lochranza. He's planning to go to his sister's in Brodick if your skipper hoves into view. There's folk in fear all up and doon the West Coast, and that's a fact.'

'It was an accident, nothing more.'

Robertson eyed Hamish with suspicion. 'Man, you're jumpy the day, eh? Too much o' the drink?' He gazed at the tarpaulins. 'Or have you something to hide, young fella?'

'What on earth would I have to hide, Davie?'

'Och, when I was a younger man, my father had that wee skiff. She'd been a ring netter, but he kept her for nostalgic reasons. I can tell you, there was no better way to spend some time alone wae a young lady. I'd some good times on that wee boat, I'll tell you.' His face took on a faraway look as he brought to mind past romantic encounters. 'Don't worry, I know fine what Kinloch is like. Everything you do is scrutinised, and that's a fact. Yor secret's safe wae me, Hamish.'

Unfortunately, at that moment, Hoynes, who'd been suppressing a cough for longer than was healthy, could do so no more. Made worse by the pile of filthy tarpaulins under which he was concealed, it was a chesty, unhealthy, hacking noise that issued from his throat, indicative of a regular user of tobacco.

Robertson looked on in surprise. 'Are you sure you should have the lassie oot in this weather, Hamish. Man, that's some cough. Reminds me o' my auld grandfaither, so it does. And he had croup!'

Resigned to the fact that Robertson was now sure there was someone else aboard, Hamish had to think on his feet. 'She's recovering fae the pleurisy, Davie. Had a right bad doze, so she did. The doctor said she should get the morning air.'

Under the tarps, Hoynes was rooting for his first mate, though he was doubtful that the excuse Hamish had come up with held water. He felt the cough reflex kick in and reached for his pipe – the only thing guaranteed to stop the convulsion in its tracks.

Davie Robertson looked down on the *Golden Dawn*'s deck once more as a cloud of blue smoke issued from under them, drifting up in the cool, dark air. The familiar odour of tobacco drifted between the boats. Robertson sniffed at it like a dog. 'Aye, she likes a good shag, that's for sure.'

'I beg your pardon?' said Hamish, balling his fists in anger. 'I'll no' have you speak like that aboot the lassie!'

'Tobacco – she has a fine taste in tobacco. You must have heard it called that. Don't you be getting your knickers in a twist, young man. Anyway, I better be off and leave you to your romancing,' said Davie with a wink. 'Here, her name isn't Sandra, by any chance? Sandra Hoynes, that is.'

'Eh?' said Hamish, but his question was lost in the rumble of the *Sea Harvester*'s engines. Robertson waved a jaunty hand out of the wheelhouse, and in a churn of water was off on his way to Kinloch.

Hoynes waited until the sound of the engines drifted off on the breeze. The coast being clear, he pushed his head up. 'Man, you should try your hand at espionage, Hamish. You have a flair for making folk think what you want them to think.'

'I do? Thanks, Sandy.'

'I'm being sarcastic. There's no' a man or woman alive would have fallen for that parade o' nonsense. I might as well have stood up and shouted, *look, it's me on the run!*'

'Well, you didna help matters by puffing at your pipe and coughing your lungs up. Goodness knows what kind o' lassie Davie thinks I'm knocking aboot wae.'

'Davie knows fine what's afoot. He might no' know why,

but when he gets back to Kinloch, he'll put two and two together. *Is her name Sandra?* Did you no' get that?'

'What will we do?'

'You keep your own counsel, Hamish. We stick to the story, and that's that. Anyhow, knowing your record wae the opposite sex, there're maybe folk willing to believe you're trawling aboot wae a lassie suffering fae chronic bronchitis and a love o' good pipe tobacco. In any event, there's nobody can prove otherwise.'

'If you say so, Sandy.'

'Aye, I do. Come on, let's press on to Portroy beach before the sun's up. My thoughts are wae those poor folk o'er on Arran – fair suffering the dirges Davie comes oot wae on thon banjo o' his, they must be.'

They sailed on: Hoynes deep in thought as to the consequences of their unfortunate encounter with Robertson, Hamish fretting about what his mother would say if she heard tell of the unhealthy woman under the tarpaulin.

13

After a spell of quiet sailing, Hoynes puffing at his pipe as Hamish made sure all was in order with navigation, they happened upon a sandy cove, dotted with rocks.

'This is it, Hamish. Ease her into the sand,' said Hoynes.

Hamish did as he was asked, kissing the *Golden Dawn* to halt on the beach.

'I've taught you well, no doubt about it. I couldna have done that better myself.'

Unused to such praise – any praise – Hamish smiled with satisfaction. He admired his skipper, and to be congratulated for his nautical skills made him proud.

Hoynes looked about, just as the sun, yet to rise, was making its presence felt in the sky. Fewer stars were visible in the firmament, and the moon looked less bright than it had done when they'd left Kinloch. Morning was almost upon the fugitive Sandy Hoynes.

'There's a spot up on the machair that will make a decent place for a tent.' Hoynes produced two ample kit bags, the type used by sailors during the war. 'You take this one, Hamish. There's a couple o' boxes, too. One has food in it, the other has some chopped wood to get a fire going. Stow them on the beach and we'll take things up one by one.'

The fishermen went about their business in a seamanlike fashion, methodically and efficiently. Soon, up on the rough grass, just behind a large rock, Hoynes began pitching the old bell tent.

It was only when they'd laid the groundsheet that Hamish realised how big it was. 'You could fit an army in here, Sandy.'

'I should think so, too, for it came from the army in return for herring. You can fit five in here, at a push.'

This wasn't the discreet hideaway Hamish had imagined. When he picked the next item from the bag, it became obvious that Hoynes had no intention of slumming it in his impromptu camp. 'What's this, Sandy?'

'Man, what a device this is. A wee camping stove, Hamish. It sits inside the tent and fair warms the place up. Aye, and you can cook on her, too. I'll be snug as a bug. The chimney is o'er there – just fit the pieces together, and away we go.'

By the time the tent was assembled, it looked more like something a Bedouin tribesman would call home, rather than a Kinloch fisherman on the run. Hoynes even unfurled a fireside rug, which he spread out in front of the stove. There were two stout camping chairs and a little cot, likely courtesy of the army. Hoynes spread a pile of thick woollen blankets on it and stood back to admire his handiwork, all illuminated under the warm flickering light of an old oil lamp.

'No' bad at all, eh?'

'It'll be cosier when you get the fire going, Sandy.'

'It will that. But I can handle that myself. I want you to come and restock me with supplies and wood every couple o' days, Hamish.'

'How long do you plan to hide out here?'

'As long as it takes Campbell to sort things out. He told me it would take a few days.'

'You're surely no' considering spending Christmas and New Year here?'

Hoynes stroked his beard. 'Well, you could spend it in worse places. Aye, and the cost o' presents alone justifies the inconvenience. No' to mention all these buggers that descend on the hoose at Hogmanay and decimate my whisky. No, things could be worse.'

'What about your wife?'

'Aye, I'll need to clean and cook for myself. But I couldna expect her to suffer such hardship at this time of year.'

'No. I meant, she'll be fair lonely. You know, you hiding out and her all alone o'er the festive season.'

'Och, she'll be fine. Marjorie is great at amusing herself. She'll likely get the cards oot and play some solitaire. Aye, and there's always the wireless.'

Hamish looked at him doubtfully. 'It doesna sound like much fun to me, Sandy.'

'You're a young man, Hamish. Excitable. It's all drugs and the free love to you. For people oor age, well, we'd rather have a good bowl o' cock-a-leekie soup. Here, have a dram and stop your havering.' Hoynes reached under the covers of his cot and produced a bottle of whisky.

'I'll have one – just to banish the cold, you understand. Mind, I've got to get Willie's boat back to Kinloch, Sandy.'

'A true lifeline, so it is. Don't forget – come back the day after tomorrow, same time. Aye, and bring any news o' Campbell the lawyer and bloody Dreich.'

'No' this early, surely?'

'Most definitely! The fewer folk see you going aboot

your business, the better. And don't worry about Davie Robertson. He canna prove that wisna your young squeeze under that tarpaulin.' He sipped his dram. 'Hopefully, Campbell will come up wae something and I'll be home in no time. But meantime, Willie MacEachran's boat is pivotal to the operation. Man, I've never seen a man fonder o' a vessel. It's breaking his heart that he canna get aboard wae that leg in plaster. It's a credit to us that we're trusted wae the thing.'

Hamish finished his dram, feeling its warmth in his chest. It was cold, but he was sure that once Hoynes got the fire raised, things would warm up.

'Right, you get back to Kinloch, Hamish. Take a wee trip up to see Campbell. He's expecting you. He'll give you all the latest on my legal difficulties. Keep your ear to the ground and make sure to rubbish anything that bugger Robertson has to say. Come on, I'll walk you back down to the boat.'

They left the tent and stepped back into the morning. The sun was now above the horizon, though the moon still loomed large in the sky. A patch of stars still shone in the part of the heavens yet to be liberated by light. The sound was still, not a wave to be seen, its surface like glass.

Hamish was first on the beach. But the sight that met him sent his heart into his mouth. 'Oh dear!'

'What are you *oh dear*-ing aboot, eh?' Hoynes followed Hamish's gaze. There was one vessel to be seen, bobbing as though at anchor about five hundred yards from the shore. Normally, this wouldn't have been worthy of a mention. But the fact that the craft in question was the *Golden Dawn* saw Hamish's jaw drop and the pipe slip from Hoynes's mouth.

'I thought you put her at anchor, Sandy.'

'You were skippering the barky. It was your job to make sure she was secure!'

'I suppose I'm used to you giving me the order.'

Hoynes shook his head. 'Here was me praising your skills as a mariner when you kissed the beach, while all the time I'd have been as well having Marjorie at the helm.'

Hamish threw off his pea jacket and began pulling his jumper over his head.

'What on earth are you doing?' said Hoynes, liberating his pipe from the sand.

'She's no' that far oot. I can swim to her and get her back to the shore.'

Hoynes clamped his hand on Hamish's shoulder. 'Man, don't be daft. That water will freeze you solid. It's bad enough having Dreich on my back, without having your death on my conscience into the bargain.'

Hamish pulled his jumper back down. 'Thanks, Sandy, I appreciate it. I'm so sorry aboot the boat.'

'Don't get carried away. At the moment I'm swithering as to whether to ram this pipe doon your throat or not. How could you have been so careless? That's us lost two boats in a matter o' days. Back to the tent. Aye, and you better get used to it, for we'll likely be here for the rest o' oor lives. Forget the legal consequences, the shame will keep us here for ever.'

Hamish looked on as Hoynes stomped back up the beach to the campsite. There had been many moments in his life he'd been happy to forget. This was, undoubtedly, one of them.

14

By lunchtime, Kinloch was awash with gossip. Not only had Willie MacEachran's boat disappeared from Dalintober pier, neither Sandy Hoynes nor Hamish were anywhere to be seen.

Peeny stood at the bar of the County Hotel, a mug of tea in front of him rather than a dram. When Malcolm Connelly appeared through the door, he eyed this spectacle quizzically.

'Have you taken the pledge, Peeny?'

'No, that I have not, Malcolm. You'll have heard the stories about Sandy and Hamish?'

'I know they've gone. You want to hear Galbraith doon at the slip. He swears that Hoynes has decamped so he doesna have to pay the repair bill.'

'Och, his backside. The man must take some o' the responsibility in all this. After all, it was him that made the repair.'

'And it was the repair that shot oot the hatch and sank Dreich's boat. You're right enough. You know Sandy as well as I do. He'll be up to something.'

Peeny stroked his chin. 'Based upon previous experience, you'd think so. But I'm no' so sure. Remember, the man's no' been the same since Dreich appeared back in the toon. He took to his bed for nearly a fortnight. They tell me Marjorie had to get Hamish to pull him from under the sheets and drag him into a bath. Fair stinking, he was. Aye, hair straggling doon his back and a beard like an oak tree in full leaf.'

'Away! I canna believe that, Peeny. He didna look any different to me the other day.'

'He'd put things to rights by that time. I'm telling you, I saw a change in him.'

'Is that why you're on the tea?'

'No, my wife's away to get my pension. That miserable bugger behind the bar wouldna advance me the price o' a dram.'

'I'll sort you oot wae that, man.'

'Very kind o' you, Malcolm.'

'When will she be back?'

'Who?'

'Your wife wae the pension.'

'Just directly, I reckon.'

'Great, you can pay me back when she arrives.'

Peeny eyed his old friend. He was famous for his parsimony, and it was clear that nothing had changed.

With their drams, they took a seat at the back of the bar to discuss Hoynes's plight.

'I think it's time for us to stand up and be counted, Malcolm,' said Peeny. 'We all know fine what a rascal Sandy can be. But there's no' one o' us he hasn't helped o'er the years.'

'Aye, he kept my boat going when I'd the mumps thon time.'

'And he ran my Janice up and doon to Glasgow when I had to get my appendix oot.'

'No' forgetting the time he bailed us oot the jail on Islay.'

Peeny winced. The infamous Battle of Bowmore was still

talked about. The Kinloch football team had been on the island to play their Islay counterparts. Unfortunately, following an away victory, things got out of hand, and the Kinloch contingent, holed up in a bar in the centre of the town, did a fine job of defending themselves against angry locals.

'Man, that was a day and a half. Hard to think it's o'er thirty years ago.'

'Och, the weans these days are too soft to do the game justice, Peeny. They all want to be George Best. Mair interested in strong drink and women than they are in football.'

The pair took a gulp of their drams in unison.

'The drink, if you canna handle it, it's a curse, right enough. Best is throwing away his talent, and that's a fact,' said Peeny.

The door swung open, revealing a bleary-eyed Davie Robertson.

'You've no' got that banjo wae you, I hope?' said Connelly.

'I've had enough o' that for a while. I played two Christmas parties on Arran. My fingers need a rest.'

'We should be thankful for small mercies,' said Peeny. 'We're discussing Sandy and Hamish. Nowhere to be found, apparently.'

'I saw them this morning. Well, Hamish was at the tiller o' Willie MacEachran's lobster boat, and Sandy was hiding under a pile o' auld tarpaulins. Hamish tried to make out he was on a mission wae some lassie. But she must smoke the same baccy as Hoynes, and besides that, she has one hell o' a smokers' cough.'

'Where were they headed?' asked Peeny.

'It was top secret, wherever it was. Hamish wisna for saying, and Sandy was staying put, playing deid. The pair o' them must think I'm half daft.'

409

Peeny smiled. 'Nobody can say you're half daft, Davie. You canna sing, and you get a terrible racket oot o' that banjo, but you're no' daft.'

Davie Robertson was about to protest when once more the door was flung open.

Peeny's wife Janice rushed into the bar. 'Thank the Lord you're still here. I came as quick as I could.'

'Man, you're desperate for your pension, right enough,' said Connelly.

'What's the matter, Janice?' said Peeny. 'You're as white as a sheet.'

'They found auld Willie MacEachran's boat in the sound about an hour ago. Just fair floating like the *Mary Celeste*, so she was. The daft bugger likely tried to take her oot wae that broken leg and got into difficulties. Poor old soul. He fair loved that boat.'

Peeny gave Davie Robertson a knowing look. 'It's no' Willie we have to be worried aboot, is it, Davie?'

'What are you three at?' said Janice, looking between them.

'It's a long story, dear. Suffice it to say, I think we should get ourselves doon the pier and speak to Mitchell the harbour master.'

'Aye, you're right.' Connelly nodded in agreement. 'I'm thinking this whole episode sounds wrong. Maybe the accident, and all that's happened since, has sent Sandy oot his mind.'

'To be fair,' said Robertson, 'considering the amount o' whisky he can put away, he was rarely in it.'

'Kidding and swanking aside, he's oor pal, has been all oor lives. And Hamish isna much mair than a boy – despite the way his hair's retreating at a rate of knots,' said Connelly. He looked at Peeny. 'You better let herself gie you that pension. Mind, you still owe me the price o' a dram.'

'That's the spirit, Malcolm. Poor Sandy and Hamish have maybe drawn their last breaths, and all you can think aboot is money. Gie him two shillings, Janice,' said Peeny.

'Oh, I forgot all aboot your pension. You'll need to queue up at the Post Office and get it yourself. I've folk to tell as to the truth o' this matter.' Janice got to her feet, and before her husband had time to protest, she was off at a clip to keep Kinloch informed.

'What were you saying aboot money, Peeny?' said Connelly.

'The pension can wait. Let's get down and tell Mitchell what Davie witnessed. I'm thinking we need to rally round. There's no' a man or boy in the fleet who won't sail out for Hoynes.'

15

On Portroy beach the mood was one of despondency. Hoynes was sitting on the camping cot drawing on his pipe thoughtfully, while Hamish whittled away with his penknife at a piece of wood he'd found on the shore.

'I think this looks like one o' they moon rockets they keep talking aboot,' said Hamish, admiring his own handiwork.

'You've some imagination, right enough. No common sense, but plenty imagination.'

Hamish threw the little piece of wood to the ground. 'I'm going for a walk. It would pay you to remember that you were the one who conceived this ridiculous plan. If you ask me – and I hate to say it – but you're just avoiding your responsibilities.'

Hoynes eyed his first mate with disdain. 'You should have been there to advise me, Hamish. You know how carried away I get when it comes to Dreich MacCallum. You should have been there to talk me doon, and no' had me racing oot onto the loch like some madman. Any engine repair must be treated wae respect.'

'So it's my fault! That's it, I'm off!' Hamish pulled his cap down on his head and ducked out of the tent.

Hoynes shook his head. He knew that the entire predicament was down to his foolhardiness. Normally, he was a man of quiet calculation, who weighed up his options and the likelihood that his plans – not always entirely legitimate – were achievable. MacCallum's presence seemed to have robbed him of this innate sensibility. He left the tent and wandered down the beach to the water's edge.

Like most men of his profession, Hoynes could observe the sky, feel the wind on his face, sniff the air and be able to foretell the weather. As he stood, he saw the Isle of Arran obscured by pearlescent cloud. The breeze – already cold – carried the promise of something more visceral, a chill that would work its way through to the bones and remain there until the weather changed. It was going to snow.

'Damn me!' he cursed to himself. 'If it's no' one thing, it's the next.'

Hoynes heard the cry of a bird and looked up. High above, a great gull was circling. Silhouetted by the low winter sun, it looked like a crucifix in the sky, its long wings outstretched as it rode the wind.

'I'd love to be as free as you,' he whispered to himself as he gazed at the seabird. He thought back to being young, with few cares and worries. Time and tide were odd things. The older he became, the more he felt the cold of winter and the heat of summer. The rain made his joints ache, and no number of jumpers and jackets could keep out the chill of frost and snow.

'But you can be free.'

Hoynes looked round. The beach was deserted, save for a seal lumbering into the sea a few yards away and the bird that still hovered in the fading yellow of the sun.

'Everyone will be free one day of the cares that hold them down.'

As he gazed across the sound again, the sky seemed to change. The pearlescence remained, but it took on a darker, purple hew.

'Sometimes you have to let go, Sandy.'

Though he knew the voice was in his head, it was distinct, familiar, not some stray thought or fancy.

'Hona, is that you?'

The question was greeted with silence.

It was as though the world had stopped turning. Nothing moved. The seal had disappeared, and instead of the gull circling in the sky, it hung there, motionless, in quiet benediction.

'Is it my time?' said Hoynes.

'No, not yet. But one day it will be. It will be here, in this place.'

The words should have shocked the old fisherman, but instead they were strangely comforting.

'Everyone must face the end with as much strength as they can muster. It's fear of the unknown that makes us scared to face this day. But there need be no such emotion. In life, we all have purpose, no matter how small or insignificant that may seem. In the end, the meek and the mighty, the weak and the strong are as one. And there is peace.'

Hoynes closed his eyes. It would be so easy to let go. The thought had crossed his mind during his self-imposed exile in bed.

'You don't want to lose those you love. But love can never be lost, not ever. It stays in your heart for eternity, as do all you care for.'

'But what about your enemies? They have a knack of appearing just when you don't expect them.'

'Friend, foe – what does it really mean? A lifetime spent

slaying demons leaves only the shell of a man who is intimately acquainted with those things. Seek out not those who make you happy, but those you love.'

'Aye, makes sense, I daresay.'

Laughter echoed in Hoynes's head. 'Of course it makes sense. Why on earth would you want to be with those who drag you into the depths? For you, the time will be slow. But for me – well, it will happen in an instant. I will see you soon, my friend.'

In a split second, it was as though the world sparked back into life. The breeze was fresh on his face, birds called in the grey sky, and he saw the distant hull of a ship somewhere off the Ayrshire coast. As he made his way back up the beach, he was deep in thought. Flakes of snow landed on his jacket and settled there, white and sparkling.

Did he fear death – the end? Yes, any sane person would. But somehow, Hona's voice in his head had allayed those fears. After all, this man, this entity – whatever it was – must come from somewhere.

Could Hona be a figment of his own imagination? Did the man that so fascinated him only exist in his mind?

But that couldn't be. After all, he'd escaped many problems – near death, even – thanks to his distant ancestor. He'd seen the man before he read about him in a book. He seemed as real as any creature – maybe more so. Nature, red in tooth and claw, as he'd heard said.

'There are more things in heaven and earth,' he whispered to himself.

As he made his way back to the tent, Hoynes was aware that time had passed. The sun was in a different place in the sky. He puzzled on this as he ducked back into the bell tent.

415

'Where on earth have you been, Sandy? I was beginning to get worried,' said Hamish.

'I was only down at the shore.'

'Which shore? When you didn't appear back, I took a wander down, and there was no sign o' you. Man, you must have been gone for o'er three hours.'

'Away and stop your havering, man.' He looked back out of the tent flap. It was snowing heavily now. They'd need to find more wood to burn.

'How do you like this, Sandy?' Hamish was holding up the top branches of a small fir tree. 'I reckoned that if we're to be here over Christmas, we'd best have a tree. I found these pine cones – they'll do as decorations.'

Hoynes looked at the tree, then back at his first mate. 'Can I ask you a question, Hamish?'

'Aye, of course.'

'Do you believe in something different – you know, otherworldly, that sort o' thing?'

'I know I've had feelings about things before they happen. You know that.'

'I do. Well, pour yourself a drink and sit by that fire, for I've a tale to tell.'

16

Dreich MacCallum watched his wife as she brushed her hair in the mirror. She was a beautiful woman, of that there was no doubt. Kind, gentle, affectionate, Tabitha was everything he could have wished for and more than he deserved. But she'd been brought up in the bosom of a privileged family. Many would have put her outlook on life down to being a spoilt only child. But, as he'd discovered, the woman he'd met as a young captain of a small charter vessel just assumed that life was filled with nice things. And despite himself, he couldn't hold it against her.

'Oh, James, I'm so angry about the boat. You sailed her all the way here and this happens. Rotten luck, if you ask me.' Tabitha applied a touch of rouge to her cheeks.

'I know, bloody bad luck. I couldn't wait to take you out in her and show you where I'm from.' Dreich was shuffling through some papers that he'd spread across the bed. He picked one up, sighed and tucked it into the breast pocket of his jacket.

'What does one eat in Kinloch? Fish, I suppose,' said Tabitha.

'You'd be amazed, Tabby. I saw a man eating a beef sandwich the other day,' he said sarcastically.

She stared back at him, not sure if he was being genuine. 'Don't be mean, James. I'm starving.'

'Well, once you're ready, we'll go for lunch.'

Tabitha checked her reflection in the mirror and smiled. 'All set.'

Locking the room door behind them, the MacCallums made their way down to the spacious dining room. They took a seat under a tall window with panes of stained glass, through which diffused an amber light that spilled onto the white linen tablecloth.

'Now, let's see if your tales about beef sandwiches are on the money.' Tabitha picked up a lunch menu from the table.

As she was taking it in, a young waitress appeared. 'Good afternoon to you. I have a message for you, Mr MacCallum.'

'Oh yes, who from? Hoynes, I hope.'

'No, it's from Mr Campbell the lawyer. He's waiting in the lobby. Just arrived.'

Dreich had been waiting for a meeting with someone representing Hoynes. This was his chance. The man could run, but he couldn't hide. 'I'll be with him directly, thank you.'

The waitress left, and Tabitha turned to her husband. 'I thought we were having lunch together, darling?'

'And we are. I'll only be a few minutes with this Campbell chap. He'll be pleading poverty on Hoynes's behalf, I'm sure.'

'Oh dear. I mean, it's such bad luck. But this fisherman chap, how can he afford to pay you back?'

'He has a boat of his own, dear. Get yourself a G&T, and I'll be back in a jiffy.'

In the lobby, an old man in a suit that had seen better days was sitting at a table on his own, a cup of coffee and ream of papers before him.

'You'll be Mr Campbell,' said Dreich, holding out his hand.

'Aye, that I am.' Campbell struggled to his feet and shook Dreich's hand firmly. 'It's a pleasure to see you again, Captain MacCallum.'

'Again?' Dreich studied the man before him. He was overweight, with a stained tie and suit collar spotted in grey ash. He had no recollection of Campbell at all. But he supposed that people changed over nearly half a century.

They took their seats.

'I remember you as a young lad. Your late father, too, God rest his soul.'

'He was a fine man,' said Dreich.

'He was,' said Campbell, not entirely convincingly.

Irritated by this, Dreich bridled. 'I'm having lunch with my wife. Couldn't we have arranged a more convenient time for this meeting?'

'I'll not keep you a moment, I promise, Captain MacCallum. I just have a couple of questions – from Mr Hoynes's insurance company, you understand.'

'I see. To be perfectly honest with you, I'm surprised he has insurance.'

'Mr Hoynes is a stickler for the rule book, I can tell you.'

'That's a bigger shock.'

Campbell donned a pair of half-moon spectacles. 'You sailed to Kinloch from Glasgow before tying up at the pier, am I right?'

'I did. The cruiser was in dry dock for repairs. That yard in Glasgow was where she was originally built, Mr Campbell.' Dreich shifted uncomfortably in his chair.

'That would be Marshall and Sons, Boat Builders. Just off Anderston Quay?'

'Yes, that's correct.'

'Excellent. Now, you work as a ship's captain with the Wiston Steam Packet Company, I think I'm right in saying?'

Dreich nodded.

'Sailing from Southampton?'

'Yes! What is this, twenty questions?'

'Och, I'm just compiling the facts, nothing more.'

'Please be a bit quicker about it.'

'Just so, Captain MacCallum, just so. In that case, let me express my sympathies. It's never easy to lose one's employment.'

'I beg your pardon?'

'I'm sorry. I was under the impression that you were made redundant in September. Is that incorrect?'

'Semi-retirement. I want more time to spend with my wife and children. But I'm still sailing, I assure you. I don't know where you get your information, Mr Campbell.'

'From a Mr Stones. I believe he's the man in charge of personnel at Wiston's. Or am I again mistaken?' Campbell removed a large cigar from the breast pocket of his jacket. 'You don't mind if I smoke, do you?'

Dreich waved his hand. 'Do what you like.'

As Campbell lit his cigar, Dreich fidgeted with his tie. 'Mr Stones isn't the most reliable of men. He's old and has a memory to match. If you're finished, I'd like to get back to my wife and lunch, if you don't mind.'

'Absolutely. I thank you so much for your time, Captain.' Campbell paused. 'Although . . . is that title still appropriate now you're on the beach, so to speak?'

'I'll ignore that. I realise you're only trying to goad me. For the last time, I'm only semi-retired!' Dreich stood, ready to leave.

420

'Just one final question, if you don't mind.'

'What?' Dreich's irritation was plain.

'If I could have the address of your insurers, please? Just following procedure, I'm sure you understand.'

'I'll have their card sent to your place of business, Mr Campbell. But I think you'd spend your time more profitably working out how to defend your client. Though I doubt you have the wherewithal. Now, if you'll excuse me.' Dreich strode off in the direction of the dining room.

Campbell puffed on his cigar. 'Aye, a bad lot, the MacCallums. Just like his father before him.' He brushed ash from his lapel.

17

The situation at the quay was fraught. Mitchell, though responsible for the harbour, and even the launching of the lifeboat, had no jurisdiction beyond that point. The Coastguard, anxious to discourage a parade of vessels unsuited to the hazards of winter sailing from piling out of port to look for Hoynes, refused to authorise an official search. In any event, heavy snow was already falling in the sound and forecast to reach Kinloch soon. Instead, the local lifeboat and its counterpart from Brodick would search for the missing mariners, so long as conditions permitted.

Malcolm Connelly glared at Mitchell. 'You'll have those men's lives on your conscience. How can you be part of such a thing?'

'You know very well that I have absolutely no authority in this case. The three of you must know what will happen. Folk will be taking off in pleasure craft and all sorts if they hear there's an official search on for Hoynes – and you're more than aware of the sea at this time of year. It's already blizzard conditions further up the coast.'

Peeny looked heavenward, just as the first fat flakes of snow began to fall. 'And if this gets worse, the lifeboats will be called back to port because o' visibility. These men could die o' cold, even if they have managed to reach safety onshore.'

'And they'll be in no condition to seek aid on land,' said Robertson. 'Cold, starving. I widna like to be you having this to think o' as you sit doon wae your goose, Mitchell.'

The harbour master, knowing full well what the consequences of the Coastguard's decision were, lit a cigarette, a slight tremble in his hands. 'There's nothing I can do, and you know it.' He took a puff. 'But I can suggest *something*.'

'Like what?' said Peeny.

'Well, there's nothing to stop you leaving the harbour. I can't stop you, that's for sure. Neither can the Coastguard.'

Peeny caught Robertson's eye. 'Right, Davie. Are you up for it?'

Robertson nodded. 'I was thinking the very same thing myself, Peeny. And there's no time like the present.'

'I'll come too,' said Connelly. 'Have you supplies aboard, Davie?'

'Are you kidding? I came back wae pies, Christmas cake, two geese and a partridge.'

'Are they all in a pear tree?' said Peeny.

'No, and there's nae French hens, neither.'

'I'll just pretend I never heard this conversation,' said Mitchell, turning to head back to his office.

'Will we go now or round up some more fishing boats?' said Connelly.

'You know folk at this time o' year, Malcom. They'll either be half cut or away somewhere. We could rouse a few, but it would take a while.'

'You're right, Peeny. It's best we just get out there before this snow sets in proper.'

'Don't worry, if we get stuck and forced to heave-to, I've got the banjo on board. We can have a singsong.'

Peeny glared at him. 'We already have two missing colleagues. It would be a tragedy to make it three.'

'You men are sore on me. I'll have you know my playing is admired all the way up the West Coast.'

'Please add "and beyond", for that's what we're hoping for.'

'Right, come on, boys. Time's pushing on – let's dae the same.'

Before long, the *Sea Harvester* was chugging out of the loch, as snow fell with evermore determination.

Mitchell watched them until they passed the island at the head of the loch and disappeared from sight. 'Aye, godspeed to you, boys. Bring them back safely.'

✧

Sandy and Hamish had limited success finding wood. The fishermen, unused to life on land, hadn't taken into account that firewood was best when it was dry. In fact, as they'd discovered, when they tried to light some of the branches and twigs they'd scavenged from the woodland above the beach, they sparked and spat, but refused to catch fire.

'Damn me, Hamish. The logs I brought wae me are near done. It'll be a bloody cold night if we canna set light to this wood.'

Hamish looked on with a sigh. Being a man acquainted with the thin places and notions that there may well be something more, beyond the realm of human understanding, he'd listened to Hoynes's tales about Hona the Viking with great interest. But then he began to wonder if the last few weeks had just been too much for his old skipper. The appearance of Dreich MacCallum had changed him, of that there was no doubt. Gone was the man so confident in his own abilities he seemed almost indestructible. The very fact they were holed up in a tent to avoid Dreich as the days turned to Christmas was proof enough of that.

Hoynes stroked his beard. 'It's clear that you'll be a while coming up wae a workable solution, that's for sure.'

'Why would you expect me to know anything aboot this caper? I've never been camping in my life. Well, apart fae a few Scout camps, and they were just up the hill. I could see the hoose fae the tent. And my mother isna fond o' creepy-crawlies. The nearest we ever came to this was going away on my faither's boat and sleeping on it.'

'Hardly an adventure, for sure. When I was a lad, we'd be up the hill every summer. Man, we'd camp under old coats held up wae a stick and eat fish we'd caught roasted o'er a bonfire.'

'Fine in July, Sandy. No' just as easy in December.'

Hoynes, though he wouldn't admit it, had to agree. Many things hadn't gone to plan in his life. But few had ended as disastrously as this predicament promised to. 'We should pile the wood up next to the fire. That way, it might dry off a bit. You be aboot that, while I pour us a dram. Either way, we'll be warmer than we are now, and that's a fact.'

Acknowledging that Hoynes was right, Hamish did as he was asked and piled the paltry collection of broken branches and twigs around the little camping stove. At the moment, it was cosy enough. But it wasn't hard to imagine what would happen when the only wood that would burn ran out.

Hamish took a seat beside Hoynes on the cot. Each of them had an enamel mug containing a decent pour of whisky.

'This reminds me o' a story my faither telt me,' said Hoynes.

'Oh aye, what was it aboot?'

'Wae back, och, in the early eighteen hundreds, three fishermen left the toon. Hale and hearty young men they were. Good lads with promise o' greater things at the fishing, right enough. In fact, one o' them, Donald, was off my mother's side o' the family.'

'They're out at the fishing, so what now?'

'Well, the day wore on, and the weather turned. It had been a middling October morning, but by the afternoon, there were gales, thunder and hailstones. Och, just hellish, all together. As the evening approached, there was no sign o' them.'

'Where were they fishing, Sandy?'

'No' far fae here, as it turns oot. Just out in the sound.'

Hamish automatically looked towards the sound, even though his view was blocked by the flapping canvas of the tent. 'There'd have been a search, eh?'

'No such thing. It was considered too risky. Men wanted tae go, but the womenfolk put paid to that. The young men just had to take their chances.'

'Man, that's a bit rough, is it no'?'

'Hamish, you must understand that things were different then. Life was often short and tragic. Och, we don't know we're living, what wae all oor home comforts and that.'

Hamish looked about the tent. In the flickering light of the gas lamp and the stove, it was hard to see any of the comforts Sandy had mentioned. 'Aye, carry on.'

'As the story goes, nothing was seen o' them for a fortnight or so. They had a service in the Wee Kirk, the lot. The grieving families did their best to carry on, and the whole sad business was relegated to the past.' Hoynes turned to face his first mate, eyes narrowed. 'But as it turned oot, it was far from the end.'

'What?'

Hoynes's voice was low now, almost a whisper. 'On the fifteenth day after they'd disappeared, a farmer oot on his field wae some oxen saw something strange.'

'Oxen? I'm no' sure there were ever many oxen roon here.'

'You're such a pedant, Hamish. Fine, let's forget the oxen. He was oot wae a few coos – does that make you happier?'

'Mair plausible, I think, Sandy.'

'Can I carry on?'

'Of course.'

'Thank you.' Hoynes put the mug to his lips and downed a fair swallow. 'Anyhow, the farmer is oot in a field wae his *coos*, when he sees a man coming towards him. Bedraggled, he was, dressed in filthy clothes – slathered wae blood, so they say.'

'Oh.' Hamish's eyes widened with the excitement of the tale.

'At first the farmer was a bit leery. He didna recognise this fella at all. And you must remember, back then it was worse than it is now. Wae fewer folk aboot, everybody knew every soul on the peninsula. Aye, right doon to the clothes they were wearing that day, I daresay.'

'I find that a bit much, Sandy.'

'You do, do you? Is it a bit like the oxen you couldna get your heid roon?'

'A wee bit, aye.'

'Well, please shut up, or I'll tell you nae mair.'

'Sorry.'

'Right, where was I? Aye, this farmer doesna recognise this

lad fae Adam. But he notices that he's fat, which was unusual in they days.'

'How so?'

'Because there wisna much grub aboot due to the unfortunate lack o' oxen!' Hoynes's lips flattened in displeasure.

'I get the message. I won't interrupt again, Sandy.'

'Good!' He took a puff of his pipe. 'The farmer doesna recognise the lad until he's almost upon him. Then he takes a step back in horror, for this is Donald, one o' the missing lads I'm telling you aboot.'

'The one related to your mother?'

'The very man. Anyway, he approaches the farmer, who asks him where he's been – aye, and how he's turned into a great beefer into the bargain.' Hoynes moved his face a bit nearer Hamish's.

'"You'll need to forgive me," says Donald. "I've done a wicked thing."'

Hamish opened his mouth, about to speak, but Hoynes's warning look was enough to silence him.

'The farmer enquires as to what wicked thing he's done. The lad looks at him, his face taking on this demonic look – pure evil. '"We were shipwrecked," says he, quite jocose, so to speak. "We found shelter in an auld cave. But we were beset by a terrible thirst and hunger." The farmer looks at him, but he carries on. "I had to live, I didn't want to die. So I killed the pair o' them, drank their blood and ate them o'er the last couple o' weeks. That's how I've become so fat."'

Hamish shrunk away from his skipper at the horror of it all. 'That's fair disgusting, Sandy.'

'Aye, it is so. But, och, you know folk here. They were having none o' it. They thought Donald had lost his mind.'

428

'He got off wae it?'

'Well, no' really. He couldna shift the weight and he died o' a coronary in his early forties.'

'Did he eat them or no', Sandy?'

'As I say, folk didna believe him. They assumed that whatever terrible accident had befallen the rest o' the lads had robbed Donald o' his right mind. That was, until fifty years later, when the crew of a fishing boat put in beside the same caves looking for fresh water. One o' the crew took a dander in to have a poke aboot, and there were the remains o' two men, the teeth marks still showing on the bones where the dirty deed had taken place. Donald had been telling the truth all along. He'd eaten his friends to save himself.'

'Good grief!' said Hamish, shaking his head at the inhumanity of it all. 'How did he cook them? He must have managed a fire, Sandy?'

'That's the worst bit. They found no trace o' a fire or of cooked bones. He'd eaten them raw!' He puffed on his pipe thoughtfully. 'Ach, in my opinion, once you go to the lengths o' killing your friends to save yourself, there's nothing a man won't do. So I'm no' that surprised. But it fair scunnered the people o' Kinloch at the time.'

Hamish looked into the dying flames of the camping stove. 'You say this Donald was off your mother's side o' the family?'

'That he was. Though all the time I knew her, I never saw her eat anyone.'

Hamish rushed over to the drying twigs and branches and stoked the fire with them.

18

Marjorie Hoynes was in a state of agitation. Reluctantly, she'd agreed with her husband's plan to escape Dreich MacCallum and his machinations. But when she heard that Willie MacEachran's boat had been found adrift in the sound with no sign of Hamish aboard, panic began to set in.

Thinking on it in her chair beside the fire, she tried to reason everything out. Was there anyone more resourceful than her husband? No. If there was, she certainly hadn't met them. Would he have been forced to adapt the plan to fit prevailing circumstances? Aye, that he would do, if required. So, she reasoned, the fact the lobster boat was found abandoned must be part of a revised plan.

Marjorie made herself more comfortable and decided to catch up with some of the sleep she'd lost since her husband chose to go on the run. All was well, she was sure of it.

Yet when she closed her eyes, dark thoughts began to nag. For a start, if Hamish was with Sandy for some reason, how could they stock up on supplies? The food, water and firewood he'd taken with him wouldn't last long – especially in this weather. What if Sandy had waved his first mate farewell, only for some freak accident to befall Hamish?

Marjorie shook her head in an attempt to clear it of these

harrying thoughts. In truth, though, she felt guilty. She should have gone down to the pier and explained the whole sorry mess to Mitchell the harbour master. But that would only place Sandy in even more trouble.

The whole thing had turned into a nightmare, and one she'd known would transpire as soon as she heard the name Dreich MacCallum. For she was only too well aware of the contempt her husband held for the man, even though he hadn't seen him for so many years. It had become an obsession, verging on madness. In fact, she worried that Sandy rigged the engine on purpose to sink Dreich's boat. But, she assured herself, even her Sandy couldn't construct a missile – could he?

She jumped at the loud knocking at the door. It was official-sounding, like that of a policeman or fishery officer. She wrung her hands as she padded out into the lobby to answer it, fearing the worst. When she opened it, the tall figure before her was picked out against the settling snow by the bright glimmer of streetlights.

'Mrs Hoynes, I hope you don't mind my calling at this time in the evening?'

Though she could hear traces of a Kinloch accent, it had all but been subsumed by an English twang. She stared at him, motionless.

'May I come in? It's a bit chilly out here, and I'd like to have a word with you, if possible.'

Marjorie Hoynes, despite the circumstances, remembered her manners. 'Yes, please come in, Dr— . . . Mr MacCallum.' Though she only remembered Dreich fleetingly from her childhood, it could only be the man himself.

She showed him through to the living room, onto the chair

that was normally occupied by her husband. Instantly regretting this, Marjorie thought about asking him to sit on the couch instead, but she couldn't think of a suitable excuse in time.

'Could I get you some tea, eh, Mr MacCallum?'

'That would be very kind, Mrs Hoynes. White with two sugars, please. Just the thing on a night like this. That snow's getting worse.'

'Yes, it is.' The thought of her husband out in this weather with nothing but an old, moth-eaten tent to keep him warm flashed into her mind.

'Please, call me James. Everyone else does.'

'It's nice to put a face to a name. I don't remember you, I confess. I was only a girl when you left Kinloch.'

'I'm sure you've heard only fine things about me, Marjorie.' Dreich smiled. He watched her bustle off to get the tea, taking his time to look round the room. It was like stepping back in time. A thick rug sat before the roaring fire burning in the stone grate. The wallpaper was a floral chintz pattern, one that would have long been considered passé where he lived. There was a display cabinet containing some crystal vases, silverware and a selection of faded black-and-white photographs. A sideboard sat against the back wall, upon which was a Bush radio – a stout one made in wood veneer, no doubt a relic of the forties. A small television set was positioned in the corner of the room. There was a tiny artificial Christmas tree, with a few festive cards dotted here and there.

Dreich had forgotten how things were in Kinloch. And despite the odd mod con, like the TV and radio, this place reminded him of his mother's front room, from so long ago.

That this brought a lump to his throat surprised him. To fend off this sudden burst of sentimentality, he leaned forward and picked up the copy of the *Kinloch Herald* from the low coffee table before him.

He smiled at the headline: *Dog Toilets To Be Installed in Kinloch.* Just how these facilities were to be discerned by passing dogs puzzled him. He read some more headlines. *Russian Satellite Visible Before Christmas. Frank MacLeod's Sheep Are Champions. Kinloch United Beat Oban Thistle Again.*

He smiled and laid the paper down just as Marjorie appeared with a tray of tea and sweetmeats.

'You shouldn't have gone to so much trouble, Marjorie. Homemade shortbread. Goodness me, I haven't tasted that since I left.'

'Please, help yourself. Made fresh today.' Marjorie sat down opposite her guest.

'I'll not bother you for long. But I have to ask you a question,' said Dreich.

'Oh yes,' she replied, dreading it.

'Marjorie, if you know where your husband is, you should speak out. What happened the other day with my boat must be resolved. Sandy can't just run away from his responsibilities, you know.'

She felt like saying that he'd been doing that since the day they were married, but managed to resist the temptation. 'My husband is away on business.'

'Oh, come on, you can't really believe that.'

'I can and I do.'

'He was spirited off in the middle of the night in a boat that didn't even belong to him. I know you know where he is.'

'Are you calling me a liar, Mr MacCallum?' Marjorie raised her chin. She was from a family that had fished the waters around Kinloch for as long as anyone could remember. She was determined not to let this effete exile call her honesty into question.

Dreich decided to change tack. 'I apologise. But you must see the position this leaves me in. I'm out of pocket. And whoever is to blame for the sinking of my vessel – either your husband or Mr Galbraith – it has to be sorted out.'

'Aye, well, Sandy will deal with it on his return. In the meantime, Mr Campbell the lawyer is looking after the matter on his behalf. I'm sure he'll be more than happy to help you.'

Dreich forced a smile and looked uncomfortable. 'Yes, I've already spoken to him.'

'So I believe. He tells me you were made redundant. I'm sorry to hear that.' Though Marjorie's face was all sympathy, she felt nothing but disdain for this man. Who did he think he was, coming into her home and casting aspersions on her husband?

'I'm semi-retired, Mrs Hoynes.' Dreich tried to keep his voice neutral, but it was raised all the same.

'That's a shame. No doubt, you'll have been intending to spend mair time on your wee boat.'

'It wasn't a *wee boat*, Mrs Hoynes! I'd just had her refitted at great cost, and now she's at the bottom of the loch.'

'Aye, but isn't sailing just the most dangerous thing?'

'It is when your husband's about, Mrs Hoynes.'

'You're safe then, as he's away at the moment.' She smiled benignly.

Dreich had had enough. It was infuriating to find that the

wife was every bit as thrawn as the husband. 'Aren't you at all worried for Hamish?'

Marjorie must have let her mask slip, because she noticed a flicker of satisfaction on Dreich's face. 'Sandy knows this coast like the back of his hand – aye, and so does Hamish, come to that.'

'Hmm . . . I remember tales of Hamish's grandfather sitting in the corner of the bar at the County telling stories in return for drams. He knew *that place* like the back of his hand. And from what I hear, his father was worse. You'll forgive me if I've little faith in that family.'

'Hamish is a fine lad, and my husband's a good man. He's never cheated anyone out o' anything. He leaves that to others.' Though she said this with great certainty, Marjorie crossed her fingers, not really sure how many people Sandy had got the better of by fair means or foul.

Dreich shook his head. 'My lawyer arrives tomorrow. If you have no regard for your husband's safety, please be concerned about your own responsibilities, *Marjorie*.'

'Why so?'

'Because I hear you have a full share in the *Girl Maggie*, therefore you are partly responsible for her.'

Marjorie wanted to say that she'd only agreed to that on the advice of her husband. He'd been told that his wife having a share would help with his tax. But this was a new worry, something which she hadn't considered.

Dreich stood. 'I'll bid you goodnight, Mrs Hoynes. But if I were you, I'd have a good think about what you're doing. No need to show me out. Thanks for the shortbread.'

With that, he was gone. She heard the front door close on the latch behind him.

'Sandy, you better have a plan – that's all I'll say,' she whispered to herself before draining her cup of tea. But though she was concerned, in her heart of hearts, she knew the man sufficiently to be sure he'd have something up his sleeve.

19

'I'm damned if I know what to dae now, Hamish,' said Hoynes as he watched the last of the wet wood splutter and die in the little stove. The old tent was getting cold – very cold.

'We could go out and see if we can find any good stuff, Sandy.'

'We couldna find any earlier without snow on the ground. How are we going to do it now there's a blanket o' the stuff? No' to mention that it's pitch-black outside into the bargain.'

'You'll have to give me a couple o' the blankets, Sandy.'

'Can you no' wrap yourself up in that fireside carpet? Man, I'm thinking that will be rare and warm.'

'I don't doubt it. But then I'll be lying on the cold ground. I need some blankets, Sandy. Damn, you must have five!'

Hoynes sighed. 'This reminds me o' the boys in the *Gloria*.'

'Don't tell me – one o' them ate the rest.'

'You see, it's that cynicism that'll get you nowhere, Hamish. It's well known that lassies canna stand that type o' person. Fair recoil, they do.'

'Marjorie seems to have stuck by you well enough. You're the maist cynical person I know, skipper.'

'I'm a realist, Hamish. I'm accustomed to the exigencies of life. Aye, and I've experienced plenty o' them o'er the years.'

'If you don't mind me saying, it's your loose grasp o' reality that's got us here in the first place. I mean, who else would have considered making themselves scarce by slipping away in a tent in December?'

'Everything would have worked fine and dandy if it hadn't been for your neglect o' basic seamanship. You'd have been tucked up wae your teddy, and I'd have been cosied in here with a full complement o' blankets.'

Hamish folded his arms. 'I don't have a teddy.'

'Aye, well, I'll apologise for that. It was an overly harsh thing to say.'

'It's a stuffed donkey, if you must know. My mother gave it to me when I was four.'

'Are you being serious?'

'I am. I put him at the back o' my neck on the cold nights. Better than a hot water bottle, so he is.'

Hoynes took time to light his pipe and consider what his first mate had just revealed. He'd never had stuffed toys when he was a wee boy. He supposed they weren't popular back then. And even if they had been, his mother had always been keen that he wasn't mollycoddled as a child. Like her mother before her, a formidable woman, she was convinced that offspring should grow up aware of the many challenges life had in store. His father was a softer, kinder man. But Hoynes had his mother to thank for the steel in his bones, and his never-say-die attitude. He'd needed that often in his life, not least now.

'Are you going to tell me aboot this *Gloria* or not, Sandy?' Hamish knew when it was time to pour oil on troubled waters. Not that they had much of that left, either.

Hoynes furled himself in an old army blanket. 'It had been

an uncommon cold winter – back in nineteen forty-seven, just after the war. You were no mair than a wean, I'm thinking.'

'I was that.'

'The boys in the *Gloria* volunteered to take supplies to Islay. The ferries had all but stopped because folk couldna get to their work for all the snow blocking roads at Tarbert and the like.'

'I mind making a cracking snowman that year. It was bigger than my uncle Donnie,' said Hamish.

'I daresay. But it has to be noted that Donnie was never the tallest o' men, right enough. A fine fellow he was, but hardly of the Samson variety.'

'Samson who?'

'The biblical strongman! What kind o' religious education have you had, eh? The poor man had terrible problems wae his hairdresser, or some such thing. Can I carry on?'

'Aye, I'm with you now, right enough.'

Hoynes shivered and pulled the blanket tighter about himself. With the fire in the camping stove down to nothing more than a glimmer of embers, the only light came from the guttering gas lantern, hung from the apex of the tent. It cast shadows about the place, spinning and dancing on the canvas walls. 'The brave boys – the skipper was a MacAllister – left the quay, fair stocked wae provisions. They made the sail quite easy, the water being calm. A local spotted them a few miles away fae the island, all looking well. But as they waited in Bowmore, the *Gloria* never appeared.'

'What on earth happened?'

'There were many theories at the time. All of them as far-fetched as the last. But the answer came in nineteen sixty-three.'

439

'How so?'

'There was a man here called MacNair. He'd been clever at the school and ended up at Glasgow University.'

'Clever, right enough,' said Hamish.

'Oh aye, a heid like a prize turnip. Folk used to remark on the size o' it. But he needed a noggin that big to accommodate those brains o' his.' Hoynes stared into the flames, as though bringing the tale from the core of his very being. 'He was that clever he ended up on the Arctic survey team. Are you aware o' such a body, Hamish?'

'Oh aye,' said Hamish confidently. 'They're the fellas that go and count polar bears, penguins and the like.'

'You're half right, Hamish. Man, if you found a penguin in the Arctic, you'd be the biggest celebrity on the planet. Mair famous than that McCarthy chap you like. Him that sings aboot blackbirds.'

'McCartney! His name's Paul McCartney, Sandy.'

'Just so. Well, maybe if he'd sung more about penguins, you'd be better acquainted wae their natural habitat.'

Hamish rolled his eyes, anxious for Hoynes to get on with his story.

'Anyway, your boy MacNair heads off into the frozen North wae his notebook, pen and a decent pair o' gloves, I shouldna wonder.'

'You'd need decent gloves in those climes, Sandy. No doubt aboot it.'

'He's there for a couple o' weeks when he sees this great iceberg a mile or so away. He gets his binoculars oot and, damn me, he sees something lodged on the top o' it.'

'On top o' the ice?'

'Aye, right there on top o' the ice.' Hoynes puffed on his

440

pipe pensively. 'He gets the captain o' this icebreaker to sail nearer the thing.'

'He'd no' be happy aboot that. There's much more of an iceberg under the surface, you know, Sandy.'

'Aye, and maybe a couple o' rogue penguins. Perhaps that's why no bugger sees them in the Arctic, eh?'

'There's no need for sarcasm, Sandy.'

'You're a dreadful man for lecturing, Hamish. As if I wouldna know that there's mair o' the iceberg underneath the water than there is above it.' Hoynes glared at him.

'Right, a point well made. How did all this end up?'

'The captain o' the icebreaker took her as near as he dared. They were still a distance off the iceberg, but MacNair had a fine pair o' binoculars. He put them to his eyes, but he couldn't believe the evidence o' them.'

'What on earth?'

'There was a fishing boat perched atop the iceberg.'

'Away!'

'Aye, and that's not all. There was a wee trail o' smoke twirling oot the lum at the wheelhoose.'

'Och, I'm no' believing this.'

'As true as we're sitting here in a tent, that's what happened, I'm telling you.'

'Was it the *Gloria*?'

'Aye, that it was. And there was MacAllister standing at the bow, waving his hands like a wild thing. A great beard straggling doon to his feet.'

'But how did she get there? The boat, I mean.'

'You'll remember what a cold winter it had been in forty-seven. Well, for the first time, icebergs began to form oot in the Atlantic, just off Islay.'

'I'm no' sure that's how it happens, Sandy.'

'You wae all that accumulated knowledge, eh. As it turns out, the great thing snagged them, and they were dragged north. They spent years living off the supplies intended for the folk on Islay. But they were found just in time. They were down to a few tins o' rice pudding and no whisky for five years. Can you imagine such a thing, Hamish?'

'No' really, it has to be said.'

'But all three were as fit as fiddles. They say the cold air does wonders for the constitution.'

'As we're aboot to find out tonight.' Hamish lifted his cap and scratched his head. 'It's funny I never heard that story before. Aye, and what happened to them afterwards? I'd know if all three o' them had been in Kinloch.'

'Och, they couldna stay in the toon. Didna get a bit o' peace. People just wanted to hear their tales. Plus, it was too painful, as all their wives, assuming they were deid, had married other men. For the good of all concerned, the three of them moved to Oban.'

'Why Oban?'

'You know fine – the only things they're interested in up there is shinty and the ferry timetables. They were just left to their ain devices.' Hoynes took another triumphant puff of his pipe, another tale well told.

Hamish stared into what remained of the little fire in the camping stove. It was only a spark or two of burning wood now, the glow coming from the accumulated ashes. 'But they had coal and plenty food, Sandy. We have none o' either.'

20

Aboard the *Sea Harvester*, spirits had waned. The snow was still falling, if somewhat lighter in nature.

Peeny stood at the prow, wrapped up in a thick sheepskin jacket. He shook his head at the visibility and walked back to the wheelhouse, where Robertson was strumming his banjo.

'Mitchell was right, Davie,' said Peeny. 'There was no point coming out in this. The deck looks like a winter wonderland. I'll set to wae a shovel shortly and clear the worst o' it.'

'Is Malcolm still below?' said Robertson.

'He is that. You know Connelly. A couple o' slices o' Christmas cake and a dram or two and he's lashed to the mast for a fortnight.'

'Mind you, there's no' much needing done, apart fae clearing the snow.'

'I've a good mind to wake him up and get him at it.'

'Mair bother than it's worth, Peeny. You know fine he'll just moan and groan. I'd be happier doing it myself.'

'Aye, true, very true, Davie.'

They looked out of the wheelhouse windows, all framed in snow.

'I wonder how Hoynes and Hamish are faring, Peeny?'

'I wonder if they're *faring* at all, to be honest.'

443

'This is Sandy we're talking aboot, mind.'

'There's no' a man alive that can outsmart everyone and everything. The minute I heard that Dreich MacCallum was back in the town, I thought o' Sandy. It's like some kind o' prophecy coming true.'

'I never knew there was any prophecy,' said Robertson.

'I was being metaphorical. I mean, they're like these star-crossed lovers you hear all aboot.'

Robertson narrowed his eyes and stared at Peeny. 'I'm no' too sure what you're driving at, Peeny.'

But Peeny's attention was elsewhere. In his late sixties he may be, but there was nothing wrong with his eyesight. 'Would you look at that, Davie.'

Robertson followed the line described by Peeny's finger. Sure enough, held within a perfect circle of cloud sat the waxing moon, bordered by the dark velvet night beyond. 'She's clearing, Peeny!'

'Aye, that she is. I'm away to wake Malcolm. All hands on deck, if we're to find them!' He hurried below as Robertson placed his banjo back in its case and patted it shut.

Connelly stumbled onto the snowy deck, half asleep. 'What's going on, Davie?'

'She's clearing. Hopefully, we can get some idea where Sandy and Hamish are.'

Connelly searched the sky. It was true: the white snow clouds were beginning to break up, revealing a sprinkle of stars. The moon was reflected in the sound and on the white deck, making the accumulation look almost blue in colour.

'What's up wae you?' asked Robertson.

'She might be clearing, Davie, but oor task is every bit as

difficult now as it was when we started out. We still don't know where they are.'

Robertson nodded his head. The thrill of seeing the night sky had been replaced by grim reality. Though he knew Hamish had sailed this way in the lobster boat, there were a myriad of little coves and outcrops upon which the pair may have sought refuge. Then came the darkest thought of all. One of them would have to scan the calm waters for their bodies.

Peeny arrived back on deck with three steaming mugs of tea. 'This'll wake us up,' he said, as he handed one to Connelly and the other through the wheelhouse window to Robertson.

'What hope have we of finding the pair o' them, eh?' said Connelly. 'It's still dark, the snow's piled high on the shore . . . Och, it's just an awful thing.'

The three of them drank their mugs of tea, deep in thought. The sea was cold enough to kill in a handful of minutes. Parted from their boat in this weather, what chance did Hoynes and his first mate really have? That aside, what calamity had befallen them that forced leaving or, more likely, falling out of the vessel?

'I canna imagine what parted them from Willie's boat,' said Peeny. 'It's snowing, but Hoynes could sail through that, no problem. Plus, there wasn't a mark on her when she was found, so it wasn't a collision.'

'Any manner of catastrophes could have befallen them, Peeny. A man overboard, for instance. Hamish is a clumsy bugger at the best o' times. Sandy would do the decent thing and dive in to save him,' opined Connelly.

'Can I ask you a question, Malcolm?' said Davie.

'Aye.'

'See when you were born, did they whack you wae the

pessimism stick right away or hang on until you were a wee bit older?'

'Look over there,' said Peeny. To the east of the vessel, the coast was emerging from the gloom.

'That's fair enough, Peeny,' said Robertson. 'But they could be anywhere up and doon the length of the peninsula – or beyond.'

'But look above, man!' Sure enough, hanging in the air above the dark coastline was an improbably bright star. It seemed to twinkle red as they looked at it.

'It's no' the Pole Star, anyhow,' said Connelly. 'She'll be up there somewhere.' He pointed high into the sky.

'No, nor Venus or any other planet. Man, I've never seen a star as bright as that in the evening sky.'

Peeny looked between the other two men. 'You don't think – well, yous know the time o' year.'

'You think it's the light fae the Firdale Christmas tree?'

'No! Think aboot it, man.'

Robertson was drumming his fingers on his banjo case. 'Do you think it's a flare, Peeny? Is that what you're saying?'

'Man, you pair must either be heathens or the densest folk that ever lived. What happens every Christmas?'

Connelly was first to reply. 'I get hammered and herself goes to her bed.'

'No, try and think a wee bit mair traditionally.'

'Archie Douglas closes the pub at six. Many a year I've been scunnered by that,' said Robertson.

'Hopeless! Think o' the manger, the newborn baby. Ring any bells?'

'Now you're in the realms o' fantasy, Penny. And apart fae

that, it would spell the end o' Christianity. I mean, nobody's going to believe that Hoynes is some kind o' deity.'

'What aboot Hamish?' said Robertson. 'All that seeing into the future lark. Man, that could be significant.'

'You're going to disappoint a lot o' people at the Wee Kirk, Peeny.'

'Look at it, just hanging there. What else can it be?'

Peeny was right; the star was motionless in the sky, as bright as the Ardnamurchan lighthouse on a stormy night.

'Here's something worth considering, given we don't have any better ideas. I reckon we have a good look closer into shore.'

'You're right, Davie. There's nothing lost by having a look. Man, we're fishermen. Every man and boy o' us is as super-stitious as they come. Malcolm, you canna see the turn o' the month without shouting "white rabbit!" seven times in a row. And as for you, Davie, I've never known you to take to the stage without a good half-bottle inside you.'

'That's nothing to dae with superstition, Peeny. I just like a good drink.'

'Even so. Pull her in as near to the shore as you can. We can have a look through that big torch you brought. You know the one wae the spinning red light at the top in case you're marooned wae the car.'

'Who died and made you Admiral o' the Fleet?' said Connelly.

'Oh aye, that's right. We should have chosen you, Malcolm. A man o' decision and swift action. Come on, we've lives to save!'

21

In the tent, things were reaching crisis point. As the skies cleared, so the temperatures plummeted. Reluctantly, Hoynes had given Hamish two old army blankets. Not through altruism exactly, but because he feared his second-in-command may perish if he wasn't offered some kind of protection against the biting cold. The camping stove offered nothing save a feeble glow, its flaming potency long expired.

'You'll be fair basking in warmth now, Hamish,' said Hoynes, who as well as sleeping off the floor in a cot, was wrapped up in three blankets. It was also true to say that his more substantial frame gave him an advantage over Hamish, who was naturally thin and wiry, lacking the fatty protection against the cold Hoynes enjoyed.

'Aye, Sandy. It's like the tropics doon here.' The first mate was shivering as he lay swaddled in the blankets atop the old rug Sandy had recovered from his loft. 'But it's a consolation to know that if I die, you'll likely eat me. Though I advise you to warm me up over a low flame so that I'll defrost.'

'Damn me, I've never heard such histrionics. You should be on the stage.'

'I'm at the last stage o' hypothermia, if that makes you feel better.' Hamish had heard about chattering teeth before, though he hadn't really experienced them. Now, he was enduring that very thing, and amazed that he couldn't stop the constant rattle of tooth on tooth.

'There could be a solution – a partial one, at least,' said Hoynes.

'Which is?'

'You'll have to come and share this cot wae me.'

The statement was enough to stop Hamish's teeth clattering off one another. 'Och, you're okay, Sandy. I'll be fine doon here. There's barely enough room for you in that thing, never mind me.'

'That's the whole idea, man. It's that oor body heat is shared. If you were lost in the Alps wae me, that's just what we'd be doing, right this very minute.'

'What on earth would we be doing in the Alps? It's aboot as far away fae the sea as you can get in Europe.'

'Well, you never thought you'd be here this morning, did you now?'

Hamish had to admit that his skipper had the right of it. And, when Sandy Hoynes was about, the oddest things were likely to happen. So, he supposed that their presence in the Alps could hardly be ruled out. In fact, reviewing his circumstances, perhaps it did make sense to remove himself from the cold ground that seemed to be eating away at any heat his body managed to generate. 'We could try topping and tailing, I suppose, Sandy.'

'Now, Hamish. I know we live in a world where things are mair permissive than they were when I was your age. Aye, and that's likely a good thing for folk, but you canna teach an old dog new tricks. So, whatever inclinations you have, I'm afraid

I don't share them. Though I think nothing less of you for making the proposition.'

'It's nothing like that, Sandy! I mean, I'll lie wae my heid at one end o' the cot, and yours at the other.'

'So I'll be staring into your rotten feet?'

'But this way we'll have a modicum o' privacy.'

Hoynes pondered on the subject of topping and tailing for a moment. 'Can I ask who it was that passed on this piece of advice to you, Hamish?'

'Mrs Green, the minister's wife.'

'Man, you've no shame. Intimate wae the wife of a clergyman! There are depths to you I'm feart to confront, Hamish.'

'Eh? She taught us in the Scouts. What else were you thinking, Sandy?'

'I've always thought she'd the glad eye, if you know what I mean. Forbye that, the Reverend Green must be one of the dullest men I've ever met. I couldna blame the lassie for taking up wae a younger man.'

'I think you might be suffering fae that hypodermia, Sandy.'

'It's *hypothermia*, you dolt. Are you going to come in wae me or not? Because I could fair do wae the warmth o' these blankets back.'

There followed a complicated dance that saw Hoynes lift his legs in the air, while Hamish slid underneath them and tried to find a comfortable position in the camping cot. He twisted and turned, eventually reaching something approaching relief.

'Sandy, you've still got your seaboots on,' said Hamish, faced with a large yellow Wellington boot about an inch from his nose.

'And I should think so, too. The only time a fisherman

should be without his boots is when he's at home in bed wae his wife or being laid oot at Smith's the undertaker.'

'If you say so, Sandy.' Despite his discomfort, Hamish had to agree that it did feel warmer. It had been an exceptionally long day, and he felt fatigue creeping over him. His eyelids fluttered and closed.

✧

Aboard the *Sea Harvester* it was all go. Peeny took Robertson's car lamp and shone it on the shore. The broad beam revealed a beach, rocky in parts, mostly covered in thick snow.

'This could be the place, right enough. I've heard Sandy banging on aboot Portroy beach before,' said Robertson.

'Did he no' come here wae his faither when he was a boy? There's a good trout river no' far away,' said Peeny.

'Look!' Connelly was pointing at the beach. 'See, just above the waterline – footprints!'

'Man, you're right enough. The snow's no' been able to lie so close to the sea. I'll be damned.'

'I'll get the rowing boat. We canna get in any closer than this, and I don't fancy wading out in this cold.'

Soon, the rescue party were afloat on the *Sea Harvester*'s rowing boat, reserved for access to harbours lacking in suitable facilities and jaunts onto beaches like this.

Peeny stared skyward. The star was still visible through the trees. 'I must admit, wae Christmas nearly upon us, and that star up there, well, I'm feeling quite overcome.'

'It's odd, to say the least,' said Connelly.

'I'm telling you, if Hoynes is some kind o' deity, I'm changing my religion,' said Robertson.

'To what?' said Peeny.

'I might as well have a crack at Hinduism. I'm sure they'd have no truck wae Hoynes.'

Peeny shook his head. 'There's things aboot this world we'll never know.'

They rowed the little boat ashore, then slid it up onto the sand out of the freezing seawater and secured it. The little party made their way up the beach and stepped into the snow.

'I'm thinking that if Sandy is here, he'll be having a bloody hard time o' it,' said Peeny. 'It's the coldest I've felt for many a year, and that's no joke.'

Robertson took in his surroundings. 'If you were looking for shelter, you'd surely head into those pine trees?'

Collectively, they looked up past the machair and into the treeline. It was obvious: any man would have sought the protection of the forest, given the circumstances.

Connelly wasn't convinced. 'I'm thinking we're on a fool's errand here. We've followed a star and ended up on this beach. I'm sad to say there's a large part o' me that thinks the pair o' them are much mair likely to be at the bottom o' the sound than up in those trees. It's all wishful thinking, lads.'

'Man, you're the cheeriest bugger that ever walked,' said Peeny, glaring at his companion. 'For good or ill, we're here now, so we might just as well have a poke aboot.' He began to trudge up the beach.

'I'm no' sure this is a good idea, Hamish,' said Hoynes. 'I mean, I'm warm enough, but I canna move, and I've got that tingling in my left foot that doesna bode well. No, not at all.'

'What's going to happen to it – spontaneous combustion?'

'The tingling is a harbinger o' cramp. And I tell you, Hamish, I fair dread the sensation. The pain's unbearable. My legs shoot aboot all over the place of their own accord – and that's a fact.'

Hamish stared at Hoynes's yellow boot once more. 'Well, try and give me some warning, at least, so I can remove my face and no' get booted to death. But, mind you, I'm no' going back on the floor o' this tent for love nor money.'

'In that case, be prepared. That's all I'm saying.'

They lay still for a few moments, a wave of tiredness drifting over Hamish yet again. But just as he felt himself drifting into sleep, he was jolted into wakefulness by a sudden flinch from Hoynes.

'I feel the cramp coming on, Hamish!' yelled Sandy.

'Wait and I'll get oot.' Hamish tried to push himself free of the camping cot. But as he did, Hoynes's nearest leg described an arc in the air and pinned him down by the neck with some force. 'Sandy, you're choking me!' he squealed.

The sound that came from Hoynes was akin to that of a boiler about to explode. It began as a deep rumble in his chest, then manifested itself in strangled cries in his throat. As the cramp took hold in pulses of agony, his cries of pain syncopated to it, Hamish's whimpers acted as a counterpoint.

'Did you hear that?' said Peeny, stopping in his tracks in the snow.

'It sounds like some kind o' animal,' said Robertson.

'It'll be rutting stags,' said Connelly. 'They go through a

right performance when they're at the rutting.'

Not listening at all, Peeny hurried ahead with the lamp, the other two close on his heels.

'Look, there's a tent behind that rock!' Peeny shouted amidst the yells and moans coming from inside.

'We better get in there, quick smart,' said Robertson. 'It sounds like murder.'

They made for the tent. Peeny stopped and wrenched the tent flap open, sending a button spinning into the cold night air, then shone the torch inside. Robertson and Connelly looked over his shoulder.

Illuminated by the beam of light, the sight that met their eyes was hard to describe. One yellow Wellington boot was thrust in the air. In the crook of the other leg, Hamish's face, contorted with pain, was visible as he screeched and moaned. At the opposite end of the cot, Sandy Hoynes's head was thrown back in the excruciating agony of cramp. The sound that issued from his mouth approximated the first paroxysms of someone about to sneeze, though much more voluble.

'In the name o' the wee man!' Peeny exclaimed, staring at the writhing tumble of legs, arms, heads and blankets, his mouth agape.

'We should let them have their privacy,' wailed Connelly above the racket.

Hamish's eyes shot open. 'Get him off me!'

As one, the three fishermen were galvanised by this cry for help. At first, Peeny and Robertson tried to prise Hamish's head from the tight grip of Hoynes's leg. But this proved more difficult than first anticipated, as the older man's limb seemed set like steel.

'Sandy, you're choking Hamish to death. Move your leg, man!' Robertson shouted.

'I canna help myself,' said Hoynes through his pain.

'In that case, just pull yourself together, man. I'm no' sure what's got into you, but now's the time to stop it. No wonder the pair o' you came a way oot here in a tent. I've never seen the like,' said Peeny.

There was something in the undertone of what his old friend said that afforded Hoynes a brief respite from the crippling cramp he was experiencing. He managed to move his leg enough to free Hamish's head. The first mate shot from the cot like a bullet and landed on the hard ground. Meanwhile, Hoynes's release from pain was a brief one. His leg shot into the air again, catching Connelly square on the nose. The latter fell back, blood pouring down his face.

'Hamish, how are you?' said Peeny. 'What's got into your skipper? You don't have to tell me if you don't want to, son.'

'He's got cramp. Pull his legs straight and it should give him some relief, Peeny,' said Hamish amid the commotion.

'Aye, I've heard it called that, right enough.' But, doing as Hamish had asked, he and Robertson grabbed a leg each, almost pulling Hoynes off the cot.

'Oh, that's better,' said Hoynes, the cramp beginning to ease.

'Speak for yourself,' Connelly groaned as blood from his nose dripped through his cradling fingers.

22

It took two trips to get them back aboard the *Sea Harvester*. Hoynes insisted on bringing back certain items, including three bottles of whisky, the little stove and the cot. The tent, it was decided, had seen better days and was as well left where it was.

Peeny sat with Hamish and Hoynes, as they warmed up below with hot tea.

'Now, there's no need to explain yourselves, lads. It's nineteen sixty-eight, and folk have the right to let it all hang oot if they want.'

'What does he mean, Sandy?'

'He's trying to imply that you and I were involved in biblical congress when they arrived in the tent.'

'We should have prayed, right enough,' said Hamish seriously. 'But, och, it just all happened so quickly, didn't it?'

Peeny looked between the pair as though he was seeing them for the first time. 'So, you were kind o' caught up in the whole . . . moment?'

'I had cramp! Plain and simple, Peeny.'

'And why was Hamish in there wae you?'

'We were topping and tailing, Peeny. Mrs Green the

minister's wife taught me how to do it when I was in the Scouts,' said Hamish.

Peeny, who had just taken a gulp of tea, now proceeded to spray it everywhere.

'Hamish was freezing to death wrapped up in my fireside rug. We had to huddle together for warmth, plain and simple. Shared body heat, man! Now, enough o' your innuendo. Aye, and you can tell your pals up in the wheelhouse the same thing,' said Hoynes.

Peeny decided to change the subject. 'We followed a star, you know.'

'Like in the Bible?' said Hamish.

'Aye, that's how we found you. I'm no' telling a word o' a lie, son.'

'What do you make o' that, Sandy?'

'There must be a desperate shortage o' Wise Men, if you ask me.'

Ignoring this, Peeny continued. 'We'll be back in Kinloch before you know it, Sandy.'

'As long as it's still dark, I'm no' bothered.'

'Why dark, skipper?' Hamish asked.

'Because Dreich MacCallum's still on my tail, that's how. That's why we were where we were – or had you forgotten?'

'Aye, of course.'

'You'll just have to face him, Sandy,' said Peeny.

'I'd rather have a few hours in bed and a good cooked breakfast before I do. So, you can keep this quiet until later.'

'But Davie's had to call the harbour master. The lifeboat was oot looking for you. We canna have folk risking life and limb just to keep you fae Dreich,' said Peeny.

Hoynes made a face and slurped at his tea.

457

'But you're fine. It'll be damn near six o'clock in the morning before we get back. There won't be a soul aboot to worry you.'

✧

Peeny couldn't have been more wrong. They were halfway along the loch when they saw activity on the piers. The closer they came to the harbour, the clearer it became that a large crowd had gathered to welcome the lost mariners home.

'Sandy won't be happy about this,' said Robertson.

'Bugger him,' said Connelly, nursing his nose through a hankie. 'This damn thing will have to be reset. I wonder why there's so many people aboot at this time o' morning? I know Sandy's popular – in some quarters – but the place is hoaching.'

Robertson stayed tight-lipped, avoiding Connelly's gaze.

'Hang on. You didna mention anything aboot that bloody star to Mitchell, did you?'

Robertson inclined his head. 'Och, I might have let it slip a wee bit.'

'In that case, we're for it now.'

'What dae you mean?'

'Christmas miracle, that sort o' thing. You wait, Davie.'

As Robertson came alongside the pier, he could see more than a hundred people huddling in the cold, awaiting their return.

'Sandy!' Peeny shouted below. 'There's a few folk aboot. Davie's just tying her up and we can get going.'

'Is Dreich there?'

Peeny pulled his head from the hatch and scanned the crowd. 'I canna see him.'

'Do me a favour, Peeny. Get Mitchell to give us a hurl back hame in his Rover.'

'I will, don't worry.' He stepped away from the hatch and leaned through the wheelhouse window. 'Sit tight just now. I'm going to cadge a lift for Sandy.'

With the skill born of years at sea, Peeny stepped across the gap between the boat and the pier. The first person to greet him was an eager-looking young man with a notepad and pencil poised.

'I'm Craig MacIntyre from the *Kinloch Herald*.'

'I know. I was at school with your grandfaither. Man, I was at your christening.'

Ignoring this, MacIntyre continued. 'Can you tell us something about your experience with the star that led you to the missing men?'

'Och, there was nothing to it. There it was twinkling away, so we just followed it.'

'The three of you?'

'Aye, the three o' us.'

'This is going to make such a good story.'

'I'm glad you think so. We were doing what we could to save oor friends. Something any decent person should be willing to be aboot.'

'Quickly, can I ask you, what condition were Mr Hoynes and Hamish in when you found them?'

Peeny hesitated. 'It's fair to say they weren't themselves, that's for sure.'

'Distressed, likely?'

'Aye, you could say that as well, right enough.'

'And how did they greet you? Were there tears, hugs?'

'It's fair to say there was some hugging on the go, for sure.

Aye, and a lot o' wailing, into the bargain.' Peeny looked rather discomfited.

'Can you describe the star? Did it appear in the east?'

'It was just there, in the sky. It looked like a star. Och, I'll need to go, son. And before you ask, I never saw Balthazar at his feast neither.'

The young reporter watched Peeny hurry off. Everybody needed a break when they were starting out on a career. A star. Christmas. A rescue against the odds. Craig MacIntyre's break was surely here and now. He ran back up the pier, anxious to get to work on the story of a lifetime. But the story about the appearance in the sky of a Russian satellite in last week's edition suddenly dawned on him. MacIntyre felt his chance of fame slipping away. But he considered his story so sensational, he resolved to go ahead anyway.

Mitchell the harbour master just wanted the pier cleared of people, so he told Peeny he was happy to offer Hoynes and Hamish a lift home.

'We'll have to force oor way through all these folk, Sandy,' said Hamish.

'I'd happily force my way through the Red Army, so long as Dreich's nowhere to be seen.'

'Definitely no sign o' him at all.'

'Good. Then there's no time like the present,' said Hoynes.

With Peeny taking the lead, Hoynes and Hamish followed, the collars of their pea jackets up round their faces, and bunnets pulled down low, like armour against the throng.

'It's a miracle!' shouted Maureen Gillespie.

'Hoynes is anointed, so he is,' commented Alan Cunningham, using the old Kinloch saying intended for those who enjoyed extraordinary fortune.

'The luck o' the devil, mair like,' said someone anonymous in the crowd.

'Away! They saw a sign – a star!' Jean Monteath, a pious woman and a pillar of the Wee Kirk, was having none of it.

'Damn me,' said Hamish. 'We'll need a miracle to get through this lot.'

Though progress was slow, they soon reached the harbour master's office and were glad to get in out of the crowd.

'Man, that was hectic, and no mistake,' said Hoynes. 'This bloody star nonsense is all they're interested in. We could have frozen to death and it wouldna have mattered. Were the three o' you on the whisky when you saw it?'

'I swear to you, Sandy. It was there – a great big thing, fair twinkling right o'er where yous were – well, where yous were *camping*.' Peeny adopted an innocent expression.

'Can you take us home now, Mitchell? I could sleep for a week – the sleep o' the just, mark you. Aye, and Hamish's mother will be waiting to tuck him in.'

'And Mrs Green the minister's wife, I shouldna wonder,' said Peeny, earning a glare from the *Girl Maggie*'s first mate.

'Follow me,' said Mitchell. 'We can use the back door. Hopefully it'll be quieter.'

They stepped back into the chill, dark morning and headed to Mitchell's Rover, parked beside a stumpy metal bollard.

Hoynes was about to open the car door when he felt a tap on his shoulder.

'Let me get in this bloody thing, will you, Hamish? Time is of the essence.' Hoynes turned, ready to berate the younger man. But it wasn't Hamish who was picked out in the lamplight. Dreich MacCallum stood tall, his gaunt frame draped in an expensive overcoat.

'Have you been away on a wee holiday, Sandy?' said Dreich, his signature sickly smile spread across his face.

'I was off on business, as well you know.'

Dreich snorted a dismissive laugh. 'What kind of business is to be done in a tent camped at Portroy? It sounds to me as though you were on the run.'

'Run fae you, Dreich MacCallum? There'll be green snow and yellow hailstones the day that happens, for sure.' Hoynes stared back at his tormentor, gimlet-eyed.

'I have news for you, Sandy. You'll not have forgotten you sank my cabin cruiser with your reckless behaviour?'

'Not true – it was an engine malfunction.'

'Not in my lawyer's opinion. He's here in Kinloch, you know. We're suing for compensation. I know you don't have the money. But I'm a fair man, and I want to give you a chance to redeem yourself.'

'I've nothing to redeem myself for, Dreich.'

'Under the circumstances, I think I'd prefer *Mr MacCallum*. But it's a simple choice. You're all here to bear witness to my extremely generous offer.' He turned to face Hamish, Peeny and Mitchell.

'We'll need to hear it before we decide how generous it is, Dreich,' said Peeny.

'Extremely so, I'd say. Perhaps too generous – certainly more than this old rascal deserves.'

'Och, just spit it oot,' said Hamish.

'It's time to put an old story to bed. I'll race you to the buoy at the head of the loch. Just the two of us in rowing boats – like back in the old days. If you win, I'll walk away, Sandy. I'm a rich man, and I daresay the insurance will cover part of the cost of my boat, if not all.'

'And if I lose?'

'I take possession of the *Girl Maggie*. Outright, you understand. No half-share or employing you to do the fishing. I'll have her and do what I want with the tub. Just think, she'd make a fine display at Hogmanay, burning out in the loch, the way the Vikings used to do, eh?'

A pool of light from the lamppost held them motionless: five men from the same wee town, the air heavy with tension. They seemed frozen in time, a tableau vivant at the end of the pier.

'You're on!' said Hoynes. He spat on his meaty right hand, Dreich did the same, and they shook on the agreement.

'How about Christmas Eve? As good a day as any, and the forecast is fair. It'll be cold, but the loch will be like a millpond, Sandy.'

Hoynes gave a curt incline of the head. Saying no more, he turned and ducked into Mitchell's Rover.

23

The few days leading up to Christmas Eve were charged with excitement in Kinloch. Some thought the whole thing foolhardy. Others reckoned it to be nothing but a stunt and swore that Hoynes was set to gain financially, somehow. After all, his track record of coming up smelling of roses was so long as to have achieved legendary status.

However, those closest to the skipper of the *Girl Maggie* wrung their hands and fretted over the whole arrangement. Marjorie pleaded with her husband not to be so foolish. After all, he was no longer an energetic teenager, and the price of failure was high.

Hamish wondered when Hoynes had last rowed any real distance. His memory was full of awkward attempts to manoeuvre their little tender back to the *Girl Maggie* in places like Lochranza or Gairsay. He told himself that Hoynes would at least be sober on this occasion, though he was by no means mollified by the thought.

Not only did Hoynes stand to lose his fishing boat, but they would also lose their employment. Though the first mate didn't give it voice, he thought the whole arbitrary notion of it all rather selfish. Hoynes was nearing retirement and would have a pension to meet his needs. Hamish had no such luxury.

The subject was also a hot one round the bar of the County Hotel. To such an extent, in fact, that a book had been opened on the race. Though Hoynes was a friend to almost every customer, the betting was heavily against him. Especially so when Dreich was spotted ploughing up and down the loch in a sleek rowing boat he'd borrowed from the boatbuilder in Tarbert. He was getting himself in shape for the contest.

But Hoynes was intractable on the subject. Not only did he refuse to put in any practice prior to the race, he hadn't even sourced a suitable craft in which to participate. No matter how Hamish, Peeny, Connelly and the rest tried to coax him, he adopted a studiously laissez-faire attitude to the whole thing, happily indulging in drams and pre-festive fare in abundance. The suggestion that he might be advised to put in some time on the oars was greeted with a puff of tobacco smoke and a raised brow.

To put it mildly, those closest to Hoynes considered that he'd temporarily lost his mind. Hamish was more inclined to think that the condition was of a permanent nature and found himself leafing through the Situations Vacant page of the *Kinloch Herald*, especially after the latest edition of the paper appeared, complete with a mocked-up star on the front page.

But inexorably, the fateful day dawned. As Dreich had predicted, Christmas Eve did so dry and cold with little more than a light breeze to ripple the still waters of the loch.

That Hoynes had asked to use Davie Robertson's tender as his weapon of choice in the upcoming contest did little to discourage those betting against him. Though a sizeable wager laid by Margaret Patterson – a kind woman who always supported the underdog – in Hoynes's favour did raise an eyebrow or two, it did very little to alter the odds: Dreich MacCallum remained the overwhelming favourite.

As they had so many years before, a large crowd gathered at Kinloch harbour, ready to see the contestants battle it out. Though the weather was bitter, Pallini's ice-cream van was doing a roaring trade in crisps, confectionery and cigarettes, while George's fish-and-chip van sold everything from pies, haggis, tea and, of course, its eponymous wares. Children ran about, energised by chocolate and Christmas, while the older townsfolk cast a leery eye over the adversaries. Such was the level of anticipation and excitement, the bar staff at the County Hotel had been allowed to close, to witness this spectacle at first hand, for as long as the contest endured. In any event, the bar would have been empty as Sandy Hoynes and Dreich MacCallum slogged it out.

Dreich was the first to appear. He strode out of a rented motor car in a bright blue tracksuit, white plimsolls and a brightly coloured scarf, in the colours of the shipping line for whom he captained – or so it was said.

As those assembled awaited Hoynes's appearance, critical eyes were cast over the boats to be used in the race. The Tarbert rowing boat to be occupied by Dreich was freshly varnished and looked as sleek as a birlinn. Beside it, the *Sea Harvester* appeared short, squat and poorly turned out. But, still, there was a race to be won and sport to be had.

When Hoynes appeared, he did so in a surprising fashion, coming straight off the midday bus from the scheme. As he forced his way through the spectators, it was clear he'd made very little effort to dress appropriately for a sporting contest and he looked very much the same as he normally did. His one concession was the abandonment of his oilskin, so he was stripped down to his usual moleskin trousers and fisherman's jumper – though he had refused to part with his sou'wester that was aligned fore and aft to aid wind resistance.

'You'll be turning oot for the Oxford Boat Race next,' shouted one wag. But Hoynes ignored that and every other taunt, as he stood beside Dreich at the top of the sea-stairs awaiting the harbour master. Mitchell had been deputised as starter and umpire, and his decision on any foul play or incident would be final and indisputable. An arrangement agreed upon by both participants.

Hoynes cast his eyes to the New Quay, where the *Girl Maggie* still sat on Galbraith's slip. Some said there was a tear in his eye, others that it was merely an effect of the cold weather. The speculation was soon halted when the door to the harbour master's office was seen to swing open, and Mitchell made his way up the pier to a ragged cheer.

On arrival, he put his whistle to his mouth and issued forth one long blast, hushing the chatter of the crowd.

'When this next sounds, you must make your way to your boats and commence the race. Is that understood?'

Dreich, jogging on the spot, nodded enthusiastically, while Hoynes merely inclined his head.

'I want a fair contest, as befits the gentlemen concerned.'

That induced much hilarity, which Mitchell ignored.

'Mr Hoynes, Mr MacCallum, please take your positions at the top of the stairs.'

Dreich dashed to his spot, adopting the stance of a sprinter waiting for the gun, while Hoynes ambled into position, hands in pockets.

Again, Mitchell put the whistle to his mouth, but he was

momentarily distracted by the appearance of Donnie in the ambulance. The local doctors were of the collective opinion that while Dreich MacCallum looked in good shape, Hoynes gave the impression of a coronary waiting to happen. And to this end, the lifeboat was standing at anchor in the loch, ready to assist any participant in difficulty.

Composing himself once more, Mitchell put the whistle to his lips and blew.

Dreich pelted down the steps and was soon in his rowing boat. He pushed himself off the harbour wall with gusto and was quickly into his stride, vigorous strokes propelling the boat out of the harbour.

Still looking unruffled, Hoynes eased himself into the little rowing boat, angled it off the wall with a feeble push and set about the oars as though he was embarking upon a leisurely plooter across to the New Quay.

Marjorie, standing beside Hamish, hid her head behind his arm. 'Please tell me he's putting more effort into it.'

Hamish grimaced as the distance between Hoynes and Dreich stretched. 'Just you keep your heid roon there, Mrs Hoynes. Come on, Sandy!' he shouted, hoping his cries might engender a spirit of competition in his skipper. But Hoynes was into a regular, if somewhat pedestrian stroke pattern. There seemed to be little effort behind his rowing, though he had pushed his sou'wester to the back of his head as, perhaps, an indication of determination.

The crowd roared, cheered, laughed and booed by turns, as Dreich MacCallum turned round mid-stroke to see how his competitor was faring. He shook his head and aimed a sarcastic wave at Hoynes rowing oh-so-steadily behind.

'What on earth does Sandy think he's doing?' said Peeny,

standing in a small group of fishermen. 'Man, he's making a laughing stock o' himself. No effort whatsoever.'

'That's the *Girl Maggie* a goner,' said Connelly. 'We should have left him in the tent.'

The crowd were becoming restive, too. They'd come to enjoy a spirited race to the finish: before them was a drubbing – no contest, a farce.

'Too much booze, Hoynes!' shouted Derek Kelly. 'You're paying the price now!' He and the skipper had a poor relationship since Hoynes had accidentally fallen onto his car bonnet after a particularly refreshing night in the County Hotel. Though the fisherman had paid for the broken wing mirror, the animus between them continued.

Both contestants were out in the loch now, though Dreich was forging ahead. Hoynes, on the other hand, maintained his unfaltering pace, pulling the boat forward but losing ground by the second.

'What's happening, Hamish?' said Marjorie, her head still tucked behind his back.

'You'll no' like it, Mrs H. Dreich's fair pushing on, and Sandy's just oot for a dander.'

Marjorie let out a muffled wail. 'I knew this would happen. He'd been too jocose about it all. Had a few drams by the fire last night as though nothing was happening. He's just given up.'

Hamish had to agree. Though he'd never expected Hoynes to win the race, he'd hoped his skipper would at least try.

Then, something happened that sent a gasp of disbelief through the crowd. Hoynes stowed his oars, delved into his pocket and produced his pipe, which he proceeded to tamp down as though he'd not a care in the world. He set light to it and puffed away contentedly, as Dreich disappeared up the loch.

There were howls of derision from the crowd, and some spectators began to drift away. All were disappointed that this pre-festive spectacle had turned into a damp squib.

'What on earth's happening now, Hamish?'

'Well, Sandy's having a wee breather, as far as I can tell.'

'What?' Marjorie whipped her head from behind Hamish's back and gaped at her husband as he placed the oars back in the blue waters of the loch and, with pipe clenched between his teeth, resumed his stately progress.

Unseen by many spectators, a venerable black Bentley turned off the roundabout and made its way down the pier. If anyone had been looking, they'd have seen Campbell the lawyer step out of the car, puffing on his cigar. He made his way towards Mitchell, the pair exchanged a few words, then the harbour master reached for his whistle and blew one long, shrill blast.

Out on the loch, near enough to hear it, Hoynes turned round. He saw the distant figure of Mitchell waving in a beckoning motion. Hoynes took a long puff of his pipe, turned the boat round by use of one oar, and headed back to the Old Quay. Dreich, well out of earshot of the whistle, ploughed on, racing for the buoy which marked the turning point and the halfway marker in the race.

Hamish and Marjorie couldn't believe what they were seeing. Though they weren't sure why Mitchell had blown his whistle, the fact that Hoynes was now rowing in the wrong direction left them open-mouthed.

Marjorie moaned.

'I'll take a wee wander doon the pier, Mrs H, and see if I can find out what's going on,' said Hamish.

By the time Hoynes had tied up his craft at the far end of the pier and ascended the ladder there, Dreich had navigated the buoy and was on his way back to finish the race. Mitchell, Campbell and Hoynes waited for him at the end of the pier.

Before Dreich was in the harbour, another car drove down the Old Quay. It pulled up beside Campbell's Bentley, and a man in a trilby hat and raincoat exited the vehicle.

Hamish, who'd remained an observer until now, thought it time to have a word with his skipper. He made his way over to Hoynes, who was enjoying a quiet puff of his pipe atop a bollard.

'What on earth is happening, Sandy?'

'The victory of light o'er darkness, Hamish. A wrong righted after many years.'

Still none the wiser, Hamish looked on as Dreich crossed the notional finishing line between the twin piers. Soaked in sweat, despite the chill of the day, he raised his arms in triumph, though looked puzzled to see Hoynes sitting calmly on the bollard with his pipe.

Mitchell put a loudhailer to his mouth. 'Come in, Mr MacCallum. I've people here who want to speak to you.'

Dreich secured his boat beside Sandy's and climbed the ladder to the pier.

'You're finished, Hoynes! You'll hand me the ownership papers to your boat at your earliest convenience.' He laughed, eyeing those present.

It was Campbell the lawyer's turn to speak. 'I wouldn't be so sure about that, Mr MacCallum. Some irregularities have come to light.'

'What?'

'Such as: the company who fabricated the part of Mr

Hoynes's engine that subsequently sunk your cabin cruiser has admitted liability. But, as it turns out, the vessel wasn't seaworthy in the first place. Aye, and you knew it, too.' Campbell turned to the man in the trilby.

'My name is Inspector Black from the Glasgow Police, Mr MacCallum. I'm here to place you under arrest.'

'I'm sorry, what are you talking about, inspector?' said Dreich.

'Your cabin cruiser was taken into dry dock in Glasgow in November, is that right?'

'Yes, what of it?' Dreich's manner was still defiant, but a shadow had crossed his face.

'The yard told you that there were major structural problems with the vessel that would take some thousands of pounds to correct.' Black consulted his notebook. 'Undeterred by this, you sold the craft to a Mr Simon McGeady in Oban. I believe he was to take delivery of her on January the sixth.'

'Yes, but what's that got to do with you?'

'The boat was dangerous, not seaworthy. You were told to take her out of the water in Glasgow. You have no insurance, and you misrepresented its condition to Mr McGeady. There's a lot to talk about here, Mr MacCallum, so I'd be grateful if you'd accompany me to Kinloch Police Station. This way, please, sir.' Inspector Black caught Dreich's wrist and began to pull him away.

'But I still won the race fair and square. It was a wager agreed upon by gentlemen. The *Girl Maggie* is mine!'

'I had to terminate the contest, Dreich,' said Mitchell. 'It's now null and void.'

Dreich MacCallum glared at Hoynes. 'You think you've

won, Sandy, but you're wrong. Wait until my solicitor sorts this out. You'll see!'

'If you're talking about Mr Fincher, he's gone back to London,' said Campbell. 'Turns out that you owe him money – a great deal of money. When he heard my tale about your losing your job, and your attempt to defraud Mr McGeady, well, he thought it best to cut his losses. And I believe your wife returned to London with him.'

Dreich MacCallum was still ranting as he was escorted to the police car.

Hoynes put another match to his pipe. 'You see, Hamish, there's nothing to be gained by dishonesty, right enough. Let that be a lesson for the rest o' your life. Always be an honest man. It's the only way.'

Hamish, Campbell and Mitchell looked at Hoynes, each man lost in his own thoughts.

Epilogue

Some years later . . .

The old man cursed as he pushed his foot down on the accelerator. He coughed weakly as the elderly Austin Cambridge chugged up the hill, then followed the winding road down towards a forest of stout pine trees, the blue sea of the sound sparkling beyond.

He parked the car on a verge and patted the steering wheel.

'Goodbye, old friend,' he said, a tear meandering down his hollow cheeks into his sparse beard.

He made heavy work of exiting the car, pausing to pull up his trousers, which hung from braces over his wasted frame. The illness that had haunted his last two years was winning the race, and its end was near.

The old man made his way to a wooden gate, pushed it open, and wandered down a grassy path towards the sea. He stopped, leaning on the two sticks he'd brought to ease his passage. Sniffing the air, he could smell rain on the way. He turned on his heel, taking in his surroundings. The heather on the hills, the green grass where cattle grazed peacefully, the trees, the sky in which a large gull soared: all were precious to him. He could hardly bear the thought he'd never see them again.

The distance to the rocky beach was short – a hundred yards at most. But by the time he felt the sea breeze on his face, he was breathing so hard that he was forced to take a seat on a rock, ready for one last effort.

As he gazed out to sea, watching its colour change in the fading light of the gloaming, many faces crossed his mind's eye. He remembered a cold, snowy night in a tent, and again had to wipe away a tear.

Having caught his breath, the old man forced himself up and shuffled along the sand to the water's edge. He took a deep draw of the salt air into his lungs and began to cough once more. The great gull circled overhead, its plaintive cry echoing from the hills beyond.

'Aye, it's all been grand,' he said, stepping into the gentle waves.

He waded out, the ocean supporting his weight like a lover. The time for tears was over.

At first, he saw the flames at her prow. Then he heard the chatter of the men as they rowed towards him.

'Sandy! It's time, my friend.' The Viking, dressed in shining leather, his long blond hair pulled back into a ponytail, leaned a foot on the low gunwale.

'I hate to say goodbye, Hona.'

'There is no such thing as goodbye, Sandy Hoynes. Your spirit will live forever with mine and those who you've loved and lost.' The big Norseman held out a hand and pulled the dying fisherman aboard the sleek longship.

The Sandy Hoynes who stepped onto its deck was wrought anew. Gone was the pain, the struggle for breath, the dread in his heart. He stood tall and strong, his fair hair shining in the low sun, as the longship made for the open sea.

For up-to-the-minute news
and information about
Denzil Meyrick's books
and projects find him here

f   DenzilMeyrickAuthor

𝕏   LochLomonden